OCTOBER'S

CHILD

OCTOBER'S CHILD

by
Ward Tanneberg

VICTOR BOOKS

A DIVISION OF SCRIPTURE PRESS PUBLICATIONS INC.
USA CANADA ENGLAND

Editors: Carole Streeter and Barbara Williams
Design: Paul Higdon
Cover Illustration: Larry Selman

Library of Congress Cataloging-in-Publication Data
Tanneberg, Ward M.
    October's child / by Ward Tanneberg.
      p.   cm.
    ISBN 1-56476-398-6
    I. Title.
    PS3570.A535O27 1995
    813'.54—dc20   95-21729
                                                CIP

---

1 2 3 4 5 6 7 8 9 10 Printing/Year 99 98 97 96 95

This book is a work of fiction. Names, characters, places, and incidents are either the product of the author's imagination or are
used fictitiously. Any resemblance to actual events, locales, or
persons living or dead, is entirely coincidental.

This One
Is Dedicated
to
Jessica and Katrina

Acknowledgments

There are several people to whom I am indebted for their interest and assistance in research and resource materials. Eric S.H. Ching, Jan Kinzel, Ken Moore, Markku Pelanne, Paul Beckendorf, Dr. James Johnson, and Mehlika Seval.

There are others who shall remain unnamed, to whom I give thanks for their observations and viewpoints while researching in Greece, Turkey, Israel, and California. In addition, Linda Lenz, my friend and able assistant during the past eight years, for proofreading and manuscript preparation. Carole Streeter and Barbara Williams for their considerable skills in editing. Greg Clouse, editorial director at Victor Books, who once again has been my advocate in affirming the concept that fiction should entertain, educate, and inspire.

Days devoted to research, meeting new people, travel, formulating ideas, and ultimately writing the story require the insights, criticisms, suggestions, and support of a best friend. My special thanks go to my wife and best friend, Dixie, who willingly puts up with and even encourages this minister/writer's life. All for the sake of telling a story that I hope sheds light on a greater story.

WT

Cast of Key Characters

....

- John Cain, senior pastor, Calvary Church in Baytown
- Jessica Cain, the Cain's twelve-year-old daughter
- Faridah, terrorist member, Palestinian Islamic Jihad
- Marwan Dosha, world's most wanted terrorist
- Syd Hershey, Texas oil worker in the Middle East
- Charles Rodeway, Political & Diplomatic Section, State Department, Washington, DC
- Leila Azari, terrorist member, Islamic Jihad, Holy War movement in Iran
- Carla Chin, firearms instructor
- Jeremy Cain, the Cain's seventeen-year-old son
- Reza Fardusi, Iranian businessman
- Arun, converted Hindu, leader of Christain house church in Iran
- Rashad Raufbar, Arun's friend, Jordanian businessman
- Jim "Grandpa" Brainard, New England innkeeper
- Herschel Towner III, security director at OCEANS
- George Callimachus, captain, M/V *Evvoia*
- Timothy Marcos, *Evvoia* crew member

Prologue

....

This October, northern California's rolling hills are not the proud color of honeyed gold for which they are renowned. They are a pallid gray, gaunt and cheerless, huddled like burnt ashes from a million fireplaces. The searing heat of summer has added its burden to four years of negligible rainfall. Lawns are rarely green. Flowers fade quickly.

Nestled high in perpetually snowcapped Sierra peaks, due east of San Francisco Bay, the Hetch Hetchy Reservoir stands at its lowest level in twenty-seven years. Wapama Falls, usually pouring a year-round flow of water into the lake, shows alarming signs of depletion. Due west of Wapama, every winter and spring Tueeulala Falls drops gossamer-like over a sheer cliff into the reservoir. This year there is hardly a trickle. Great mountain streams that usually roar westward out of the snows and glaciers have dwindled to beds of mud and gravel.

Digger pine, California bay canyon oaks, yerba santa, and poison oak still dot the parched hillsides, but grass has long since wilted into the drab, brown earth. Blackened trails from recent fires meander indiscriminately through forests now fallen victim to the holocaust of nature. It is known that this perpetual source of water, taken for granted by the millions who have depended on it, is now predictably endangered by nature's insolvency.

Not known, however, is the fact that the one hundred forty-nine miles of engineering genius that carries San Francisco's enviably pure mountain water supply to the sea is even more endangered by the devilish designs of a few men.

Certainly John Cain did not know. In a hundred years he could never have guessed at how intricately involved he already was in the schemes of those bent on the destruction of a city and the breaking apart of a nation. His mind was elsewhere as he drank a last sip of water and stared pensively at the empty glass.

Someone has done the unthinkable.

First it was Jenny. That nearly tore us apart. And now it is Jessica.

John looked up at the black oak that reigned like a king over the far corner of the backyard patio. Through its branches and leaves, he glimpsed the fading rays of the evening sun.

Where have they taken her?

Why don't You answer? Why won't You tell us?

Refilling the glass, he set the pitcher down on the Middle East map spread out on the patio table beside his Bible.

Has she been beaten? Raped? Is she dead? Has her body been tossed like garbage into some nameless grave half a world away? When I left her, I asked You to protect her and help her get home safely. I trusted You. What happened to Your promise, God?

Familiar words flashed across his mind. *"Do not throw away your confidence; it will be richly rewarded. You need to persevere so that when you have done the will of God, you will receive what He has promised."*

It was a verse John had read earlier from Hebrews, a biblical injunction to the faithful to persevere while passing through hard times.

Did the writer have any idea how hard the times could get? Maybe God's promises don't cover this sort of need.

He turned the glass slowly in his hand, afraid of transferring blasphemous thoughts into spoken words.

Promises made can also be broken. Maybe even God's promises?

He lifted the glass to his lips and drank deeply. It was good mountain water. It had always been there, until now, that is. Now it appeared that the promise of water relied on for so many years might not be enough to meet the Bay Area's needs. No one knew for certain.

But there was one thing John Cain did know. However bad the lack of moisture, it could not compare to the drought in his soul.

Maybe there aren't any guarantees after all.

He put the glass down, thrust his hands into his pockets, and stared longingly at the map.

Four weeks. . . . Weeks of helplessness and growing hopelessness. Weeks that seared one burning question into his mind.
What has happened to Jessica?

ONE

SUNDAY, 18 SEPTEMBER
SOMEWHERE IN ISRAEL

Jessica was positive that her eyes were open. So why couldn't she see?

She shut them again, felt her eyelids press tightly together, then opened once more, just to be sure.

I must be in bed.

No. The surface she was lying on was too hard for that.

Did I fall out of bed onto the floor?

Her head throbbed with each pounding heartbeat, forcing a wince of pain.

She lay perfectly still, feeling the darkness with her senses, straining to see something, but there was nothing.

No light in the window. No stars in the sky.

Only the darkness. And the voices.

At first they were nothing more than a quiet murmur. Jessica could not make out what was being said. She closed her eyes again, pushing everything to the back of her mind. Her head swirled and she felt groggy.

Still, the voices remained. Low. Distant. Unintelligible. Their words sounded strangely . . . foreign!

Maybe Daddy's watching television in the other room.

The voices grew louder and it sounded like two people quarreling. Though she did not understand what they were saying, Jessica could detect the argumentative tone. Then she recognized the language.

They're speaking Arabic. But how do I know. . . ?

The mental cobwebs in the dark corners of her mind slowly detached and in their place one terrifying memory leaped forward.

The bus. The tour group left the hotel in the bus. Without me!

Her thinking became jumbled again, running together in kaleidoscopic patterns, as she tried to grasp that incomprehensible fact. It did not make any sense.

Why? Why didn't they see that I wasn't in the bus? I always sit in the front seat near the door.

She remembered the stunned feeling as she stood in the entrance to the hotel lobby, staring in disbelief toward the place where the bus had been parked.

Bewildered, and more than a little frightened, Jessica approached the desk clerk. When he first looked up, the man appeared as surprised to see her as she was at being there.

"How did you miss your bus, Miss Cain?" he asked, his eyes never once leaving her, even as his hands fumbled for the handle of an open drawer.

"I don't know. I told my father where I would be. I don't understand. What should I do?"

Reading the concern on her face, the clerk's demeanor rapidly changed from obvious shock to one of kindly sympathy. With a smile, he assured her that she was not the first passenger to miss a bus, and he was confident that as soon as her absence was discovered, the driver would return for her. If, however, the hotel did not hear anything within a couple of hours, he would personally contact the tour agency representative. Together, they would make whatever arrangements were necessary to reunite her with her father and the others. He even volunteered an unused room in which she could rest while waiting.

Then he offered her a glass of orange juice. Now . . . try as she might, Jessica could not think past the orange juice.

She hadn't been feeling well. That's why she had gone to the restroom just as the others were walking out of the hotel to board the bus. Her father had reminded her that it was a two-hour journey to Jerusalem from the Dead Sea resort at Ein Bokek and there were no facilities on board. Having had an upset stomach all day, she wanted to be ready for the journey. Then, when she came out, they were gone. For this she was not ready!

The juice.

It was such an uncomfortably hot day and a glass of orange juice sounded great. Besides, it was probably the one thing that would stay down. Earlier, while stretched out in the shade by the pool, she remembered her father cautioning her not to get dehydrated.

"Drink lots of liquids, honey. If you don't, this heat will make you feel even worse."

Now, as she lay in the darkness listening to the strange voices, she tried to remember what came after the orange juice.

Did that man put something else in it?

Suddenly, fear tore through her stomach, clawing and flaying at her insides. Jessica tried sitting up, but was unable.

What's the matter with me? Why can't I get up? If only I could see . . ."

Questions, like pirouetting ballerinas, danced randomly across her mind, only to disappear as though whisked away by a magician's hand.

That's when the awful realization hit her! She couldn't move because her arms and legs were bound tightly!

Now, totally stricken with fear, Jessica shut her eyes and cried out for help, but she heard only muffled sounds. Tape covered her mouth too, barricading her cry against its escape.

A motor started up. Seconds later, as she felt herself moving, it dawned on her. She was not in a room at all, but in some sort of vehicle.

Is this a truck? Maybe that's why the air smells funny. But what am I doing in a truck?

She bounced helplessly over each pothole in the road as the vehicle gathered speed.

Panic pierced her brain. Fright played boogeyman in the darkness.

Who are these people? Where are they taking me? What are they going to do? Daddy! Where are you?

But Daddy did not answer.

Jessica's unprotected head banged painfully against the truck bed, while the roar of the engine, the scraping of gears, and the sounds of wheels on pavement filled her mind with such terror that she began convulsing. Instinctively, she tried to fight back the bile that threatened to erupt, sensing that she could very well choke to death if she didn't get control.

Jessica closed her eyes tightly. Slowly, the panic receded as she breathed deeply through her nose. Again . . . again. Her heart hammered as though making a desperate attempt to escape her body.

O God. How can this be happening?

I want to go home. Daddy, where are you? Mom, oh, please, help me. Dear God, don't let this keep happening!

In this dark room on wheels, far from the home she now frantically wished for, Jessica's natural enthusiasm for adventure vanished. Instead, a consuming terror stalked through her mind like a character from a horror movie.

Tears broke free, running unchecked into her hair and ears, as the silent screams of all the world's missing children fought to escape her lips.

Twelve-year-old Jessica Cain knew she was being kidnapped!

TWO

How long had it been?

An hour? Two?

It was impossible for Jessica to determine. What time of day was it? Had she dozed off?

The only thing she knew for sure was that her body ached from the beating it had taken as she bounced up and down on the truck bed. Occasionally, her head banged against the side wall. With every turn in the road, her stomach tried to twist itself into knots.

Where are they taking me? And where is Daddy? The Andersons would have noticed I wasn't with them. So, how could they just go off and leave me behind?

Tears continued to fall as Jessica scrambled to sort out her patchwork of thoughts. Suddenly, her mind skidded to a stop.

What if something has happened to Daddy? And the others too? That might explain . . .

Her inert body slid forward, banging against the truck's front wall, as the driver suddenly applied the brakes.

We must be stopping. Oh, please . . .

Jessica desperately wanted to be outside in the open air. But she was also afraid, dreading to see whoever had taken her. This could not be a nice person. No one who would do such a thing as this could possibly be nice.

Why would anyone want me? Is there only one person out

there? No. There are men's voices, and they're arguing. What will they do to me?

A name pushed its way forward. *Polly Klass!*

Panic set in again, filling her mind with even more fear. She remembered seeing Polly's face, and that of her father on television. The tragedy of Polly's abduction from her home, and her subsequent murder, had gripped the hearts of a nation. Jessica thought of how they had prayed for her at school.

That's it! They're going to rape me and then kill me! O God, please . . . please help me!

The truck was moving slowly now. She rolled onto her side as it took a sharp turn and went off the paved road. Then the truck stopped and the motor was turned off.

Jessica felt a wave of relief roll over her. She heard the truck door open and the driver step down. He slammed the door shut.

There were voices at the back of the truck as someone fumbled with the locked door.

It opened and she saw a flashlight waving back and forth on the ceiling above her. In the distorted shadows, she became aware of several boxes surrounding her. Someone was in the truck now, grunting as he pushed some of the boxes to one side.

Suddenly, there he was. No, not just one but two of them. One held the light on her face as she squinted into its bright glare. Then he spoke to the other, who grunted in reply.

The man reached down and scooped her up. Even through the binding tape, Jessica could feel the strength of his hands and forearms. As he turned and started to carry her out, she glimpsed a dark beard covering his chin. His breath caused her to gag, and she turned her face away.

A moment later, he turned her up over his shoulder, like a sack of potatoes, and proceeded to drop from the truck to the ground. Jessica groaned as her stomach slammed into the bony part of his shoulder. Her head was in an upside-down position so that all she could see was the back of his body, the movement of his legs, and a dirt path.

They were on a cement slab now, pushing through an open doorway.

Another voice.

A woman! Oh, thank God. Maybe . . .

The man lifted her away from his shoulder, dropping her on an old sofa. Dust flew from the cushions as she landed. They were in a room dimly lit by a single lamp in the far corner, fairly good-sized, with a cement floor that long ago had received a coat of green paint. Several worn rugs were scattered about.

The woman came over to Jessica and stared down at her. She looked very old, but it was hard to tell in the diffused light. She was dark-skinned, her face creased with lines, and snips of un-kempt hair strayed from the scarf around her head. Heavyset, she wore the long, traditional garments of an Arab woman.

Jessica's eyes pleaded with her.

The woman looked away and said something to the men who stood off to the side, talking in low tones.

The one who had carried her inside replied curtly. The old woman's response was sharp.

The man grunted and then shuffled across to Jessica. He bent over her, frowning. To Jessica's surprise, he spoke in heavily ac-cented English.

"I am removing the tape from your mouth. If you try to scream or make any noise, I will break your neck right now," he said in a menacing tone. "Understand?"

Jessica blinked and gave a half nod.

"You will be quiet?"

She nodded again.

The man tore the tape away with one smooth motion. Jessica held back a cry of pain for fear he would do exactly as he had threatened. She breathed deeply through her open mouth.

Her eyes traveled from the two men who turned their backs to her and continued their conversation, to the Arab woman, stand-ing alone by a wooden table. Jessica mouthed a silent word to the woman.

Please?

Slowly she came over and stood next to her, never taking her eyes off the young girl.

"I need to go to the bathroom," whispered Jessica, feeling both embarrassed and more desperate about this necessary bodily function with each passing minute.

The woman did not move.

"A restroom. I need a restroom," Jessica whispered again.

No response.

Perhaps she doesn't understand English. And the man who does said he'd kill me if I say anything.

Jessica's mind raced back over the few Arabic words and phrases she had learned on this trip. What was the word for bathroom?

"Toilet . . . taewaelit?"

The woman's eyebrows lifted and a look of concern flashed

across her face. She turned and said something to the men. They stopped their conversation and stared at Jessica. The man who spoke English reached into his pocket and pulled out a Swiss Army knife. Opening it, he walked over to her.

"You need the toilet?"

Jessica nodded.

"All right. I will remove the tape. If you try to get away, I cut your throat. You understand?"

Jessica nodded, flinching at the thought, and whispered, "Yes."

The man slid the sharp blade through the tape wrapped around her body. It came off quickly, tearing free from her clothing. Fortunately, instead of the usual shorts she had worn for most of the trip, she had put on a pair of pants today, in preparation for going up to Jerusalem. But her arms were bare and felt the sting as body hair pulled away along with the tape. Jessica grimaced but said nothing.

Her relief at being able to move her arms and legs was overpowering.

"Go with her," the man said, nodding toward the woman.

As Jessica stood, the room swayed back and forth. Her legs suddenly gave out and she started to fall.

The woman caught her as she fought to regain her balance, then nudged her forward, pointing to a doorway at the far side of the room. Jessica walked toward it slowly, taking stock of her surroundings as she went.

At the opposite end was a wooden table with four chairs. A small stove. Some cupboards with dishes and pots and pans all stacked on open shelves. It looked odd to Jessica. She couldn't remember ever having seen cupboards without doors.

On the wall was a picture of the man she recognized from television news. Double chin, unshaven, looking like a soldier, with a gun strapped to his side. She couldn't remember his name, but he looked like trouble.

Jessica paused in the bathroom doorway. There was a shower to the left, framed in rusty metal, with a faded plastic curtain across the opening. The stool was on the opposite wall, and it looked filthy. She shuddered, and the memory of her own pretty bathroom at home flashed through her mind. She looked for the familiar paper roll near the seat. There was nothing. Only a small bucket half-filled with water. Then, she noticed the small window above the stool and to the left.

It was open!

Her eyes darted from the top of the stool to the window, then back again, gauging the distance.

Maybe . . .

Jessica stepped into the small room and reached for the door.

"No!"

Startled, Jessica turned and looked up. The man who had spoken to her earlier in English was shaking his head now and motioning with his hand.

"Leave it open."

Jessica started to protest.

"No," the man repeated and started toward her.

Jessica quickly removed her hand from the doorknob.

Now, instead of the possibility of escape, she faced the embarrassment of using the toilet without the customary privacy. Taking two additional steps, she stood by the stool, her hand on the wall. Then she turned and looked back into the other room. The men were talking again, seemingly oblivious to her predicament. Only the old woman was watching.

Jessica's body was making a last desperate call for relief. She sighed, noting that the men had moved away from her line of sight. She looked around one more time for a paper roll, paper towels, anything. The only thing within reach was the half-filled water bucket. She stared at it for a long moment, grimacing as its purpose finally began to dawn.

THREE

TUESDAY, 20 SEPTEMBER
SOMEWHERE IN ISRAEL

Voices.

Jessica stirred, shifting her uncomfortable position on the filthy couch. Two days had come and gone since her arrival. She remained unbound, but was confined to sitting or reclining on the couch. She could stand and stretch, but if she moved more than a step away, the old woman shook her finger and motioned for her to go back.

Her longest journey consisted of twelve steps to the toilet. She knew them by heart. By now she had resigned herself to that little cubicle's filthiness and inconvenience. At least it was there for her to use. And she was feeling better. The upset condition experienced earlier in the week had passed. The first day and night she had slept very little; it was not until well into night two that Jessica had finally drifted off into a dreamless sleep.

The old woman was constantly nearby. One of the men was also always present in the room, although they completely ignored her. The woman brought her a small bowl of fruit on two different occasions. In the evening, there was a watery, brownish soup. In the morning, plain pita bread and goat's milk. She gagged over the milk, thinking it must be spoiled. Eventually she got it down, reasoning that she needed to eat and drink whatever was offered. Keeping her strength up was important.

Stay alert. Daddy will come after me soon. I need to be ready when he does.

Opening her eyes, she saw the men sitting at the table, eating cheese and drinking orange juice, the old woman attending to their needs. Noticing that Jessica had awakened, she picked up a plate and walked over to her. Jessica saw that the plate held more pita bread, a substance that had grown familiar during the past week. She reached up and took it from the woman.

"Thank you," she whispered. Then, she remembered that the old woman apparently spoke no English.

"Shokran," Jessica added, using one of the few Arabic words she had learned since her arrival in the Middle East.

The woman's face was expressionless as she nodded and turned away.

The pita bread pocket was filled with a strange-looking mixture, but it was food, and Jessica discovered that she was very hungry. Biting into it, she decided that there was pickle or cucumber mixed in with something, she wasn't sure what. Maybe chicken.

The woman went back to the table and took down a glass from the nearby shelf. Jessica watched as she withdrew several oranges from a basket and proceeded to cut them open, squeezing the fresh juice into the glass. Silent and still unsmiling, the woman carried the juice across the room and handed it to her.

For a moment, Jessica wondered if the glass was clean. The one she had first been given, filled with goat's milk, had looked dirty. But when Jessica examined it, she saw that it was stained but clean. Her mind flashed back to the glass of juice she had been given at the hotel. Her abductors must have knocked her out with that drink. Could there be something in this one too?

No. She couldn't have put anything else in without my seeing.

Finally, thirst overcame hesitation. Taking it, she drank eagerly, handing the glass back to the woman when she was finished.

"Shokran," she said again. "May I have another?"

Her answer was the same expressionless stare as the woman took the glass and walked away.

At that moment, a third man entered the house, struggling with a large, wooden crate. He placed it on the floor, saying something to the others in Arabic. The man glanced over at her as he reached into the box and lifted a thin blanket roll, shaking it loose.

The man who had earlier spoken English said something to him. He shrugged and tossed the blanket aside. Then, he took a knife from his pocket, opened a blade, and bent over the crate.

Jessica's apprehension increased as she watched.

What are they doing?

Her eyes widened as the others rose and walked toward her. The man who spoke English had a hypodermic needle in his hand. Jessica felt a sudden spasm of fear.

"No!" Jessica spoke out loud as she pushed herself off the couch and started for the door.

The second man's rough hands grabbed her, pulling her up off her feet. She thrashed helplessly, kicking at his shins. She heard him grunt in pain as he pinned her arms and held her back against his belly. Now the other one moved in and, before she could cry out again, the needle sank into her arm. She felt a burning sensation as the syringe emptied into her system.

The man holding her threw her back onto the couch. Crying now, with a mixture of fright, anger, and pain, Jessica continued to kick her feet and swing her fists, as she rolled off the couch and fell to the floor.

I've got to get out of here. They're going to kill me. Run . . .

But the shot was starting to take over. She fought back gamely until the room began turning. The sickening feeling in her stomach returned. She felt someone's hands gripping her arms.

Kick. Fight them. Do . . . something . . . oh, please. . . Daddy?

Jessica slumped forward helplessly, eyes refusing to focus as she lost consciousness.

THE OLD WOMAN WATCHED in silence.

"She's a little vixen," the first man exclaimed, the empty syringe still in his hand. "Here. Put her back up on the couch."

"I'll tell you where I'd like to put her," grunted the one who had held her, rubbing his shin with a free hand. "I'd like to bash her head in and drown the little witch in the Jordan!"

"Just bring her here," the third man said. "The box is ready."

"Don't be such a bad sport, Ahmed," the first one chuckled. "A little girl has bruised your shin. Maybe she has bruised your spirit too?"

"Does anyone know why we are going to all this trouble for her?" the man by the box asked, taking Jessica's limp form.

"It was not understood at the beginning that she would be important; but since the mission in Jerusalem has ended in failure, she is all that is left. The girl is the daughter of the man from America. He was one of the hostages."

The third man paused. "You mean that Christian minister from California? The one whose face is in all the newspapers and on television?"

"Yes. She was left behind by accident at the hotel. Now, our instructions are to get her out of the country. That is all I know."

"But, it is too dangerous. Everyone will be looking for her."

"Exactly. They will be looking for her because she is important. If we are successful in removing her, perhaps she will be even more important negotiation material later."

"And if we are not successful?"

His comrade shrugged, but did not answer.

"So she goes to Jordan this morning?"

"As soon as the bridge is open. We want to be there early, before the line is long. The authorities often let the first trucks go through with minimum examination, so the line does not become bogged down too soon. Especially since the 'new accord' between the Jews and King Hussein. The truck you are driving has been across many times in recent weeks. That should help us."

"What if they search and find her?"

"That is the chance we take. Certainly it is dangerous, but our leaders have made the decision. Ahmed, this is the most important assignment we have ever been given. Allah will guide us and make a way!"

The old woman continued her surveillance from across the room as the man by the wooden crate chewed his lip, thinking about what he had just heard. Then, without further comment, he lowered Jessica into the box. Turning her onto her side, he forced her knees up into her stomach. Her arms were pulled behind her and taped at the wrists. Then, her feet. Finally, a piece of tape was placed over her mouth.

"The lid. Bring it to me," the man said to Ahmed. "And the hammer too. They are in the truck."

As the top was being nailed into place, the old woman turned away with a sigh of resignation and busied herself at the small sink.

Such a pretty little girl ...

THE DRIVER GLANCED ABOUT nervously as the four trucks in front of his were visited by border security personnel. The authorities didn't seem to be in any hurry this morning. The third truck in line had just been motioned over. One entire side of the truck's load of oranges was being removed and opened. A uniformed soldier was examining under the hood of the second truck for possible weapons or illegal drugs.

It did not bode well at Allenby Bridge for the driver of truck number five.

Things had been more relaxed at this crossing since the peace treaty between Israel and Jordan and the PLO occupation of the region surrounding Jericho. However, since the near catastrophic events in Jerusalem of the past forty-eight hours, there was noticeably more tension in the early-morning air.

Little more than a one-way crossing from the West Bank to Jordan's Hashemite Kingdom, the Allenby Bridge spanned one of the world's smallest but best known waterways, the River Jordan. It was no more than two or three trucks or buses in length. Ugly block buildings, showing signs of severe deterioration, stood on either side. Some palm trees. Everywhere, plenty of sand and dirt underfoot.

The area was a no man's land leading into Israel on the west bank of the river and Jordan on the east. Sandbags were piled high, shielding a machine-gun nest in which two soldiers sat, casually observing the chaotic but normal scene. They appeared to be having breakfast atop their desert post; in a small office at the side of the bridge crossing, soldiers shouted and strutted back and forth, looking and feeling a good deal more important than they really were.

At least, that's the way the driver of number five saw it.

Now, one of these soldiers strolled up to his door.

"Sabah el-khir," the Israeli greeted the driver in Arabic. *Good morning.*

"Toda, boker tov," the Arab replied politely in Hebrew. *Thank you and good morning to you.*

"Please, get out and open the gate of your truck."

Reluctantly, the driver pushed open his door and dropped to the dirt below. Tiny dust clouds puffed up around his feet with each step as he moved to the back of the truck and unlocked the rack. Orange crates were stacked on top of each other and surrounded by a wooden, open-slat rack.

"Take that crate down from up there. Yes, that one, on the right. Open it, please."

The driver understood that while it was phrased as a request, he had just received a direct order, and he proceeded to remove the lid until the oranges inside were visible. The soldier ran his hand down into the crate, feeling for concealed weapons or other contraband. He found nothing.

"Over there, please. Yes, that one next."

The driver and the soldier continued this security ritual for the next twenty minutes. All in all, thirteen crates were randomly selected, removed, opened, and examined. Nothing out of the ordinary. The truck was a familiar one, making this trip every few days. Even though this was not the regular driver, his papers were in order.

"Where is the man who normally drives?"

"He is sick."

"Too bad. Hope he's better soon," said the soldier, checking to see that the appropriate stamps and signatures were placed on the man's documents.

"Naharak sae'id." The soldier handed the papers to the driver and stepped back. *Have a good day.*

"Shokran. Ila liqa," the driver smiled, climbing up into the truck. *Thanks. See you later.*

He started the engine and released the brake. Soon he was inching his way across the narrow bridge toward the Jordanian checkpoint. An hour later, he was back on the highway, slowly making his way up the long, winding grade that led away from the river toward Jordan's capital city of Amman.

Every crate on his truck was full of the finest Jaffa oranges, ready to be delivered to the marketplace.

Every crate except one.

HER EYES FELT ALMOST too heavy to open. Her head was spinning. She felt sick to her stomach as a wave of nausea swept through her. By the time she recognized the familiar feeling of tape over her mouth, the nausea had passed.

She closed her eyes and then opened them again. It was so dark. Briefly, a ray of sunlight penciled its way into her vision. The sudden brightness caused her to squint. Then it disappeared. Where had it come from?

Where am I?

The hole through which light filtered was not far from her face. She could hear the roar of the truck's motor, the down-shifting of gears, and the sound of wood against wood.

What is that?

She tried to stretch out, but couldn't. Wedged in so tightly, with her hands bound and helpless behind her back, there was no room to maneuver. Her feet were taped together too. The feeling of panic returned in earnest.

The box at the house. They must have put me in the box!

As the reality of her predicament intensified, she began gasping for breath.

It's so stuffy and hot in here. I need air. I need to get out!

Jessica pushed desperately against the end of the box, but there was no way to gain leverage. She tried changing positions, but the right side of her face was pressed against the bottom of the crate, with her shoulder curled underneath. There were spasms of pain every time the truck bounced. With a muffled groan and a twisting motion, she finally was able to push her shoulder out from beneath her so that she rested partially on her chest with her face angled toward the small hole.

Thoughts raced across her mind like a runaway train.

Will they bury me alive? Does anybody know where I am? Of course, they don't. O Jesus, I'm so scared!

The truck continued its arduous climb up the narrow, twisting highway, avoiding cars and trucks descending on the left toward the border. Occasionally, a car pulled out from behind and passed the slower moving vehicle. Jessica started at the blast of an air horn, feeling the truck veer sharply and then continue up the hill.

THE TOUR BUS WAS FILLED with Americans, most of whom were from the Merryweather Baptist Church of Savannah, Georgia.

Since yesterday, whenever their Jordanian guide was not pointing out some special location, or offering up a bit of local history, the talk among these religious pilgrims was about the newspaper stories concerning Reverend John Cain and his heroic effort in turning terrorists away from the Western Wall. It was an amazing story, augmented by potentially devastating attacks in America, and it provided no end of exciting conversation. This was a good day to be an American in Israel. And that was fortuitous, they decided, because in another hour or two, they would be there themselves, many of them for the first time.

Sitting in the front seat nearest the door, Pastor Harvey Drake had withdrawn from the animated discussion. His thoughts drifted ahead to Jerusalem, where a colleague in the ministry searched anxiously for his missing daughter. He did not know the man personally, but he could not get him out of his mind.

What must he be going through right now? According to the news reports, his wife is hovering between life and death. His church has been shot up. He is under a doctor's care, after being beaten while a hostage. And now, his daughter has disappeared. The man must be going crazy!

Pastor Drake stared out the window toward the Jordan River far below, covered over with a sultry summer haze. His eyes moistened at the thought of what it might be like to be in that man's shoes, then closed in silent prayer while their bus continued down the steep grade.

Lord, I am so deeply moved right now for my brother in the ministry. Please undertake for this man's wife and young daughter. Let Your healing flow through Mrs. Cain in the hospital, and be with Pastor Cain and his group here in Israel. Undertake for each one of their needs. Especially, Lord, be with that little girl, wherever she is. If she's really been kidnapped, then watch over her. Only You can do that. Keep her safe and bring her home to her family once again. They've all been through much too much. Thank You, Jesus. Amen.

Pastor Drake looked up just in time to see a truck, loaded with crates, creeping around the corner, its wheels well over the middle line. The bus driver honked the air horn, stepping on his brakes as the truck veered back across the line. Its driver waved apologetically as they squeezed by each other.

"Stupid farmer!" muttered the driver, loud enough for those in the first rows to hear.

Pastor Drake chuckled. "Oranges," he called back to his tour group. "Those are Jaffa oranges, some of the best in the world. Maybe we can get a case in Jericho."

He turned back again, facing Israel's desert hills, which loomed ever larger as the bus continued its descent into the Jordan Valley. The truck loaded with oranges was quickly forgotten as Pastor Drake opened a leather pouch and began searching for the crossing papers they would need at the border.

IT WAS NEARLY NOON when the truck turned off the main highway and trundled along Amman's suburban streets, the driver keeping more of an eye out for the delivery site than for the potholes in the pavement. Whitewashed apartments lined the rocky hillside on both sides of the street. Once again, he checked his destination address.

There. Just ahead.

The market was situated on the corner, crowded with shoppers and hagglers, a mélange of colors, smells, and sounds. Varieties of fruits, vegetables, and herbs were stacked on top of rickety wooden tables, arranged in rows on the street in front of a two-story building. Pickled foods and pita bread at bargain prices. Exotic annonas, fijoyas, persimmons, and star fruit heaped alongside bananas and oranges.

A few feet off to one side, a man squatted in the dirt. He appeared to be planting a seedling. Sleeves were rolled above his elbows and dark-rimmed glasses gripped his ample nose. A cloth cap perched askew on top of his graying hair. As the truck rolled to a stop, the would-be gardener stood and wiped his hands. His friendly smile revealed unusually white teeth for someone in this part of the world, where teeth are often permanently stained by tobacco juice or lack of personal hygiene.

"You made it," he shouted, over the combined sounds of the marketplace and the truck motor. "No problems?"

"None at all," the driver grinned, as he jumped down from the truck, relieved to be here at last and hand over his cargo.

"Is she all right?" the jovial man asked, his voice lower now.

The driver shrugged. "I don't know. She was drugged when we left. The soldier at the border came within one case of finding her. I thought for sure we would all be history. Allah was with us, however, and I made it through. I've been on the road up from the valley ever since. There was no place to stop and check on her."

"Then let's hurry," said the man, whose face would let him pass for any child's grandfather, but whose eyes had now narrowed into two dangerous openings. "I don't want to have to bury her here, dead from suffocation. Quickly now. Which one is she?"

They walked to the driver's side of the truck where he pointed to a crate, about midway from the back.

"That's her."

The two men worked quickly to remove the wooden rack. The driver climbed up and began handing down crates of oranges to the other. These were stacked along the ground, beside the truck. In a matter of minutes, they had reached the bottom crate.

The driver dragged the box to the edge of the truck bed and then jumped down. Each man took one side of the box and lowered it to the ground, pausing briefly to catch their breath and adjust for a better hold. Picking it up, they carried it through the large, open door located just behind the fijoyas, persimmons, and star fruit.

Once inside, they climbed up a narrow stairway, proceeding along a hallway to a door that opened into a small apartment. Once inside, they put the box down in the center of the room and quickly closed the door behind them.

From a drawer in the tiny kitchen, the man from Amman retrieved a sturdy knife and began working on the box's lid. A minute was all it took to break it loose.

Dropping the knife, he removed the cover and peered inside.

The girl was wedged in tightly, her hair matted with sweat, clothes soaked through, and her face drawn and pale.

Her mouth was pressed against the solitary air hole, but there was no indication of breathing. No sign of life.

The man from Amman swore softly as he shook his head. The little girl had not survived. He reached in and lifted her limp form from the box.

FOUR

Four weeks. Actually, twenty-nine days, if you count today.

John walked to the edge of the patio. The low garden lights cast a soft glow on the flowers and trees surrounding the pool.

Quiet water . . . the half moon reflecting prismatically on its surface in glasslike luster.

Dark water . . . a repository of mixed messages.

His eyes followed the path of light across the pool's surface, upward into the early darkness of the autumn evening.

The moon . . . marked forever with the footprints of man.

The stars . . . tiny torches in angels' hands.

The backdrop . . . black and cold and vast.

It all seemed to work together, giving his mind permission to open the road to the past, an act that did not often meet with his approval these days.

How many hours had he and Esther spent here with their children? He smiled at the memory of splashing and screams of laughter filling the air as family members "cannonballed" into the pool, each attempting to outdo the other in the amount of water they displaced.

Happy hours . . . a lifetime ago.

John was pretty good at it. Actually, everyone agreed that the cannonball, requiring very little skill, was probably his best diving form. But there was never any question as to who was the real family champion. Jeremy remained the consistent winner, able to spray water all the way to the patio table, something no one else had ever accomplished. Though his feats were legendary, they were not appreciated by everyone.

Jessica liked to read by the patio table. She also did her schoolwork there in the afternoons, until it was too cold to sit outside. Jeremy's antics exasperated her and she told him so in no uncertain terms. Of course, the more infuriated she became, the more her older brother tantalized her. Mom was the one who usually called a halt to these sibling spats.

They took on a familiar kind of ritual. When Jeremy's antics were brought to a halt, he would get out of the water and stretch out in the sun on a lounging chair. After a few minutes, the last droplet of water would disappear from his tanned, muscular body.

It would not be long now. In the ritual, timing was everything.

Jeremy always knew what was about to happen, but pretended not to. He dozed, enjoying the warm rays of the sun, eyes ostensibly shut, yet all the while watching as Jessica made her way toward him on tiptoe, the ritual pitcher of ice water in hand. It was all Jeremy could do to lie still.

With a squeal of vengeful delight, Jessica dumped the icy water on Jeremy and ran for the family room door. She never once made it all the way inside. Jeremy was up, sputtering and yelling and chasing after her. She screamed as his strong arms wrapped around her and swept her off her feet. While she squirmed and tried to get away, he carried her to the pool's edge, holding her over the water while she kicked playfully and cried out, "No, Jeremy, no. Don't do it. We're even now!"

"No," was Jeremy's inevitable reply. "I managed to get a few drops on you and your book. You nearly drowned me in ice water, little girl. So, in you go!"

At that point in the ceremony, Jeremy would toss her into the center of the pool, careful never to let her fall near the edge. When she came up, she was always laughing. Jeremy then jumped in after her and for the next half hour, he and his sister created memories. Not just for the two of them, but also for Mom and Dad and anyone else who might be watching.

The noise would occasionally awaken baby Jennifer from her afternoon nap. Jenny's face was aglow with excitement as she waddled out in her diaper, holding tightly to mother's finger while her feet continued their adjustment to the fine art of walking. Her eyes sparkled as she watched her brother and sister splashing together in the pool. John and Esther thought that it must look like great fun to Jenny, something that she would one day enjoy doing with them.

Tragically, that would never be.

One day, eighteen-month-old Jennifer managed to unlock the screen door and wandered onto the patio in search of her favorite pink ball.

It was waiting there for her all right, at the edge of the pool.

It was only a matter of minutes until her mother came looking for her.

No time at all, really. But long enough.

Esther found Jennifer's lifeless body at the bottom of the family pool. That discovery had nearly destroyed them all.

Yes, this place was indeed a repository of memories.

John looked at his watch. *Ten after eight. That means it's ten after six, tomorrow morning in Israel.*

After a predawn chill in Jerusalem, it would be pleasant and warm along Galilee's shores, stretching farther south toward the Dead Sea, and all the way down to Eilat.

As John's mind shifted to Ein Bokek and the Salt Sea Hotel & Spa, he felt the customary heaviness return to his chest. Every detail was vivid.

Sunday, September 18.

The day the world had been introduced to terrorism in a suburban church in California, in the metropolis of Boston, at a seaside village in Maine, and on a bus filled with Americans in Israel.

Etched forever in the minds of people around the world as the day of the infamous September Strike!

His thoughts ran to another pool, where he sat in the shade with Jessica, their shoes tossed to one side, feet dangling in the warm water. A quiet lull before resuming their journey toward Jerusalem. Time for complimenting Jessica on how well she traveled as a child among adults. Time for thinking of how glad he was that she had come with him on this trip. No doubt it would become one of their most treasured memories.

Late afternoon in Israel. John had planned the group's arrival in Jerusalem to coincide with the sunset. It would be a spectacular sight and he was anxious for his people to experience it.

Jessica was not feeling well. It appeared to be a relatively light case of "traveler's revenge," a discomfort experienced by every adventurous soul wandering through a far-off land. Tomorrow, she would be fine. He was sure of it. . . .

John brushed at a patch of unruly hair. Every remembered detail possessed a torturous clarity.

Shortly after four they entered the hotel lobby. Everyone was there, ready to board the bus. John reminded Jessica that they had a two-hour journey ahead. She excused herself to go to the restroom one last time.

Then, the unexpected message. David Barak, their guide, had been called away to a family emergency. The hotel volunteered to send one of its employees along as an interim guide. Soon John was making his way across the parking lot, his slow, sure stride keeping pace with an attractive female employee of the hotel, now their designated guide.

He remembered the exact instant when he thought of Jessica.

In the surprise of the moment and the concern he was feeling for David, he had momentarily forgotten about her. Stopping abruptly, he turned to go back.

He would never forget the first time he felt a handgun digging sharply into his side.

The attractive hotel employee had suddenly become John's worst nightmare, forcing him across the sun-bleached parking lot and into the bus. He remembered the pale, frightened looks on the faces of his group, as they stared at automatic weapons in the hands of two strangers. Someone had even taken the place of Amal, their driver.

There had been a split second in which to make the decision.

He saw it now as a moment he might live to regret for the rest of his life.

Rather than bring Jessica into this calamitous situation, he determined to say nothing. To leave her. Surely she would be safer at the hotel than here, with these armed terrorists. And, in the harrowing hours that had followed, it seemed to John that he had made the right choice.

The hostage drama, in which he and his group were suddenly cast as major players, was filled with danger and little hope for survival. It was no place for adults, much less a twelve-year-old girl. He became more and more convinced that he had made the right choice for Jessica.

Only after events played themselves out did John discover the terrible truth. Jessica was gone. She had disappeared off the face of the earth!

Investigators went to work in an effort to find her. In a matter of hours, they concluded that a clerk from the hotel in Ein Bokek was also missing. Putting two and two together was not difficult. An inside contact from the hotel staff would have been invaluable in providing the terrorists with a necessary base for their operation. After the bus had departed, that same person must have recognized Jessica. Perhaps she even went to him for help after realizing the bus had left without her. No one knew for certain. Perhaps they never would.

John's spur-of-the-moment decision to leave her behind had proven disastrous. He could hardly bring himself to accept the horrible reality of this added loss.

First, Jenny.

Now, Jessica.

What more could possibly happen to further destroy his world?

After several days of fruitless searching in Israel, John returned home. Esther was hovering between life and death from wounds suffered during the dangerous rescue operation at Baytown's Calvary Church.

Jeremy had kept close watch over her until his father returned. Strained relationships had marked their family prior to September Strike. Following their remarkable experiences, however, the family had begun to draw new strength from each other and from the Lord.

Especially the Lord!

Now, Esther was almost completely recovered from her physical wounds. The emotional scars resulting from Jenny's accidental death seemed to be healing as well. Jeremy had also reached a new level of peace within his young spirit, and he and his father were experiencing a togetherness they had not known in months. Maybe not ever before.

Yes, a lot had happened around this pool. Around the world.

John looked up at the night sky one more time. The moon and stars were blurred by the moistness in his eyes, as the familiar feeling of unspoken hopelessness swept over him.

Where are you, sweetheart? Daddy is sorry. So very sorry!

FIVE

TUESDAY, 18 OCTOBER
BAYTOWN, CALIFORNIA

As with all stories deemed worthy of massive attention by those invincible and invisible heads of the world's news bureaus, September Strike's impact reached its crescendo quickly. And, as quickly as it had climaxed, interest began to wane. Last month's high tension drama, fueled by the all-consuming, color coverage of national and international television, and chronicled by daily papers and weekly magazines worldwide, had eventually given way to the reporting of new crises.

During his first week home from Israel, John had been inundated daily with news interviews and television appearances. Network magazine shows clamored for attention. "Good Morning, America," and the "Today Show" featured interviews with John in their prime-time viewer slots. "Sixty Minutes," "Dateline," and "20/20" also worked the story with features surrounding the event. "American Journal" and "Estra" offered substantial sums of money for exclusive interviews. When money was received, the full amount was deposited in the "Bring Jessica Home Fund" that had been hastily established by Baytown community leaders with the assistance of a local bank.

Although the media were generally sympathetic to the plight of the Cain family, John occasionally found himself facing interviewers who were not particularly enamored by his Christian faith. It happened on the popular "Kris Lauring Show." Lauring was a young, rising star in the talk-show business. His reputation for probing, sometimes embarrassing questions touching all aspects of life, including politics, religion, and personal lifestyles, made him a "must see" for many of the Bay Area's under-thirty crowd. John thought this particularly interesting in light of the fact that this TV host and his sister were originally from Baytown and had attended youth camps sponsored by Calvary Church. The last he had heard, Lauring's sister was attending seminary. He wondered what Lauring's parents thought about their son's ultra-liberal and at times even Machiavellian views. His father pastored a small, fundamentalist church on the other side of town.

He could tell by the caustic edge to Lauring's interview that, given a different event than a missing child, John would most likely have been confronted with intense religious cynicism. That the young man was sharp there was no doubt. It was too bad the Christian message had not captured his heart.

Initially, John was repulsed by the idea of accepting money for interviews. However, the cost of printing and mailing posters to countries throughout the Middle East, North Africa, and Europe was eating up their small personal savings. Keeping Jessica's terrifying plight before the world's conscience was critical . . . and expensive. Yet, somewhere out there, an innocent twelve-year-old girl had become the unwitting victim of international terrorism. His girl! And he was determined to get her back, whatever the cost.

Media attention continued well into the following week, with Calvary Community Church's telephone lines jammed by reporters seeking more information, well-wishers offering heartfelt condolences, and the usual crank calls that go along with something of this magnitude. In self-defense, John and Esther had placed their home telephone on voice mail. Volunteers from the congregation took turns gathering the calls and determining how best to answer them.

After Esther was released from the hospital, she continued convalescence at home under the watchful care of John, Jeremy, and a task force of women from the church who cooked, cleaned, answered mail and did what had to be done. Their presence enabled John to interact with an interested media to keep Jessica's plight in front of the public.

Turning their quiet home into a beehive of activity, however, removed the last vestige of retreat, and the physical and emotional stress of it all was taking its toll. John needed to get away, to go to the beach or the mountains. He needed time off for the sake of his own recovery, and so did Esther, but there was no opportunity for that now; too much depended on the moment.

By the beginning of week three, as telephone calls started to subside, John sensed that their window to the world was closing. By week four only occasional media calls were being received, though volunteers from the church still came by on a daily basis to check on the Cain family and to bring a hot evening meal. On Thursday, two women had come to clean house and wash and iron clothes.

Yesterday had been John and Esther's first entire day alone since early September. Most of it was spent in their backyard, near the pool. It was their favorite place. At least it had been.

John had relished the thought of their finally being alone together. He was almost recovered from the beatings he had sustained in Israel, but remained exhausted from the nonstop tension of these last weeks. Gradually, taut muscles loosened and his set jaw relaxed as they dozed in the warm October sun, sipped iced tea, and let their hands touch now and again. Yet, the day had given way to long periods of silence and, at times, a feeling of awkwardness between them.

When first reunited in Esther's room at the hospital, they had spoken reassuringly of their love and devotion for each other. It was easy to see that Esther had been dramatically changed by what she had gone through. Transformed for the better, he thought. She seemed to be at greater peace with herself, no small miracle, considering their present circumstances. It was different for John. He didn't know what he felt, other than an overwhelming sense of responsibility and loss where Jessica was concerned. There was no time to deal with personal feelings. All of his energy needed to be directed toward the crisis at hand.

The anxiety of Jessica's disappearance, and the myriad activity surrounding their traumatic adventures, had left little time for anything other than surface conversation. The consequence was an awkwardness that neither of them had yet felt safe enough to break through. They had managed to speak at length about Jessica, trying to imagine where she might be and what she was doing. Then they swam together in the pool, for the first time since Jenny's death.

Later, they showered and went to bed.

John was mindful of Esther's freshly healed bullet wounds and the scars still tender to the touch. His lips brushed each wound lightly as an awesome awareness washed over him once more, a reminder that his own beautiful wife had narrowly escaped being killed in their own church. It seemed as though he held in his hands a rare porcelain vase which, with a careless move, might easily be broken.

They had lain quietly, cradled in each other's arms as moonlight filtered through the window, illuminating their bed with a soft glow.

He looked at his lover's face, resting inches from his own. Her eyes were closed.

I love you so much. His lips moved silently, shaping his declaration of devotion.

But the tensions that had been set aside earlier still lurked, like demons in the shadows, ready to drain away energy and renew his state of exhaustion.

Why?

He breathed again the fresh scent of her hair, loosely falling across her shoulder. He felt the warmth of her body next to his.

Her physical injuries he could see and avoid hurting. That was easy. But there was more, so much more that he was uncertain about.

What about the other scars? The emotional lacerations that he could not see? These were the truly frightening wounds, the ones that tore at soul and spirit.

Since Jenny's drowning they had hardly been able to touch, much less be intimate with each other. The pain of her loss had drowned them both in depression.

An undeclared waiting pattern had finally prevailed between them, a tender truce upon which their very survival seemed to depend. John did not know exactly what they were waiting for, but he hoped there was something.

There had to be. Otherwise, their marriage was never going to make it.

WEDNESDAY, 19 OCTOBER
0900 LOCAL TIME

THE MORNING SUN appeared tentative as it caressed the few remaining flowers. John cleared away the fruit bowls and coffee cups from the table. After a few minutes, he returned to find that Esther had moved away from the patio table and into the sunlight, letting its warmth cut the cool edge lingering in the morning air.

"Feel like going for a walk?" John asked, smiling.

Esther nodded, releasing a deep sigh.

"We don't have to, if you don't feel up to it."

"I'm okay. I want to walk," she said, stretching her legs. "I need to walk. All this lying around and being waited on hand and foot has got to end sometime. I'm getting lazy."

"The day you can be classified as lazy, we'll both check into the old folks home," John responded, taking her hand as they walked through the garden gate and out onto the sidewalk.

"If we live that long."

Esther's words were pensive. At another time, they would both have laughed and joked about getting older, about hot flashes and failing memories and graying hair. Then, Esther would break into a run, calling back over her shoulder, "Come on, old man, see if you can keep up!" But not today.

Today they walked slowly, staring into the distance. A car drove past, windows open, radio booming unintelligible sounds from an acid rock station.

"Think that guy is hard of hearing?" John watched as the car slowed for a stop sign, then sped around the corner and disappeared.

"If not now, soon," Esther replied.

John's hand pressed against Esther's, palm flat, fingers touching but not intertwining. Now and then, they would walk like this, letting the palms of their hands feel the slight movement of the other. A sensual feeling. A message to each other in a crowd.

Esther looked over at John and smiled. They continued walking in silence for several minutes.

"Last night was wonderful," John broke the silence "Thank you."

A brief hesitation.

"No. Thank you," Esther answered.

More silence.

"It's been a long time, hasn't it?" she continued, finally.

John felt her hand move and her fingers intertwine with his.

"It's been a hard time," John answered. "For both of us."

They were walking past Caldwell Field, a neighborhood park with slides and tables and benches, designed for young families and named after Alfred W. Caldwell, a deceased city councilman.

"Can we sit down for a few minutes, John? I need to rest."

"Sure. Would you like me to get the car? You shouldn't overdo it."

"No. I don't need a car. I just need to rest . . . and to talk."

They walked across the grassy field to a picnic table and sat down. Esther touched the scar from the bullet wound along the side of her head. Early on, it had been the most wicked looking of her injuries. Now, it was well on its way to healing.

"Does it hurt?"

"Not so much."

John watched as she moved her hand away, brushing a fleck from her denim skirt, and then folded her hands in her lap.

When she looked up at him, he wondered what was coming. Her face was a mask of sadness. He started to reach for her, to reassure her somehow that everything was going to be all right. She held up a hand and he stopped short.

"I don't know exactly how to begin this, John. Actually, I'm so terribly embarrassed. I did something while you were gone. I know Jeremy hasn't told you, because I asked him. Believe me, I wish I didn't have to share this, but, we've never had secrets before, and I can't start living with them now."

John did not move, paralyzed by anticipation of what might be coming. He already understood by Esther's tone of voice and the paleness of her face that it would not be good news.

Esther swallowed as she played nervously with the corner of her shirttail.

"I tried to kill myself!"

Her words hit him with the force of a hammer.

A flood of memories. . . . Her heartrending wail when the fireman confirmed that Jenny was dead. . . . The blank stares as she sat by her favorite window. . . . The look in her eyes when they said good-bye in the airport.

"Please, John," she was crying softly. "Don't hate me. It wasn't your fault."

He closed his eyes tightly, stunned at what he was hearing. When he opened them again, he saw her in front of him, head bowed, shoulders drooped, tears falling freely onto clenched hands.

"I'm sorry," she said simply. "I'm so very sorry."

"O, dear Lord," John whispered in disbelief. "What have I done?"

He reached out and took her into his arms, pulling her off the bench and onto the grass. Clutching each other tightly, they lost all track of time, huddled together in the warm autumn sun. John wiped away his tears and hers, listening while Esther released her story of recent pain and the overwhelming depression that had followed.

Then a wonderful thing took place. For the first time in a long time, John felt himself slowly start to relax. He smiled, choking back the pride he felt as she spoke of Jeremy's strength and the role of healer he had played in John's absence.

He felt sadness, as Esther tried to explain her jumbled feelings while teetering on the edge of self-destruction.

Then it was John's turn.

He begged forgiveness for not being there in her trial. Instead, he now saw that he'd been an unwitting contributor to it. Deeply immersed in his own pain, he had failed to help Esther deal with hers. He voiced his own guilt where Jessica was concerned. And, in the same way that John had assured Esther that Jenny's drowning was accidental and not her fault, Esther spoke words of comfort to John. . . .

"You could not have known. You did what you thought was best for her at the moment.

"The whole thing is unimaginable . . .

"We can't go on blaming ourselves for what has happened, can we?

"Where is God in all of this?"

It was nearly noon when they rose from the grass and slowly retraced their steps. They moved to one side of the walkway as two women approached, out for a late morning stroll. So intent on each other, so lost in their thoughts, they didn't return the greeting that was offered.

"NOW, THERE'S A COUPLE IN LOVE, Emily. Don't you wish Henry would look at you like he was looking at her?"

"They probably aren't married."

"Yes, they are. I saw a ring on the man's finger."

"Okay, so they're married, but maybe not to each other!"

Laughter.

"Actually, the last time Henry looked at me like that was nine months before Carl was born."

More laughter.

"Did you see the way they were holding hands?"

"Yes. Didn't it look strange to you?"

"Different, anyway. I've never seen anyone do it quite like that."

"Maybe they're aliens, Doris, from another planet. That's it. That's what they are. And the only way to tell the difference between them and us is the strange way they hold hands."

"You and your science fiction novels! You've got to stop reading that stuff."

"Well, you don't know. It could be."

"O, Em, as my granddaughter would say, 'Get a life!' "

IT WAS NEARLY FOUR-THIRTY when Esther reached over to refill their glasses from the pitcher of iced tea. She smiled at John, absorbing the warmth of his gaze in return. It was a most satisfying look of love. This had been an unforgettable day. They would never have another quite like it. Desire and devotion had merged as they searched for each other.

Healing. Restoration. Passion.

Esther could not remember having felt like this before. Ever. She relished this blissful interval.

The afternoon had left her feeling beautiful and whole. At last, the two of them were truly one again. Not just in name or address or mission in life, but with each other. She knew it with such certainty. Incredibly, she also felt a oneness with God that was fresh as well. In the act of human love, her soul had touched the divine heart as well.

These hours spent in each other's arms had awakened within her an unexpected flood of emotion . . . instinctive . . . elemental.

She drifted along a river of Edenic primitiveness. Earth and heaven mingled together with the seasons of their love.

"What?" John smiled questioningly, looking into Esther's glowing face.

"Nothing," she replied.

Then, laughing, she kissed the tip of his nose.

"Nothing, my dearest. And everything."

Esther laid her head against his chest. Contentment. When was the last time they had done this?

As she mused, there came a smile. She was not sure about the last time, but she could remember one time, thirteen years ago.

That day they had created a child. *October's child!*

SIX

Prayers were being chanted in a nearby mosque. Jessica had no choice but to listen to their mystical cadence. She was also growing accustomed to the sounds of the minaret. Was someone actually in the tower, calling the people of this city to prayer? She doubted it. She had been told by her father that most prayers were prerecorded and played back at the appropriate hours.

In any event, these appeals to the Almighty helped her to keep track of the hours and days. She awakened each morning at sunrise to the Muslim call to prayer. Shortly after the noontime call, her food was delivered. In the middle of the afternoon, the third call to prayer was offered. Next, at sunset. Last of all, came the evening prayer. Five times every day.

The whole thing was amazing to her. And depressing. . . .

The first thing Jessica had felt in this room was a cool, damp cloth being applied to her face and body. When she opened her eyes, the walls and ceiling swirled in sickening circles. She shut them quickly, then opened again slowly, trying to halt the sickening movement and to focus on something. Gradually, the room slowed its circular motion and came to a stop.

Her eyes were drawn to an attractive woman who bent over her cot. She was dressed in a blue, one-piece cloak that covered all parts of her body except her hands, feet, and face. A strangely familiar sight. Jessica remembered Arab women in Israel also wearing something similar. It was called a chador.

"Aehlaen, Jessica," said the woman. Her teeth were even and white, her smile warm and friendly.

Jessica lay quietly, staring at the woman's face.

How does she know my name?

Her mind kept turning pages, trying to find something that would help her remember. Nothing.

"Hel tetekellem arabi?"

Jessica moved her head to signal that she did not speak Arabic. She winced in pain as again the room turned topsy. The combination of the earlier drug dose and subsequent dehydration, while being transported in the back of the truck, had left her with a major headache. Gently, the woman placed her hands on each side of Jessica's head and held her steady, pressing in on her temples ever so slightly. That felt good.

"If you do not speak Arabic, you must listen to my poor English," she said softly. "Do not move your head just yet. You have been very ill, Jessica. The others thought that we had lost you. They did not know how strong you are. I breathed into you the breath of life. You call it something. . . . I do not know what is the term. Finally, you come back to us. But, you have need to rest now, and you must drink. Here is water. I will lift you slowly until you can take some."

Jessica felt the woman's hand slip beneath her head and neck. As she was lifted, a bottle was pressed against her lips. She tried to swallow, but most of it ran down from the corners of her mouth and onto her shoulders. That's when she noticed that her blouse had been removed. In its place, a damp towel was draped across her chest.

Another sip. This time, the water ran cool down her throat.

The woman took the bottle away and lowered her back again on the cot.

"Where am I?" Jessica's voice sounded strange and far away to her.

No answer.

The woman busied herself by carefully placing a cool, moist cloth over Jessica's face.

Pictures flashed across her mind. . . *A blanket. A box. Men looking at me. One with a syringe. He . . . he . . .*

Shards of recent memory stabbed her consciousness, causing Jessica to flinch. She struggled to rise, instinctively sensing both danger and her need to escape.

The woman's hands were on her shoulders, forcing her gently back on the cot. "Please, Jessica, try to remain still. You are safe."

The woman's words were soft, reassuring.

She settled back, trying to remember what came next . . . after the man with the needle. *Darkness. A truck motor. Can't move. A hole with light coming in. Hot. Get to the hole for some air. Bouncing. It's so hot. O God, please help me!*

Jessica clinched her fists and struggled to control the panic.

The woman took away the facial cloth and lifted her again, ever so slightly, placing the bottle to her lips, letting the water trickle over her tongue and down her throat.

A few minutes passed and, exhausted, she had slipped back into a fitful sleep. . . .

That had been then. This was now.

Looking at the collection of tiny marks near the boarded window, she saw that nearly a month had drifted by. Each day, Jessica scratched the block wall with a tiny stone. Four scratches. A fifth crossed through the other four. Then, four more. She recounted just to be sure.

Twenty-seven! She figured that she missed two or three days at the beginning, when she almost died.

The kind woman in the chador came every day. Jessica had asked her name, but she simply smiled and shook her head. Occasionally, she arrived at mealtime. Once a week, she stood guard at the door of the toilet while Jessica took her shower. On the first such occasion, she gathered up Jessica's clothes and, in their place, presented her with a hejab. It was made of dark blue cloth that draped loosely on her body and formed a hood over her head, leaving only her feet, hands, and face uncovered. She looked like a young Muslim girl.

Jessica assumed that her own clothes were gone forever. But, the next day, the woman had returned them washed and folded.

One day, after having regained most of her strength, she heard someone talking over a loudspeaker. It was considerably longer than the usual prayer to which she was becoming accustomed. She knew that one of the men who guarded her door and brought her food spoke English, so she asked him what was happening. He told her it was Thursday, and that every Thursday a sermon was delivered at the mosque. It was the longest conversation she had had with any of her captors, but now, at least, she knew what day of the week it was.

The next day, at Friday morning prayers, another lengthy address boomed out across the area. She wished that she understood Arabic. The sermon and the prayers made her think of her father. She longed to be home again, to hear his full, rich voice fill the sanctuary as he led the people in prayer or invited them to "join with me today in God's Word." Every Thursday evening and Friday morning were the same. The routine became the confirmation of her calendar scratches.

One day Jessica asked for a book to help her learn Arabic. No. No book.

Then she asked for books or magazines in English. Still nothing.

The days stretched out interminably, and since she was not chained, she walked. Each time someone came to her room, she studied the face, inscribing every feature in her mind. She wondered about their willingness to let her see them. Surely they knew that she would be able to identify them later. That is, of course, unless they knew that later they had nothing to worry about.

Across from where she sat, Jessica stared at the boarded-up window. Through the cracks she could see when it was daylight. The mosque had to be somewhere nearby. Occasionally, she overheard faraway voices. Was it a school? No, the voices were older. It sounded more like a marketplace.

The handle on the inside of her door had been removed. A single light bulb hung down from the center of the room, its pale glow the only nighttime illumination in her otherwise gloomy prison cell.

She was thankful not to be tied up. Circling the room, she paced it off, measuring its length and breadth. She even tried to calculate how many times she would need to walk in a circle to complete a mile.

At home, she had occasionally walked with her mother. The route that they normally took was two miles long. It had never taken them more than thirty minutes. Now, however, her watch was gone—she assumed that her captors must have stolen it. She counted from one to sixty as she walked, attempting to establish the length of one minute. Then she kept track of the "minutes" until fifteen of them had been counted. Six times around the room in a minute. Ninety times equaled one mile.

The cell was musty and surprisingly cold at night. After the woman brought back her laundered clothes, she immediately removed the hejab and donned them. But, as the chill became increasingly uncomfortable, she put the hejab on over her clothing.

I wish I had my suitcase with all my things in it.

Her cot had a foam rubber mattress and a thin blanket. When Jessica complained to the woman about being cold, she was given an additional blanket, in much better condition than the other one, and a small pillow.

The men who took turns guarding her left her alone, except for the youngest. Their post was just outside her door. She could not tell the ages of the others, but the oldest one had gray in his hair and few good teeth. The older guards smiled and nodded to her, but they rarely spoke more than a word or two. That was okay with Jessica—she didn't want to talk with them anyway.

The times Jessica needed to use the toilet were the worst. At first, she was embarrassed; but eventually, necessity forced her to become more assertive.

She learned to pound on the door in earnest.

A key would turn in the lock. She was always relieved when it was one of the two older men.

"Sit," they would say.

She sat.

"Why you make noise?"

"I need the toilet."

"Not make noise."

"If I don't make noise, you won't open the door."

"No noise."

"It's urgent. I need toilet."

"Later. Not now."

"No. Now. I need to go now."

This argument took place on a regular basis. The exception was when the woman with the kind face was there. She permitted access without question.

The guards followed her down the hallway each time to the toilet and stood outside while she went in. The door was always left ajar. When she had finished, they followed her back to her cell. As soon as she walked through the doorway, she heard it close and lock behind her.

Today, she knocked on the door. The key turned.

When it opened, the youngest guard was standing there, his automatic weapon slung over his shoulder by a single strap. She was surprised to see a grin on his face.

"Sit."

She sat.

"Why you make noise?"

"I need the toilet."

The guard let his eyes roam up and down Jessica's body. She had folded the hejab on the foot of the cot and was wearing her own clothes. Suddenly, she wished that she had thought to put on the dark, shapeless garment. His stare made her nervous.

"Not make noise."

"It's urgent. I need toilet."

"Later. Not now."

"No. Now. I need to go now."

"All right," the guard said reluctantly, still leering insolently at Jessica. "Go."

He did not back away from the doorway.

Jessica bit her lip. She wished she could hold it until one of the other guards was on duty, but her bladder was full and she needed to go. Desperately.

"Excuse me."

The young man didn't move.

"I said excuse me."

He continued blocking the doorway.

Jessica started past him. Turning sideways, she pressed her back against the doorjamb as far as she could. There still was not enough room to get through without touching him, so she put her hands in front of her and nudged him away. He smelled bad and she wanted to gag.

Suddenly, he grabbed her wrist and twisted, causing her to drop to her knees.

"You're hurting me. Stop it!"

"How badly do you need to go?" the young man stood over her, laughing at her discomfort.

"I said quit it. You are hurting me!"

"American whore!" He leered at her, laying his gun on the hallway floor. Dropping to his knees, he yanked her forward until her face was next to his and tried to kiss her. His mouth was wet and his breath was bad. She felt his hands fumbling with her shirt as she twisted and struggled to push away.

Then his mouth was on her lips again. This time she bit him! With a cry of pain, he fell back.

Jessica scrambled to her feet as the guard felt his lip and looked ruefully at the blood on his fingers. Angry, frightened, and without thinking, she aimed a well-placed kick at his groin. It hit the mark, causing him to double over with a groan. As she turned to run, he grabbed her ankle, wrenched it, and made her fall to the floor once more.

All at once, she heard other sounds and then, as quickly as it had started, it was over.

The woman with the kind face yanked the young lad backward, causing him to sprawl across the hallway floor. Her face was flushed with anger as she stooped to pick up his weapon. Only she did not point it at Jessica but at the guard.

"That's mine," he said, reaching up for the gun.

"It *was* yours, you stupid donkey. Not any more. Get out of here!"

"You can't tell me what to do."

She brandished the weapon under his nose, in a way that clearly indicated she knew how to use it.

"I can and I am. You're finished. Get out now!"

The young man pushed himself to his feet, glaring sullenly at the woman and then at Jessica. Without a word, he turned, walked the length of the hall, and disappeared down the staircase.

Now the woman turned and looked at Jessica who was shaking and crying.

"Are you all right?" she asked.

"Ye . . . yes," Jessica stammered. "I just need to go to the toilet."

"Go."

Jessica turned and ran to the other end of the hall. At the door, she paused and looked back. The woman with the kind face had not moved. She still held the guard's weapon in her hands. With her head, she motioned for her to go in. Jessica went inside and closed the door. For the first time, she was alone. She had not been this far from her guards since having been brought here. Her breath came in short bursts. Looking down at her shirt, she saw that the top two buttons were missing, and she shivered at the thought of what had just happened.

When she was finished, Jessica opened the door and stepped back into the hall. The woman was in front of the door to her cell, talking to someone Jessica had never seen before. The stranger looked up as she came out, then returned to his conversation with the woman. As Jessica approached, the man took the gun from the woman and turned toward the staircase.

The woman extended her hand to Jessica. In it were the two missing buttons. Jessica took them as the woman guided her back into her quarters.

"Are you all right now?" she asked.

Jessica nodded.

"You are certain? He did not hurt you?"

Jessica looked up, tears rolling down her checks.

"He twisted my arm, called me a name, and started to put his hands all over me."

"He touched you? Where?"

"Here." Jessica motioned with her hands.

The woman's face clouded over in anger.

"And he called you a name?"

"Yes. He said I was an 'American whore!' He frightened me. But *that* made me mad!"

The woman suppressed a smile.

"Yes. I could see that you were mad. And I saw what the boy was doing. He will not return. They know you were not trying to escape. No one will bother you from now on. I have seen to that."

Jessica crouched on the edge of her cot. She was still quivering from the fright she had just experienced. The woman with the kind face moved closer, and placed a hand on Jessica's head. Jessica leaned forward, releasing a surge of emotion, as she buried her face in the folds of the woman's chador and wept uncontrollably.

The woman put her arms around Jessica and gently rocked her back and forth.

SEVEN

Her long, disheveled hair fell unevenly across bare shoulders as she reached for the open pack of cigarettes on the night stand. Shaking one out, she placed it between her lips and struck a match. Touching the match to the cigarette, she inhaled deeply, then shook out the flame with a practiced flick of her long fingers.

Settling back into the pillows, she pulled the bed covers even with her waist, filled her lungs once more with the familiar taste, and exhaled as she examined her reflection in the mirror across the tiny room.

A nice face. Not beautiful, but nice. A bit girlish for a woman of nineteen, Annie thought, but men seemed to like it. Blue eyes, oval-shaped nose a bit too small, and mouth a bit too large. She smiled as she admired her "look." Her friends thought that her skin was her greatest asset, the color of fresh milk, in stark contrast to her dark brown hair now cascading loosely across the pillows. She guessed they were probably right—most of her customers felt the same way.

Tonight was no exception.

She moved slightly, in order to position the man's reflection in the mirror. He had been here with her for two hours.

At first, he'd stood outside her rented cubicle for several minutes, watching through the large display window. She thought he looked interested, and so she began moving more sensuously than usual.

Here, in the heart of Amsterdam's infamous red-light district, Annie danced to music played on a portable tape recorder. Clad only in revealing lingerie, she smiled from behind the plate glass that faced out onto the street, and made certain that her audience was aware of what she could offer. Up and down the street, similar scenarios were being acted out in dozens of look-alike windows.

She had been right. He signaled her and asked to come in. As it turned out, he insisted on going to a nearby hotel, rather than the shabby little room in which she normally plied her trade.

Quiet and strong. And very handsome. She had guessed him to be a Middle Easterner, with his dark skin, black hair, and nicely trimmed beard. Muscular and fit. Piercing eyes, even when he smiled. She was intrigued by the eyes and the rakish-looking scar trailing across his cheek.

The money was folded under a wine bottle on the night stand. US$200. Not bad, considering some of the nights that she endured in her line of work. Not bad at all.

Now he sat with his back to her, speaking into the telephone. His Middle Eastern heritage was confirmed as she overheard the conversation. At times he spoke in English, then in Arabic. She understood most of the conversation in both languages, though she assumed her client would be surprised at that. She actually paid little attention to him, thinking of what she would do with the money. Perhaps a nice new dress. Then, she remembered that the rent was due on Tuesday. Oh, well . . .

She tuned into the one-sided conversation, watching in the mirror as the man's eyes narrowed. What had caught her attention? Had it been the sudden change in the tone of his voice? He was glaring into a corner of the room now, moving a finger back and forth across the scar on his cheek.

"Don't argue," he burst out angrily in Arabic. "Just do it. Get the girl out of there. . . . Of course, it's a long way to Iran. . . . No, I don't care how you do it. . . . Just don't lose her. She's all we have left. . . . Yes, I know everyone is looking. . . . We'll tell them how to get her when the time comes. . . . Yes, I'll be in touch in a few days. . . . Look, if you have not heard from me by the time she arrives, get word to Gazeb. . . . That is right. It is most important. Good luck."

The man replaced the receiver and stood. Tucking his shirt into his slacks, he slipped sockless feet into a pair of sandals and reached for the jacket he'd hung earlier on the hook by the door.

"Thanks," he said, looking at the girl.

She smiled and coyly waved a hand.

The door closed behind him.

Annie sucked on the cigarette again, then crushed it out in the ashtray under the bed lamp, blowing the last of the smoke toward the ceiling.

I wonder what that was all about.

She went into the bathroom, turned on the shower, and stepped into the spray of hot water. Scrubbing, soaping, and rinsing herself clean, she closed off the tap and wiped dry with a thin hotel room towel. She took another from the counter and briskly dried her hair. A few minutes later, she was dressed and ready to walk out the door. Through the entire time, however, something continued to nag at the back of her mind.

Gathering up her jacket, she stood with her hand on the doorknob, surveying the room. Thinking back over the events of the evening, her gaze passed over the telephone, then returned to it.

That conversation was unusual, to say the least. Who was he talking to? Why did he suddenly get so angry and leave? And what was all that about Iran? Who could possibly want to go there? What girl was he talking about, anyway?

She shook her head and opened the door, then hesitated again.

Could it have been . . . no . . . surely not. The girl in the papers and on TV . . . this couldn't have been about her, could it?

Like the rest of the world, Annie had gotten caught up in the CNN story dubbed September Strike. It had been a nerve-racking crisis, and everybody was talking about it. When the worst was over, an announcement was made concerning a girl named Jessica, who apparently had been kidnapped by the same terrorist group that had nearly touched off an international conflagration.

It was the girl's picture that had haunted her.

First on CNN, then in the local Amsterdam journals. On the cover of *Newsweek* and *Time.* Even some of Europe's major news magazines. The fate of a solitary twelve-year-old American girl enthralled the world. Where was she? Was she still alive?

After seeing her face in the media at least a dozen times, Annie was almost certain that it was her.

She looks so much like the little girl who waved to me through the window last month. Her eyes were so expressive . . . their color . . . I wish I could be sure. They were unusual, though. What if it was that preacher's kid from America? She was with a man that night. Was that the preacher? And she was kidnapped in the Middle East, wasn't she? The news people said they came through Amsterdam on their way to Israel. And this john tonight was speaking Arabic. He sure looked the part too....

Her heart beat faster as she started down the hall toward the elevator.

It could just be her imagination. Even if she went to the police, would they believe her, considering who she was?

Why should I care, anyway? Getting involved in people's problems is always bad news. Still, if it was her ... the kid deserves a break.

Through the night, she tossed restlessly on her bed. The girl was there with her, and evil men were doing bad things. Annie buried her face in the pillow and tried pushing little Jessica from her dreams.

By seven the next morning, Annie had made up her mind. She dressed, put on her makeup, walked down the stairs and out onto the street. A brisk ten-minute walk along the canal and across the footbridge to the opposite side. Climbing the steps of the neighborhood police station, she took a deep breath, pulled open the door, and walked in.

The small reception area looked familiar. Annie Heergaren had been there before.

TWO HOURS LATER SHE WALKED OUT, closing the station door behind her. She stood on the landing for a moment, admiring a rare burst of October sun, feeling more alive and excited than she could remember.

Retracing her route across the footbridge, she stopped at mid-point and put both hands on the iron railing that overlooked the drop-off into the canal. She breathed deeply of the fresh morning air. Sunlight accented an oily scum mixed with pieces of litter floating in the canal's dirty water. The canal itself was bordered by narrow, tree-lined streets and charming three-story row houses painted in an array of bright colors.

Every window was curtained with white lace. In most cases the lace was pulled back to permit strollers the enjoyment of a fine painting hanging inside on the wall, or an ornate vase purposely set before the glass pane for all to see. Window boxes offered passersby a blossoming riot of color, defying the impending depression of winter grayness that every Hollander knew was just around the corner.

She had seen all this before. But today was special. For the

first time in a long time, Annie Heergaren knew that she had done
something truly worthwhile. It felt good.

....

20 OCTOBER
THE STATE DEPARTMENT
SENSITIVE

Local Authorities in Amsterdam report information re
JESSICA CAIN, American citizen, missing in Israel since 18
September, believed to be possible terrorist kidnap victim.

Source: Ms. Annie Heergaren, Dutch citizen, age nineteen,
prostitute.

Information Quality: Good
Thursday, pm, 20 October, Ms. Heergaren overheard a
client's telephone conversation with unknown party. Became suspicious when client gave an order to relocate a
"girl" to Iran. Further questioning indicates that Ms.
Heergaren believes she saw Jessica Cain when she and her
father passed through the city in September. This is unveri-
fied and considered speculative.
In photo search, client identified by Ms. Heergaren is
Marwan Dosha. Repeat: MARWAN DOSHA. Police are following leads produced by interview with Ms. Heergaren.

Action Steps:
In the Netherlands, police are alerting airport and train
officials and auto rental agencies. The most recent Dosha
photo is accompanying general APB. Orders are to approach with caution and detain. May be armed and should
be considered extremely dangerous.
Police in Belgium, Germany, and France have been informed. INTERPOL, CIA, and MOSSAD have been
contacted.

....

FRIDAY, 21 OCTOBER, 1025 LOCAL TIME
BAYTOWN, CALIFORNIA

AS THE LAST OF THE GROCERIES were put away, Esther
reached for the telephone. While at the store, she had decided to
talk to John. When he left for the church office, earlier that morn-

ing, she had sensed his depression.

I'll see how he's doing. Maybe we can sneak away later for an early dinner at Hunters. I'll see if they will give us a table in the back corner where no one will bother us.

Picking up the receiver, she heard the familiar beep-beep that indicated messages were in the voice mail box. Hesitating for a second, Esther began punching in the numbers that opened the box. There were times when she hated this task, but it did catch a lot of otherwise missed messages.

The automated voice could be heard saying, "You have one new message . . ."

Oh, good. Only one.

Esther punched the code number for "listening," and prepared to write it down.

" . . . sent today at nine twenty-three," declared the familiar recorded female voice.

Next, a man's voice with a deep southern drawl.

"Reverend or Mrs. Cain. It's about twelve twenty-five here in Washington. Please call Charles Rodeway at 202 . . ."

Esther quickly scribbled down the name and number.

"We have some information we'd like to discuss. Please call right away. I'll be waiting to hear from you. Good day."

Esther's heart skipped a beat. She stood, staring first at the receiver in her hand, then at the freshly written note.

Information? It's Jessica. It's got to be!

Esther listened for the tone, then pressed the number for John's office.

"Hello. This is Grace speaking. How may I help you?"

"Hi, Grace. Is John there?"

"Oh, hello, Esther. How are you?"

"I'm fine. But I need to talk with John." Esther knew there was an impatient edge to her voice, but didn't bother trying to cover it up.

"He's with the staff right now. Would you like for me to buzz him?"

"Yes, please. I need to speak to him right away."

"Just a second. I'll get him for you."

Esther did not normally like to bother John when he was counseling or with the staff. However, he had always made certain that Esther and the children knew they could call him, even if it interrupted a counseling session. It was one of the ways he tried to temper the long hours and numerous evenings spent away from the family.

"Hi, hon," John's voice greeted her.

"John, there was a message on the telephone when I got home from the store. It's from a Charles Rodeway."

"The name doesn't ring a bell. Are we supposed to know him?"

"He's calling from Washington."

Silence.

"Did he leave a number?" John's voice had taken on a cautious tone.

"Yes, he did. He called just over an hour ago." Esther repeated the area code and phone number.

"Okay. I've got it."

Esther hesitated.

"Honey, are you all right?" asked John.

"I'm . . . okay. Would you come home, please? Let's make the call here together." Her anxiety was clearly evident in her voice. "I . . . I don't want to be alone right now."

"I'm on my way."

FIFTEEN MINUTES LATER, JOHN WALKED through the door. Without a word, he took Esther in his arms. They held each other tightly, her face pressed against his chest.

"How are you doing?"

"I'm okay. No, that's not true. Actually, I'm frightened. Petrified. Scared to death!"

"The message didn't contain any other information?"

"No, nothing."

Slowly, they pulled away from each other, and their eyes went to the phone.

"Well, let's do it," John said, lifting the receiver. "Get on the extension. Maybe this is good news."

He flashed a thin smile at Esther. Forcing a weak one in return, she hurried into the other room.

"CHARLES RODEWAY? MAY I SAY who is calling, please?"

"John and Esther Cain. We're returning Mr. Rodeway's call.

"Thank you. One moment."

The woman's voice was pleasant enough, but John sensed that he had just invaded a different world, one in which this woman was comfortable, but he was not. Was this a State Department official? Or the CIA? It didn't really matter. There probably wasn't that much difference between the two.

"Hello, Rodeway here," boomed the voice with the southern drawl.

"Hello, Mr. Rodeway. This is John Cain returning your call."

"Oh, yes, thank you for calling back, Reverend Cain. Is your wife there with you?"

"That's right."

"Good. Well, first of all, let me add my congratulations and admiration to that of the rest of the world for the way you both conducted yourselves last month. You are heroes. Our country . . . actually the whole world . . . owes you a debt of gratitude. We're all walking a little taller around here in Washington."

"Thank you, Mr. Rodeway," John responded, a tinge of impatience in his voice. "But I'm sure you have something else to tell us."

"Right you are, Reverend Cain. Actually, something has turned up. We're not certain as to its value at this point, but I wanted to let you know and to verify a part of the story. Yesterday evening, a prostitute in Amsterdam was servicing a client . . . excuse me, ma'am. . . ."

"It's all right," Esther's voice broke in. "Go on, please."

"Well, it seems the girl became suspicious when she overheard her client talking to somebody on the phone. He probably thought she wouldn't understand him because he was speaking in Arabic. Turns out that she has a fiancé at the University who is from Saudi."

"Wait a minute," John interrupted. "She has a fiancé? Like in marriage? I thought you said she was a prostitute."

"You heard correctly, reverend. It's a strange world! Anyway, she heard him say, 'Get the girl out of there.'"

"Did he mention any name?" asked John.

"No, he didn't. That's one of the weaknesses in this story. But he did mention a destination."

"What?" queried Esther anxiously. "What was it?"

"Well, I'm sorry to say that it is one of the most difficult to get at places on the globe, Mrs. Cain. The man supposedly indicated Iran as the destination point."

"And you think the girl might be Jessica?"

"It's a possibility. We can't be certain, but I wouldn't be here talking to you if we didn't think that it was likely your daughter that the man was talking about."

"Iran," repeated John incredulously. "Are you serious? Why Iran?"

"It may not be as far-fetched as it sounds. You see, the Iranian government is one of the chief financial backers of the Palestinian Islamic Jihad, the group that has claimed responsibility for all the activities of this past month. I guess you both know them better than I do."

"But, Iran?" Esther echoed. "What will they do with her there?"

"We aren't sure of anything, Mrs. Cain," Rodeway's voice softened a little. "I'm sure this is terribly difficult. I have a ten-year-old son. I can only imagine what you must be going through."

"If it is Jessica, where in Iran would they take her?" John persisted.

"We don't know. We're just beginning to call in some of our markers on this case now. If we find out anything further, we'll call you, of course."

"Yes, of course. Thanks very much."

"There are a couple of other things," Rodeway continued. "This girl who reported the story—she claims to have seen your little girl last month. It seems a bit unlikely, in that she works in the red-light district. Says she saw her there with an older man. Recognized her picture in the media. Thinks you might be the man. Is any of that possible?"

John's heart was beating rapidly.

"It is possible, Mr. Rodeway. We went out for a walk the night we arrived in Amsterdam. I became disoriented and, before I knew it, we were in the heart of the red-light district. Jessica was taken by it all, especially one girl who looked very young. I doubt if she was more than twenty or twenty-one. Long hair, brown, I think. Fair skin. I remember that Jessica decided the girl's parents must be very sad about what she was doing, and that she would pray for the girl every day during our tour through Israel."

"Do you recall anything Jessica might have done while she was there?" asked Rodeway. "You know, to catch the young woman's attention?"

John tried to think back to the exact scene. It seemed so long ago. He remembered holding Jessica's hand as they stood in front of the window.

"No . . . I can't think . . . wait. I remember that Jessica waved to her. A kind of timid, little wave. And she smiled up at the girl."

There was a long pause on the other end of the line.

"Reverend Cain, that's exactly what the young woman told the police. It sounds like it's the same girl. She remembered seeing you and your daughter standing there."

John's thoughts were spinning now, reliving that night together with Jessica in Amsterdam. This bit of news was incredible.

"Wait, Mr. Rodeway," said John. "You said there were a 'couple' of things. Is there something else you haven't told us?"

"Well, yes, there is. It's the woman's client. We think we know who he is."

"You know the man? Who is it?"

"His name is Marwan Dosha."

John's heart skipped a beat.

"Dosha?"

"Yes."

"The terrorist connected with the Boston incident?"

"One and the same."

John's heart sank.

"You mean our Jessica is in the hands of the world's worst terrorist?" The volume in John's voice rose, as did the sick feeling in the pit of his stomach.

"We're not sure about anything, Reverend Cain. But it looks like that's the way it may be."

Through the receiver, John heard a noise in the background, a voice saying something. Then Rodeway was back.

"I have a call on another line. I need to go. Reverend and Mrs. Cain, I want to thank you for returning my call. Please rest assured that we are doing our best to find your daughter and bring her home. If you are contacted by anyone, let me know, will you? I'll be in touch whenever I have something to tell you about her whereabouts."

"Thank you, Mr. Rodeway."

"Yes, thank you very much," Esther chimed in. "Good-bye."

John hung up the phone, his mind racing in all directions at once.

Dosha! I can't believe it. The same man who lived for a week with three other terrorists at Jim Brainard's Hill House in Maine. The mastermind of September Strike!

John stared up at the ceiling.

Dear God, when will all this madness stop?

Esther's steps were slow as she returned to the kitchen.

"She's alive," her voice cracked with emotion. "I've been trying to keep believing, but it's been so hard. O John, Jessica is still alive!"

John was silent, lost in a mental scramble, as they held one another.

EIGHT

Officer Martin Leideveen leaned against the wall near the Hertz Auto Rental customer service counter. His back was sore from having worked in the garden the day before. It had been perfect weather for pruning and preparing for the long winter months, so he had spent the entire day off digging, hauling and, in general, making his wife very happy.

During roll call at the station this morning, Leideveen learned that the world's most wanted terrorist was believed to be in his city. Along with a dozen other officers, he had been assigned to Schiphol Airport. This gateway to the world was a likely place for Marwan Dosha to pass through; and though Leideveen usually viewed this sort of duty as extremely boring, today was an exception. The thoughts of apprehending an internationally known criminal of Dosha's stature gave him an exciting adrenaline rush.

Leideveen shifted his stance, in order to give his aching back some relief. A light but steady of stream of people moved in and out of the central doors. He watched as a family, obviously Dutch, pushed a luggage cart filled with suitcases. An attractive woman, probably in her forties, French beret perched on her head, black blouse, tan suit and leather boots, was directly behind them.

From his vantage point, Officer Leideveen had a good view of the outdoor area beyond the main entrance. Taxis queued up, waiting to take tired travelers to downtown hotels. A group of pedestrians, most carrying luggage, was hurrying toward the entrance from the train station across the way.

An elderly man, dressed in rumpled trousers and jacket, and walking with the help of a cane, fell behind the others as he shambled toward the entrance. A bag hung from his bent shoulder. The man looked as though he could use some help, but none was offered by those overtaking and passing him on either side. So much for Dutch hospitality.

Suddenly, Leideveen spied the suspect. He came up behind the elderly man at a rapid pace, brushing by without a word. Dark-skinned, black hair, beard, open shirt, an expensive-looking gray sport jacket, and dark slacks. He carried a suitcase in his left hand. Now he was past the old man and nearing the entrance. Two young fellows in jeans strolled through the door ahead of him and went straight for the KLM ticket counter.

Leideveen took a step forward to get a better look at the man in the gray jacket. He glanced down at the picture in his hand, then up again. As he did, his heart began to pound with excitement.

It could be . . .

As the automated doors slid open, the man passed through and headed directly for the KLM counter, stopping behind the two young men. He put his bag down on the floor and pulled a ticket folder from his pocket.

By this time, the Dutch family and the woman pulling her suitcase had reached the exit, nearly colliding with the elderly man as he made his way in from outside. The commotion distracted Leideveen for what felt like only a split second. But, when he looked back toward the man in gray, he was already well away from the ticket counter, hurrying toward Concourse B.

Officer Leideveen spoke into his two-way radio, giving instructions to the policemen stationed on that concourse. There were two, one halfway along the concourse, the other in the boarding area at the far end. He began jogging after the suspect at the same moment that he disappeared around a corner. Leideveen rounded the same turn, just in time to see him step into a restroom. He waved his partner over and they approached the entrance together.

"When he comes out, you take the right side and I'll be on his left. Be careful. This could be Dosha. If it is, he's dangerous."

The other officer nodded, eyes on the restroom exit.

The door swung open and two young boys ran out, chasing each other as their mother called from across the corridor. Seconds later, the man in the gray jacket came through the door.

By the time he realized what was happening, the officers were on either side of him, and it was too late.

Leideveen spoke.

"Please. May we have a word with you?"

The man paused in mid-stride, looking first at one, then the other.

"What's the problem, officers?"

"May we see your passport, please?"

"Is there a difficulty. . . ?"

"Your passport, please."

The man's hand went toward a pocket inside his jacket.

"Sir!" Leideveen spoke sharply. "Please move your hand slowly and keep the other one where I can see it."

By now, a few passersby had noticed the altercation and were slowing down or stopping altogether in order to see what was happening. Even the old man paused for a moment, to watch and to catch his breath. Then, he shuffled on, stepping carefully onto the beltway and letting it carry him down the long concourse, while he recouped his flagging energy.

Minutes later, a disappointed Martin Leideveen made his way back to his station near the main entrance. The dark-skinned man, the only one he'd seen who looked the part, had turned out to be an American citizen on his way home to Chicago. Lamenting his bad luck, he leaned against the counter and resumed his watch.

THE OLD MAN SMILED at the flight attendant as she helped him settle into his seat. Then she placed his carry-on in the overhead compartment.

"When we arrive in Paris, Mr. Contaviani, I will get your bag down for you. You're sure you won't need anything before then?"

His wrinkled face, looking a lot like a throwaway sandwich bag, broke into a pleasant smile as he shook his head.

"All right then, make yourself comfortable. I'll be back after takeoff to see how you are doing. Enjoy your flight."

The attendant patted his shoulder, moving past him along the aisle, as the plane started to back away from the concourse loading dock. The old man leaned back in the seat and looked out the window, squinting against the unusually bright sunlight of this splendid October day in Holland.

Having arrived only yesterday on his way from Canada and ticketed all the way to Rome via Amsterdam and Paris, he decided that even though his visit to the land of tulips had been brief, it had certainly been agreeable.

21 OCTOBER
THE STATE DEPARTMENT
SENSITIVE

Additional confirmation re Marwan Dosha's presence in Amsterdam. Local authorities report a second photo identification confirmed by one Ferdinand Ternzen, night clerk at the Canal House Inn.

Information Quality: Good.
The clerk witnessed Ms. Heergaren enter the lobby with Dosha, who was registered there as Mansour Qudzik, a businessman from Cairo, Egypt. The passport number is currently being checked.
The clerk does not remember seeing Dosha leave although he does recall Ms. Heergaren passing through the lobby sometime after midnight.

Action Steps:
In the Netherlands, an APB has been issued. Police are watching airports, train stations, and auto rental agencies. Orders are to approach with caution and detain. May be armed and should be considered extremely dangerous.
This update has also gone to police in Belgium, Germany, France, and Egypt, as well as INTERPOL, CIA, and MOSSAD.
Will keep you advised.

1605 LOCAL TIME
CHARLES DE GAULLE AIRPORT, PARIS

MR. CONTAVIANI SHUFFLED across the concourse slowly, stopping every so often to catch his breath and lean on his cane. Eventually, he reached the telephones and waited patiently for a young man to finish setting up his date with someone who sounded as though she was worth waiting for.

Hanging up the receiver, the young fellow ignored the man with the cane as he brushed past, anxious to get on with his plans for the evening. The old man's eyes followed him for a few seconds. Then, he hooked his cane over the edge of a metal tray, pulled a number from his pocket that was scrawled on a small piece of torn paper, and, inserting the appropriate coins, proceeded to dial.

"Hello?" a male voice answered the ring.

"The night is dark," said Mr. Contaviani.

"The sun does not shine at night," was the cryptic reply.

"Only the crescent can light our path."

"This is certain, Allah be praised."

"We are booked on Aeroflot, tomorrow, at 0930 hours. I have the tickets with me."

"Do you know for certain that they can provide us with a sufficient amount of the required substance?"

"Yes. All parts of the shipment are ready for transport. They expect payment when we meet tomorrow evening. You are ready?"

"Is the amount the same?"

"Of course."

"Then I am ready. I will have the final installment in $100 increments of US currency, together with the receipt of deposit at the bank of their choice."

"Good. I will join you in front of the Passport Control at 0830. Listen for the name Contaviani. And bring your long underwear. Where we are going, it will be cold."

"I will be there."

Without saying good-bye, the old man hung up the phone and started toward the beltway. *An old man like me needs all the help he can get,* he thought, on the way to finding a room for the night.

NINE

"Why?"

The woman with the kind face said nothing.

"Do you know why they brought me here? What is happening? Where is my father? And the rest of the people from our church? It has been over a month, but you will never talk about it. If you know, you should tell me." Jessica's voice wavered a little, though she tried very hard to sound grown-up.

"Do you have any idea at all?" the woman countered. "Have you overheard the men speaking?"

Jessica shook her head as she sat down on the edge of her cot.

"I don't even know where I am. It must be a city, but where? Are we in Jerusalem? No one will tell me anything. Please, I deserve that much at least, don't I?"

The woman was silent. Then she turned and knocked for the door to be opened.

"I will return shortly, child, with your dinner."

The guard outside poked his head around into the opening and grinned at Jessica. As quickly as it appeared, his face was gone and the door closed. Jessica threw herself down on the cot, overwhelmed by a feeling of despair.

She stared up at the boarded window, the bare walls, the door. Everything felt hopeless. All she wanted was to get out of this place and find her father. Then everything would be all right.

Where is he? Did they take him prisoner too?

The totality of her emotional isolation closed in on her. So did the reality of physical exhaustion. Her eyes closed and she fell into a restless sleep.

SHE AWAKENED AT THE SOUND of the door opening and saw the woman carrying a food tray. The guard reached around and closed the door behind her.

Jessica wasn't hungry.

"Eat, child."

Jessica didn't move. She stared at the ceiling, an ache in her stomach, as she hovered near the breaking point.

"Jessica."

She turned her head slightly and looked at the woman just as she withdrew something from under her chador . . . a piece of paper.

Jessica pushed herself up on one elbow, curious.

The woman held a finger to her lips, with a knowing glance at the door, as she handed her the folded paper.

Jessica threw her feet over the edge of the cot and sat up as she unfolded it, letting out a cry of surprise at what she saw.

"Shh," the woman whispered anxiously. "You must be quiet."

Jessica looked up into her eyes, back to the paper, then up again. It was a news article, complete with headline and the *International Herald* masthead. There, on the front page, was her father, shaking hands with a man she did not recognize!

Her hands actually quivered.

"It's my father," Jessica exclaimed, looking up at the woman.

"Read it quickly, child. If we are discovered, it will not go well for either of us."

"Oh, please, let me keep this."

"No. It is too dangerous!"

"But you can't take it from me," Jessica pleaded. "Leave it at least until tomorrow. It's about my father."

The woman hesitated, gazing back at Jessica.

"Put it under your mattress when you are done. Fold it tightly and place it here." She lifted the edge of the thin mattress, near where Jessica would lay her head. "If they come for you, do not carry this on your person. Do you understand?"

Jessica didn't really, but she nodded.

"Are they taking me somewhere?"

Again, she saw the woman hesitate.

"Soon. I'm not sure when, but soon you will leave this place."

Jessica felt a twinge of apprehension.

"Where are they going to take me? Are they releasing me? Are they taking me to my father?" She glanced down at his picture.

"No, you are not going to your father. I'm not sure where you will be taken. All I know for certain is that it will be far away."

"Why? What have I done?"

"You have done nothing, child. But your father has done something and Hamas is very unhappy with him. The story is there. Put it away now and eat. You can read it after I have gone, but be careful. Do not let the guard see you reading it. Understand? You will take great care, Jessica?"

"Yes, I will. And, thank you."

The woman seemed nervous.

"This is dangerous for you, isn't it?" Jessica asked. "I mean, bringing me this newspaper story."

She said nothing, but looked down.

Jessica carefully folded the precious paper and slipped it under the mattress. Her appetite was gone. She hoped the woman soon would be, as well. She nibbled at the roasted chicken and picked her way through a side dish of raw onion, chilies, and olives. Finally, she pushed the tray back.

"Shokran," she said, in a loud voice.

The woman smiled at Jessica's attempt to express thanks in Arabic. "Afwan," she said, and started to reach for the tray. As she did, Jessica's hand moved to the mattress, just above the hidden newspaper. The woman did not miss the movement. Their eyes met for a long moment.

"Shokran," Jessica said again, this time whispering softly, her eyes brimming with tears of gratefulness.

A look of concern flashed briefly across the woman's face. She started to say something, appeared to think better of it, turned and walked to the door. Without looking back, she knocked. The door opened and she disappeared into the hallway.

THE SOUND AWAKENED JESSICA. Light from the hallway cut a path through the door opening and into the darkness of her cell. Shadowy human silhouettes. She made out at least two of them. One reached for the pull chain on the bare light bulb hanging from the ceiling. Brighter light filled the room, dispelling shadows. Squinting, she recognized the man that the woman had spoken to in the hall following her attack by the young guard. The other was a stranger.

To her relief, she saw the woman enter behind the men and stand by the door.

"Get up," ordered the one she had seen before.

"What do you want?"

"Get up!" The man started toward her and Jessica scrambled out from under the thin blanket. The floor felt cold to her bare feet.

"Is this all she has to wear?" The man directed his question to the woman. She nodded.

"Get her a coat or something."

"Where are you taking me?" Jessica asked, mustering up as much defiance in her voice as she could.

"Shut up," the man growled.

"I want to . . ." Jessica stopped as she caught a glimpse of the syringe. She shrank back onto the cot. "Please, no more of that stuff. I'll be quiet."

The woman wrapped a woolen jacket around Jessica's shoulders. Then she turned to the man and said something in Arabic. He hesitated, looked over at Jessica, and then responded to the woman with what seemed to be a question. She nodded quickly and turned to Jessica, who by this time was standing against the wall.

"Child." Her voice was stern, but the look in her eyes was one of concern. "If you do not wish to be put to sleep, you must promise to be absolutely quiet. Will you do this?"

Jessica nodded, never taking her eyes off the syringe.

"You must do exactly as you are told."

She looked over at the woman.

"Your life depends on your obedience, Jessica. This is not a game. Do you understand?"

"I understand," she answered. She started to ask a question, but stopped short.

"Do you want something?" the woman asked.

Jessica nodded.

"What is it? Speak up."

"May I go to the toilet before we leave?"

"Of course, but hurry."

The men were standing by the door, conversing in Arabic. Jessica slipped her hand under the mattress and withdrew the telltale news story. The woman started, her hand moving involuntarily to her lips as she observed what Jessica was doing. In an instant, the paper was hidden inside the sleeve of the woolen jacket.

Slipping into her socks and shoes, she walked past the men

and down the hallway, turned on the light and closed the door. Reluctantly, she pulled the crumpled newsprint out from her sleeve.

There was the familiar face of her father. His smile. The story of his heroism. She stifled a sob.

I love you, daddy.

Tears splashed down onto the picture.

I love you so very much!

Everyone she loved was gone. And now this too. A last look. Jessica brought the photo to her lips and kissed the inked imprint of her father's face. For a brief moment she hesitated, then crumpled it and dropped it into the stool.

Her hand pulled the flush chain. She watched to be sure it disappeared.

Wiping at her eyes, she opened the door, turned out the light, and walked to where her captors stood waiting.

JESSICA SAT IN THE BACK OF THE TRUCK. She was relieved to see that the woman was climbing in beside her. Moments ago, coming out of the building where she had been held prisoner for over a month, the feeling of fresh, cool air on her face had been indescribable. She had forgotten how good a breeze could feel. The outdoors gave her a sense of freedom, even though she knew she was far from free. She glanced around quickly at her surroundings.

Empty tables. *I thought I heard people at a marketplace.*

Lights in the distance. *It's a city of some kind. Watch for signs. Maybe they will tell me where I am.*

A tower across the alley. *That must be the mosque!*

The truck was a single seat affair, green in color, its sides caked with mud. The carrying space behind the cab was covered with canvas across the top and was open at the sides. She guessed it to be about the size of a small pickup truck back home in California.

California! Home. Every time she thought about it, the overwhelming depression that followed was so painful that she had begun to shut thoughts of home out of her mind. Now they came back with monsoon force, threatening to sweep her away on a riverbed of lost dreams.

As Jessica waited alongside the woman, one of the men carried a cardboard box around to the back of the truck and dropped it inside. She had glimpsed its contents as he walked past her.

Packages of potato chips, crackers, and bottles of water. From the shape of one item, wrapped in butcher paper, she guessed it had to be cheese.

At least they don't intend for us to starve.

"Here, girl, put this on." The man handed Jessica a dark, wrinkled chador.

"You need a black one where we are going," the woman said. "Here, I will help you."

"Where are we going?" asked Jessica.

"Hurry up and get in," the man ordered impatiently, standing by the driver's door. "In the back. And don't try to attract attention or get away."

They climbed up into the vehicle and the woman sat down on the floor of the truck bed, crossing her legs as though reclining in front of a campfire. Watching her every move, Jessica followed suit. The man leaned over the edge and looked at them. Grunting his satisfaction, he spoke to the woman in Arabic.

"Faridah."

She looked at him steadily.

"You must keep an eye on the girl."

The woman nodded.

"And you, Jessica Cain, had better behave." The man was looking at Jessica now, his voice low and threatening. "I am leaving you unfettered. If you try anything, you'll make the rest of the journey bound and gagged. Is that clear?"

Jessica nodded, indicating that she understood, but her mind was suddenly racing in an opposite direction.

Faridah. Had the man called her by name? Faridah!

As Jessica absorbed this unexpected revelation, the two men climbed into the cab and started the motor. Soon they were bouncing along poorly paved streets, heading toward the lights at the center of the city.

"Do you know where we are going, Faridah?"

The woman glared at her, obviously displeased that Jessica had used the name she had successfully kept secret for a month.

"We are at the western edge of Amman. We are going through the city and into the desert."

"Where is Amman? Am I still in Israel?"

"No. You are in Jordan, but not for long."

"Where are we going?"

"Be quiet. It does not matter. Soon enough you will find out."

Jessica tried to control the fear that bubbled up from the cauldron of her stomach.

"Do you have the paper?"

"No."

"Where is it?"

"I threw it away."

"Where did you throw it? Will anyone find it?"

"No. I flushed it down the toilet."

It was one of those moments that occurs unexpectedly.

Faridah's gaze seemed to slip past Jessica's eyes and into her heart. The silence that followed was disturbed only by the sounds of the city and of the truck as it rolled through Amman's dimly lit streets.

A woman. And a child-woman.

While only inches separated the two in distance, light years divided them in culture, faith, and life experience. Something they both knew was so precious to her had been sacrificed in a way that seemed almost a sacrilege. Flushed down a toilet! The only thing remaining was a shared feeling of loss and guilt. Loss for one by destroying the last tangible link to her family. Guilt for the other by making the sacrifice necessary.

A familiar sign broke the sudden, unexpected emotion that flowed between the two of them . . . a red and white sign reminding Jessica of another world. Kentucky Fried Chicken.

They turned left onto Sulleman an-Nabulsi Street. The truck jerked forward as the driver gunned the motor and ground his way through the gears. After a while, Jessica noticed an impressive-looking building.

"It is the qasr, the palace," Faridah volunteered, motioning with her hand. "It reaches back to the early eighth century, though no one seems to know for certain what its function was."

The truck banged across a huge pothole, jarring the two women who had only a folded blanket between them and the metal flooring.

"Look over there," she pointed in a southerly direction. Jessica noticed fencing, cranes, and rubble outlined in the shadowy light. "That is the temple to Hercules. You have heard of him?"

Jessica nodded.

"A group from the United States is working to restore it to its former glory. They will have spent over US$600,000 by the time it is finished. Some of the ancient columns and parts of the temple walls will be standing when the work is complete. Actually, the temple dates from the reign of the Roman Emperor Marcus Aurelius, in the second century."

Jessica observed her carefully as she listened. "You know a lot about things," she said, taking in the sweeping night views of the theater and the center of town. There also appeared to be countless backyards, some still full of last night's washing and assorted debris.

Soon the lights of the city faded as the stony desert plain opened in preparation for swallowing up the three travelers and their young prisoner.

After what seemed an endless night, while the sky was still dark and dotted with stars, Jessica noticed the traffic was increasing, with huge trucks rolling along the desert highway. For the most part, they were going in the same direction as their own vehicle.

"Where are all these trucks headed?" Jessica asked, thinking that an answer might give her some further idea of where she was going, but expecting nothing. To her surprise, Faridah answered.

"From Aqaba to Iraq."

"Aqaba? What is that?"

"It is our seaport. In the south. It was thought, initially, that you might go there. Eventually, however, the desert route was chosen. The trucks you see are part of a major supply effort, ever since the Gulf War. There is still an embargo levied against Iraq, but people there must continue their lives. Families must eat. Most of their supplies come through this backdoor route."

"Is that where we're going? Iraq?" asked Jessica. Suppressed fear began to mount once more. The little she knew about Iraq came from the unending television images of Desert Storm. It had been so very real, almost like being there. Except that she had been safe and secure in her own family room. She was not safe now, and the possibility she might be headed for Iraq made her mouth go dry.

How will Mom and Dad ever find me there?

2345 LOCAL TIME
MOSCOW, RUSSIA

MOST OF THE LEAVES had fallen from the trees lining the city streets. A dark-colored automobile slowly rounded the corner and pulled over to the side of the street. The lights were turned off, but the driver left its motor running, the exhaust forming cloudlike patterns behind the car.

From the automobile in which they waited, about a hundred feet farther down the street, it was impossible to tell how many were inside. Dosha and his companion, François Genet, scanned the surrounding area. Nothing seemed out of place.

"Okay," said Dosha, opening the passenger door. "Watch for anything out of the ordinary and keep me covered."

Genet opened his door and got out as Dosha walked around to the front of the car and waved. The dark-colored automobile pulled away from the curb and moved toward them, its lights still off. Left windows, front and back, rolled down simultaneously, revealing the driver and three other passengers. Dosha walked over and bent down to look inside.

"You have the money?" The nearest rear-seat passenger looked up at Dosha as he spoke, his English heavy with a thick Russian accent.

"And you have completed arrangements for the shipment?"

The front-seat passenger emerged from the other side and came toward Dosha. His features were distinctly Arabic, as was the language he spoke. "I have confirmed with my own eyes, Marwan. The shipment is on the way."

The two men smiled as they greeted one another in traditional Middle-Eastern fashion.

"It is good to see you again, Wafa. It has been a long time."

"Indeed. Too long, my friend."

"There is no chance of any problem with the shipment?"

"I assure you, there is none.

"It's going by rail?"

"Yes. Things have continued smoothly since our conversation last month. We acquired three surplus tankers and prepared them for our use. Three tractors for these tanker trucks have been leased in Canada. We also managed to get a sufficient amount of surplus borosilicate ration rings."

"What is their purpose?"

"They prevent nuclear criticality reactions by absorbing neutrons."

"I still do not understand," Dosha said as he fumbled for a cigarette.

"Each one of these rings is a small glass pipe about the length of your thumb. There are thousands of them and they cost us a good deal more than the tankers, I might add. We poured these glass pipes into each tanker unit. Over time, they will absorb neutrons and become radioactive. Their purpose is to enhance the "shelf life" of our product so that it does not deteriorate before we are ready. Without them, it is also possible to accidentally get a chain reaction going. It would be like dropping a Ping-Pong ball onto the first of fifty thousand preset mousetraps. An instant later, there would be mousetraps snapping everywhere. But, in our case, instead of mousetraps we would have a blue flash."

"An explosion?" Dosha interrupted.

"No, not an explosion. Just a tremendous fatal flash of nuclear energy that would kill everything and everyone within its proximity in a matter of a few hours."

"If such a thing were to happen, would it be seen?"

"If there was nothing to obstruct the visual line," Wafa answered with a grin. "If there was, say, a cement wall in between you and the flash, then you would not see it. The wall would not stop it from killing you, however. And the plutonium would remain every bit as deadly after the flash as before. It would be useless to us, however."

Dosha's hands were getting cold. He rubbed them together briskly, sensing that the man in front of him was enjoying his moment of professional triumph as a trained terrorist. Staring at the exhaust vapor rising from the rear of the car and disappearing into the darkness, he listened as Wafa continued.

"There is a modified PUREX process that produces significant amounts of plutonium chloride solutions. My scientist friends here work with that process at Complex 300 in Majak. I doubt that you have been there?"

Dosha shook his head.

"Few outsiders ever have. It is one of Russia's closed towns, quite a ways southeast of here. It's close to Lake Karatsay, but you wouldn't want to spend your summer vacation there. They've been dumping liquid radioactive waste into that lake for years. Before the Soviet breakup, Majak was its largest production site for weapon-grade plutonium. There have been lots of accidents, and it's one of the most radioactively polluted areas of the world. For sure, if we need more of this stuff, there is plenty. Over the last several weeks, our friends here were able to shunt approximately two thousand curies of the plutonium isotope 239Pu into each of the three tankers. That's six thousand curies altogether, Marwan. Believe me, it is more than enough to do the job."

"Are you certain it will arrive safely?" asked Dosha, growing impatient to be on his way. He glanced around to make certain they were still alone on the street.

"No problem. The tankers have been placed on railcars and leave early this morning. Their route takes them north to Severodvinsk and then to Murmansk where they will be loaded on a ship. From there it is in the hands of others."

"One thing. How can we be certain it will not be discovered en route?"

"We poured a layer of diesel fuel on top of the plutonium. This stuff is like oil and water. It doesn't mix. Officially, each tanker is carrying five thousand gallons of fuel. This is done on occasion so as to make such a transfer of scrap metal even more profitable to its buyer. They will have to use a Geiger counter before the plutonium can be discovered. It is highly unlikely that they will be so thorough. Relax, my friend. It will be a success."

"You have done well," Dosha replied, patting the man's shoulder. "And your friends in the car?"

"These scientists are too honest to be crooks." Wafa chuckled at his little joke, winking at Dosha. "Or too stupid. They just want to get rich and get out."

Dosha reached inside his coat as he turned to the car.

"Gentlemen, we wish to thank you for your assistance," he said, reverting to the English he knew each of the occupants understood. He handed the rear-seat passenger a brown envelope. "Inside is the final payment for your services. As we agreed, you will also find the number of your new bank account in Zurich on the receipt of deposit. The rest of the money is there. We have followed the instructions that you gave us. You have received verification, I am sure. Yes?"

The man nodded.

"Then you are three very rich men. It is what you wished?"

The man did not smile, or even look directly at Dosha, as he took the envelope. He opened it quickly, glanced inside and then nodded.

"We are done here, Wafa," Dosha said, patting his friend on the shoulder. "I have some news that will sweeten things even more, I think. We have unexpectedly come into possession of yet another item that should help us break the resolve of our enemies. If you will join us for the ride back to the hotel, I will tell you about it."

"I will be delighted." He turned to the three Russian scientists who had just received payment. "It has been a pleasure doing business, gentlemen."

None of the Russians said a word. These scientists did not look happy as their car moved away. With the economy out of control, the cold war ended, their skills no longer needed, these $50-a-month professionals had just sold their souls, and maybe the lives of countless thousands, for short-term gain. The only question remaining was whether or not two hundred thousand dollars each would be enough to assuage their consciences for placing in the hands of known international terrorists six thousand curies of deadly plutonium chloride.

TEN

A gray jungle of booms, masts, antennas, and cold steel hulls, fringed by icy waters, lay exposed by the early morning light that pushed against the encroaching of darkness at this time of year. Ships were lined up on either side of the rusty freighter, awaiting their turn under the loading crane. Around the *Grodno*, the rancid smell of oil, dead shellfish, escaping steam, and rubbish hovered in the cold air as dock workers stumbled over random cables and hoses strewn across the wooden planks. Tractors rumbled past, their drivers huddled against the stiff, north wind. Bells clanged in the distance, as the last of the shipment was lowered onto the deck.

Standing to one side, the crewman in charge of cargo placement instructed the crane operator to shift farther to the right . . . a little more . . . there. Down three feet. Good. It's done. Cable hooks were released and the crane swung slowly away from the ship, leaving its final deposit on the ship's forward deck. The crewman glanced down at the manifest in his hand and nodded.

The last of the three scrap tankers, each loaded with "diesel fuel," was now being tied down in preparation for the long voyage ahead.

0645 LOCAL TIME
AZRAQ, JORDAN

JUST OVER 100 KILOMETERS east of Amman, the wide, shallow valley of the Wadi Sirhan stretches southward toward

Saudia Arabia. In previous centuries it served as a major caravan route. Today, it lay shrouded in silent desolation, occupied only by memories of past glories.

The sun rose on a tired oasis community of desert dwellers as the citizens of Azraq were beginning to stir and make preparations for facing the inevitable heat of another day. Early rays of light crept across the landscape, feeling for signs of the only water source in the eastern desert. Nature's relentless search was on, but growing more difficult with each passing day. At one time, Azraq's morning skies had been filled with birds migrating between Africa and Europe. No longer. The water buffalo, bear, deer, cheetah, ibex, and the gazelle had once lifted their heads to greet each new morning. Not today.

During the past decade, man's insatiable thirst had taken without giving back. Large-scale pumps sucked the life-source from wells in an effort to supply city-dwellers in Amman with drinking water, reducing the once lush swampland to little more than a muddy pond.

As the reddish sphere climbed above the horizon, shimmering ominously, flora and fauna alike braced in anticipation of its fiery blow that daily threatened to vaporize the last vestige of desert life. On this morning, birds flew over without stopping to rest, on their way to the Sea of Galilee in Israel. The sounds of their flight caused a few upward glances, followed by a collective human sigh of resignation.

Still, there was hope. Workers could be seen leaving their modest homes and making their way to the nearby Shaumari Wildlife Reserve, as they had most days for the past twenty years, carrying out a nation's belated attempt at reintroducing wildlife into this region from which it had all but vanished. They were the vanguard of the future, the last hope of a land in its death throes.

Standing in the center of it all, the large Qasr al-Azraq lifted its stolid face to the sun. Built in its present form in the thirteenth century out of black basalt, inscriptions in Greek and Latin identify earlier constructions on the site, dating as far back as A.D. 300. Shaken by an earthquake in 1927, some of its original three stories lay crumbled, a mute testimony to the unremitting will of the desert, and man's refusal to succumb to its persistent power.

This morning, the castle's elderly caretaker put a cigarette between his lips and lit up. This had been his turf for many years. Some of the locals swore that he was older than the castle itself. There might not be many visitors today, but he intended for those who did come to have a memorable experience. As on every other day, he would regale them with his Lawrence of Arabia stories, the same ones he had heard from his father, who had himself been one of T.E. Lawrence's Arabian officers. He checked to make certain that his supply of Lawrence snapshots was ready and available. While at it, he gathered up a few old magazine articles about himself. He was ready for anything and anyone.

As he approached the old castle, he was surprised to see the green truck. It was unusual for any vehicle to be here this early in the morning. He stopped a few feet away and called out.

"Sabah al-khayr." *Good morning.*

Someone stirred inside the truck. Then a man poked his head through the driver's side window opening.

"Marhaba." *Hi.*

"Min wayn inta?" *Where are you from?*

"Amman," the driver replied, stretching, as he opened the door and stepped out. He rubbed sleep from his eyes and squinted into the low sun. "We arrived too late last night to try for rooms in the hotels. Who are you?"

"I am Majid, the guide here at Qasr al-Azraq. I was surprised to see your truck, as I do not normally find people here so early."

By this time, another man had stepped down from the vehicle, walked away a few paces, and lit a cigarette.

Hearing movement in the back of the truck, Majid glanced in that direction, just in time to see a woman's face come into view. Obviously, she too had been sleeping. Then, a second face appeared. Both women were dressed in the dark chador. Only the eyes, nose, and the upper part of the older woman's mouth could be seen, but the younger woman's face was entirely visible.

Just a girl, barely come of age, guessed Majid. He smiled at her. She did not return his kind look.

"Ahlan wa sahlan. Kayf haalik?" *Hello. How are you?* he asked the young girl. It was not the usual custom for an Arab man to speak so casually without first being introduced. Female children, especially those come of age, were not spoken to in public by one who was not a relative. But Majid was used to talking with children in his line of work. He enjoyed them and was not about to change.

The girl's gaze was steady, but she said nothing.

The driver gave a curt order to the woman who spoke softly in the girl's ear. Majid could not hear what was being said, but slowly the child disappeared below the side of the truck, never taking her eyes off him until she was gone from view.

Strange, Majid thought.

"We must be on our way," the driver announced. "Can you recommend a place to eat that has good food, but is not expensive?"

"The Al-Zoubi Hotel is the best for you. About one kilometer south of the old junction road on the way to Saudi. You are going in that direction?"

"Aiwa. Shokran jazeelan." *Yes. Thank you very much.*

"Afwan." *You are welcome.*

The two men stepped up into the vehicle and the woman settled down in the back. Majid watched as they turned the truck around and headed away from the castle.

Strange. Very strange indeed. What was it about them? Why did they stop here instead of getting into the line last night if they intended to cross the border this morning? And, that young girl . . . was she just shy? Why did she not smile? Perhaps I am losing my touch with the girls.

Majid's face broke into a toothless grin at such a thought.

He walked over to the southern door of the castle, a single massive slab of basalt. Later today, someone would pass by here and he would tell them how Lawrence declared that this door "went shut with a clang and a crash that made tremble the west wall of the castle." Majid loved to quote that historic line. Inside, he paused to pick up a stray piece of paper from off the familiar paving stones. The stones were pocked with small indentations, carved out by gatekeepers of old, who played an ancient board game with pebbles to pass the time.

Majid walked toward the small mosque in the middle of the courtyard, thinking just how much he truly loved this place. Suddenly, he stopped and began scratching his beard as he stared at the mosque.

That's it! That's what was different.

He started toward the storerooms, opposite the entrance.

It was the girl's face. Her skin was so much fairer than the woman's.

Then he stopped.

No. That's still not tt. It was her eyes.

Majid turned and stared thoughtfully out through the castle entrance and into the desert beyond.

Her eyes were green!

THE NUMBER OF TRUCKS AND CARS lining the road at the border crossing was moderate, but the drivers had come prepared. Each truck had a well-stocked food box attached to the side, complete with teapot and gas stove. They came together in small groups of three or four, making a brew and having a chat while sitting out the wait.

Faridah and Jessica remained in the back of the truck, under the canvas, sensing that the early morning coolness was rapidly giving way to the inevitable onslaught of desert heat. Earlier, at a huddle of felafel and shawarma stands near the Al-Zoubi Hotel, one of the men had purchased additional food for the journey ahead. Some of this store had been passed back to them, the rest placed in a small bag under the seat in front. Jessica ate quietly, surprised that she was hungry and that the local food tasted as good as it did.

By now, she had become familiar with felafel, a Jordanian staple at breakfast, lunch, or dinner. This morning, it was filled with deep-fried balls of chickpea paste, mixed with spices and wrapped in pieces of khobz, or unleavened bread. The operator of the felafel stand had inserted a few pickled vegetables and tomatoes as well. Jessica washed down the simple fare with bottled water. Although the water was not cold, Jessica drank deeply.

"Don't let yourself get dehydrated, sweetheart."

She had begun listening for her father's voice each time she placed a bottle of water to her lips. It would have been hard for Jessica to describe, but there came a feeling of belonging whenever she did it. She did not belong here. Not here in this truck. Not with these men. Not in this godforsaken place.

She belonged there. Back home. With her mother and father! With Jeremy and her friends at church and school.

How can this possibly be happening to me? What are Mom and Daddy doing to get me back? I'll bet they're sad. They miss Jenny so much. And now, me. But what can they do? They don't know where I am, or even if I'm alive.

I hope Jeremy will be on the starting team again this season. I want to see him play. It's his last year. I'll bet Amy and Shawna are at school right now. No, wait. It's probably nighttime where they are. I wonder if they'll still be my best friends when I get back. Maybe they've already found someone to take my place. School has been going for two months now . . . my first year in junior high. I've missed so much, I'll never catch up. It may not matter. I may never get back.

Jessica reached up and brushed a tear from her cheek.

"What's wrong, child?" asked Faridah.

Jessica said nothing.

"Is the food not to your liking?"

"The food's okay."

"Then, why are you crying?"

"I'm not crying," Jessica replied sharply. "Just leave me alone."

Faridah sat quietly, watching Jessica. A few feet away the two men crouched, drinking hot tea and making conversation with other drivers.

"Perhaps you are homesick?"

Jessica looked at Faridah. Her lip quivered as she tried to steel her emotions against the unexpected power of those four words.

"I'm not homesick," Jessica retorted, biting her lip. "I . . . I'm . . ."

Words failed, but the tears came all too easily.

Faridah reached her hand over and took Jessica's.

"I'm sorry, child."

Jessica didn't move for a long minute. Then she dropped the remaining piece of felafel on the floor of the truck bed and, for the second time in recent days, buried her face in the folds of Faridah's chador. Her shoulders heaved with uncontrolled sobs. Faridah put her arms around her and drew Jessica in until she rested against her breast.

Hearing something, one of the men looked over at the truck. He stood up, drink in hand, to get a better view. Moving closer, he saw the girl huddled in Faridah's embrace and heard her sobbing. Faridah looked across at him and shook her head. *No need to come closer. Leave us alone.* He turned back to the circle of drivers and squatted once more on the ground.

Nearly two hours later, the green truck and its four passengers had passed through the border crossing. First, on the Jordanian side and then, at the entry checkpoint in Saudi Arabia. Soldiers. A few nondescript officials. Vehicle registration papers, drivers' licenses, passports. Everything was in order.

The fact that the registration papers, passports, even the vehicle's license plates were all forged or stolen escaped the scrutiny of the disinterested border guards. By the time the discrepancies were uncovered, it would be much too late. The two men chuckled with relief as they headed out into the open desert, on the road to Riyadh. All that money for false documentation had paid off.

FOR THE NEXT TWO DAYS, the exhausted quartet traversed the Arabian desert, making their way through a land, the likes of which Jessica had never dreamed existed.

For the most part it was flat and uninteresting. At other times, huge sand dunes, poised like golden ocean waves, seemed ready to swallow up their tiny, desert ship. The vastness of the terrain soon grew monotonous, however, and hours later she was wishing it would all go away. Little vegetation and lots of desolation . . . would it never end?

Daylight hours were unbearably hot. Temperatures soared unrelentingly around the intrepid travelers, who consumed large quantities of water. The men periodically stopped the truck and walked a few steps away to relieve themselves.

The first time, Faridah motioned to Jessica and they got out of the truck. Jessica followed after her as Faridah walked away from the men to the opposite side of the truck and proceeded to do the same. At first, Jessica stood there appalled, casting embarrassed glances toward the truck and the men just beyond. But finally, necessity overcame convention while the chador maintained a modicum of modesty.

Jessica had lost track of time long before they stopped at a gasoline station. As they pulled in, she sighed with relief. A real restroom! A small boy and his sister followed her around the corner of the building. They waited, curious, smiling shyly at her. Jessica looked at the hole in the ground and the surrounding filth, and quickly decided the desert was definitely the lesser of two evils.

Around in front, there were warm soft drinks with straws sticking out of glass bottles. Jessica took the one she was offered.

"Use the straw, child," admonished Faridah, when she saw that Jessica had removed it.

She looked at Faridah questioningly.

"It is clean," she said simply.

Jessica put the straw back in the bottle, at the same time wondering how long these bottles had been sitting in those wooden crates. No matter.

"Drink, honey. Don't let yourself get dehydrated."

As they continued on, Jessica could feel the others slipping into the rhythm of the desert. The quietness. The loneliness. The stark landscape. The effort required for survival. It appeared to be so natural for her captors. She wished that she could say the same. Still, she had to admit that being out of her dreary cell in Amman was an improvement. And, as evening approached, the desert sky gave way to the most spectacular sunset that Jessica had ever seen!

The nights were opposite the days, so cool that Jessica shivered in her chador. She pulled the blanket up around her chin and huddled close to Faridah for warmth.

What was it that made Faridah different from her other captors? Was it because she was a woman, the closest thing to a mother in Jessica's precarious life right now? No. It was something else. Jessica had felt her caring.

In Amman, when the guard had tried to grab her, Faridah's angry intervention had felt good. Then there was the newspaper article. Faridah had placed herself in jeopardy so that Jessica could know a little of what was going on. There was a bond of sorts forming between them. Jessica sensed that it was important to resist it, but she needed somebody.

I wonder how old she is? Probably about Mother's age. How old is that? Was it last year or the year before that Daddy had friends over for her fortieth birthday?

Jessica tried to sleep, but the desert stars left her wide-eyed with wonder. The first night out, as she lay staring up at the sky, her mother's face seemed to appear. Jessica imagined watching as she combed her long hair. Her eyes were radiant, dancing with merriment, and she tossed her head the same way each time she broke out in laughter. She was the most beautiful person in the world. At least she had been, before Jenny died. After that, she always seemed to be somewhere else.

She used to look at me. Even into me. Now she looks past me.

The memory became mixed with anxiety over what might be happening with her mom and dad back home. She knew lots of kids whose parents were divorced. It was hard to imagine that happening to her parents, but the possibility had worried her for some time. All the signs were there. She decided it was wrong for kids to have to worry about their parents like this. Still . . .

Jessica trailed the moon across the velvet darkness. Tonight, she was empty. Forlorn. Numb with repressed feelings of fright.

She pressed closer to Faridah.

DURING THE SECOND DAY, IT WAS EASY for her to guess the direction they were traveling by watching the sun's position as it inched its way across the heavens. Sometimes east but mostly south, she estimated. Not that this knowledge would do her any good. Jessica didn't have a clue as to where she was headed. She tried to remember the maps in her geography class at school. Recalling the days her class spent studying the events of Desert

Storm gave her some perspective.

East of Jordan. Okay. We must be in Saudi Arabia. Iraq is somewhere around, but I would have known, if we had gone there, wouldn't I? Goodness, I hope we're not going to Iraq.

She could occasionally see a large pipeline and periodic clusters of oil wells. These were familiar sights, similar to California's central and southern oil producing areas; only here, they were multiplied in number. She pictured the Standard Oil Refinery, only twenty miles from her house, and the huge oil tankers that plied the San Francisco Bay. Had they been transporting oil from the fields that surrounded her today?

Jessica dozed off, physical exhaustion merging with the heat and the constant movement of the truck, as they cruised this sea of sand.

Late in the afternoon of the second day, they arrived at another border crossing. This too was clogged with vehicles of various kinds, but they moved along more rapidly than before. The road signs all seemed to be in Arabic. Looking away from the signs, Jessica suddenly sat up straight and stared out over the edge of the truck.

Water!

As they drew closer, she saw that it was no mirage. Nor was it simply a pond or lake. It was larger. Much larger. They were driving along a stretch of well-kept roadway, within sight of the beach and the shimmering water just beyond. The sun was behind them now.

We must be headed east.

The sunlight was brilliant on the water, causing Jessica to look away every once in a while. Still, she was drawn back to its contrasting beauty as the shore scenes rushed by. They were entering a city where people strolled along the beach, looking very much the way people did in America. There were office buildings and hotels.

A Sheraton! We stayed in one of those back home! If I could only get to the Sheraton, they would help me.

Her body, stiff and sore from the day's journey, tensed as she saw a street light coming up just ahead.

Yellow . . . yellow . . . red!

She glanced over at Faridah.

Still sleeping.

Go for it!

As the truck rolled to a stop, Jessica made her move. Instinctively, like an animal discovering an open gate, she scrambled over the side, dropped down onto the street, and began running.

She stumbled, regained her balance, and dodged between two cars.

A horn blared.

Then another.

The door of the green truck flew open.

She had reached the sidewalk by the time the man shouted.

Footsteps!

Another horn sounding.

Run, Jessica. Run for your life!

ELEVEN

"Run, Amy. You can do it! Don't give up!"

Amy Foster's lungs were ready to explode. Her feet were flying as she rounded the final turn and headed for the finish line. Only one girl was ahead of her . . . the tall, African-American from Benton Christian, the one she knew would be her greatest challenge.

Amy had been on the Benton girl's heels from the sound of the starter's gun. That's what Coach Staley had told her to do. *"Stay with her into the final turn. Then pour it on!"*

The time had come. Amy's arms pumped in runner's rhythm. The distance between them narrowed.

Each girl glanced at the other from out of the corner of their eyes. Amy couldn't help grinning. This was fun!

The other runners were dropping farther back. This was the moment.

Shoulder to shoulder, the two girls flew across the cinders.

There was nothing else in the whole world. Just the track. And, the far-off sound of schoolmates cheering them on.

Amy broke the tape a fraction of a second ahead of the Benton girl!

A few steps beyond, her arms flopped loosely as she ran off the track and toward her coach whose own arms were stretched high above her head in celebration.

"Great job, Amy. You were terrific!" Coach Staley exclaimed, as she hugged her twelve-year-old protégé. "You ran like the wind today. That Benton kid is an eighth-grader. A year older than you. And she was the fastest girl in the league last year. Congratulations!"

Amy laughed breathlessly.

"Thanks, coach."

"Go take your shower. It's chilly today and I don't want you catching a cold. I'll see you later. I've got to make sure Susan and Becky are ready for the last race."

"Okay. See you. Thanks again."

Amy looked over at the stands where she had last seen Shawna Pickett. There she was, smiling and waving her book in the air. Amy waved back and jogged in her direction.

Shawna was Amy's best friend, though the two of them were total opposites. Amy was outgoing, athletic, her short hair bleached from the sun and the chlorinated water in which she had spent hours this past summer, while working out with her neighborhood swim team. It didn't actually matter what the activity was—if there was competition, Amy was right there in the middle of it, all the while gaining energy.

Shawna was fair-skinned, quiet, and an "A" student. Amy had long ago decided that Shawna was a hopeless geek. Always on the honor roll. Always with a book in her hand. Amy had tried to get her to turn out for some sports activity, even Ping-Pong, but to no avail. Shawna had no real interest in sports and put up with physical education class only because it was required. Amy had often wondered how the two of them had gotten to be so close. But she knew the answer to that question now. There was one important thing they had in common.

"Hi, Amy. You were great today!" Shawna called out as she stood up.

"Thanks. I was lucky. That Benton girl can really run! Coach said she was the best in the league last year."

"Wow. Does that mean you're the best this year?"

"I don't think so," laughed Amy, a musical lilt in her voice. The exhilaration of winning was still flowing, along with rivulets of perspiration.

"So, are you done now?" Shawna asked.

"Yes. That was my last race for the day."

"Then go shower and let's get out of here."

"You'll wait for me?"

"Sure. We'll walk home together."

The girls headed up the hill toward the gymnasium and the shower room.

Suddenly, Amy stopped and looked at Shawna.

"You know what I miss right now?"

Shawna closed her book and returned it to her backpack.

"Yeah, I think so. I miss her too."

"What do you suppose she's doing right this very minute?"

"I don't know," Shawna said, her voice pensive, as they scrambled up the incline. "I pray for her every night before I go to bed."

"Me too."

"Maybe they've got her tied up somewhere in a dark room."

"Do you think so?"

"It could be. I saw that in a movie once. They must have taken her to some secret place. No one seems to know anything. I asked Mrs. Cain at church last Sunday. She doesn't have any idea where Jessica is."

"That must really hurt her parents, huh?"

"How do you think your mom and dad would feel if it was you?"

Both girls fell silent over that thought as they opened the door to the gymnasium and went inside.

1735 LOCAL TIME
SHARJAH, UNITED ARAB EMIRATES

SYD HERSHEY HAD THE SHERATON HOTEL in sight for the last two blocks. His pulse quickened at the thought of a cool shower and a warm evening by the pool. It was the beginning of a four-day holiday away from Kuwait's oil fields.

Syd was from Texas. Originally, he had signed up to help fight the terrible fires set by Iraqi raiders. It was good money. He'd told Helen that he would be in and out before you knew it. But the promise of even better money, if he stayed on a while longer, lured him to extend his contract, room and board included. The countryside was so remote that there was no place to spend what he was making, which was more than twice what he would be paid back home. It would be worth it to stick around, he thought. However, he hadn't figured on the boredom factor, and now he was counting the days until his contract was complete and he could get out.

Ever since coming out here, Syd had heard about the United Arab Emirates. It had quite a reputation among his working buddies, and what he'd heard sounded good to him. He'd been told that high-priced, European call girls were flown into the Emirates on a regular basis and were readily available to anyone with money enough to buy their services. They were allegedly some of the world's most beautiful women, checked medically, and under contract to service the male citizens of the Emirates as well as the nearby Saudis. It had been a long time since he and Helen had been together. A very long time. So, a week ago, Syd decided to visit the Emirates and see for himself.

When it came to the morality of his impending holiday plan, Syd was more of a pragmatist than a theologian. Religion had really never fit into his thinking all that much. Yet, he couldn't avoid being confronted by the effects of religion in this part of the world, and he was often amused at its contradictions. How, for example, could this sort of behavior be tolerated in the midst of the strictest of Islamic cultures? At best, the whole thing seemed a dualistic, chauvinist morality.

Score one for the men's side, he thought. *No pun intended.*

On the one hand, Syd knew that the Holy Koran, Sura 24, 2, calls for serious punishment to be meted out to those who commit sex crimes:

The woman and the man guilty of adultery or fornication,
flog each of them with a hundred stripes.
Let not compassion move you in their case,
in a matter prescribed by God.

The breach of this moral code carries an additional stigma, according to Sura 24, 3:

No man guilty of adultery or fornication may marry
but a woman similarly guilty, or an unbeliever,
Nor let a woman marry any one
but a man similarly guilty, or an unbeliever.

Arab women are jealously subjected to this commandment by their male protectors, who themselves conveniently overlook it. Syd's mentor on this subject, however, had made clear to him that many male Muslims in the Middle East, maybe even most, live by some other unwritten code that permits them a hedonism not open to their female counterparts. The Koranic law appeared to Syd, to be upheld only against females. Men could, and generally did, carry out their acts of sexual infidelity without recrimination.

Still, while it seemed there was nothing that kept Muslim men from dalliances with non-Muslim women, it was crucial to a foreigner's well-being that similar liberties with Muslim women were not engaged in. At the very least, it could result in deportation. Syd, and every other foreign worker in that part of the world, knew that the end result could be much worse.

Thus, it had become a familiar sight in the city of Sharjah,

UAE, to see Western workers enter its modern downtown area and prowl the hotel district, looking for sexual liaisons with European prostitutes. *Let the infidels lie with their own kind, and not with our Muslim women.* That was the code, and Syd intended to live up to it during his four-day holiday.

He could see the waters of the Persian Gulf off to the left, as he scanned the boulevard through the open window of his pickup truck. The street was modern and well kept, as were the surrounding buildings. Just ahead of him was a dirty, green truck, with two women in dark chadors in the back. One looked as though she was sleeping, her head slumped forward, chin against her chest. The other one glanced back at his truck, then, out over the edge of her vehicle.

The truck was slowing now for a street light.

He saw the younger woman look over at the one who was sleeping. Then, as the truck rolled to a stop, she suddenly leaped over the side, dropped onto the street, and began running.

Syd slammed on the brakes to avoid hitting her.

She stumbled, and reached a hand out against the front of his pickup. He saw her face clearly for an instant as she regained her balance and proceeded to dodge between his pickup and the next car.

A young face!

Somebody's horn blared. Then another. The door of the green truck flew open. A man jumped out and chased after the woman. Or was it a girl?

As Syd watched the strange scene unfolding in front of him, the part of the chador that covered the woman's head fell away, causing her hair to drop free as she ran. It was long hair, a light chestnut in color, its reddish highlights flashing in the sun's reflection. Syd caught his breath.

It's just like Helen's. Same color. Same length.

A sudden wave of guilt pushed its way through his earlier resolve to party and proceeded to upset his stomach.

He watched as the woman reached the sidewalk. The man shouted for her to stop. He called out in English.

English? That's strange.

Another step and he had her. His hand flashed in the sunlight and Syd flinched as the man hit the woman hard. Her body sagged and she would have fallen had he not grabbed her. Roughly twisting her around, he picked her up and started back toward the green truck. Syd got another good look at the woman as they passed in front of his pickup and started at what he saw. It was not a woman at all, but a young girl. And she was fair-skinned, with European features.

The guy must have knocked her unconscious when he hit her. Now, that makes me mad! And everyone just sits around and lets him do it. If we were back in Texas ...

Another horn sounded.

The man was standing by the truck now, glaring at the woman in the back who crouched on her knees, gripping the side of the vehicle with both hands. He said something to her that Syd couldn't catch. Then, he pushed the girl inside the cab and climbed in behind her. The light turned yellow again, and then red, just as the truck roared through the intersection and disappeared.

Syd waited for the confusion to clear from the cross streets, and then continued on slowly toward the Sheraton. His mind was no longer on high-priced European women. He couldn't shake the thoughts of that young girl and the man who had hit her. And the fact that nobody seemed to care.

What kind of a world is this, anyway?

Minutes later, he was inside, leaning against the registration desk, watching as the clerk checked him in. He fingered his blue-covered passport.

The good old US of A!

A dull ache had started to press in directly between his eyes. She was there in his mind. The young girl with the fair skin and the long, chestnut-colored hair.

Helen's hair!

THE NEXT MORNING, SYD WOKE UP alone in his room. The sun was streaming through the window as he stepped into the shower. A half hour later, he locked the door behind him and headed down the hall to the elevator.

The gift shop was on his left as he stepped out of the elevator. A stack of *International Herald* newspapers were on the floor by the door. It had been weeks since Syd had taken time to look through a paper. He picked one up, paid the clerk, and folded it under his arm as he walked across the lobby toward the restaurant.

The maitre d' smiled and led Syd to a table by a window overlooking a large, fresh-water pool. Already, a few hotel guests were settling down at poolside. Three young children splashed in the water, reminding Syd of his two kids in their younger days.

Now, one's married and the other is off to college, generating the last of the big bills that climax the childrearing experience. All the more reason for me being over here, I guess.

A uniformed employee finished straightening the chairs and tables.

Syd sat for a moment, appreciating the ambiance of the place. High windows looking out onto the pool and beyond to the sea. An attractively displayed breakfast buffet. Even a tablecloth. How long had it been since he had been served on a tablecloth? He smiled contentedly.

Putting the newspaper down, he pushed back his chair and stood. Stretching, he wiped his hands on the cloth napkin and dropped it by the utensils. He sauntered over to the buffet and checked it out. Toast. Cereal. Hard-boiled eggs. Some scrambled eggs too. Cucumbers and fresh tomatoes. Butter and jam. He glanced up and saw the waiter coming with coffee.

Syd gathered up his first round of breakfast goodies and returned to the table. Sitting down, he watched as the waiter poured coffee.

"Yes, I'd like cream, thank you."

He broke open a hard-boiled egg. A dash of salt. A little pepper. Then, he relished the first bite.

Not ham and eggs and hotcakes, but it'll do.

Picking up the *Herald*, he scanned the first page. Arafat was in Jerusalem yesterday.

The guy's got guts. Not much brains, but guts.

Police quelled several riots staged in protest of the man's presence.

I'll bet they did. Arafat in Jerusalem is like a wolf in a pen full of sheep.

The president was spending a week vacationing at Camp David.

Well, at least that'll get him out of the way for a while. Maybe someone in Washington will get something done while he's gone.

Yesterday, at Camp David, he met with Britain's prime minister. It was not known what full range of topics they discussed, but an undisclosed economic package benefiting both countries was believed to have taken up the bulk of their time.

Like who's going to loan who how much? Both of them are broke, so who are they trying to fool? Each other?

He snorted in disgust at the meaninglessness of politics and politicians, pushed the remainder of the egg in his mouth and turned the page.

What the. . . ?

He stared at the face that looked out of the newsprint. It was the girl from yesterday.

That's her. The one the guy knocked unconscious.

Syd was stunned as he looked at the pretty face of a twelve-year-old girl named Jessica Cain from Baytown, California, near San Francisco, missing since September 18. He read the story of Reverend John Cain's daughter. Cain was the man who had gotten involved with terrorists in Israel in September. Syd had heard that story and then quickly forgotten it.

Now, he ran his fingers over the printed image of the girl's features, still finding it hard to believe.

It's her all right. I got a good look and I'll never forget that face. It's the same girl. She was right there in front of me!

Hurriedly, he read the rest of the story. It was datelined Azraq, Jordan. An elderly Jordanian caretaker-guide, at the Qasr al-Azraq, reported seeing a young girl answering the description of the missing Jessica Cain. The guide, whose name was Majid, said that it was her fair skin and green eyes that caused him to be suspicious. As it happened, he had been following the story from its inception on local Jordanian television. Authorities believe that she may have been taken into Saudi Arabia. They were last seen traveling in a green truck, outfitted for desert travel.

Fair skin. I couldn't see her eyes, but she did have fair skin. And it was a green truck too. It was her!

By now, Syd had forgotten his breakfast. He had also forgotten his reason for being in Sharjah in the first place. Excitedly, he scooped up the paper and rushed out of the restaurant toward the registration desk.

"May I help you, sir?"

"Yes. How do I dial 911 in this country?"

"Sir?"

"I need to speak to the local police!"

"Is there something wrong, sir?" asked the young lady behind the counter, a look of concern crossing her face.

"Yes, there certainly is. Now, hurry, please."

TWELVE

Her head throbbed. Her left cheek and jaw were especially tender. She remembered the man twisting her around and his fist coming down at her.

Slowly, she turned her head. A large picture window filled her view. Blue sky beyond.

Looks like a nice view.

Nicer room than she had been in since Israel, seven weeks earlier.

How did I get here? We were in the street. I was running . . . then he hit me . . . must have carried me back.

She started to sit up. That's when she felt the noose around her neck. With the movement, the rope had suddenly tightened and Jessica began choking. She tried to reach for it, only to discover that her wrists were bound by another rope that ran underneath her body. She could not raise them higher than her waist. She tried moving her feet. They were tied to the foot of the hotel bed.

"Please . . . help me," she gasped.

Faridah was on her feet, reaching for Jessica, when one of the men pushed her away.

"Let her alone!"

He moved over to the bed and watched as Jessica struggled to get her breath.

Reaching into his pocket, he pulled out a cigarette and casually lit it, blowing the smoke toward Jessica's struggling form. He watched as her face turned dark red.

"Help her!" Faridah was on her feet again. "That's enough!"

The man watched a moment longer, then reached down and loosened the noose.

Jessica coughed repeatedly as she gulped air into her oxygen-starved lungs.

"How do you like that, Jessica Cain?"

She tried to respond, but broke into spasms of coughing again. She twisted forward as she coughed, causing the rope to choke her once more. This time, the man moved quickly to loosen the noose-grip.

"Do not move, girl!" He spoke roughly. "If you move, the noose will tighten. It will not release itself when you stop. It will remain tight. The more you move, the tighter it gets. Unless some-one releases it, you will choke to death. Is that clear?"

Jessica forced herself to settle back on the bed.

"Yes."

She whispered the word, fearing that any other response would destroy the delicate balance within her at the moment. She was utterly helpless. That was what he wanted her to feel, and that was what she felt. But there was more. Despondency and fear had controlled her emotions and actions for the past seven weeks. Now something else was stirring deep within her, something terrible and dangerous. She felt it, but didn't understand it. It was completely out of character, a darkness she had never known before.

Sweet Jessica Cain. Where did we get you, darling? You're the most lovable person in our family. Sweet, lovable Jessica.

The man leaned over, exhaling another cloud of smoke into her face. Jessica turned away, but with even that slight movement, she felt the rope tighten again. She could feel the sensations of desperation building inside her now. She wanted to scream or cry out, but something inside made her unwilling to do either, for fear it would give the man standing over her a controlling edge.

Then suddenly, from deep down, buried underneath layer upon layer of despair, the secret darkness broke to the surface. Jessica's twelve-year-old eyes blazed with hatred.

"You are a . . . a . . . an animal!"

She spit out the words, her entire body quivering as it had many times before. Only this time, it was not fear that caused her to tremble. It was indignation, fueled by the fires of an intense, out-of-control rage. Jessica was as astonished as anyone at the sudden outburst.

The man slapped her face with his open hand.

"You're not a man. Not like my father. You're a pig!"

Jessica screamed it out, incapable of stopping things she had never said before from rolling off her tongue.

Never. Not on a dare. Not to show off. Not to spite anyone. Not ever . . . until now.

His second blow hit her with enough force to cause her neck to pop as her head twisted sideways. Her upper body lifted off the bed, just for an instant, but that was enough to draw the noose tight again and begin choking her. She fell back, but it was too late. The man was angry now. He hit the opposite side of Jessica's face with his other hand.

At last, the total prisoner of a rage she would never have believed existed within her, she saw the man bend toward her and, as he did, she spit what little saliva she had remaining directly into his face!

The man flinched as the spittle found its mark.

Jessica saw his fist double and clinched her eyes shut. She tensed to receive the blow she knew was surely coming.

"Amal, stop it!"

Jessica opened her eyes in time to see the driver wrap his arms around the other man and drag him back out of her line of vision. Faridah was at her side a second later, loosening the rope around her neck. Jessica fell back, gasping for breath, suddenly exhausted from the physical violence and the emotional volcano that had so unexpectedly erupted from within.

She could hear the voices. There was angry shouting. They were all yelling at once. Jessica tried to stop shaking. She didn't care anymore. She couldn't understand them anyway. One new fact burned its way into Jessica's memory, though. As she lay panting for breath, she realized that she now knew a second name in her trio of abductors.

Amal. His name is Amal.

"SHE'S ONLY A LITTLE GIRL," FARIDAH declared, her voice raised angrily and her face mere inches from Amal. "It's bad enough that we must keep her a prisoner. There is no excuse for abusing her further still. She is a twelve-year-old child!"

"She's old enough to marry and have children," Amal retorted insolently, glaring across the room at the form on the bed.

"You know nothing," Faridah shot back. "Among her people, she would wait for another twelve years before marriage. Besides, what has that to do with anything?"

"Both of you, back off and cool down," ordered the other man. "It has been a long journey. We are all tired. Faridah, you were remiss in letting the girl get away in the street. If we had lost her, your life would be the price. Don't forget that!"

Faridah looked away, biting her lip.

He turned to Amal and smiled. "Control your emotions, my friend. You got the girl back. No one was the wiser. Anyone who saw us would assume it was a little family squabble. Let us not forget, my friends, that we are under orders to deliver the girl in good condition tomorrow, not in tiny pieces. A few more hours and this will all be over. We can come back to Dubai, do some shopping, and then catch a plane home. Amal, go out and get some air. And bring some food back with you. We are all hungry, no?"

Amal turned and walked out of the room, slamming the door behind him.

The other man walked to the window and gazed silently out toward the sea, where sailboats danced across the water, pushed along by a warm evening breeze.

Faridah went to check on Jessica.

THE NEXT MORNING THEY LEFT the green truck, now caked with a layer of desert dust on top of mud, on a side street close to the ferry dock. The four of them walked down the street to the corner and turned right, toward the dock. They saw the ferry-boat near the end of the dock, lying quietly on the calm sea. According to the schedule they had been given at the hotel, it was still thirty minutes before it sailed. Plenty of time.

Faridah and Jessica, dressed in chadors, walked behind Amal and the other man. As they approached the small crowd of waiting passengers, Faridah checked again to be certain that Jessica kept it close around her face, showing none of her hair. For the first time since leaving Amman, the two men wore jalabiyyehs, the full-length robes preferred by fundamentalist Muslim men.

A short way from the line of those waiting to board the vessel, the man without a name stopped. He turned to Jessica, his eyes hard.

"Do you remember what I told you?"

Jessica nodded.

"If you do anything to draw attention to you or us, I will kill you. Is that clear?"

Jessica swallowed, then nodded.

"I will shoot you in the head with this revolver," said the man, pulling a black handgun just far enough out from under the jalabiyyeh so that it could be seen. A second later, he produced a short dagger. "Or, I will drive this into you and tear your heart out. Understand?"

"Yes," Jessica answered, her voice strained. She glanced at Faridah and saw a worried look in her eyes.

"You must do as he says, Jessica," Faridah spoke quietly, but firmly. "You have no other choice. Don't try to do again what you did yesterday. All right?"

Faridah placed her hands on Jessica's shoulders and stared directly into her eyes.

"You will promise?"

Jessica bit her lip, then her shoulders sagged in resignation.

"I promise."

"Good. Now, stay close beside me. If you must say something, whisper it in my ear. No one must hear you speak English."

With that, they continued walking toward the dock. As they drew near, people began boarding the UAE ferry. Amal had visited the Oasis Freight Company the evening before and purchased their tickets. He handed these to a man standing at the foot of the gangplank.

"Momkin tasif li at-tariq daraja awla?" *Can you direct me to first class?* "Aelæ tul," the crew member responded, pointing along the narrow walkway. *Straight ahead.*

"Shokran."

A few steps farther, they came to a door and entered a small private cabin. The solitary round window was quickly pushed open as far as it would go. The room was already sweltering. Faridah motioned for Jessica to sit. A worn seat, designed to accommodate two, had been attached to each wall, together with a fold-down table that rested on a wobbly chrome leg.

Jessica watched as drops of perspiration formed on their faces. The man without a name said something to Faridah; then both men left the room, shutting the door securely behind them.

Faridah and Jessica sat quietly for a while, feeling the throb of the ferryboat's engines as they moved out into the Strait of Hormuz. Finally, Jessica broke the stifling silence.

"Where are we going?"

Faridah remained still, looking toward the porthole.

"Faridah?"

Slowly, she turned and faced Jessica.

"It has been a long journey, hasn't it?" she responded, ignoring Jessica's question. "Would you like something to drink?"

"Yes, please."

Faridah produced two small bottles of water from a cloth bag. Opening one of them, she handed it to Jessica, then proceeded to help herself to the other.

"Faridah, I want to know where we are going."

"Will it make any difference to you, if you know?"

"I'm not even sure where I've been. I think we are somewhere in Arabia. Is that true?"

Faridah paused, taking a deep drink of water. Then, giving the appearance of having decided to make a profound revelation, she put the bottle down on the tabletop and folded her hands ceremoniously in her lap.

"For the past two days, we have traveled across Jordan and Saudi Arabia. Yesterday, we came into the United Arab Emirates and stayed in a city called Sharjah. This morning, child, we are in the final stage of our journey. When we have crossed the channel, we will dock in a city called Bandar-é Abbâs."

"Is this in Arabia too? Or the United Arab whatevers?" asked Jessica.

"No."

Faridah waited, then went on.

"There is something else," she said. Her face assumed a look of sadness that gave Jessica a fresh twinge of apprehension.

"What is it?"

"I will be leaving you today. When we arrive, our orders are to turn you over to the people who will meet us. They are expecting you."

Jessica fell silent. Faridah become her safety in a frightening and hostile world, the only person who had acted toward her with any degree of kindness. Jessica had felt some sense of security with her, no matter how tenuous. And now, she would be leaving her?

"Who are these people?"

Faridah said nothing.

"Where am I going?"

She looked out of the window, in silence. When her gaze returned to Jessica, there was a hint of regret in her voice.

"We are taking you to Iran."

Early morning light had successfully overcome the darkness that had tormented John most of the night. He was wide-eyed as he lay staring at the ceiling. His mood was foul as he consciously tried to relax the knotted muscles in his body.

Last Sunday had not been a good day. Normally, he could shake off a bad Sunday by Wednesday, but not this week. John allowed his thoughts to pile up like dark thunderclouds against a tall mountain. The weekend services had gone reasonably well, but he knew he had not been at his best. Concentration had been hard to come by. Jessica was at the forefront of his mind, not his message from God's Word to the people. Normally, he could put distractions aside, no matter how significant they might be, but not this week. Not Jessica.

He rolled over and stretched. As he did, one of the knots in his back cramped. With a groan, John leaped from the bed, placing both hands against the wall, stretching again in an effort to control the pain. As the cramp subsided, he gradually relaxed the muscles, remaining ready in case the cramp returned.

Esther leaned forward on one elbow.

"Are you all right, hon?"

"Yeah. I'm okay. Go back to sleep."

"What happened?"

"Just a cramp. Sorry I woke you up. Had to move fast."

"That's all right. Tense, huh?"

"An understatement."

"Here. Lie down and let me rub you."

"No. It'll be okay."

"Lie down. Don't be so stubborn. It's the middle of the week, John, but you've been moody for days. You're acting like it's still Monday, the day every pastor resigns from his church."

Esther stood and pulled back the covers, and John stretched out on the bed while she disappeared into the bathroom. He closed his eyes and once again tried to concentrate on relaxing. Then, Esther was back, climbing up on the bed until she was perched over him. Her strong fingers began working their magic.

"Goodness, John, your back has more knots than a Boy Scout rope."

"Tell me. I've been tying those knots all night."

She touched his hand.

"Loosen up, sweetheart."

It was his first realization that the fingers of both hands were pressed together tightly. He let go and breathed in deeply.

Gently, the firm, penetrating strokes worked their healing power.

HE WASN'T SURE HOW LONG Esther's relaxation program had gone on, but suddenly he realized that he was alone.

Must have dozed off.

Ten minutes? An hour? He looked at the digital clock by their bed.

Oh, great. It's nearly eight!

John started to get up just as Esther came in with a cup of coffee in each hand.

"Here you go," she said brightly. "A little pick-me-up."

Setting the cups on the night stand, she fluffed the pillows and John leaned back. Esther sat across from him in her favorite reading chair.

"So what is it? The services went well enough on Sunday, didn't they? People have left us pretty much alone so far this week, haven't they? The coffee's your favorite blend, isn't it? And we're good for each other, aren't we?"

John smiled as he sipped the hot drink, thinking back over the past month.

Yes, we are. Better than I can remember in a long time.

"It's Jessica, isn't it?"

It wasn't really a question. John's vacant stare reached across the room, honing in on an imaginary spot. Finally, he turned slightly in order to include Esther in his line of vision. Her hair fell around her shoulders. The sunlight through the window behind her greeted each tumbling strand with a golden kiss.

"You're beautiful, you know?"

"Don't change the subject. Am I right?"

John took another sip, his brow furrowing as the hot liquid burned across his lips and tongue.

"Yes. I can't get her out of my mind. Furthermore, Sunday's services weren't all that great. I did a lousy job. Every time I tried to focus on the message and the people, she was there. The last two days at the office have been the pits. We've got some problems that need solving at the school. The bills for repairing the sanctuary are higher than we first thought. The insurance company is reviewing our coverage. They say they're not certain that 'acts of terrorism' are covered by our policy. The board is anxious about security now, with all this publicity, and rightly so. And me? All I can think about is the last time I saw her at Ein Bokek."

"I know. Since that State Department call, I've been the same." Esther put her cup on the lamp table by the chair. "Darling, look at me."

Esther caught John's eye.

"I'm aware of just how careful you've been, when talking about Jessica." Her voice was flat and low. "At first I thought it was because you weren't sure if I could deal with it. That's really not the case, is it?"

John didn't answer.

"Is it?" Her voice rose slightly, edged with determination.

John looked down. It was obvious that the time had come. When Esther spoke in that tone, nothing but the whole truth would suffice. There was no getting out of this. He let out a deep breath.

"No, it isn't."

"So just what is it that you are carrying around, John?"

Esther waited, her eyes never leaving him.

"It's . . . well . . . it's just that I . . . "

"Can't bear to think that she may be undergoing the same sort of treatment you experienced in Israel?" Esther finished his sentence. "Imprisonment? Or worse? You're afraid they might . . . abuse her by raping, or even killing her. That's it, isn't it?"

The words scraped discordantly across John's raw emotions. *Rape? Kill? Please don't put those words in the same sentence where Jessica is concerned. But, that's what they did to that woman who worked for Jim Brainard, isn't it? How can we really imagine that they will treat Jessica any differently? They are beasts. And this Dosha character . . . what does he want with a little American girl?*

When he started to speak, his voice cracked in hoarse response.

"Yes. I am afraid. I'm afraid of all those things." John cleared his throat. "These people are killers, Esther. Fanatic killers. They are trying to purge the earth of evildoers in the name of Allah. Life doesn't hold the same value for them as it does for us. Jessica is only a pawn . . . a tiny, helpless pawn in a game that we don't really understand. A game soaked in politics and ignited by religious fanaticism. No one understands it . . . except maybe this Dosha character."

Now it was Esther's turn to sit in silence. She moved her toes back and forth, then smiled wanly.

"Thanks. I know we've discussed some things before, but we can't stop talking now. If we do, things begin to build up. The hurts, the anger, the fears. Believe me, I live with them every single day. The same demons that you wrestle with, I'm fighting too. At times, I don't think I can bear it. That's why I need you to keep talking to me. The worst words must be said, at least to each other. We have to own them. They are the potential realities of this situation. John, it is possible that she . . . won't come home." Esther's voice faded into a plaintive whisper. "I need to be able to talk about all this to someone. I guess you're it."

They came together then, wordlessly, into each other's arms and clung there in an embrace tinged with desperate fierceness.

"We're all we've got right now, along with Jeremy and Jesus," she added tearfully, looking up at the only man she had ever loved. "So, go take your shower and get dressed. By the time you're finished, breakfast will be ready. Maybe we can finish this conversation then."

John nodded and started for the shower. Just before rounding the corner, he stopped and turned.

"I love you, do you know that? And, I'm sorry."

"Sorry? That you love me?"

"No, of course not." His voice grew husky. "I'm just so sorry I came home without Jessica."

Before she could respond, he disappeared around the corner.

Esther didn't move. Seconds later, she heard the water running. Then, slowly, she started for the kitchen, shaking her head, remembering the guilt that she had carried for so long over Jenny's accidental drowning.

Esther felt a sharp hurt, deep within.

Dear God, help us. He's going through the same agony of feeling responsible for Jessica's kidnapping that I have been suffering over Jenny's death. Lord, is there no end to this? I need to help him. But how? What should I do?

Esther reached into the cupboard and pulled out a cereal box, her mind far away from the task of serving breakfast.

God, do You know where Jessica is? Sorry. Foolish question. Of course, You do. Please, Lord, I'm begging You. Let us know too, so that we can bring her home. Meanwhile, keep her safe.

A tear dropped onto the counter.

Yes, Lord. Please, keep her safe!

FOURTEEN

Faridah had never been to Bandar before. Wiping at the beads of perspiration that formed tiny rivulets along the crevices of her body, she agreed with those who said there's not a lot of reason to hang around this place. The ferry powered its way into the busiest port city in Iran, overlooking the Strait of Hormuz and acting as a stepping-off point for Jaziré-yé Hormuz and other islands.

She stood in the cabin doorway, watching the approaching outline of the city that is the year-round home for over two hundred thousand Iranians. It stretched along a narrow coastal strip, shimmering in the heat and humidity. Even on this October day, the sweltering dampness was relentless.

"Why am I being taken to Iran?"

Faridah turned to look at Jessica.

"Isn't that the country that once held a bunch of Americans hostage?" Jessica asked, remembering a lively discussion about this in her class at school last year, and about something called the Iran-Contra scandal. Iran did not sound like a place in which she wanted to be left alone.

"Please. I need to know why. What you are doing is not right. But you know that, don't you?"

Faridah remained silent.

"I don't understand any of this. All I want to do is go home!"

"Hush, child. You are not going home. You must stop thinking about it. You'll only make yourself more miserable. If you want to survive, you must be strong."

Jessica stared at Faridah.

"What do you mean? How can you say I'm not going home?"

"Because it is true. Get used to it. You are a hostage. Do you understand what that means?"

"Of course. I'm not stupid. You are holding me here against my will. But surely you can't believe that what you are doing is right."

"It may not seem right, but it's a fact of life. You are a little girl whose father got in the way of an important mission for my people."

"You mean destroying the Wall in Jerusalem? That's your idea of an 'important mission'?"

Faridah looked away.

"My dad did a good thing. He helped save people from going to war. He saved the lives of my friends from back home. He . . ."

"Be quiet."

"No," Jessica retorted. "I will not be quiet."

Faridah's hand flashed with rapier swiftness, stinging Jessica's face. Jessica flinched at the blow. Faridah saw her fight back the tears and instantly regretted having let Jessica's defiance provoke her. Disturbed by her feelings, she reached out to touch Jessica apologetically. The girl had become more than a prisoner to her. She felt a grudging admiration for the child and, at the same time, remorse over the course of action taken by the Palestinian Islamic Jihad.

Is all the violence and bitterness really necessary? And now we have this young girl. To what end? Will the leaders ransom her? Kill her? What?

Faridah watched the girl wipe her eyes, saw the set of her jaw. She wanted to tell her how sorry she was, then decided against it.

Outside the stifling cabin, the mournful sound of the ship's horn signaled that docking was only minutes away. Soon it would be over. The girl would be gone. Probably forever.

JESSICA STOOD NEXT TO FARIDAH, watching the passengers disembark. The citizenry on the dock were mostly of Middle-Eastern and African stock. There did not appear to be a single Euro-American in the group, but she was growing used to that. She could think of no reason why any white person in their right mind would be here. At the same moment, she caught herself. It was the first time she could remember ever having thought in terms of color.

Isn't that strange. Back home, I never gave the color of a person's skin a second thought. In fact, I've been taught to treat everybody the same way.

Edgar and Jill Anderson, both African-American, were two of her favorite people, just like grandparents. They accepted her as one of their own and she loved them dearly. Now, however, she was very conscious of race.

I'm the oddball here. It makes a difference how you feel about things. If I . . . when I get back, I'm sure going to see others differently than before. First off, I'll tell the Andersons how neat they are and just how much I love and admire them!

Thoughts stopped and started, then stopped again, like misdirected traffic facing off at a dangerous intersection. Actually, she decided race and being a foreigner was of little consequence. Here, everyone was the enemy. It didn't take long to figure that out. Faridah surprised her, though, because she didn't fit the stereotype—she had been too kind. Even the incident that had just occurred could not change that. The woman with the kind face had risked a great deal to smuggle in that story of her father. Jessica would never forget that act of kindness. She had to constantly remind herself that Faridah was "one of them."

The breeze, caused by the ship's forward movement, gave no relief from the heat. As the rumble of the motors decreased, signaling their arrival, the air hung even heavier around them. Wooden docks and vessels of all shapes and sizes loomed on the shoreline. They were coming into the east side of the town, though Eskelé-yé Shahid Bahonar, the main docking area, could be seen off to the west.

"What is this place called?" asked Jessica.

"Bandar-é Abbâs. 'Bandar' means port or harbor. Shah Abbâs I founded the town in the seventeenth century."

"How big is it?"

"It is approximately two hundred . . . how do you say it in English?"

"Two hundred? Oh, you mean thousand?"

"Yes. Two hundred thousand."

Amal and the other man were standing a few feet away, watching as the boat closed against the dock. Moments later, deckhands tossed ropes to men standing on the landing and Jessica heard the vessel grind against the pilings. A gangplank was dropped and the safety chain removed, permitting the passengers to make their way to the landing.

While Jessica and the others waited their turn, she noted several of the passengers being greeted by waiting relatives, a kiss on both cheeks, and hands eager to help with tattered luggage and cardboard suitcases.

Contrary to Sharjah's distinctly modern look, the women of Bandar appeared conspicuously plain and tentlike in their black or dark blue chadors.

Some of the younger girls on the dock were wearing jeans under the hejab. Many were barefoot while some wore loose-fitting sandals. All the men were dressed in long-sleeved shirts buttoned at the wrist, even though the docks were sweltering in the heat.

Jessica caught herself searching the crowd for her father. There was always the chance.... There *must* always be the chance....

"Come."

Jessica felt Faridah's hand on her shoulder, propelling her forward. They followed the two men across the gangplank and onto the wooden dock. She flinched as the sound of a nearby ship's horn startled her, and looked up just in time to see the ferry to Jaziré-yé Gheshm gradually move away from the dock and head out to sea.

The line through customs moved fairly quickly. Amal showed passports and the necessary visa permits. Jessica had a strong feeling that they were false, and she hoped someone would notice and raise questions. The man in uniform glanced up briefly, his hand busy stamping an empty page on each passport. Moments later, they were through.

On Jaddé-yé Eskelé, they paused while Amal purchased sodas from a street vendor. They were warm, but Jessica took hers appreciatively, drawing deeply on the straw as she drank.

"Don't let yourself get dehydrated, sweetheart."

From out of the heavy flow of traffic, a dusty blue van pulled up alongside and stopped. Jessica saw the man without a name hesitate for a moment as he scrutinized the driver. Then, opening the side door, he motioned for the others to get in. He climbed in last of all, pulling the door shut, as the van moved out into the traffic.

"Salâm" said the man. *Hello.*

"Salâm aleikom. Esmam Sardar-é. Hastam dust-é Massumeh," the driver answered. *Peace be upon you. My name is Sardar. I'm a friend of Massumeh.*

The driver stepped on the gas as he squeezed the van between a taxi and a bus. Then, just as quickly, he pumped the brakes to keep from hitting the rear of another bus.

Jessica remembered a television movie she had once seen, in which the heroine kept an eye out for street signs as her captor drove her through a strange city. Later, when the heroine escaped, she was able to call her fiancé and direct him to her location. Jessica watched out the window for signs. Unfortunately, even when one presented itself, she could not read the lettering. Then she tried to encapsulate landmarks in her mind until a forlorn feeling swept over her. It all seemed too hopeless.

She recognized numerous posters of the late Ayatollah Khomeini. It was a face she remembered from school and from looking through her dad's old *Time* magazines. Heavy eyebrows, glowering face full of deep lines, and a thick beard, all under a turban-style head covering.

What a sinister-looking man! He wasn't a very happy camper, that's for sure.

Jessica turned her attention back to her surroundings. An office building. A mosque. Another office building. Straight ahead, she saw a large market and bazaar.

Just then, the van turned left and stopped in front of a building that looked considerably older than those surrounding it. The drab sign in front declared that this was Hotel-é Homå.

"Come," the man without a name motioned to Jessica and the others. "Move quickly."

They stepped out of the van and walked into the lobby. It was relatively empty, giving the impression that rooms were plentiful and guests were few. She looked around with distaste. Jessica knew about the star system of hotel rating—the more stars the better the hotel. The worst hotel she had ever been in was better than this. Amal went to the registration desk and signed them in.

They crowded into an antiquated lift and rose to the fourth floor. The hall was musty and bare electric light bulbs hung from dangling cords. Amal opened the door to the room and entered, the others following him in single file. Here, as in the lobby and the hallways, the paint was flaking and fixtures were cheap. Jessica went straight to the lavatory, only to discover that the stool was without a seat. Amal fiddled with the air-con system control; it did not appear that guests had much control over air circulation.

When Jessica emerged from the lavatory, she walked past the others and stared out the window. Across the street and beyond were countless rooftops of drab buildings and, still further, the glistening waters of the Gulf. Below their window was a swim-ming pool and, off to one side, some tennis courts. It all looked run-down, with an air of elegance past.

One by one, the others were moving in and out of the lavatory.

Jessica sat down on a worn, cloth-covered chair and waited. By the way the others were acting, she sensed that this must be their destination. Tired of the long journey, she was relieved to think that the end was at hand. And yet, her anxiety level kept building.

What is going to happen next?

"Amal and I are going out for a while," the man said to Faridah, ignoring Jessica as though she were not even present. "We'll find Massumeh and make the necessary arrangements. When we come back, we'll bring food."

Faridah said nothing, but wiped perspiration from her fore-head with the back of her hand.

"Amal, tie up the girl," he ordered.

Amal reached inside his cloth bag and withdrew a roll of tape. Jessica's eyes widened as he pried the end of the tape from the roll and moved around behind her. He pushed up the cloth of her garment until her arms were exposed. Roughly, he twisted them behind her, encircling them with the tape.

"Wait," said Faridah, looking at the other man. "She needs to shower. Let her be free to do that. Then, I'll bind her."

Amal paused, his eyes on the other man.

"No. You almost lost her in the street yesterday. I cannot trust that you will be able to control her by yourself."

"That was not my fault," Faridah protested, feeling all the while that she probably was to blame. At least in part.

The man without a name ignored her.

"Hurry up, Amal. The sooner we leave, the sooner we get back. I am already anxious to leave this godforsaken country. Let's do what we have to do and get out of here."

Amal finished taping Jessica's arms behind her back, from wrist to elbow. Then he proceeded to twist tape around her ankles. As he bent in front of her, Jessica fought off the temptation to kick his face; she knew she was helpless and that retribution would be swift and brutal. He concluded the task by tearing a final strip of tape and pressing it over her mouth.

Fear that she had fought off in past weeks was now back in full force. As Amal grinned wickedly at her, she wanted to scream. Panic tore at her stomach. She squeezed her eyes shut while try-ing to regain control of her emotions. Swallowing, she pushed down the bile that once more threatened to erupt. She opened her eyes as the door closed. Faridah was busy locking it behind the men who had just left.

She turned and gazed at Jessica for a long moment.

"I am sorry, child. I cannot disobey his orders."

Jessica furrowed her brow and made unintelligible sounds as she attempted to plead from behind the tape.

Faridah stood in the center of the room, rubbing her hands nervously, watching. Finally, she came closer.

"I do not think anyone can hear you, even if you try to cry out. And, believe me, child, even if they could, no one would care! Not in this place. You must promise, however, that you will not cry out if I remove the tape from your mouth."

Jessica nodded her head vigorously.

"You promise?"

Jessica nodded again.

"This may sting."

Jessica felt the woman's finger tug gently at a corner of the tape. Then, with one swift motion, she peeled it back away from her face. Jessica flinched at the stinging sensation.

"Thank you," she exclaimed breathlessly.

"Don't ask me to do any more," said Faridah, her countenance dark with worry. "This, in itself, is enough to cause me great trouble."

"Faridah, I know your name and the name of that evil man, Amal. But, who is the other one? What is his name?"

"You should not know any of our names, child," Faridah responded. "You would be much better off not knowing."

"Well, I do know them, so nothing can be done about it. But, how is it that you can be alone with these two men? I thought, from what Daddy told me, Arab women are never to be alone with men other than their husbands. Is that true?"

Faridah nodded affirmatively.

"Then how can you . . ." Jessica paused. For the first time, it dawned on her. "Do you mean that the other man is . . . your husband?"

A weak smile crossed Faridah's face.

"Yes."

Jessica tried to assimilate this new piece of information. She was totally surprised.

"But, you are never alone together. You do not act like a husband and wife toward each other."

"He is my husband. Being a wife in my country is sometimes

a very complicated thing, child. In our culture, it is permissible for a man to have as many as four wives.

"Are you serious?"

"Very."

"Why would anyone want to be married to a man who had three other wives?"

Faridah shrugged.

"There are worse things."

"Does your husband have four wives?"

"No." She smiled at that, giving Jessica the distinct impression of being relieved at her own answer to the question. "Generally speaking, it is only the very rich or the very poor who have more than one wife."

"Why is that?"

"The Koran teaches that each wife and her children must be treated equally. They must be accorded the same worth and value. This may mean an extra tent for the very poor man or an extra palace for the very rich. The middle-class man cannot usually afford more than one wife, under those conditions."

"But why doesn't he ever talk to you like a husband? He doesn't kiss you or treat you like a wife. I've never even seen him touch you. He orders you around and treats you like a servant."

"In our country, each wife is subject to her husband's authority in every aspect of life. I know that your Bible talks about women being submissive to their husbands, but Christian women don't practice this, as we know."

"You don't know anything. My mother lives this way with my father."

"She may be the exception. We too have such a teaching in the Koran. However, we are not like you in America. We who live out our belief in Allah practice what the Prophet Mohammed has taught us. We do not show affection publicly. We do not kiss or hold hands where we will be seen by others. To do so would be considered highly improper. Even immoral by some."

"Immoral to hold hands in public?" Jessica repeated incredulously.

"Yes. And certainly we know this is true by observing women in the West, where public affection is casually acceptable and leads to all kinds of immoral acts."

"How can you say that? Have you ever been to America?"

"No. But, I have seen some of your movies and your television programs. And I've read your books and magazines. Your women spend all their time talking of equality with men. They demand equal rights and then are expected by their husbands to work outside the home. They are rebellious in spirit, dress immodestly, and live in open immorality. Perhaps your parents are different, I don't know. And you're only a little girl. You would not know of such things."

"But . . ." Jessica started to protest.

"Be quiet. I do not wish to talk of these matters any further with you."

She turned and walked away.

Jessica watched her pace back and forth, this woman of many contradictions. One moment she was warm and friendly, even caring. Then suddenly, she could be cold and distant. Jessica felt disquieted by the conversation they had just had. She wanted to explain to Faridah that Hollywood was not the American norm. At least, not the American norm she knew.

Faridah had withdrawn into herself. She went to the door, opened it and peered outside. For an instant, Jessica thought of screaming, then decided against it. It would do no good and would probably just get her into more trouble.

The familiar wave of hopelessness swept over her once again. She bit her lip as she turned her head away.

Jessica felt like crying, but was determined not to permit herself any further show of weakness.

The next two hours dragged by slowly. Faridah had shut off any further conversation with Jessica. The humidity was oppressive and Jessica's body was damp with perspiration. She was thirsty, but refused to ask for something to drink. She wasn't certain why, but something inside caused her to reject her obvious dependency on her captors.

When the door opened, Faridah's husband and Amal entered ahead of two strangers. Amal frowned as he looked over at Jessica and saw that the tape had been removed from her mouth, but he said nothing. The other men spoke in low tones. Faridah stood nearby listening.

Arms aching from being kept immovable, Jessica shifted to a more tolerable position. Resentment. Anger. Frustration. Fear. Slowly they stirred within her like the ingredients in one of her mother's mixing bowls.

The stranger on the left handed an envelope to Faridah's husband. The two men with whom Jessica had crossed the desert opened the door and walked into the hall without even looking her way. Faridah started to follow them, then hesitated. She turned and walked over to Jessica. For a brief moment their eyes met. A young girl full of questions and a woman bereft of answers. Faridah's hand brushed Jessica's face ever so lightly. Then, without a word, she turned and followed after the others.

The door closed. Jessica was alone with the two strangers. Her emotional mixing bowl was ready for the oven.

FIFTEEN

The first ring sounded as though it came from far away. She started at first, then settled back. The second ring was shrill, jarring Esther's already jangled nerves into semiconsciousness. Her eyes struggled to open as once again the phone rang.

On the night stand, numbers on the digital clock glowed red in the darkness. Five forty-seven. Reaching, she brushed against her rings and a writing pen, knocking them onto the carpeted floor.

Her fingers fumbled with the receiver and finally lifted it on the fourth ring.

"Hello?"

Her voice cracked and then she coughed before clearing her throat.

"Hello," she tried again, dropping back on the pillow with a sigh.

"Good morning." The voice was feminine, pleasant and, Esther noted with no small sense of loathing, wide awake. "I am calling for Reverend or Mrs. John Cain."

"This is Mrs. Cain."

"Mrs. Cain, I'm calling from Washington, for Mr. Charles Rodeway. What is your mother's maiden name, please?"

"What?"

"Your mother's maiden name."

"Why do you want to know that?"

"Due to the nature of this call, I am required to verify the identity of the person with whom Mr. Rodeway will be speaking."

"Stevens."

"Ma'am?"

"My mother's maiden name is Stevens."

Esther was sitting up when John turned on the light and looked over at her quizzically.

"Your social security number?"

Esther repeated the number.

"Thank you, Mrs. Cain. Is your husband there also?"

"Yes."

"If there is an extension phone, please ask him to come on line with you. Mr. Rodeway would like to speak with you both."

"All right."

Esther covered the receiver with her other hand.

"It's Washington. Rodeway wants to talk to both of us."

John rolled out of bed and disappeared into the hallway. A moment later, Esther heard him lift the extension in the family room.

"I'm here." His voice sounded reassuring.

"Still waiting," answered Esther.

They sat in silence, in separate rooms with separate thoughts, wondering what had happened to give cause for this early morning call.

Hopeful. Afraid.

"Hello. Reverend and Mrs. Cain?" Rodeway's familiar voice and southern drawl came booming through.

"Yes," they answered simultaneously.

"Good morning, Mr. Rodeway." Esther heard John's voice over the extension, and sensed the edge of anxiousness in it. "What do you have for us?"

"First, the bad news. I wish I could report that we have found your daughter, but I'm sorry. I cannot. However, there is some good news, I think. I'm sure that you have read the *International Herald* article regarding a possible 'Jessica sighting' near the Jordanian/Saudi Arabian border. I can now . . ."

"Wait a minute, Mr. Rodeway. We've neither heard nor read of such a sighting. Are you sure about this?"

"You mean you were not notified about this earlier?"

"You are the first."

"All right then." Esther could feel the man reaching for the right words. Her anxiety was very quickly turning into anger. Someone in Washington had fouled up. At the same time, she felt empathy toward the deep-voiced, southern stranger who had recently become their personal Washington connection.

"My deepest apologies. I was out of the office for a few days during the time when this reached us. I had instructed my assistant to contact you immediately with any fresh news, knowing how important it would be to hear an update, even though there was little hard information to go on."

"I assure you, Mr. Rodeway," said Esther, "there has been no contact and no message left for us either at the church or here at home."

"I'm sorry." His voice was apologetic. "I will definitely make certain that a similar snafu does not occur again. Okay, let me bring you up to date."

Charles Rodeway proceeded to tell them about Qasr al-Azraq and an elderly guide named Majid. He detailed the encounter between the guide, and two men, a woman, and a young girl.

"At first the guide assumed the girl to be Arab," he droned on. "She was dressed in a chador. It's being worn by an increasing number of fundamentalist Arab women these days. But something was different about the girl, though by the time he figured it out, they had gone."

"What was it that made him curious?" asked John.

"It was her eyes, reverend. He insists that her eyes were green."

Esther felt her heart skip a beat. *It was Jessica. It had to be!*

"This Majid fellow further states that he saw a wisp of hair underneath her head covering. He describes it as reddish brown, more light than dark. Her skin color was, as he put it, 'pale,' compared to the usual darker skin tone of an Arab girl."

"Did she say anything? Did she speak to the man?"

"No, I'm sorry, Mrs. Cain. She apparently didn't say anything at all, though that in itself doesn't mean much. An Arab child might not say anything in that situation either. Anyway, local authorities have investigated the man's report and they believe it authentic. The man has a good reputation in the community. Based on all we know, this 'Jessica sighting' looks to be genuine. Especially, now."

"Why now?" asked John, finally.

"Because she's been sighted again!"

"Where? When?" John and Esther both blurted out their excitement and concern together.

"It happened late afternoon their time on Tuesday, early morning ours. Seems there is this oil company employee who was on a long weekend out of Kuwait. His name is Syd Hershey and he's from Texas. We've verified his identity with his employer. We've had him checked out stateside as well, and there doesn't seem to be any reason to disbelieve his story."

There was a break in the conversation and the sound of papers being shuffled could be heard. Esther and John waited impatiently for him to continue.

"Hershey says he drove down to the United Arab Emirates on a holiday. The UAE is notorious as a playground for boys who want to play, if you get my drift. I'm not sayin' that's why this guy was there. He's got a wife and family back in Texas and all, but, well, who knows? Anyhow, what's important is what happened after he got to Sharjah."

Rodeway went on to relate the story, pausing periodically to answer questions.

"So, once again, we have a guy describing in detail features that are identical to your daughter's. It corroborates the prostitute's story in Amsterdam. She said that she overheard our Mr. Dosha telling someone to take the girl to Iran."

"I'm a little rusty, Mr. Rodeway. Just where is the United Arab Emirates?"

"Next door to Iran, across the Bay. That's one reason we think they may have gone by boat. They could have flown from points further inland—there are regularly scheduled flights. Could even have chartered something. But they went all the way to Sharjah and that says 'boat,' maybe the regular ferry system, maybe a fishing boat. It's only a guess at this point. They might even still be in Sharjah, but I doubt it. No, I think they've made it across already."

"Has anyone been looking for her since she was sighted?" asked Esther.

"Yeah, the locals jumped on her case as soon as it was reported. Two days now and nothing. They've been checking out people going to and from Iran, by air and sea. No sign of them. The same is true of the hotels in the area. It appears they are doing their best, but one never knows for sure. Hard to read from this distance, as I'm sure you can appreciate. Yet, everyone seems to be cooperating."

"So, what happens now?" John asked, the strain sounding in his voice.

"We keep working. You keep praying. Hopefully, our works and your prayers will do the trick. Look at it this way. We don't have her, but we now have a good idea of where she's at, or at least where she's headed."

"Iran," John's voice echoed with remorse at the thought.
"One more thing to be thankful for."
"Yeah? What's that?"
"She's alive!"

CHIN IN HANDS AND ELBOWS on the table, John stared into his half-empty coffee cup. Across from him, Esther looked out through the family-room door, watching two bluejays flash through a kamikaze routine over the patio.

After thanking Rodeway for the call, Esther had joined John in the kitchen. The coffee had brewed quickly and the dark, hot liquid burned with each sip. It was John who finally broke their silence.

"I've got to do something."

Esther looked across at her husband. His face was strained, new lines furrowing deeply in his brow and around his eyes. Indian summer's end was near, and normally, John would still be looking fit and tan from an occasional game of golf or tennis. Instead, he looked pale, almost ashen.

Maybe it's the light. No. That's not it. He looked better than this when he got home from Israel. And then he looked pretty pathetic.

"What?" she asked. "What is there that we haven't already done? We've contacted our congressmen. We've written to the Secretary of State and sent letters to the White House. We've encouraged others to do the same, and they have, by the hundreds and thousands. We've had her face and story featured on every major television network in the country. What else can we do?"

"Not we. Me!"

"You? Don't leave me out of whatever it is you're thinking. Okay?"

"I'm not leaving you out, but this is one time I'll have to go it alone."

"What are you saying?"

John took a long sip from the coffee cup, then pushed back his chair and began to pace back and forth.

"I can't keep up with this 'business as usual' routine. I can't keep my mind on the church's needs because our own needs are so much greater right now. I'm losing it, sweetheart. I've got to focus on one thing and that's getting Jessica back. Everything else has to go. There's no way to keep all the balls in the air until we get Jessica back."

"Translate all that, John. What are you saying?"

"What am I saying?" John repeated her question slowly. "I'm saying that if no one else can do anything, then I've got to. We can't keep living like this. I'm saying that I'm going to Iran and bringing our daughter back myself!"

0815 LOCAL TIME
HALIFAX, NOVA SCOTIA

"THANKS. I CAN HANDLE it from here."

The driver of the truck waved at the crane operator, while stuffing his gloves into the pocket of his jacket. He pulled the wool stocking cap down over his ears again and checked the couplings between the tractor-trailer unit. The remaining two drivers were already inside the other trucks, awaiting their leader's signal.

The crane swung another unit toward the *Grodno* and began lowering it into position, alongside the others. The driver watched for a few seconds, then climbed up into the tractor portion of the unit which was unmarked and painted white. The tanker itself was grimy and red with rust. The other two looked exactly the same. He started the motor and released the brake. Satisfied that everything was in order, he moved the gearshift and let out the clutch, heading away from the noisy dock area toward the center of Halifax. Glancing at his watch, he grunted his approval. He had forty minutes to make it to the warehouse where four out-of-work painters were waiting to begin a task that promised each man a much-needed week's pay for a job that should take only a few hours. Glancing in the mirror he saw the other trucks behind him, slowly making their way off the dock and up the grade.

SIXTEEN

A small lamp and lamp stand had been dragged next to the door. On the stand was a tray filled with ashes and cigarette stubs, an international English edition of *Newsweek*, and a Daewoo DP-51 semiautomatic military pistol.

Any soldier and most law enforcement officers would have immediately recognized the handgun as a NATO special, the standard issue of the Republic of Korea Armed Forces. To the twelve-year-old girl, the steel blue weapon was simply another link in the fence that continued to separate her from those who truly loved her.

Before leaving California, she had never seen a real gun. At first she had been frigthened by them; now, they were part of her life. She had not touched one yet, but sometimes her hand actually ached as she stared at the handgun.

If only . . .

Blinking, she drove away her fantasy. How would she ever get hold of the gun in the first place? Even if they handed her this one, what would she do with it? She knew enough to point it away from herself, but how do you hold a gun in order to fire accurately? She understood that you had to pull the trigger in order for it to fire, but wasn't there a safety or something? Where was that, and how was it released?

How many bullets are in that handgun? One? Five? Ten? Wait a minute. Get a grip, girl. . . . Jessica attempted to rein in her thoughts. Anyway, what difference would it make if she knew? Still, her mind wandered. . . . *More than ten?*

The young guard was thumbing through a local newspaper. *What do you suppose goes through his head? This has to be as boring for him as it is for me.*

She had already tried conversing with the two guards who took turns sitting just inside the door of her hotel cell.

"Do you speak English?"

The men shook their heads. "Engelisi ballad nistam."

Jessica took that as a "no." Beyond those few words, there was nothing. It was the only conversation she had until her bladder could no longer afford her to be silent. Many times during the past few weeks she had asked herself how a normal body function could be such a constantly embarrassing problem.

"I need to go to the bathroom."

The guard looked up and then returned to his magazine.

"Hey. I need to go. Understand?"

He ignored her.

"Toilet? I need the toilet! Hey!" Her voice rose a decimal. The young man stood up, a questioning look on his face. He pointed to her and then to the bathroom.

"Yes. Yes. The toilet, please."

Glancing at his watch, he then moved toward the bed. From his pocket, he pulled out a Swiss Army knife and flicked open the longest blade. He held it up in front of Jessica and began speaking.

"I don't understand what you are saying," Jessica interrupted. "If you are telling me not to try to run away, I won't. If you're asking me do I need my arms and legs untied, the answer is, 'Yes.' And, if you're trying to say something to me in English, forget it. I'll die from an exploding bladder long before I ever understand you!"

Having verbalized that embarrassing possibility, Jessica began to giggle. She couldn't stop the nervous release that had broken loose from deep inside. Here she was, talking to a guy who couldn't understand a word she said, and she was desperate to go to the bathroom. The personal nature of her problem simply added fuel to her giggle, and pain to her abdomen. She closed her eyes in an effort to stop it.

Jessica shuddered involuntarily as the guard's hands rested briefly on her shoulders. He rolled her over on her stomach and she felt the knife blade against her arms. He cut through the tape and her arms fell free. Seconds later, her ankles were also released.

Now, Jessica lay on the bed, unable to move. Her arms had been taped behind her back for so long that they would not function. She tried pushing herself up, only to fall back again.

Suddenly, she felt herself being lifted from the bed and placed in an upright position. Blood began rushing to her extremities. How many hours had it been? She swayed uncontrollably.

I'm going to faint!

But, the young man did not let her fall. Instead, he kept her balanced as she gingerly tried first one step, then another.

"One small step for man . . ." Jessica mumbled to herself with a chuckle, wondering all the while what was so funny about all this. Finally, she was at the doorway to the lavatory.

What if he goes in with me?

Another involuntary giggle erupted at the thought.

"This is ridiculous," she said, her voice breaking the sticky stillness that hung oppressively over the room.

At the sound of her voice, the young man let his hands fall away and he stepped back. Jessica turned, the giggle still tickling her voice box.

"Thank you," she said.

"Khosh amadid," he said, still watching her.

"Whatever," Jessica answered back and closed the door.

At least she had been spared that embarrassment. Eventually, feeling much better, she sighed with relief. Then, tears suddenly filled her eyes.

What's going on? First, I can't stop giggling and now I'm crying.

She buried her face in her hands, shoulders shaking spasmodically as each new wave of emotion rolled over her.

O dear God, I am lost. I'm really lost. I don't have a clue as to my whereabouts, and Dad and Mom won't know either. What am I going to do?

Carefully, Jessica tore away the last remnants of tape and put them in a wastebasket near the sink. Next, she turned on the faucet in the sink and let her arms, still stinging from the tape removal, feel the soothing warmth of the water. She took a bar of soap and gingerly washed her arms, hands, ankles, and feet. She looked longingly at the shower, but was afraid that the guard might decide to come in if he heard her running the water.

In fact, at that very moment, there came a knock on the door and a voice on the other side said something.

"I'll be just a minute," she called out, wiping her hands and arms. Hanging the towel back on the hook, she took a deep breath and opened the door. The guard was standing in the middle of the room with the handgun that had been on the lamp stand. He motioned to her with the gun, indicating that she should sit on the bed. Jessica was afraid that he would bind her again, but he did not. When she was situated to his satisfaction, he grinned and returned to his position by the door.

THAT HAD BEEN TWO DAYS AGO. Since that time, Jessica remained free, but with no possibility of escape. The phone had been removed, though she knew she probably would not have much success in trying to use it. She had never made an international telephone call.

It appeared as though her attempted breakaway in Sharjah had served only to heighten security efforts. In spite of her questions, the guards made no attempt to respond in kind. They remained seated at the door, most of the time tipped back against the wall on the chair's rear legs, reading a book or newspaper, or simply staring off into the distance.

An ancient television on the opposite wall was never turned on. She had asked about it, pointing and making gestures toward the set. Did it work? Could she turn it on? A shoulder shrug and a head shake. Those were the only responses to her pleadings for relief from the continuing boredom.

At eight o'clock on the evening of the second day, she was wondering what would come next.

When the door opened, five minutes later, she had her answer.

1130 LOCAL TIME
WASHINGTON, DC

TO:	CIA, Office of the Director
	State Department, Office of the Secretary of State
FROM:	Charles Rodeway, SD Political and Diplomatic Security Section
RE:	Jessica Cain, Missing American
DATE:	28 October 1130 EST

Incident Report Update
   Unconfirmed reportings of "Jessica sightings" have slowed somewhat in the last two weeks. A Sunday, 23 October sighting, believed authentic, placed the 12-year-old

near Azraq, Jordan, in the company of two men and a woman. They were traveling in a green truck, model unknown. The woman and girl were dressed in chadors, customary for female members of the Muslim fundamentalist Shia sect.

Tuesday, 25 October, late afternoon, Mr. Sydney Hershey, USA citizen temporarily deployed to Kuwait by an American oil company, confirmed the second sighting of Jessica Cain. He witnessed what appeared to be an attempted escape in Sharjah, UAE. Details of Hershey's testimony are being forwarded from our embassy in Dubai and will be sent to you under separate cover. The incident was not reported until the following day when Hershey saw the Cain girl's photo in the *International Herald*. No further contact with the missing girl has been reported. The most likely possibility is that she has been removed from UAE and relocated in Iran.

Action Steps

Continued monitoring of the situation. Available information to be relayed between Mossad and security agencies in Middle Eastern Arab countries. Cooperation good so far. Telephone contact made with the Reverend and Mrs. John Cain, Jessica's parents.

Outlook

That the girl is alive has come as a surprise. Reasons why she is being held are unclear. Iranian contacts have so far proven unproductive. If whereabouts are known by officials in Tehran, they are a closely guarded secret.

Will advise as further information is available.

SEVENTEEN

"You're going to what?" Esther gripped the edge of the table and leaned forward, her countenance frozen with a look of disbelief. "You can't be serious, John."

"Well, I am," John replied, returning her gaze.

"How in heaven's name can you ever hope to do something like that?" Esther exclaimed, her tone nettled and tinged with exasperation. "You're not James Bond, for goodness sake. You're John Cain, a preacher. Do you think the Iranians are going to welcome a Protestant preacher with open arms? Especially a preacher whose face they've already probably used for target practice? 'Oh, yes, Reverend Cain, we're so pleased you have come. We're the people who funded the kidnapping of your little daughter so that we could thank you appropriately for thwarting our righteous attempt to assist the Palestinian Islamic Jihad in regaining their sovereignty and their homeland. Welcome, Reverend Cain. Now that you're here, we want to admit our wrongdoing, beg your forgiveness, and give your daughter back.' Is that what you think?"

Esther could feel herself sliding into an abyss of emotional darkness. She was babbling and she knew it, as a sudden rush of resentment boiled to the surface. Banging her hands on the table, she stood up, rattling the cups and splashing coffee onto the table-top in the process.

"Esther, look . . ."

"No! No, no, no!" Esther was crying now, her hands shaking. "You look! I've lost Jenny. Jessica is somewhere out there, God only knows where. A few weeks ago, I thought I might lose you and Jeremy as well. John, I can't bear the thought of your leaving us . . . me . . . and maybe never coming back. There has got to be another way!"

John reached out and took Esther's hand. Her tears fell on the table. He stood and gently drew her to himself. She buried her face in his chest and felt his arms encircle her as she tried in vain to control the sobs that racked her body. How long did they stand together like this? She wasn't sure. She didn't care. Long enough for her body to empty itself of tears, to halt its reflexive spasms, and complete the release of pent-up tensions that had been lurking inside.

The room became quiet. Esther did not want to move.

Let the world turn on its own. I can't be responsible for it any longer. This is safe. This is where I want to be.

She caught her breath as John's strong hands moved to her shoulders and slowly parted them from their fierce embrace. She forced herself to look up at him, ashamed now at the way her emotions had boiled over. His face was damp with tears as well.

"I'm sorry," she said simply.

John picked up a napkin and wiped her cheeks.

"It's okay. There's nothing for you to be sorry over. We're both living on the edge these days."

He ran the napkin over his own face and then dropped it on the table.

"Come on, love. Let's sit down and talk about this."

Arms around each other, they walked over to the couch and sat down. Esther's hand instinctively brushed under her eye, to wipe away any mascara run. Then she remembered she had not yet put on any makeup. She pushed her hair back from her forehead.

"Do I look as bad as I think I do?"

"Darling, you look great."

"Be honest."

"Well, maybe a bit worse for wear, but you'll get over it."

Esther offered up a thin smile.

"Thanks. I needed that."

"No problem. Compliments of my extensive sensitivity training."

"Now I know you're lying," she came back, with a half sigh, half shudder. "But God will forgive you."

John chuckled.

Another long pause as their emotional hurricane blew itself out, and a gradual calm took its place.

"Okay, so what is this crazy idea about going off to Iran?"

"Actually, I've been thinking about this for days. Ever since we heard that they might be taking her there. I've had the feeling that if she is in Iran, our government won't do anything. Rodeway and the others in Washington will keep holding our hands and being sympathetic, but what will they do? What *can* they do?"

Esther remained silent, staring at the floor as John continued.

"You mentioned a minute ago about the Iranians and how they would feel if I showed up on their doorstep. But what we have to keep in mind is that this is not about a nation of people. Honey, there are probably two hundred thousand Iranians who live right here in the Bay Area. Most of them are good people. They have children themselves and will hate what is happening to us, once word gets out that she may be held in their homeland. This whole madness is not about racism. It's about radicalism!"

She leaned back against the soft couch pillows, unaware of her fingers twisting the loose end of her blouse, looking at John with interest now.

"I've done some checking around this last week. I spoke with Jerry Handover at our denominational headquarters."

"I don't know who he is," Esther said, feeling herself being drawn toward what he was saying.

"He's one of the guys at the Foreign Missions Department. I met him a couple of years ago when I taught at that regional conference in LA."

She nodded, remembering the time.

"He tells me that the church does exist in Iran. It is not very organized. In fact, it is mostly underground and the Christians stay pretty invisible because of persecution. But it's there, nonetheless. Maybe, if I can get to some of them. . . ." His voice trailed off as he thought about the odds.

"Does anybody even know who they are?"

"God does."

"Could we ever get in touch with them? And, even if that were possible, what could they do to help us?"

John leaned forward, elbows on his knees, fingers interlocked. Carefully, he began laying out his proposed plan. For the next two hours, they discussed, disputed, and defended their crisscross speculations. At last, they grew silent, studying the floor as if it were the womb of every deep thought they had ever conceived.

Eventually, Esther stood to her feet and looked down at John.

"This is absolutely the most ludicrous thing we have ever considered. It's too risky. What kind of a chance for success do we have, really?" She looked away, then back again at John, her lips slowly forming into a half smile. "I guess if the Lord is with us, we're not supposed to be able to fail. Isn't that the way it works?"

"That's the idea anyway," John agreed, getting up and walking over to the window that looked out onto the pool.

That's the idea, but is the idea really going to work in this case? It's a whole lot easier to preach to others about trusting the Lord than it is to live out that trust yourself. Especially with something like this where so much is at stake.

He took in the dance of the sun's rays on the water's surface. Then his gaze was drawn to the familiar object at the bottom of the "swimming hole," as Jeremy used to call it in those happy times in which he and his sisters splashed and played there together.

It's still there, he thought. The pool sweep rested quietly beneath the water, its reflection a dark shadow in an otherwise bluish-white world. *Our beloved ghost. I miss you, Jenny. We both do. And now we've lost your sister too. It's almost more than I can deal with, even though I know you're with Jesus. What do you understand up there in heaven, Jenny? You were so little when you left us. Do you have grown-up knowledge now? Do you ever get to look down and see us? Do you know where Jessica is today? If you do, put in a good word for her, okay? And us too. We need to get her back.*

John smiled. His understanding of Scripture and theology clearly precluded any spiritual contact with the dead. Still, once in a while, he felt extremely close to Jenny, almost as though she were physically near at hand. When it happened, the sensation of her nearness was a pleasant one. *Maybe Jesus has her in His arms during these moments when I feel especially close to her. . . .*

"Where are you, sweetheart?" Esther's voice broke through his momentary reverie. She slipped her arm around his waist.

John looked down, flushed slightly with embarrassment. "Sorry. Guess I was . . . out there . . . with the girls somewhere."

Esther understood. Their beloved ghost had returned. But October's child had not.

Her lips moved in soundless prayer. *Pleading. Please, Jesus, take care of our girls. Please?*

EIGHTEEN

At the time of the Iranian Revolution in 1978–79, Leila Azari had been eleven years old, living in Tehran with her parents and two brothers. The Holy War raged back and forth through the cities and countryside, profoundly affecting her childhood. She vividly remembered the recurring reports of Muslim women literally throwing themselves into The Cause as suicide assassins and female warriors. Her mother repeatedly spoke of being ready to sacrifice her own children for Islam, if called upon to do so. During Leila's childhood and youthful years, the whole mood in Iran became one of the modern era's most mysterious phenomena.

The classical image of women in Islamic society as subordinate, weak creatures, dominated by the rule of men, was broken. In its place stood a new woman, armed and fanatically supportive of war. The reality of women displaying zealous, martial qualities was totally alien to conventional views on what constituted womanhood. Part of the conundrum resulted from the fact that their struggle was not directed at Islam, even though it had discriminated against them for centuries. Instead, they were displaying an impassioned defense of the faith.

The veiled women of the Iranian Revolution did not bewilder the Western World alone, but other Muslim societies as well. In Islamic countries, where segregation of the sexes was strictly imposed and women were confined to duties at home, these Iranian women were a confusing enigma.

The chador came to symbolize a form of political protest, an identity with Islamic values, and a return to Muslim fundamentalism. It also symbolized a reversal of the Westernizing process undertaken by the Shah. Students began wearing the chador, as did working women. It was largely the Iranian woman who imprinted the Revolution with an Islamic character by wearing her black veil and calling for the establishment of an Islamic republic.

This fundamentalist fanaticism drove thousands of women to join their men in the streets of Tehran on 8 September, 1978. Leila's mother was there among them, carrying a flag in one hand and Leila's younger brother in the other. It was the dawning of a new day, and people were eager to demonstrate their opposition to the Shah. To do so, they defiantly faced American-trained Iranian soldiers armed with American weapons.

People did whatever they could to help the Revolution. Even the blind woman who stood on the corner by a phone booth with a bowl full of two-rial coins, offering them for use by the demonstrators if they needed to make a call.

On this day, later to be known as Black Friday, the marchers seemed to feed on the energy their mass created. They moved stridently up the boulevard, spilling over into Jaleh Square. Women in Islamic dress walked in the front lines, protecting their husbands who marched behind them. They believed that because they were women, the soldiers would not fire their weapons.

They were wrong. Incessant machine-gun fire shook the streets as the massacre got underway. Soon, hundreds of blood-soaked bodies were scattered everywhere, among them countless women, grotesquely draped in black chadors that became death shrouds.

In the midst of the horror, one woman fell, mortally wounded. She clutched her small son to her breast, hands sticky with blood from the bullet hole through his heart. She looked up to see her husband staring at her in horror, hands stretched toward heaven, whether signaling prayer or surrender, she could not be sure. A moment later, a hail of bullets slammed into his chest.

She did not cry out. She did not whimper or complain. She repeated "Allah-Akbar" until she died.

She was Leila Azari's mother, and the little girl never forgot!

By the time Leila celebrated her seventeenth birthday, 10 April, 1985, she had become a committed revolutionary. That's what made the events of that birthday so poignantly beautiful. One could even say it was a sign from Allah. Leila knew it would remain forever etched in her mind, symbolizing what was to be her mission in life.

It was on that special day, set aside to celebrate the joy of life, that a young woman drove up to an Israeli checkpoint known as Bater-al-Chouf, twenty-four kilometers east of the port of Sidon, Lebanon. As the Israeli soldiers approached the car, the driver closed her eyes, listened to the pounding of her heart, whispered the name of Allah, and pushed a small button. The fiery explosion that followed blew her into tiny pieces, along with two of the soldiers. Two other soldiers were critically injured. The suicide attack, and its reverberations felt around the world, had been carried out by a sixteen-year-old Shia girl.

The Western World was shocked. Why would a young girl in the bloom of life engage in such an act? Who could understand this sort of thing?

Leila Azari understood.

It had been eloquently stated for her and for thousands like her by Gohar Dastghaib at the Interparliamentary Union in Havana, Cuba in September 1981. She wore the black veil and declared herself to be the representative of millions of Muslim women who carried the heavy burden of the Islamic Revolution of Iran upon their shoulders.

Dastghaib spoke passionately of those women who had stood in the front ranks during the Tehran riots of 1978. She painted a stark picture of those who bought freedom by accepting in their bodies the bullets of the Shah's troops. Their veils had become their burial clothes; their clenched fists and the cry of "Allah-Akbar" heralded the ousting of the Shah.

The most moving part of her speech so stirred Leila's young spirit that she memorized each word and often repeated them with reverence. "Our young people are in love with martyrdom and we mothers will never tire of producing martyrs."

Leila understood what her Shia sister-in-the-faith had done. And she understood why. Inflamed by this sixteen-year-old's holy sacrifice to the Islamic cause, Leila vowed a similar determination to serve notice on the arrogant, disbelieving world of the West. The antihuman forces of the USA and Israel, together with their sordid Western allies, deserved her eternal hatred.

They had killed her mother and father and little brother!

In October 1985, Leila was recruited into one of the Shia commando camps. In a matter of weeks, undergoing rigorous physical and technical training, she became proficient in handling automatic weapons like the American M-16 and the Soviet AK-47, and learned how to operate machine guns and mortars. Her fervor for the Islamic Republic was consuming. "We see that women are valued in our country," she would tell her friends. "We are worth as much as any man. Probably a lot more. I'm still learning how to use our weapons, but I am ready to fight at any time."

In the summer of 1986, tens of thousands of women volunteers joined the "Bassij." These were the mobilization units of the Revolutionary Guard. Some five hundred women a month qualified as combat soldiers, so that by the end of summer there would be enough trainers to staff two thousand "Zahra Camps." Leila Azari became one of these.

A brief marriage ended tragically when her young husband was killed on the front lines, in the province of Khuzestån near the sprawling industrial capital of Ahvås, during the war between Iran and Iraq. In the same conflict, she lost her older brother. Her entire family had now been consumed by the ghastly machinery of war. It seemed to Leila that death was the only thing certain in her precarious world, and she lived with the constant awareness that Allah was probably not going to permit her a long life. So, when the call came, she was thoroughly ready to embrace the "Path of Zaynab."

Zaynab was a granddaughter of Mohammed. During the Karbala war of A.D. 680, she became a legendary example of bravery and self-sacrifice. Her brother, Imam Hussain, had declared war against the despotism of the caliphs, accusing them of turning the Islamic community into a repressive class system. Following Mohammed's death, Islam had become a world hegemony. The wealth and military power that followed soon corrupted the caliphs and other leaders.

Zaynab stood beside the blood-soaked bodies of her relatives at the close of this disastrous battle and cursed her captors, without concern for her own welfare, and blamed them for preventing the emergence of a just Islamic society guided by Mohammed's teachings.

Hundreds of years later, Leila and thousands of other Shia women militants followed the "Path of Zaynab" by taking their stand against the corrupting influences of Western capitalism. Beyond that, it meant a willingness to take up arms in the name of the Holy Cause and not shrink from bloodshed or even the sacrifice of one's own life.

Leila eventually worked her way into the Iranian militia group, Hizballah, the Party of God, a name coming from a Koranic verse that promises victory to those who join the "party of God." Mohammed had used this promise to promote his faith.

She quickly fell under the spell of the films and ideological training offered to Hizballah followers. By age twenty-three, Leila was accepted into the notorious Islamic Jihad, the Islamic Holy War movement that was terrorizing the West and its allies in Lebanon, Israel, and the entire Middle East.

Leila eventually became an instructor at a camp in which young Shia girls and boys were trained for suicide attacks. If called upon by the leaders of the nation, these children were ready to give their lives in order to carry out onslaughts against American, Israeli, or Saudi targets.

The history of their movement was recorded in the blood of martyrs and their victims. Shia suicide drivers were responsible for blowing up Beirut's US Embassy in 1983. In October of that year, American and French military units were victims of a bomb attack. In 1984, Israeli troops in Southern Lebanon became bombing targets of the National Lebanese Resistance, headquartered in a Shia slum suburb of Beirut called Burji al-Barajneh. Year after year, more and more young suicide drivers and bombers lined up to become the Islamic Jihad's bloody trademark.

Leila was recognized as a leader among leaders by the time she reached her twenty-fifth year. By then, she had been involved in a variety of covert attacks against the West. Once, she barely escaped with her life, when a bomb went off before she and her companion had a chance to get far enough away. Her cohort was killed instantly. Leila carried a small piece of shrapnel in her lower back, lodged too close to the spinal cord for surgery.

In the camp where she served as an instructor, boys and girls, men and women were trained in the devilish arts of terrorism and warfare. This, in a culture where women were traditionally confined to home and family.

It was this rediscovered strength that Leila believed to be the power behind Iran's successful revolt. Leila told her recruits that if the West were ever to understand this, it would be ruinous to the future of Islamic expansion. Then she would laugh, reassuring them of the unlimited stupidity of the West.

"It will never happen," she would say. "Not in a thousand years!"

IT HAD BEEN TWO WEEKS since Leila Azari had first been contacted by her superiors and told to report to headquarters in Tehran for a special assignment. Autumn's early chill was in the air as she drove across the central plateau and into the urban sprawl that was home to Tehran's twelve million souls. It promised relief from the hot and dry summer, but did not quite deliver. An early rain had been predicted, but there was no sign of its appearance. Instead, automobile pollution filled the air, all but obliterating the magical Elburz Mountains.

Upon her arrival, she had been ushered into the Spartan quarters of her superior officer, and offered a small glass cup of tea. "You are being given an important task, Leila. Pick carefully two of your best people and be in Bandar-é Abbâs by next week. Once you are there, further instructions will be forthcoming."

"Can you tell me anything?"

"I can tell you it involves taking into your custody that young girl the world has been looking for, the cleric's daughter from America who has been in the media these past weeks."

"We have her?" Leila exclaimed, surprise engraved in the tone of her voice.

"Yes. Our freedom fighters have successfully extricated her from Israel and are bringing her to us shortly. You will retain her in safekeeping until Marwan Dosha arrives to take charge."

"What is our purpose for holding the girl? Wouldn't it be simpler just to kill her?"

"It would seem so. However, Dosha apparently has some grand scheme that involves her. I gather she was left behind when her father's group was taken hostage. The Islamic Jihad contact in the hotel was a desk clerk. When he realized what had happened, he didn't know what to do. Personally, I think he panicked. At any rate, you know the rest. Dosha's plans for Israel were thwarted and all he has to show for his trouble is the girl."

"Dosha," she murmured, the tone of her voice almost reverent. "He really is involved in this then. I have wondered whether or not it could be true, ever since first reading about it."

"It is true."

"I have always wanted to meet him. He has the reputation for being the best."

"That is what they say. However, since this recent mission was neutralized, I have heard that some of our leaders are beginning to wonder just how good he really is. He was beaten by a Christian pastor, of all things, not even a soldier or a policeman. That he has lost considerable face is without question. I'm sure he must know this and is planning to redeem himself. The girl probably has something to do with that."

"You have met him?"

"Dosha? No, never."

"When will he arrive?"

"We are not certain, but the girl will arrive from Jordan soon. They are bringing her across Saudi when they think it is safe. The Western media has made her so well known that keeping her whereabouts a secret has been difficult. It is also extremely dangerous to move her. They have been waiting for the right moment to transport her to Bandar-é Abbâs. The word is that it will be soon. Any day now."

"Should I contact you when I have taken her?"

"Yes, but exercise extreme care. The entire world is looking for her. That is why you are to be in charge of the operation. Keep in mind that we are never sure what capabilities our enemies have to monitor our communications. Things have been very different since Khomeini died in 1989. There are traitors among us. These are uncertain times and this American girl is a prize. Do not let anything happen to her until we are ready."

"We have no idea what will be done with her?"

"No. That remains to be determined by others. For now no one else is to know that we have her in our possession. Not until Dosha arrives. Your instructions and the location at which you will hold her are in this envelope. You must go without further delay. Moraffagh bashid! *Good luck!*"

IT WAS FRIDAY, a few minutes past eight, when Jessica glanced up at the knock on the door, expecting to witness another routine changing of the watch. When the guard unlocked the door, however, three women entered the room. The first was dressed in jeans and a loose-fitting shirt that reached almost to her knees. A plain, dark head scarf covered her hair and neck. Next came a woman in a black chador. The third wore a full-length black skirt, a shirt with sleeves buttoned at the wrists, and a dark head scarf.

The one wearing jeans came forward until she stood at the edge of the bed. Her skin was the color of ivory, her face striking with a straight, narrow nose, high cheekbones, long lashes, and dark, piercing eyes that remained fixed on the young girl in front of her.

A few weeks ago, Jessica would have been very uncomfortable, even fearful, in the presence of these women. The time spent with Faridah, however, had minimized that apprehension. Still, the longer the woman in jeans stood there, the more rapidly she felt her heart beating.

"So, this is the daughter of the Great Satan's latest hollow hero, the Reverend John Cain. Your name is Jessica?" The woman's voice was low and harsh, but her English was clear enough.

Jessica was surprised to hear her speaking English. She was also shaken to hear her father's name mentioned by this stranger.

What a relief to be able to talk to someone again!

"Yes. Who are you?"

The woman ignored her question, allowing her gaze to move around the room, as though expecting to see something out of the ordinary. Jessica could have assured her that there was nothing extraordinary about this room. In fact, if the woman was interested, she could tell her exactly how many tiles were in the ceiling and how many dead flies were on the windowsill by the bed.

"For the moment, you are our prisoner," the woman said. "Gather up your things and come with us. Be sure to bring everything. You will not be back here again. Furthermore, once we have left the room, you will remain silent until I say that you may speak again. Is that clear?"

Jessica nodded.

The woman's eyes narrowed.

"In Iran, when addressing a stranger, especially one older than you, it is polite to begin your comments with åghå-yé, meaning 'sir,' or, khånom, meaning 'madam.' We know, from experience, how ill-bred and impolite most Americans are. You, however, do not have that option as long as you are with us. Is that perfectly clear, Jessica?"

"Yes."

"The word is 'baleh.' "

Jessica stared at the woman.

"Say it."

"Baleh," Jessica answered, her voice soft and uncertain.

"Speak up."

"Baleh," Jessica repeated.

"Baleh what, Jessica?"

Jessica thought for a moment.

"Baleh khånom," she said finally.

The woman nodded, pursing her lips as she did.

"Now, get your things. We must hurry. Don't forget what you have just been taught. And remember to maintain an absolute silence from this moment until I say otherwise. Understand?"

"Baleh khånom," Jessica answered.

There was really nothing for Jessica to gather up. Her only possessions were the clothes she had been wearing ever since she was kidnapped in Israel, and the chador she had been given in

Jordan. Also she had a toothbrush, a small tube of toothpaste, and a bar of hand soap.

As she stuffed the toothbrush and paste into her pocket, a mental flashback caused a brief smile.

"What do you find so humorous, Jessica Cain?"

The woman in jeans glowered over her.

"I was just remembering how many times my mother has told me to gather up my things at home. There, it takes me five or ten minutes to get it all put away. That's not my problem here, is it?"

Out of the corner of her eye, as she gathered up the chador, it appeared to Jessica that the woman's facial features changed for a split second, but it was hard to say. The beginning of a smile perhaps?

"Hurry. Put it on."

Jessica wrapped the chador over her own clothing. She knew it was going to be uncomfortable, but she took the woman's warning seriously and said nothing.

I hope, wherever we're going has air conditioning!

The guard opened the door and, without a word, the three women and the girl stepped through the doorway and started down the dimly lit hall.

NINETEEN

The smell of fresh coffee lingered over the large, mahogany table as pleasantries were exchanged between those seated around in worn, leather chairs. Cory Johnson, Calvary's business administrator, reached over each person as he poured into the mugs.

"Thanks, Cory," Harold Cawston said. "You do this extremely well."

"Yes," agreed Jerry North, with a big grin. "It looks to me like you may have missed your calling. You should have been a waiter."

The others laughed and Cory chuckled with them. He placed the carafe on a small table and pulled out a plate loaded with fresh brownies.

"All right!" exclaimed Mike Dewbar. "Now we're talking. Pass 'em this way before Peping gets his hands on them, or they'll never make it around the table."

Scott Peping grinned as he rubbed his hands together in mock anticipation. As longtime golfing buddies, he and Mike enjoyed kidding each other unmercifully about their game, weight, eating habits, and any other thing that might wander across their conversational agenda.

David Bolling had rearranged his travel schedule in order to be at the meeting. He had planned to leave for Chicago to attend a national conference, but put off leaving until the next morning.

As the brownies finally reached Scott's chair, Dennis Lanier walked through the doorway, having rushed from a City Planning Staff meeting. As Baytown's city manager, he often left one meeting a little early in order to arrive at another a bit late.

The others greeted him warmly as he sat down next to Scott and speared a brownie from off the serving plate. More banter.

As John leaned forward in his chair, the conversation gradually lessened until the room was quiet. All eyes were turned toward him, with an awareness that something unusual was afoot. For one thing, brownies were out of the ordinary. For another, they had no agenda and the only thing in front of John was his Bible.

Six men. Normally, the official board of Calvary Church consisted of seven. Attorney Ken Ralsten was the missing person tonight. Since the fateful events of September Strike, Ken had not attended any of their meetings. His depression over the events of that weekend had been devastating. John had spent considerable time with Ken, eventually introducing him to a Christian psychologist, one who often worked with him in cases requiring special training or long-term therapy. Ken's son, Geoff, was also in counseling. John understood that some progress was being made, and he tried to stay in touch with them by telephone or in person on a weekly basis. A few days ago, Ken and his family had flown to Hawaii for a three-week vacation.

"Fellows, let's get started. Our meeting should not be long, but it is important. I appreciate some of you rearranging your schedules in order to attend another 'extra' meeting. We've had our share of them these last weeks, haven't we?" smiled John, as he acknowledged the affirming nods around the table. "As we begin, let's remember Ken and his family. They have a couple more weeks in Hawaii. Let's ask the Lord to complete His work of healing there, as He has been doing for each of the rest of us. Okay? Any other needs you feel like mentioning?"

The room was silent. There was something else, but no one needed to mention it. It was permanently imprinted on their hearts, a constant part of their lives that surfaced each time they bowed their heads in prayer.

"Why" questions still lingered, but none greater than the unspoken one concerning Jessica's whereabouts. There was not one of them who failed to include her in their family mealtime prayers and private devotional periods. Her disappearance was a never-ending ache in the heart of every Calvary Church member. More than they could ever have imagined, Jessica had become a very real member of all their families.

This was true of every Calvary Church family. They all felt the loss, sensed the unfairness of it, and became angry.

Then, watching John and Esther trying to live out their faith before them, they asked God to forgive their anger in the same way that they observed the Cains had forgiven others. The last few weeks had seen a spiritual deepening in the congregation at Calvary Church that most people admitted had been far too long in coming, and purchased at far too great a price.

It was also true for Christians in other churches of Baytown. They too felt the loss, even though most had never known Jessica. It affected them in ways that went far beyond feelings of concern for a missing child.

Over the years, the area saw new churches come into being, and in some ways the work of God had expanded. But, in other ways, it had fallen far short of God's intention for His body, as carnal competitiveness thwarted the church's mission. Wanderlust drew dissident members from one church to another. The study of theology gave way to the development of church management techniques. Simplicity in worship became lost in the debate over worship styles. The church had become mired in selfishness and self-centeredness.

After that unforgettable weekend in September, however, there was something different about the body of Christ in Baytown. It had finally felt its extreme vulnerability. Not only Calvary Church, but every church. To Baytown believers, there had come a fresh sense of the fragility of the Christian community as a whole. For a while, at least, there seemed to be more warmth, more concern, and more love being shared than anyone could remember.

Christians who had not expressed feelings of love for each other before, in the safety of church walls, now hugged in the malls and supermarkets.

Christians who had not spoken in years held hands and wept as they sought each other's forgiveness for past wrongs.

Christians who had not read the Bible or prayed together as a family in ever so long a time, now sat in homes all over Baytown, listening to one of their own read the Scriptures before joining hands and hearts in prayer.

Christians were being Christians again.

Some had forgotten just how wonderful that could be. Others had never known. It was exciting.

"Jerry, will you lead us, please?" The room was silent.

Jerry began to pray . . . for the Ralstens . . . for the people of Calvary Church . . . for churches, pastors, and Christians throughout the community. John could not keep from thinking how much this prayer differed from those that had opened their board meetings before September 18.

Then, Jerry prayed for Jessica, whose human helplessness had drawn Baytown's extended Christian family together in a never-before-experienced spirit of love and unity.

WHEN IT CAME TO MEETINGS, Dennis Lanier was an expert. He had been in hundreds of them during his city government career and had a sixth sense about their importance or lack thereof. Most tended to be ordinary. Some were key to matters that moved institutions forward or backward. But a few meetings were crucial moments in the life of the entity in question.

Dennis' instinct told him that this was going to be one of those. It was in the air from the minute he entered the room. A defining moment.

He had listened to the last bits of camaraderie while eating a brownie, then leaned back and sipped the hot, black liquid in his cup. He didn't just listen to John's words as he opened the meeting; he analyzed the tone as well. It was quiet and calm, but there were telltale signs of strain around the edges.

Dennis wondered about the personal pressure in his pastor's life right now. He had been doing a great job of shepherding the flock since returning from Israel, but the situation at home had to be unbelievably stressful. He and Barbara talked about it often and wondered what it would be like if it were one of their children.

Bowing his head, he joined with the others around the table as Jerry led them in prayer. Before the amen validated their unity, a forewarning gripped his spirit.

Something significant has happened. Have they found her? If she was alive, John would be bouncing off the ceiling. If this is about Jessica, then it can mean only one thing. What else could there be, Lord?

When Jerry finished, there was silence around the table. John was the last to look up.

Dennis waited for him to open his Bible, but John didn't touch it. Instead, he sat back in his chair and let his eyes take in each of the men gathered there. Then he shifted and leaned forward, until his elbows rested on the table and both hands dropped onto the Bible.

"Gentlemen, you are all wondering why I've called this special meeting. I'm not quite sure how to phrase what I want to say, so I'll just stumble along.

"After our September board meeting, just before leaving for Israel, I wrote out my letter of resignation as senior pastor of this church. At the time, I was pretty discouraged. Jenny's death and Esther's depression had almost destroyed us. That, coupled with Jeremy and me not being able to really communicate without anger, was slowly sinking us as a family. Add to that the pressures that go with this business of pastoring and the result was . . . still is . . . what the experts call 'clergy burnout.' It's a growing phenomenon among my colleagues in the ministry. We just get to a point of not having anything to give. We're used up. No more tread left, we still try to keep running on the rims.

"At the time, I had determined that when I got home from Israel, I would get out of the ministry altogether. The price for staying in it was too high. My 'clergy account' was spiritually way overdrawn. It seemed that the only bright spot left in our lives was Jessica."

John paused and cleared his throat before continuing.

"Well, the events of the past few weeks have been something I never dreamed would happen. Not in my wildest nightmares. The truth is, the last couple of years are beyond my understanding at times. Anyway, there is some good news. Esther has experienced a positive healing, spiritually and emotionally. Our marriage has never been stronger. Jeremy and I are talking like two old men. Jenny is not simply a source of grief any longer. She is our star in heaven. But, of course, there still is Jessica."

The silence was electric as the men listened to their pastor share his personal pain, and that of his family. Dennis had never thought about his pastor quite like this before. Sure, he knew that John and Esther must experience some of the same problems as everyone else. But they worked things out differently than other people, didn't they? That's what pastors did.

Dennis watched John's body language. He had begun with his hands folded over the Bible, glancing down at it every once in a while, as though seeking some reassurance. In general, he kept his eyes on the group while he spoke and that was a good sign. He spoke clearly too, and when talking about his family, he opened his hands in an unconscious gesture that indicated he was hiding nothing.

At the mention of Jessica's name, he looked down again. Dennis saw his shoulders and chest move as John took a deep breath, in an obvious effort to keep it together.

"This last Sunday it became clear to me, brethren, that I can no longer carry out the work of senior pastor. At least, not now. Not while Jessica is somewhere out there, waiting for me to come and get her."

Dennis heard David blowing his nose.

"So, I'm going to dig out that letter and give you a revised, updated version for the official minutes. I should have had it ready for this meeting, but I just didn't have the heart for it today. I'm sure you understand and will forgive me. However, though it needs to be redone, the bottom line is still the same."

John paused and smiled at the men. *The smile is genuine,* Dennis thought, *but it is full of sadness. He doesn't want to do this, but he's going to do it and nothing is going to keep him from it.*

No one moved. No chair squeaked.

Finally, Dennis spoke up. "John, I want you to know something up front. I personally do not want to hear that you are resigning." There was an immediate chorus of affirmative voices as the intensely emotional moment was broken. Chairs turned. There was coughing and clearing of throats. Mike Dewbar stood and, moving to the window, peered out at the darkness.

"In fact, I'll go on record as saying that it's not a good idea," he continued.

He saw John immediately become tense, as the other men's voices once again attested to what he was saying. Mike turned from the window and started to speak, but Dennis held up his hand. He was not finished.

"I don't believe it's a good idea for you or for the church."

John was leaning forward now, sitting on the edge of his chair.

"Dennis," he began, "I appreciate what you are saying, but you have to understand that . . ."

"Excuse me, John," Dennis interrupted, his voice firm as he stood and moved away from the table.

"Please, Dennis, I . . ."

"John, you are my pastor and I respect and love you more than you will ever know. You will always be one of my dearest friends, though we've never had much time to spend on that relationship. However, more than being friends, you are my spiritual mentor. You are that to all of us in this room and in our church. You have been God's faithful servant among us since the day you arrived. You've taught us by word and by example. We're proud of you, John. Whatever else happens, we want you to know that. Right, fellows?"

"Yes."

"Absolutely."

"Couldn't say it any better."

"Without question."

"I agree with you one hundred percent, Dennis."

"There's got to be another way."

John dropped back in his chair and closed his eyes.

"I think there is," Dennis continued speaking, while at the same time, moving around the table until he stood near where John was seated. "There is one thing you've never done before, John."

Curious now, John looked up. "And what might that be, Dennis?" he asked, with a good-natured sigh.

"You've never taken a sabbatical."

"A sabbatical?"

"Yes. An extended leave. Call it time off for good behavior."

The others laughed and even John chuckled as he backed the chair away from the table and stood up, next to Dennis.

"Fellows, listen. I appreciate what you are saying and it is very tempting. I don't want to leave Calvary. I love this church. I know God called me here, but there are some things you don't understand. If I was only going to be away a few weeks or even months, that would be one thing. The fact is, I don't know how long I will need to be gone. I have to devote my energies, at least the energy I have left, to one task alone. I've got to find Jessica and bring her home. There's no way that I can promise I'll be back in a few weeks. That uncertainty is not healthy for a congregation. You'd better just let me cut myself loose."

Mike Dewbar was speaking now.

"John, everything Dennis is saying makes sense to me. For us to accept your resignation now, it's . . . well, it's too 'corporate' and not at all 'Christian.' Do you understand what I'm saying?" He looked around at the others. "It's the way big business does things, but we're not big business. We're God's business. We're the church. This is the time we all stick together."

He walked toward John as he continued.

"You are the example of Christ to us, in good times and in bad. It's not only what you teach us from the pulpit. I watch your life and I try to pattern myself to walk with Jesus like I see you walk. We need that, even if you can't show up in the pulpit or carry out the regular work of the church. We can bring extra help on board during this time. You have some close friends in the ministry. How about one of them? Someone we can trust to serve both you and us in this crisis."

"But I can't . . ." John started to protest.

"Furthermore," Mike continued, without waiting for John, "I believe we should continue John's full salary during this time. I know you will be drained with extra expenses while you try to find your girl. Well, you've just got to let us do this. Jessica has become almost as much our daughter as she is yours."

Dennis had never heard Mike express himself so emotionally about anything in his life. Nor had he ever known Mike to cry in public, but tears were running freely down his face as he spoke. He glanced around the room. There did not seem to be any dry eyes at the moment. He brushed his hand across his cheek and included himself, thus making it unanimous.

John sat down again and buried his face in his hands. Tears spilled out on the unopened Bible. Not a verse had been read tonight. *But*, Dennis thought, *that Bible has spoken volumes to us all. It reminds us of who we are in Christ and who we should be as Christians. Most of all, it seems to represent everything that John is about. He's God's man all right.*

In that moment, "God's man" looked up at the others.

"You guys are something else," he began, brushing tears off the cover of his Bible. "I don't know what to say. Let me think about it. I need to talk to Esther. There is one other thing, though."

As John paused, Dennis saw the look of concern, even dread, that flashed across his face.

"I don't know where my search for Jessica will lead me, or what I may have to do to get her back. To be perfectly honest, I'm wrestling with my own conscience regarding some things I might have to do. Things that I don't feel free to talk about. I don't want anything I do in the future to bring discredit to the ministry in general, or to Calvary Church. I just don't know . . ." His voice trailed off.

Every man was standing now, moving in around John. They seemed to understand what he was struggling with.

Dennis had two children of his own. He was certain as to what he would do in order to protect them.

As one, all six deacons laid hands on their troubled pastor. At another time and place in their lives, this might have seemed maudlin and maybe even a bit corny. But not here. Not now.

They waited, eyes closed, spirits connected. Real men, in touch with each other and with God.

Then Jerry, who had led them in prayer earlier, did so again. His carefully chosen words united them in a heartfelt appeal to the Lord for their wounded shepherd. And for Jessica.

TWENTY

The three drivers stood away from the vehicles while the US Border Patrol guard checked the manifest and bills of lading. Five thousand gallons of diesel fuel. Point of origin: Murmansk, Russia. Destination: Rad-Fuel, Ltd., Reno, Nevada.

"You guys from Russia?" she queried pleasantly, eyes shifting to the three white trucks, each carrying a generous coat of mud from the journey and each emblazoned with a bright red RAD-FUEL, LTD. on the sides.

"Are you kidding?" said the lead driver. "We're from Montreal. We picked this stuff up in Halifax. I guess some guys in Nevada are starting up a new fuel company or something. They bought the tankers in Russia, refurbished them, and had them sent over, full of diesel. They'll keep the tankers and, if the diesel is the right quality, they'll begin a business designed to help the Russians and compete with the big boys in a state where the tax base gives them a fightin' chance. We're just haulin' down the road."

The agent walked around to the rear of the tanker unit. There was nothing to see, but the strong odor of diesel fuel was unmistakable.

"Okay, thanks," she said, looking up at the driver, while retrieving her clipboard from the bench where she had dropped it moments before. "You can be on your way. Everything looks to be in order."

Impressing the entry stamp on the form, she scrawled her

initials at the bottom. "Here you go. And don't spend all your money on slots in Reno. Welcome to the States. Drive carefully and have a nice day."

"We will," the driver answered, reaching for the door to the tractor cab. Moments later, the trucks were grinding through their gears as they pulled out onto the highway and headed south.

0930 LOCAL TIME
BAYTOWN, CALIFORNIA

JOHN TURNED THROUGH the yellow pages slowly, not certain where he should be looking. Finally, he saw it.

> Gun Safety & Marksmanship Instruction.
> See Firearms Instruction; Schools—Gen Interest Guide Heading of Gun Safety & Marksmanship.

He proceeded back to the F's. Fingernail Salons, Fingerprinting, Fire Alarm Systems, Fire Department. Not there. Next, he went to the S section and flipped through pages of various private schools. There was Calvary Christian School. He glanced approvingly at the attractive ad design. Then came more schools. Business & Secretarial, Business & Vocational. Here it is. Gun Safety & Marksmanship. Only one place listed, Sure Shot Firing Range, located across the Bay in Santa Clara. He wrote down the phone number and replaced the directory in the drawer.

After dialing, he listened as the phone rang once, twice, three times.

Maybe they're not open.

Four times.

Maybe this is God's way of saying . . .

"Hello, Sure Shot. How may I help you?" A woman's voice.

"Yes, I'm calling from Baytown. You seem to be the only firearms instruction center in the yellow pages. Can you tell me what you offer by way of classes?"

"Sure. We have a firearms safety class every Thursday. It's open to the public. Is that what you are looking for?"

"Not exactly," replied John, hesitating for an instant. "I need an instructor to show me how to use a weapon correctly. I think that I'd like some private lessons. Do you have someone who can help me?"

"Certainly. Any specific interests in choice of weapon?"

John hesitated.

"Probably a handgun."

"Are you primarily interested in self-defense?"

"Yes," he replied, thinking as he said it that his answer was only partially true. *Maybe I'm the aggressor.*

"We have a qualified instructor who works with us. Her name is Carla Chin. She's very good."

"Your instructor is a woman?" John was surprised.

"That's right. Is it a problem?"

"No, I guess not. Just seems kind of unusual."

The voice ignored John's comment.

"Would you like her phone number?"

"Yes, please." He wrote it down, then repeated it back just to be sure. After thanking her, he hung up the receiver. His hands felt damp.

Can you believe this? I'm acting like a kid making plans he knows his parents won't approve. The idea of firing a weapon at someone, maybe even killing another human being, is unreal. I just don't know. Is it right for me to even be learning how to do this? Why am I so troubled? King David killed lots of people, didn't he? And Elijah knocked off four hundred prophets of Baal, for goodness sake, and they were not holding his daughter as a prisoner. Still, if it comes right down to it, can I actually shoot someone? Even in self-defense? Even to get Jessica back? I don't honestly know the answer.

Anxious doubts continued to plague him. When he had talked to Esther about it, she had suddenly grown very silent. He could almost see her retreating into her own private terror having to do with firearms. Barely recovered from gunshot wounds that had nearly taken her life, it was apparent that she was not prepared for a dialogue on the moral implications of killing another person, so he had dropped the subject. He'd just have to work through it alone.

He dialed the number he'd been given. The 415 area code meant Carla lived in the San Francisco region.

A voice recorder. John left a message.

He retreated to his desk and busied himself with the stack of unanswered correspondence, mainly letters, some that hadn't even been opened yet. A pattern had emerged, making the letters sound very similar, even though they came from all over the United States, and as far away as Asia and the Middle East. People wanted to express their encouragement, wishing the Cains well, pledging to pray for them regularly, once in a while enclosing a personal check or a cash gift to help in the search for Jessica.

John and Esther were especially moved by the letters from

Muslims around the world, expressing their deep sorrow over the actions of a minority of radicals within their ranks. Many of them pledged to pray for Jessica's safe return and for a calming of the tensions that the events of last September had generated.

After almost two hours, the pile had diminished somewhat. John was reaching for another envelope when the phone rang.

"Hello."

"Hello, is this Mr. Cain?"

"It is," John answered.

"My name is Carla Chin. You left a message."

"Oh, yes, Ms. Chin. Your name was given to me by the people at Sure Shot. They say you are an instructor in the use of firearms?" He framed the statement into a question by the inflection of his voice.

"That's right."

"Okay, Ms. Chin, here's my situation. Let's see if you can help."

For the next five minutes, they talked back and forth. John spoke of his basic uncertainty and lack of knowledge where firearms were concerned. He told her that he had hunted as a young man with his father, ducks, pheasant, quail. He said nothing about his real motivation and was relieved when it appeared that she did not recognize his name. The more they talked, the more John began to relax.

Eventually, the instructor suggested a time and date, and John agreed to meet her at the range in Santa Clara. Replacing the receiver, he stood and walked away slowly, his mind filled with unsettling thoughts.

It's done, he thought. *There's no turning back now.*

JEREMY WAS KEEPING A CLOSE EYE on his parents. Something was up, he knew that for sure. He just didn't know what. It was on his mind a lot, though.

Even now as he stood just outside the free throw line, bouncing the ball on the recently resurfaced gym floor, he was thinking about it. In one fluid motion, his body left the floor and he released the ball, watching its familiar arc toward the basket and smiling with satisfaction as it went through the net with a swish, not even touching the rim. He was feeling good about his game, even this early in the preseason. His chances for retaining the position he had earned last year as MacArthur High's starting point guard looked a lot better than a few weeks ago.

Out of the corner of his eye, he saw the new kid practicing ball-handling techniques on the opposite side of the court. Jim Burnett was a junior transfer from a big school in Fresno, and he was good, no doubt about that. But Jeremy had the edge in experience. Then, last week, at the first official team workout, the players had nominated Jeremy to be team captain.

He took another shot from twenty feet out that rattled the rim as it went through. Retrieving the ball, he paused to watch Jim working on his moves. *He's not only a good ball player,* Jeremy thought, *but he's got discipline. Beyond that, he's a good guy too.* Jeremy hadn't wanted to like him at first, since they were both competing for the same spot on the team. But Jim's big grin and slow, country-boy ways had proven irresistible. He was too real to be fake, too likable not to like. The feeling had been mutual. Jim admired Jeremy too, and they quickly became good friends.

All the publicity surrounding the events of last September had caused Jeremy's popularity to soar around campus. A few months before, this much attention would have gone straight to his head; but Jeremy had done a lot of growing up during his family's recent trauma. He'd stopped drinking and fooling around with pot. He and his dad had bonded like never before, and his mother, well, she was the absolute greatest! Their mutual crises while John had been in the Middle East served to bring them closer than he had ever dreamed possible.

On top of all this, there was Allison.

Thick brown hair that fell past her shoulders. Hazel eyes. Tall and slender, nearly five-nine. The outdoor type. Excellent swimmer and top student. A good chance to be valedictorian next May. Dr. Sidney and Helen Orwell's only daughter.

They were seeing each other regularly now. Daily at school, at youth group on Wednesday evenings, and in church on Sundays. Jeremy knew he had never cared for someone the way he did for Allison. She was wonderful, the type who brings out the best in those around her. That had certainly been true for Jeremy.

He liked the way their relationship was deepening. They had spent hours talking and getting to really know each other on the beach one day at Santa Cruz. During the annual Calvary Church high school outing to Disneyland, they sat together on the bus and talked about other years and other trips and how this would be their last one before college. Jeremy loved talking with Allison. She was intelligent, fun to be around, and definitely up-front with her Christian faith. Her friendship and firm commitment to Christ had been all the encouragement Jeremy needed to put into practice his own faith and values.

Early on, Allison expressed a desire to set clear boundaries in the physical aspect of their friendship. A number of her classmates had not done so and more than a few regretted it. One of her best friends was pregnant. Two others had had abortions.

Last spring, Dori, a senior classmate, had come to her crying, terrified that she might have contracted AIDS. Allison talked with her father and helped find a doctor to examine her. Fortunately, her fears proved groundless. Allison had hoped that the scare would be motivation enough to discourage her from further casual sex, and she spent hours encouraging her to commit her life to Jesus Christ. That had not happened, however, and it looked as though Dori was continuing her sexual gamble, hoping against hope that nothing bad would come of it.

Jeremy and Allison were joining the ranks of a growing number of young people across the land committing to refrain from premarital sex. Allison had taken the initiative. She told Jeremy that she was a virgin and intended to remain one until her wedding night. It was very important to her, and she wanted Jeremy to understand that right off.

Jeremy had never had a girl talk to him this way before, and it felt like the first fresh breeze of summer. For Allison to express the need for such boundaries made life much easier for them both. Her position on chastity was exactly the way he had been taught at home. To know that she was living out her firm convictions in this regard made him admire her all the more.

He'd certainly felt the pressures from some of his buddies to experience sex, but he had not given in. He'd been embarrassed by the way the guys kidded him and by some of the stories they told in the locker room of their own sexual conquests, but something held him in check. He was a virgin too, and when Allison shared the decision she had made about her own body, he was glad he could say the same.

They covenanted to keep themselves chaste until marriage. If their friendship developed into something deeper, they would have this gift to present to each other. If they eventually fell in love with someone else, they could look back without regret. It was a decision for the sake of their own health, their future mates, and the welfare of children they might someday bring into the world.

Jeremy had to secretly admit to himself that their respective decisions were so mature and responsible that, at times, he could hardly believe it. It gave him a sense of positive pride. He guessed he was growing up after all. He knew that he didn't want to disappoint Allison either, because his respect and affection for her was continuing to flourish.

A few more shots and he tossed the ball toward the locker room's open door.

"See ya," he called out to Jim, as he jogged off the court.

Jim waved back. "Later."

A quick shower and a towel through the hair. In ten minutes, school books in hand, he was out the side door and headed across campus toward the bike rack. It was generally somewhere between the gymnasium and the bike rack that he dreamed about getting a car. It had been on the front burner of his mind when he turned sixteen, but now he was glad he had waited. Biking was a great way to keep in shape. Besides, borrowing Dad's car was definitely cheaper.

Keeping a brisk pace, it was about a fifteen-minute ride home. His route took him past trees that were turning from their rich summer green to varying shades of amber and gold. Jeremy loved this time of year.

He had been surprised when his parents talked to him about taking a sabbatical, as they called it. It sounded to him more like a leave of absence, but whatever. His favorite high school teacher had taken a year's sabbatical and so he was familiar with the idea. It was usually an opportunity to go back to school or travel or strengthen professional skills. Jeremy knew that this was not the reason in his father's case.

The light turned red as he coasted up to the intersection. Waiting for the cars to clear out, he continued to process the data in his family's puzzling circumstances.

For the past couple of weeks, he had sensed that his dad was holding something back, but decided not to press the matter. He'd delay and see if his dad would take the initiative. Their relationship was a complete turnaround from the past summer, but Jeremy didn't want to press it. There was still a lot of tension in the family and probably would be until Jessica came home.

Jessica. Do you suppose that's it? Do they know something? No, if they knew anything more they would tell me. Still, what else could it be? Dad announced to the church that he had to spend more time working on the campaign to bring Jessica home. He and Mom have been making lots of calls and answering letters. Yet, what if they're on to something that they're not telling anyone? I'm sure they think she's still alive. . . . Maybe it's time to start asking a few questions.

The light turned green and Jeremy pushed forward into the

intersection. Five minutes later, he braked to a stop in their drive-way, pushing his bicycle the rest of the way onto the porch. Lock-ing the wheel, he grabbed his books and headed for the front door.

THAT NIGHT, AROUND THE DINNER TABLE, it was quiet-er than usual. Esther had prepared tacos, everybody's favorite meal. Fresh lettuce, chopped onions, tomato slices, grated cheese, and ground hamburger, each in their separate bowls. Her special hot sauce was in a small container at the center of the table. Helping themselves, John and Jeremy created tacos two at a time while Esther settled for one.

After the blessing, and the usual "Great job, Mom" and "These are really good, hon," had been passed along, conversation lagged. It felt to Jeremy that everyone was intent on something else.

"This is Jessica's favorite meal," Jeremy commented finally, his eyes darting from one parent to the other to catch their reac-tion to his reminder. He noticed a slight quiver in his mother's hand, but she did not look up. John glanced his way and nodded.

"Yes, it is," he replied, taking another bite from the taco, mak-ing sure he leaned over the plate to safeguard against the dripping hot sauce. "I hope that wherever she is, they are feeding her well."

"Dad, I've been doing some thinking since you and Mom talked with me about taking this sabbatical. I'm really glad the church is letting you do it this way. I agree that you shouldn't resign—the people need you right now. Even if you're not directly in front of them every week, they won't feel abandoned. It's like they are a part of what you are doing, you know?"

John nodded, his eyes fastened on his son, as he stuffed the last bite of taco into his mouth and chewed.

"Well, that's important, you know, to feel like you're part of what's happening. Especially if it's really critical." Jeremy paused, his statements sounding more like questions.

John swallowed and reached for the water glass.

"Go on, son."

"Well, I was just wondering . . . if there is . . . is there . . ."

"Is there something going on around here that you don't know about?" John finished the sentence.

"Well . . . yes, actually. You guys just seem so preoccupied the last few days. I know all of this is tough on you. Me too. She's . . ." Jeremy cleared his throat. "She's the only sister I've got. I want to help get her back."

"You've already been a great help, son," Esther responded.

"More than you'll ever know. But now you're back in school. It's your senior year. Basketball season is just around the corner. Graduation will be here before you know it. We want . . . well, we want at least one of our kids to be able to live a normal life."

"But you don't understand, Mom," retorted Jeremy. "Life can't be normal as long as Jessica is missing. I'm in this as much as any of you. I know that school is important, but if there is something going on that you're not telling me about, then it's not fair. I want to know."

Jeremy looked intently across the table.

"I need to know!" he added emphatically.

Esther's face was lined with concern and she reached out to touch Jeremy's hand. John, however, was smiling as he finished off the glass of water.

"I hear what you're saying, son," he began. "Let's see if I can rephrase it. You're saying that you think we're not being totally open about what we know, and you don't like it. You're reminding us that you'll soon be eighteen and ready for college and you need to be treated as an adult member of the family. You're telling us . . . in a very diplomatic way, I might add . . . that you can be trusted to keep confidential anything your mother and I know or are doing, when it comes to getting Jessica back. Is that about it, son?"

Jeremy grinned and gave the thumbs-up sign.

John's gaze did not waver. He was not smiling.

Jeremy's grin faded and his hands dropped to the table.

John pushed back his chair. With calculated deliberateness, he rose to his feet and put out his hand to Jeremy.

"Okay, son. You're in. You're in because you deserve to be, because we need you to be. But, what I'm about to tell you cannot go beyond the three of us. Understood?"

Jeremy nodded, and wondered what was coming next.

1710 LOCAL TIME
WASHINGTON, DC

TO: CIA, Office of the Director
FROM: Classified
RE: Report of Missing Plutonium Chloride
DATE: 01 November

Incident Report

    Highly placed source reports rumor that a large quantity of plutonium 239Pu is missing. Majak is 60 kilometers north of Tshelabinsk in South Ural. A production center for weapon-grade plutonium. Several accidents have been previously reported at this site. Security is minimal and inadequate. Estimates indicate as much as 6,000 curies of plutonium chloride solutions are missing. No one will make an official statement. Everything hush-hush.

If rumor is authenticated, the danger to the Western World must be considered a priority.

Action Steps

Will monitor through both official and unofficial channels. Agencies in Europe and Israel have been notified. Border agents will be asked to watch for ships, trains, trucks carrying large quantities of any liquid-based product. Primary area of concern is Israel. Land and sea boundaries of countries located between Russia and the Middle East are especially vulnerable. Cooperation in some of these areas can be expected to be minimal.

Further Recommend

Inform the State Department. Request assistance in confirming/denying this report.

....

TWENTY-ONE

Madeline was used to the impersonal relationship that often exists between master and servant. She worked quietly and efficiently, spoke only when spoken to, and secretly counted the days until her contract would be completed so that she could return to the Philippines to study nursing. Upon graduating, she intended to go to Saudi Arabia to work in one of the modern hospitals. She knew what salaries other Filipino nurses were making there, and that she could support her entire family in the Philippines with such an income. It was this dream that kept her going.

When her father was killed in a truck accident, her mother had been six months pregnant with a second child. Entirely dependent upon his income, they were left without any support. An aunt eventually took care of Madeline and her little sister, Tamara, while her mother worked as waitress and maid in a local hotel. Over and over, her mother impressed Madeline with the importance of learning. She wanted her to understand that a good education was their only hope for any future. Frugally, she saved for her children's college fund.

Then, a year before Madeline was to enroll in nursing school, her sister became seriously ill. People did not usually die of hunger in the poor area in which they lived, but malnutrition was an ever-present threat. Her sister's medical treatments and slow recovery ate away at the education fund until finally, it was empty. That's when Madeline decided to get a job outside of her country.

She was informed that a thousand Filipino workers were be-ing sent into the Gulf region. Two weeks after filling out the appli-cation, she learned that she was going to work in Iran for a well-to-do family in a place called Bandar-é Abbås.

The night she arrived at the compound of Reza Fardusi, one week before her nineteenth birthday, she was frightened and com-pletely overwhelmed by her new surroundings.

Immediately, she attached herself to Mrs. Muños who super-vised the household staff. Her initial assignment was to clean the rooms of the two youngest daughters of the house. She worked quietly and efficiently, and it wasn't long before some of the other Filipino workers took her into their circle of friendship and began filling in the details about her new employer.

She learned that before being deposed, the Shah had under-taken to develop Bandar-é Abbås' potential as a major port city. To get the project under way, parts of the surrounding desert region were irrigated and the ensuing cultivation turned a previ-ously barren countryside into a lush, food-producing region. Much of the produce was exported through Bandar's updated port.

During those years of revitalization, Reza Fardusi had man-aged to keep his hands near the reins of power while, at the same time, giving the appearance of independent distance. The Shah had been more than willing to use him for his own grand pur-poses. Fardusi, on the other hand, used the Shah to further his wealth and position.

While the Shah sought to disengage the country's political life from the religious right, Fardusi remained firm in his commit-ment to the more traditional and conservative religious values. He was baffling to many; but, in reality, it was just one more aspect of his disparate personality. Because of his connections and his great wealth, he was always viewed with some suspicion by the coun-try's new leaders. But, it was determined in the murky power circles of political leadership that Fardusi was to be tolerated, so long as he proved himself loyal to the new government. If he could be manipulated effectively, his influence would be of great value. He had many powerful friends, both in and outside of Iran. Through it all, he shrewdly kept his balance in the tricky, mysteri-ous, and sometimes lethal world of Persian politics.

By the time Madeline arrived on the scene, Fardusi was nearing seventy years of age, an aging relic in a world full of new passions. He was handsome, a vigorous man of medium height, a square chin, snow-white handlebar mustache, and green eyes, un-usual for an Iranian. He carried himself with a proud step. On those rare occasions when Madeline caught sight of him, she was always in awe. He was like no man she had ever seen.

The Fardusi compound was a place of striking beauty. At the center was a large rectangular garden, filled with colorful flowers and surrounded by poplar trees. A sparkling blue pool was positioned in the exact center of the garden, forming the base of a fountain that sprayed thin plumes of silvery water, easing the discomfort of the long, hot season when temperatures occasionally reached 140 degrees Fahrenheit.

A gravel road encircled the garden, and a ten-foot-wall, with a heavy wooden gate at the main entrance, encompassed the entire complex. Inside the walls were Reza's spacious home, the separate houses of his four wives, a workshop, and a garage. On the opposite side of the compound was a large greenhouse, from which gardeners regularly replaced flowers and other growing things that had succumbed to the unendurable desert heat.

The region's new ruling class frowned on the opulence and overstated wealth that symbolized the deposed Shah's era of multiplied excesses. Still, Reza Fardusi was a powerful, brilliant man, and he had proven to be useful.

Madeline wondered how he survived the strict and disapproving eye of the religious and political leaders in this difficult place. She had quickly learned to hate both them and their repressive ways as she observed their occasional visits and underwent their disapproving scrutiny. She decided her employer must be very powerful indeed. Or else he was the consummate diplomat.

Upon her arrival, Madeline was given a small room in the andarun, the inner area containing the living quarters of the wives and their children. The outer section or biruni, where Fardusi lived, was the realm of men. Though this kind of segregation seemed old-fashioned, it was respected and observed by all the inhabitants, family and servants, no questions asked.

At least not in public. In private, however, it was a different story, particularly in the women's quarter, where gossip flowed with the muddy strength of the Tigris River. Roshan was the eldest wife and the mother of three sons. Everyone knew the sons to be willful and spoiled. Fardusi's second wife was bedridden with a serious illness. Rumor had it that she was not well mentally, though none of the servants seemed certain what the problem was. Outside of the wives, who visited her regularly, no one else ever saw her except the old woman who worked in her home. Fateema and Delrobah were the other two whom Reza Fardusi had married. They each had children of their own, among whom was Reza's favorite, Pari-sima, whom he lovingly referred to as Pari, meaning "angel." All the wives looked upon each other's children as their own and lived out their days as best friends.

Stories of secret sexual liaisons between some of the servants and Reza's older sons were the common fodder of guarded conversations carried on in darkened corners of one of the houses or under the branches of a poplar tree. Word had it that these encounters were most often forced upon the servant girls with threats of reprisal if they resisted or spoke of them to anyone. Madeline dreaded the very thought of such an ordeal and was careful to maintain her distance from any of Roshan's sons.

During the weeks following her arrival, Madeline settled into her routine. Though the work was hard and the climate intolerable, she considered herself fortunate. But she missed her mother and sister. She missed the lush green valley that had been her home in the islands. She missed going to Mass each Sunday.

A month ago, she and two of the other servants had been given permission to go outside the compound for a Sunday afternoon walk. They were careful to cover themselves to the ankles, as well as from wrist to neck, and to wear the customary head coverings. For about thirty minutes they appeared to meander with no particular destination in view. Madeline followed the others as they turned down a narrow street and made their way to a doorway partially hidden behind a tree. At the knock, a young woman opened the door. Recognizing the servants, she glanced at Madeline and then motioned them in with the flick of her head.

To Madeline's surprise, there were fourteen people in the small room, each with a Bible in hand, listening as one of their number expounded from the Scriptures. After appropriate introductions were offered, she sat down with the others. At first, they sang "worship choruses" for several minutes. They were songs she had never heard before, but were simple enough that she was soon singing along with the others. Some closed their eyes and lifted their hands as they sang. At first, she was nervous, but after a bit, it felt all right. Then, they listened as another one of the members spoke from the Scriptures. Afterward, the people discussed it together.

It was a different kind of service than she had ever attended in the Philippines, warm, sincere, and personal. It felt to Madeline as though God was very near as they prayed for one another. She thanked her two friends, telling them that she had enjoyed the experience. When would they be going back again? Maybe next week or the week after, depending on whether permission to leave the compound was granted.

Madeline had actually been back to the tiny house church twice since the first visit. It was a sometimes thing, depending on their supervisor and their employer.

One new practice had proven to be the greatest source of inspiration for Madeline. Here, in this strange and difficult land, she was becoming better acquainted with the Bible. A tattered King James version had been given to her mother by a Protestant missionary, who had been staying at the hotel where she worked. Madeline's mother had insisted that she pack it with her things. While not thinking much about it at the time, now she was glad that she had done so. She knew how much this Bible had meant to her mother. Just picking it up and feeling the worn leather that her mother's hands had so often touched made Madeline feel closer to the ones she loved.

Each night before turning out the light, she took the Bible from under her pillow. The black cover was almost torn from the binding. Carefully, she opened its pages and removed the bookmark. The Psalms was her favorite place to read in the Old Testament. In the New, so far, it was the Gospel of John.

Replacing the bookmark, she put the Bible on the floor, where it would remain until morning, when she made the bed. Reaching over, she turned the light out, settled back into her pillow, and moved her lips in silent prayer for her mother and sister. She thanked the Lord for her job and for the dream of nursing school after she had completed her contract and saved enough money.

It was in moments like these that Madeline felt deep pangs of loneliness. She especially wondered about Tamara—how she missed her little sister! To see her right now would be perfect. But that, of course, was impossible, and anyway, tomorrow promised to be a fresh challenge to take her mind off her homesickness.

Settling back on the pillow, she thought back over the day. Just before going off duty, Mrs. Muños had informed her that she was being assigned new duties at the main house. Beginning Friday, Reza Fardusi would be entertaining visitors in his private chambers. She listened as the rooms were described, the location of the linen closet identified, and her duties outlined. Madeline was to clean, make beds, and provide for the personal needs of the guests as long as they remained.

"Whatever they want or need, you are to see that they have it. Any questions?"

Madeline shook her head.

"Enter and leave through the servant's side door that takes

you into the kitchen. Speak only when spoken to. Always be polite. And never wander into any other part of the house."

"Yes, ma'am. How many guests are there?"

"Three women. They have a young girl with them too."

"How old is the girl?"

"She must be twelve or thirteen."

The same age as Tamara. This should be fun.

TWENTY-TWO

The three white RAD-FUEL, LTD. trucks stopped in Nevada, just as the lead driver had indicated to the agent at the Canadian–U.S. border. But not in Reno, and only for one night. Thirty miles east of Reno, the tanker trucks turned off the highway and onto a dirt road. A half mile down the road, they went past a horse corral and turned into a driveway. The trucks did not slow down as they churned past the ranch house and the man donning his cowboy hat as he stepped down from the porch. Moments later, all three had disappeared inside the old barn.

The only thing unusual at the ranch that evening were the sounds of small motors and lights burning in the barn well into the night.

Early the next morning, three black trucks with the words POTABLE WATER painted on the sides roared out of the barn, passed the house, and headed up the dirt road. Upon reaching the highway, they turned west.

They had been on the road for twelve hours by the time they drove past the Interstate 580 intersection and continued south on 680, slowing somewhat as they merged with wave after wave of commuter traffic. Suddenly, a brown Ford Pinto sped past, cutting in and braking abruptly in front of the lead truck. The driver slammed on his brakes and popped the air horn as he tried to avoid a collision.

"Watch out!" he shouted at the driver of the tiny car, his

hands instinctively gripping the wheel, preparing for a crash. He cursed. It was impossible to slow down enough with as heavy a load as he was carrying. At the last moment, the driver of the Pinto saw the truck coming up fast in his rearview mirror and sped up just enough to avoid being rear-ended.

"That was too close!" he muttered to himself. "I'm ready to park this stuff and get out of here. My nerves have had it."

He glanced in the mirror. The others were still there. This had been a very long run, but the end was in sight. A mile farther, he signaled to turn off the Interstate and onto 84 headed toward Livermore. Twenty minutes later, they drove off the highway and onto a narrow, blacktop roadway, coming to a stop in front of an iron gate where a man stood waiting next to a pickup truck.

He rolled down the window as the man approached.

"Everyone is here?" the guard asked without a greeting.

"This is it," the driver answered, as he passed an envelope thick with hundred dollar bills through the opening. The guard reached up and took it.

"Follow me."

He got into his pickup, leading the others to a large, underground warehouse where he motioned them forward through the entrance. As soon as the last truck was inside, a large garage-style door came sliding down.

The lead driver shut off his engine. Stepping down from the cab, he stretched his arms and legs and looked around. Even if a search were launched for the trucks with radiation detectors, no one would think of looking in an abandoned underground storage at this former atomic research center. Even if radiation detection helicopters were used to search for the trucks, the facility's dormant reactor was an established fact and traces of low-level radiation would not be considered suspicious by anyone.

It had been a very long drive, but it was done. He smiled as he watched the others clear their things out of the trucks. It had gone so easily.

1915 LOCAL TIME
SANTA CLARA, CALIFORNIA

AS JOHN PULLED UP TO THE CURB, he glanced at his watch. Fifteen minutes early. He got out, locked the door, and walked toward the entrance of the Sure Shot Firing Range.

Upon entering, he looked over the heads and shoulders of three men whose backs were to him, and caught sight of two women behind the reception counter. They appeared to be checking the men in for range practice. He dawdled for a moment, taking in the scene, then started past the desk toward the gun displays.

"May I help you?" the short one with dark hair called out.

"I have an appointment with Carla Chin."

The woman glanced down at an open calendar on the counter. "Cain?"

"Yes."

"It's at seven-thirty. You're early."

"Right. I'll just look around until she arrives."

He started to turn away.

"Do you have any weapons on you?"

John hesitated.

"No. Nothing,"

He smiled to himself as he walked toward the displays. *Now there's a question no one has ever asked me before.* The first thing he noticed was the white-lettered sign on blue background, tacked on the wall:

YOU MUST BE 21 TO RENT OR BUY A HANDGUN
OR AMMUNITION. FOR ADDITIONAL INFORMATION
PLEASE INQUIRE WITH THE MANAGEMENT.

Just beyond the retail area, through closed doors, he could hear the sounds of gunfire on the enclosed range. He peered through one of several spectator windows and saw the cubicles, each with a hand-operated target. A man was firing a pistol at a target that John estimated to be fifteen or twenty feet away.

All around the retail area were glass display cases filled with small firearms. He had never seen this many guns in one place before. Moving from case to case, he stopped to look at several larger semiautomatic rifles. Kneeling down, he read the hand-printed tag on the one nearest him: "SPRINGFIELD M-1A— $2950—SERIOUS INQUIRIES ONLY!

Wow! For that kind of money, it would have to be serious.

"Hello. Are you Mr. Cain?"

Engrossed in reading the tag, John was startled at hearing his name.

He looked up and saw a short Chinese woman, her jet black hair clipped close to the neck and ears. She was in jeans, white pullover shirt, and a gray windbreaker open at the neck.

"That's me. And you're Ms. Chin."

"Carla, please." She motioned toward the case. "Find anything there that interests you?"

"To be honest, I don't know much about guns. That's why I called you. I decided it was time for me to learn."

"Any particular reason?"

"Well, you know how it is these days, crime on the increase and all that. I've decided that I want to learn how to protect myself and my family." John thought his answer was acceptable, even if it wasn't the whole truth.

The woman waited for a moment, as if expecting more. Then, she turned and started toward the sound of guns firing. "Come along. Let's go back and acquaint you with the weapon you will be using tonight."

John breathed a sigh of relief and followed her around the corner.

"You indicated on the phone that you were interested in both handguns and automatic weapons."

John nodded, studying examples of both that Carla had laid out on a table.

"What's your profession, Mr. Cain?"

He waited for a moment, various answers racing through his mind. Then, he sighed and said, "I'm the pastor of a church."

"A pastor?" Carla's eyes opened wide with surprise. "Isn't it a little unusual for a pastor to be interested in handguns and automatic weapons? Have you had some problems recently?"

"Some," John replied, noncommittally.

"Okay," Carla said, slowly. "I don't mean to pry, but it is important to me that I know a little about the person I'm training. That's why I ask. I don't want to teach some psycho to use a weapon."

"I can appreciate that. And I can assure you that I'm no psycho. Now, shall we begin? You said on the phone that you charge $30 an hour." John grinned. "I'm not a wealthy man."

Carla smiled for the first time and seemed to relax her attitude.

"All right, Mr. Cain. Sit down here and let me introduce you to these weapons."

Carla remained standing and reached for the handgun. "This is a Colt .45 Government Model. You've probably seen some older versions of this gun in movies. It was adopted by the US Army in 1911 as the official military sidearm. Its appearance has changed a little over the years, but the basic components are the same now as then." She turned it over in her hand and continued talking.

"You can tell that this gun has been modified. Here, see? The edges have been beveled so that it will not get caught so easily in a person's clothing. That's called 'dehorning' the edges. And here — see the extra large sights? The rear sight is a notch and the front sight at the muzzle is a post."

John listened carefully to the description of the Colt .45 as Carla went on with her explanation. "This is a beaver tailgrip safety. When it's depressed, it is turned off and the gun is ready to fire. This is an extended thumb safety. It gives more leverage and is easier to operate than the standard safety. Any questions?"

He shook his head.

"See the trigger? It has been modified also. Most factory triggers require greater than necessary pressure, an average of about six to eight pounds, to make the hammer fall. Four pounds is just about right for a combination gun, and when you pull the trigger, it should release crisply like breaking a glass rod or snapping an icicle. See?"

Carla pulled the trigger and John saw the hammer fall.

"This is the slide stop, here on the left side. You are right-handed? Good. To load, pull back the slide with your left hand after you insert a full magazine. Go ahead and try it. Don't worry. We're using inert training rounds."

John took the gun and awkwardly attempted to follow Carla's instructions. After a few tries, he began to get the hang of it.

"How many bullets in a clip?" he asked.

Carla frowned. "They're cartridges and magazines, Mr. Cain, not bullets and clips."

"Sorry. How many cartridges in a magazine?"

"There are eight, plus one in the chamber, when the gun is loaded."

"And how much would a gun like this cost?"

"Modified about $1,000 to $1,500 for a combat-modified gun similar to this one. More if you include a tritium dot-over-bar or three-dot night sight."

John let out a low whistle.

Carla showed him how she carried the weapon in an inside-the-belt holster. On the opposite side, she wore a small pouch that could contain two extra magazines.

"A pistol like this is a defensive weapon. Compared to a rifle, it is underpowered and harder to shoot accurately. Up to fifteen yards is its primary operating range." Carla put the pistol down and picked up the assault rifle. "Of course, this is an entirely different animal."

"Is that yours?" John asked as he stared at the grim-looking black gun.

"Yes. It is a Colt AR-15. You said you have an interest in automatic weapons. However, they are mostly illegal, except for the military. This one is a semiautomatic civilian version of the M-16. The fact of it being semiautomatic rather than fully automatic is its only difference. Here, hold it." She held it out to him.

"It feels heavy to me," John said, as he balanced it in his hands.

"No, it's not heavy for a rifle. That's probably not more than six or seven pounds. Feel the butt stock? It's plastic. Over here is the ejection port, and here is the safety. It takes twenty- or thirty-round magazines like this," she said, holding one up for John to see. "With a real M-16, you could probably get off several hundred rounds per minute."

John's mouth dropped. "Are you serious?"

"Very," she replied, without expression. "That's one reason the latest M-16s have been modified to three-round bursts. If you got excited with one of the earlier models, you could empty your weapon in a second. With the three-round burst, you waste less ammo.

"It might interest you to know that the first assault weapon in history was made by the Germans in World War II. Their original battle rifles had a range of well over a thousand yards, but most of their battles were at closer distances than that. So, they reduced the power of the cartridge and produced an assault weapon that is the grandfather of today's Russian AK-47 and the US M-16."

Carla dropped three wicked-looking bullets on the table in front of John. "These are all full metal jacket cartridges. No lead is exposed. See?" She held one up in the light.

"This one's for a battle rifle, and fires a 150-grain bullet at a velocity of 2,700 feet per second. Now, look at this. It's the AK-47 round. It launches a bullet weighing 123 grains at only 2,300 feet per second."

John listened, trying to grasp the magnitude of weapons like these, firing away at hundreds of rounds per minute. He was beginning to be overwhelmed by the whole picture unfolding in front of him.

"This smallest round is fired by the M-16. Its bullet only weighs 55 grains. But it moves out at 3,300 feet per second and on impact with living tissue it tends to tumble, producing more damage." Carla paused, taking the AR-15 from John and laying it on the table. "Any questions?"

John swallowed and wiped his hands on his pants. "I think I'd like to stay with the Colt .45 for now, Carla. This other one is a little too awesome."

"Good idea." She smiled again, then turned serious. "Mr. Cain. Your name and face are familiar and I think now I know why. You are the one whose church was taken hostage? And you were in Israel at the time?"

John hesitated, wishing that she had not recognized him. Then he nodded.

"And your daughter is still missing?"

"Yes, that's true, Carla. Does this make any difference in your willingness to help me learn how to use a weapon?"

"Yes. It most definitely does, Mr. Cain." Her voice became quiet and restrained. John's spirits sank. "For one thing, you can forget the $30 per hour charge. I'll teach you for nothing."

John stared incredulously.

"And for another," she continued, looking at him directly, dark eyes flashing. "I don't know if you think these people will be back, or what your reason is for wanting to learn how to shoot. But, if you will accept, I will personally work with you until you are good at this. Really good. Okay? And there will be no charge."

"But, why . . ." John stammered, all at once embarrassed by her sudden effusiveness.

"Because what these people are doing is wrong. Terribly wrong. There are better ways to right the ills of the world than to storm churches and threaten to destroy whole cities and kidnap young girls. You may find this strange, Mr. Cain, but I sympathize with the plight of the Palestinian people. They are victims of wrongs that need to be made right, but engaging in further wrong is not the answer. There has to be a better way, a more humane way than what they are doing. Besides," she hesitated before continuing, "I want to help you get your daughter back. That's what this is all about, isn't it?"

John stared back into the searching eyes of his instructor.

"Are you a Christian, Carla?" he asked.

Carla chuckled. "No, you're probably as close to 'Christian' as I've ever been. My family is Buddhist. Personally, I am not at all religious."

"Well, you are a very perceptive person, nonetheless. Yes, you have guessed correctly what this is all about. I can't say anything more. I hope my reticence to talk about it doesn't offend you?"

"Not at all. I think I understand."

"Thank you. And I accept your offer."

"Good. Now, let's go see if I can keep you from shooting yourself in the foot. When we get out there, the first thing I want to show you is the Weaver stance for firing your weapon."

"The Weaver stance?"

"Yeah. It's named after the sheriff who made it popular. I'll show you the guard position too. Come on, follow me."

"By the way," said John as they walked toward the range, "what do you do in real life? I'm sure you can't make a living teaching guys like me how to shoot."

"You wouldn't believe me if I told you."

"What? Are you military? A police officer?"

Carla laughed. "Bad guess, Mr. Cain. Actually, I'm an RN at South Peninsula Hospital. Pediatrics."

"No way. A gun-totin' gal like you is in pediatrics?" John exclaimed.

"I said you wouldn't believe me."

TWENTY-THREE

FRIDAY, 04 NOVEMBER, EARLY MORNING
BANDAR-É ABBÁS, IRAN

It was still dark as the familiar call to prayer resonated from the minarets across Bandar, urging the faithful to rise up for prayer.

Does anyone really get up to pray when that guy sounds off? What is it they call him ... oh, yeah, the muezzin. Faridah taught me what he was saying. Let's see ...

> *Allah u Akbar.*
> *God is greater.*
> *God is greater.*
> *I witness that there is no god but God.*
> *I witness that Mohammed is the prophet of God.*
> *Rise to prayer.*
> *Rise to ... fel ... felicity.*
> *God is greater.*
> *God is greater.*
> *There is no god but God.*

Faridah had told Jessica that when Islam was in its infancy, the Prophet's disciples used to gather around him for prayer. As their numbers grew, it became necessary to call them together. That's when Mohammed chose Bilal to be the first muezzin or caller to prayer. Bilal was an African slave who had been freed after accepting Islam. To accomplish his assignment, he climbed

▼▼176▼▼

the roof of a house near the mosque that Mohammed had helped build, and recited the Adhan or call to prayer.

I wonder what Faridah is doing? And if she ever thinks of me?

Jessica pictured the woman with the kind face. There had been something between them, an unspoken bond. They had talked, really talked. Under other circumstances, the woman could probably have been a friend, like an aunt or older cousin. Faridah had been a protector of sorts, even though she was in league with the kidnappers.

Faridah . . . I wish you were here . . . I wish we could talk some more . . . I wish . . . I had asked you what felicity means.

It was Friday, the holy day, and the normally bustling universe that comprised the compound of Reza Fardusi had slowed to a pace befitting this day of reflection.

Jessica had discovered that by standing on the small cot, she was able to see out of the room's only window. It wasn't very large, she guessed not more than eighteen inches wide and about two feet in height. The glass was marred by a thin, jagged crack. It was too high to be able to see down at all, unless she stood on the bed. Otherwise, the only view was blue sky. Last night she had waited until no one else was in the room before pushing on the frame. At first, it stayed in place. Then, stretching as far as she could, and pushing with both hands, she discovered that it was not locked.

The sound of creaky hinges frightened her, and she stopped short of pushing it fully open. Instead, she carefully returned it to its original state and sat back down on the edge of the cot. For weeks, she had lived in a world of locked doors, guards, and social deprivation. To think that there was a window in this room, one without bars that she could open at will, was almost too much. Her heart beat with excitement.

Maybe it's a way out of here!

This morning, she took the chance to look out the window at first light. Her heart sank. The opening looked even smaller in the light of day.

No wonder they aren't worried about it being unlocked.

Peeking out, she confirmed that she was on the second floor and there was no real ledge, only a narrow cornice, nothing to keep her from falling, even if she did manage to crawl out of the window. She pushed it open a few inches and let the powerful breath of roses from the garden below inveigle her sense of smell, tantalizing her with memories of her mother's roses on the patio.

Dropping down onto the bed, Jessica sat with her back against the wall and stared at the door. After a while, she heard voices coming through the window.

Standing on the cot, she saw the people. Four small children were running in circles around one another and laughing. With them were three older boys and three women acting very much like mothers as they made their way along the gravel road toward the house where she was being held prisoner.

I wonder who they are?

Just then, a door below her room opened.

Why are they coming here?

They quieted, almost as though on cue, as they disappeared inside. When the last person had entered, the door closed and all was quiet once more. Jessica pulled the window shut, dropped down on the cot, and cradled her face in her arms.

BELOW JESSICA'S TINY PRISON, Reza Fardusi's family waited respectfully in the foyer that led into the room where Fardusi dined and also met with visitors. They were not the least bit aware of the recently arrived young American guest secretly tucked away on the floor above.

A servant appeared to inform the mothers that their husband would be a few minutes longer, due to a long-distance call he had just received. As they lingered, the older boys walked around acting bored, looking at pictures hung tastefully on the walls, while the younger children jostled one another around the open door of the great chamber where they would soon be meeting with their father. Eventually, the servant reappeared and beckoned to them. Hastily, the mothers shooed everyone inside.

Though Fardusi seemed something of a dinosaur from Iran's past, he was nobody's fool. He had held numerous high posts in Iranian politics, deftly managing to survive both His Imperial Majesty Mohammed Reza Shah Pahlavi, Shahanshah, the "King of Kings," and the much-revered Ayatollah Ruhollah Khomeini.

For thirty-seven years the Shah had tried to westernize Iran and lead it into the twentieth century. Following Ataturk's example in Turkey, he broke up large land holdings, gave women the vote, increased literacy, made Iran a key player in the world's oil markets, and allied his country with the West, especially the United States and France. Yet, he ruled like an ancient Persian king, despite his own father's modest origins. His autocratic ways alienated many people, including the mullahs, those Shia Muslim clerics who extolled martyrdom and promised direct entry into paradise to all who fell victim to the sacred cause of the Holy War.

When opposition forced the Shah from his throne in January 1979, up to a million Iranians—military leaders, professionals, and government officials—fled as well. Khomeini's return from exile in Paris eventually resulted in the mullahs gaining power and executing or exiling their rivals. Iran was declared an Islamic republic on April 1, 1979. There quickly followed the emergence of the religious fervency of fundamentalist Islam under the mullahs, together with a debilitating five-year war with Iraq.

Through all of his nation's political and religious infighting, Fardusi had survived. Those who knew him from past business dealings with the Western World wondered how he did it. It was a question to which he simply smiled and said, "Allah is great."

That was how his public saw it, because that is what he wanted them to see. No more and no less. Privately, however, it was a different matter. He was, at heart, a quintessential Middle Eastern pragmatist. He did not like the way many things had been in the past; he disliked the present even more, but the sands of time were running out for him. Self-preservation was now at the forefront of his thinking—for himself and for his family after he was gone.

He made provisions for the best education available—private schools and tutors in reading, math, and poetry. The girls studied French and Persian cuisine under the watchful eye of Fardusi's personal chef. All the children were exposed to classical Persian music, though Fardusi knew the eldest son preferred his secret collection of hard rock and rap music. He expected that each child would develop to full potential. Anything less was unacceptable.

This morning, Fardusi looked with pride at his children and their mothers. The children lined up according to age, arms crossed respectfully over their chests. He sat in his favorite chair as he playfully challenged each of his brood with questions.

"I understand that you have been doing well with your studies," he said to the youngest and most intellectually inclined of the three boys.

"Thank you, Father. Yes, I am doing quite well," replied the boy confidently.

Fardusi spoke to the lad in French, one of the languages in his required curriculum. The boy answered quickly. They continued to spar verbally, father trying to get the best of his son, but the young lad was quick and very good. Finally, Fardusi acted as though he had given up and put his hands on the boy's shoulders. "You are doing well indeed, my son. I am proud of you."

The boy bowed respectfully and, sensing his inspection was over, he stepped backward, though never taking his eyes off his father. Fardusi turned his attention to the next lad. At last, the time spent together was over. The children passed by their father and gave a respectful bow as they prepared to leave.

JESSICA ROLLED OVER ON HER BACK and stared at the ceiling. As depressed and homesick as she was, there were no tears this morning. Would she ever cry again? Was there a secret chamber of tears still hidden somewhere inside? She pillowed her head in the palms of her hands, listening to the low, monotonous hum of the ceiling fan's electric motor, watching as it turned. Her thoughts turned with it, looking to light on something pleasant.

She summoned the cool, dampness of Holland, and contrasted its tiny green fields with the harsh desert region she had recently seen. She held her father's hand and walked through Amsterdam at night. Magical, never-ending canals. Flower vendors at the bus stops. Tiny shops, brightly lit for the tourists.

I wonder what ever happened to the things I bought for Mom and the kids in my class at school? Do you suppose that stuff ever got home? It was the first time she had considered this question since being taken hostage.

How long has it been now?

At first, she had kept track; but moving from place to place, she had become confused about dates. After deciding it must be November, and that Thanksgiving could not be far off, she let her mind return to the cool streets and dark canals of Amsterdam.

She remembered becoming lost with her dad and how embarrassed he was when they arrived in the area where young prostitutes worked. She thought about the pretty young woman in the window. She could see her as though it were yesterday.

I promised to pray for her.

Jessica felt a pang of guilt. Many days had come and gone since last she had prayed for the girl in the window. In her own stress-filled preoccupation, she had forgotten. Silently, she let her lips move in prayer in behalf of the stranger.

She retraced the steps she and her father had taken the following morning, on their way to visit the Anne Frank Haus. Thoughtfully, reverently, Jessica let herself walk through Anne's secret home one more time. She touched a table, a lamp, a book. She was there again. With Anne.

What did she look like?

Jessica tried to remember. The pictures had shown a young girl with dark hair and fair skin, but beyond that, she could not recall. So, she began filling in Anne's features herself. A pretty girl. Her eyes are friendly, but there is sadness too. A firm chin. She looks pale from being inside all the time. Anne has hidden for two years without playmates, no school plays, no sports, no sharing lunches or laughing with friends, no waving goodbye in the knowledge that she will see them again tomorrow. Her daily companion is fear.

Only fear. The fear of being discovered.

Jessica felt that fear piercing her now, like a cold knife. But, here in Iran, it was different.

For her, it was the fear of never being discovered. Or, of being discovered too late!

1000 LOCAL TIME
SANTA CLARA, CALIFORNIA

JOHN MET CARLA at ten o'clock on the range at Sure Shot. During their initial session, they had agreed that the Colt .45 ACP would be the weapon of choice. This semiautomatic pistol appeared to pack the most accuracy and penetration potential, yet it was light and relatively easy to operate.

Before going onto the firing line, Carla went over the fundamentals of firearm safety rules.

"Mr. Cain . . ."

"Please, Carla, the name is John."

Carla smiled politely.

"John." She repeated his name softly. Placing the handgun on the table, she turned to face him directly. "For me to call you by your first name, Mr. Cain, will take some getting used to. I must tell you that after our initial meeting, I went to the library and read through several of the news accounts of your action in Israel last September. I am somewhat in awe of you."

John's mouth dropped in surprise. "Carla, you can't be serious. I am the one who is in awe. I am standing here with a female firearms instructor who in real life is a pediatrics professional. You are more knowledgeable and proficient with guns than I will ever be. What you handle so professionally scares the living daylights out of me. Believe me, you have no reason to be in awe. God is the one who gets the credit for Israel. I was just the instrument He decided to use."

"I'm not sure about God deserving the credit, but if you say so, I will accept it. What I read about does seem to have been a bit of a miracle. Anyway, enough of this. Let's get to work. I am honored to be your teacher . . . John."

Carla picked up the .45 and turned it over in her hand.

"There are four things you must always remember with any gun. First, all guns are always loaded. At least, that is your assumption until you have personally inspected the weapon to be sure that it is empty. Don't accept as fact what anyone else says about it. Always check for yourself. Second, never let the muzzle cover anything or anyone you are not willing to destroy."

She paused and looked up.

John let out his breath and nodded for her to continue.

"Third, keep your finger off the trigger until your sight is on the target. Finally, be absolutely sure of your target. Don't shoot at shadows or sounds. Okay?"

"Okay."

"So, let's go out and fire a few rounds."

They opened the door and walked to the nearest vacant shooting booth. Handguns were being fired in four other locations, making Carla speak up more than normal.

"When you grip the weapon, be consistent. Learn the right way and then use that same method each time. Your right forearm should always be an extension of the barrel itself. Like this. See?" She demonstrated while John watched.

"Now, you do it," she ordered, handing him the gun.

"Put your hand directly behind the weapon . . . that's right. A little higher. Grip it as high as possible and you will minimize the recoil. See the target? It's at five yards. Take a couple of shots. Ear plugs? Safety off . . . take your time . . ."

John fired once.

"Safety on?" Carla asked, reaching to take the gun from John's hand. "Let's see how you did."

She hand reeled the target in until it hung directly in front of John. There were no bullet holes!

"I guess I failed Shooting 101, huh?" John said, sheepishly.

"There is a great difference between failing and being a failure, Mr. . . . John," Carla rejoined. "We obviously have more than a little work ahead. Would you agree?"

"I would agree," he answered.

"You will now learn to use the proper stance," she continued. "There are several, but the one I prefer is the Weaver stance. It has become the favorite for law enforcement and competition shooters. Here, take the gun."

She handed the .45 back to John, who decided upon taking it that it felt more natural than it had the first time he prepared to fire. He was starting to relax.

"Left elbow down slightly. Feet approximately even. Flex your right arm a little. Now, put your left hand over your right hand . . . no, it must be vertical. Yes, like that. Hold the thumb high. Now, advance the left shoulder . . . that's right. Are you comfortable? It feels okay?"

"It feels pretty good, considering I've never done this before," John answered.

"Your left hand is going to help keep the pistol down when it is fired. It absorbs the recoil and provides you with more accuracy. Now, try a couple of shots again."

This time, John had two marks, one in the second ring and the other at the outer edge of the third ring.

"Good job!" Carla shouted enthusiastically. "We'll make a marksman out of you yet."

For the next thirty minutes, they practiced shooting technique. When Carla announced that it was time to quit for the day, John was surprised.

"I can meet you again on Tuesday evening, if that works for you," she said, flipping the pages of a small pocket calendar. "Of course, you can come any time and practice. I think working on your own will be more valuable after a couple more lessons. But, suit yourself."

"Tuesday will be fine," John replied. "How long do you think it will take before I can at least hit the side of a barn with this thing?"

"In a few weeks, we'll have you shooting like a Texas Ranger," Carla beamed. Then, the glow of enthusiasm suddenly disappeared and she lowered her eyes. "Do you have a time limitation, John?"

He put his hands on the shelf in front of him and stared at the paper bull's-eye, ten yards out. "I don't know. I just need to be ready as soon as possible."

"How do you feel about it now that you've had your first lesson?"

"What do you mean?"

"I mean that I've noticed your tentativeness. You obviously are not afraid to deal with things that are dangerous. So, I assume it has something to do with your feelings about guns. You'll have to work that out, you know. Whatever convictions you carry about shooting someone need to be dealt with early on. Otherwise, having a handgun in your possession will only be a danger to you."

John turned his gaze from the target and looked at Carla.

"I understand."

Carla nodded, then turned toward the exit.

"Next Tuesday then. Seven o'clock?"

"I'll be here."

He followed her out into the cool autumn air, his mind swirling with the moral implications of what he was preparing to do.

TWENTY-FOUR

Reza Fardusi peered at his house guest over the remains of a large dish of steamed chelo rice. At the beginning of the meal, the chelo had been covered with a crunchy egg yolk crust, broken up and served on top. Nearby was a side dish of måst, or yogurt, mixed with diced cucumber, fresh herbs, and spices. Fardusi's guest had declined an offer of shrimp and prawns, opting instead for fresh vegetables and helpings from a plate filled with crisp and salty barbari, the elite of Iranian breads. A pitcher of boiled drinking water was off to one side, near the bowl of assorted almonds, pistachios, and hazelnuts.

As is the custom for Iranians, they ate in relative silence, with only occasional fragments of polite of conversation. A servant appeared at exactly the right moment, carrying a bowl filled with fresh pomegranates, bananas, and rosy-fleshed grapefruit, served in place of a dessert. A moment later, she returned with two small glass cups in detachable metal holders, and proceeded to fill them with scalding black tea. Fardusi believed hot tea to be one of the best and safest drinks that could be served on a hot day. The servant quickly cleared the table until only the fruit and tea remained.

"Mersi, khosh maze bud," his guest said, smiling as she looked across the table at her host. *Thank you, it was delicious.*

"Ghåbel nabüd," Reza Fardusi nodded politely. *Don't mention it.*

"It is an honor for me to sit at your table," she continued.

"The privilege is mine," he responded.

Their small talk continued for a few minutes as they savored the fruit, drank the tea, and engaged in Iranian pleasantries.

"My apologies for not being able to greet you earlier," said Fardusi. "Of necessity, I had to attend to matters in Kermån Province."

"How did you find it there?"

"Things are not so good, as you might well imagine. The economy continues to suffer severe regression. I have many friends there from the days when Bandar was the major trade outlet for thcir crops. I'm sure you understand just how dependent on ghanåtas—the underground water channels—they have become for their irrigation. The drought has been insufferable. To make life even more difficult, the water table is descending and some say the water is contaminated. At any rate, problems continue to loom over that region of our homeland. But, enough of this. Tell me, please, the nature of your unexpected visit. I understand that you have with you a young guest?"

He watched Leila Azari push back a wisp of hair that had slipped from under her head covering. In some circles, that slight indiscretion alone would have been enough to cause her arrest and land her in jail. Personally, Fardusi thought such things to be unimportant. It was just one item, in a list that was growing, that lessened his respect for the mullahs who spent their time enforcing such foolishness. She reached for the teapot, a classic piece of porcelain that was clearly British in origin, and refilled her glass cup. Looking across the table, her eyes asked if her host wished more tea, without words being spoken.

"Yes, please," he responded, holding up his cup as she poured.

"You know of Marwan Dosha?" she began, returning the teapot to the table.

"Of course," the old man answered. His eyes fluttered slightly at the mention of the name, then quickly regained their cryptic appearance.

"And you have read about the so-called September Strike operation."

Fardusi waited, never taking his eyes off her.

"Dosha was the leader of that mission," she continued. "It was the Palestinian Islamic Jihad's most sophisticated operation to date. He was the architect, working at the behest of their leaders, Hafez Tabatai and Mahmoud Assad. I know Tabatai from the training camps in southern Lebanon."

Leila paused to sip her tea.

"You probably know that an American named John Cain was instrumental in foiling the mission. He and his American followers were taken hostage. . . ."

"And ultimately escaped, if my memory serves me correctly," Fardusi interrupted, a thin smile on his weathered face.

"That's correct. All escaped, but one."

"His daughter?"

"Yes."

"And this is the little girl who is a guest in my house?"

"One and the same."

Fardusi shifted his body with a suddenness that surprised Leila, causing her to clutch nervously at her cup of tea. Leaning forward, he rested his hands on the table and spoke with deliberate slowness. "And why, may I ask, is she here? What purpose is being served by kidnapping this American child? For what reason is she being kept a prisoner in my house? Oh, and can you think why I was not first asked if this would be acceptable? Have the leaders forgotten their manners?"

Fardusi had already decided that Leila Azari was not one to be easily intimidated. She could normally depend on her beauty to distract and fluster her cohorts, especially the male variety. But Fardusi was different. He was far past the age of being physically formidable. But mental and emotional intimidation, now that was a skill at which he was a professional, and he saw no reason not to establish the upper hand with this female warrior at the very outset.

"I am a servant of The Cause, Aghâ-yé Fardusi. I follow orders." There was an edge to her tone and her eyes flashed back at his as she spoke. "A short time ago, my superior called me in from the field to entrust me with the child's welfare. She was brought to Bandar by the PIJ, at Marwan Dosha's request. I was informed that your home would be ideal. It is private, well provided for, and secure. I'm sure your full cooperation was assumed without question by our leaders."

"Our leaders assume a great deal these days," remarked Fardusi sardonically, the fingers of his right hand impatiently tapping on the table's surface. "Are you telling me that you have no knowledge about the purpose of your mission?"

He felt her hesitation. She obviously was not used to being interrogated by anyone, especially an old man. She had expected him to be more acquiescent, and she was put off by his questions. It was exactly what he wanted.

His fingers ceased their drumroll on the table. Relaxing his body, he leaned back, resting his hands with fingers intertwined on the table. He looked across at the woman and smiled so warmly that the distance between them suddenly seemed to shrink.

"Khânome Ahmadi."

Leila started at being referred to by the name of her dead husband.

"I am not married," she blurted out, before thinking.

"Ah, but you were. Your husband was killed at the front in the war with Iraq. It is regretful. I am very sorry."

Leila eyed him guardedly now, yet saw no hint of anything but genuine sympathy. How long had it been since any of the people she worked with had expressed compassion over the loss of her husband in the war? It suddenly hit her—she couldn't remember anyone ever doing so. Until now.

"How did you know of this?" she asked. "Our marriage was brief. After his death I chose to return to my family name."

"It is not important. I know many things. An old man has little else to do but to listen and to know things."

"But . . ." she stammered, fighting to regain her emotional balance.

Fardusi raised his hands, palms up, in a calming gesture.

"I would like to see the girl. Theresa!"

The servant reappeared at the first call.

"There is a young child upstairs, in the first room on the right, just beyond the landing. I want you to bring her to me."

Theresa turned and started toward the staircase that curved upward from the great room toward the second floor hallway .

"Wait," Leila called out. Theresa stopped. "The room is locked and she is being guarded by one of my team members."

"She is being guarded in a locked room?" Fardusi twisted the pointed end of his mustache, an amused look on his face. "How old is this woman who is so dangerous that she needs to be locked up and guarded?"

"She is twelve," Leila answered, angry at the way Fardusi was playing with her and yet seemingly helpless to stop the unexpected scenario. She stood and moved toward the hall. "I will need to bring her to you."

"Thank you," Fardusi responded, tilting his head slightly forward, a satisfied twinkle in his eyes. He did not like Leila. Her demeanor was too cunning and sinister, and there was a toughness about the woman that made him wary. "It will be a pleasure to meet our little guest."

Fardusi pushed back his chair and stood. He walked over to a nearby lounging chair and sat down once again. From here, he could command a view of the entire room, as well as the small garden just outside the French doors. This was his favorite place in the house. It also provided an excellent view of the staircase leading up to the second floor landing. Sitting back in the chair, he waited.

JESSICA HEARD THE SOUND of the key being inserted into the lock. Then the door swung open. Though she still did not know her name, she recognized the woman who was the unquestioned leader of her new female guards. Her face was flushed and her dark eyes flashed as she entered the room.

"Get up!" she ordered.

Jessica sat up on the edge of the cot.

"Come with me. There is someone who wants to see you."

"Who?"

"Do not speak unless spoken to."

"I thought you were speaking to me."

The woman's hand flashed out across Jessica's face with a stinging slap.

"Do not try to act smart with me. It will get you nothing but pain."

"Hey, what did I do?" For an instant, Jessica's vision blurred and her cheek began to redden from the force of the blow.

"Cover your head and come with me."

Jessica scooped the scarf from off the stand by her bed and wrapped it around her head, in the manner in which Faridah had taught her, until only her face could be seen. The woman walked out into the hall with Jessica following. They were retracing steps that she remembered, having come this way the night they arrived. As they left the room, the one who had been sitting by her door followed them. Jessica was sandwiched in between.

At the landing, the first thing she noticed was the elegant chandelier hanging over the center of a great room. Hundreds of pieces of cut crystal caught the afternoon sun, formulating prisms of golden light that danced across both floor and ceiling. Jessica faltered in stride, then came forward to the steps and began her descent behind the woman.

Her hand reached for the railing at the same time she caught sight of someone sitting in a chair. He had a white mustache and looked considerably older than her father. Her heart pounded with apprehension as she reached the main floor. They walked across the room until she was standing in front of him.

She felt the woman's hand on her shoulder, pushing her forward.

"This is the girl."

Jessica stood still, waiting. *Who is this? What does he want from me?*

"What is your name, child?" The man's voice was deep, his English clear, with a light British accent. He leaned forward and studied her face.

"Jessica."

"That's a very nice name. Jessica what?"

"Jessica Cain."

"Where are you from, Jessica Cain?"

"My home is in California. Baytown."

"That's near San Francisco, correct?"

"Yes. What is your name?" Jessica was looking directly at the man now, taking in all his features. In some way, he reminded her of Grandpa Cain, but it was not so much in looks. What was it? Mannerisms? Or perhaps it was the sound of his voice. Yes, that was it. Grandpa Cain's voice was deep like this man's.

"Jessica, you are not to ask questions!" The woman's hand was on her shoulder. Jessica twisted away from her grip and glared up at her captor.

Fardusi lifted his hand. "Stop it."

The woman halted abruptly, and Jessica turned back to the elderly man.

"I understand that this girl is your prisoner, Khånome Ahmadi," he spoke sternly, pointedly using her family name as he looked past Jessica to the others. "However, as long as you make my home her prison, I am certain that you will respect the fact that this truly is *my* home."

Leila did not answer.

His voice quieted. "She most assuredly is *your* prisoner, but she is *my* responsibility, as are all of my guests, including each one of you. And, as is always my custom, I intend for my guests to be treated in the best manner possible.

"You will be in no danger here," he said directly to Jessica. "This woman is Leila Azari. And my name is Reza Fardusi."

Jessica could feel tension slicing through the atmosphere in the room. *What this man is saying about not being in danger, and what I am feeling right now, are two entirely different things.*

"Come closer, child." Fardusi reached out his hand. Jessica took a half step, then another. Then she did something that surprised even herself. She reached out and touched the man's hand!

It was a big hand, compared to hers. And hard, not soft. A working man's hand. *He looks too old to be an ordinary laborer. Besides, check it out. This is not your average working man's home.* In fact, Jessica could not remember having been in any finer home before. This room was huge. Lots of wood throughout. Marble tile floors with gorgeous Persian rugs everywhere. Through the French doors she could see the garden with bright flowers and greenery. A stone path led to a bench beneath an arbor. It was lovely.

"How did you get such a beautiful house?" asked Jessica. "I thought everyone in this part of the world was poor."

Fardusi laughed. It was a hearty laughter. Then he took Jessica's hand and drew her closer. She pulled back nervously.

"Do you know why you are my guest, Jessica Cain?"

"No. And I am not your guest," Jessica's eyes flashed as she spit out the words. "I'm being held hostage here against my will. There's a big difference."

"Right you are, young lady," Fardusi replied. "A big difference indeed."

"I'm being held here against my will," she repeated. "I want to go home, that's all."

"I'm sure that in due time, you will get to go home. But for now, you are here with us. And as for my abode, I have worked hard to be able to provide for my family a suitable place. This has been my home for many years."

"You have a family? Are your children grown up?"

Fardusi chuckled once again, pleased at how the young girl handled herself. "My family was here a short while ago."

Jessica flashed back to the women and children she had seen earlier. Could some of these have been his family? She started to say that she had seen them along the roadway. *No, wait. Don't say anything. They'll know I looked through the window and they won't like that. If they check it out, they will discover that it's not locked.*

Fardusi saw her mouth open, then close. "You wished to say something, child?"

"I . . . I was wondering . . . how many children do you have?"

Fardusi folded his hands against his chest and leaned back in the chair.

My wife, Roshan, is the mother of my three sons. Fateema and Delrobah have each provided me with two daughters."

"You have three wives?" Jessica blurted out, surprised at this admission. She had never known anyone with three wives before.

At this, Fardusi laughed uproariously.

"Yes, indeed," he answered, and then, just as suddenly as the laughter had come, his countenance changed. "Actually, I have four wives. In our religion, Allah permits us to have up to four wives, provided that we can care for each of them equally well."

"I cannot imagine my daddy having four wives. That would be against our religion. It would be illegal in my country. In America, you can have only one wife."

". . . at a time," Fardusi concluded her comment. "Your males can marry only one woman at a time. But your divorce rate is such that many men in America have more than one wife in their lifetime. So, what is the difference, do you think?"

Jessica was at a loss to answer the question. It was true. A number of her friends at church and school suffered the aftereffects of their parents' marital breakup. It hurt her to even think about the possibility as far as her own parents were concerned. It was beyond imagining, and she chose to leave it there . . . in that dark region of "the beyond" . . . even though, before leaving on this trip, she had sensed her parents' struggles and secretly wondered if the terrible ogre of divorce was about to tear her own family apart.

"You said you have four wives," she countered, deciding not to try to answer the elderly man's question.

"That is correct."

"You mentioned only three by name."

Fardusi hesitated. A shadow seemed to cross his face.

"My fourth wife, Katya, is ill."

"Does she have children?"

The somber shadow remained. He looked away.

"There were two. They are both dead."

The mood in the room was suddenly subdued.

At last, Fardusi sighed heavily, breaking the silence. "Esak would be twenty this year. His sister, Shana, would be eighteen."

"I'm sorry." Without thinking, Jessica reached out and touched the man's hand again. All at once, he looked very old and haggard. Clearly, the memory of their deaths was distressing to him. At her touch, his eyes found hers and looked into them steadily. There was sadness, but there was something more, as well.

"Were they sick?" she asked.

He dropped his gaze and moved his hand away from hers.

"They died six years ago. In the war."

Jessica remained silent. She didn't know what else to say. She wanted to ask, *"What war?"* but this was not the time or place. Besides, this man was the enemy. She was being held hostage in his home. She tried to muster the remnants of anger and resentment that had burned a hole into her heart these past weeks, but the glow was faint. The fire was almost out. Only the ashes remained.

In its place, something else was beginning to take shape. A determination. A resilience fueled by an ever-increasing will to outlive and wear down her enemies.

Survival. Endurance.

Jessica silently gritted her teeth.

I want to go home!

FARDUSI STUDIED THE GIRL INTENTLY.

She has spirit. I like that. And this in spite of being a child alone in a land peopled with strangers. Does she have even a glimmer of understanding? Can she feel the true danger she is in?

For a long moment, the pain inside seemed deeper and more intense than any since that first day in which he had been notified of the martyrdom of his two children.

They were his oldest and, contrary to the law of the land that declares all male Iranians to be eligible for the draft after the age of sixteen, they had been conscripted into the Iranian war machine at the ages of fourteen and twelve. Esak was a gentle boy, a good student. Shana was too young and innocent to realize what was actually happening. There had been nothing Reza Fardusi could do to keep them home. At least, that was what he had told himself at the time. While Iraq's well-trained armies were pressing the battle against Iran, tens of thousands of children throughout the land were being called up.

In the customary Muslim gesture of leave-taking, Esak and Shana had kissed the Koran held by their father, and passed under it three times. With the bravado of innocent children, they declared their willingness to fight for Islam and for the revolution. Looking into her father's tear-filled eyes, Shana told him, "If I become a martyr, that is Allah's will; if I come back victorious, that is all the better."

She did not come back. Nor did Esak.

Reza had gone to tell Katya. He could still hear her mournful wail. She never recovered; something inside her snapped with the terrible news.

Her two babies had been tied together with other children at the wrist. At an officer's order, they fanned out as far as they could from one another, and started walking across an onion field, in front of the Army tanks.

The field had been seeded with Iraqi mines. Children were more expendable than tanks.

Maashallah!

INTO THE OLD MAN'S MIND THERE CAME again the familiar words of an anonymous Iranian poet who, during this apocalyptic horror that ripped the soul from his beloved nation, had written:

> That black smoke that rose from the roof—
> that was our black smoke. It came from us.
> That burning fire that swayed left and right—
> that was our fire. It came from us.
> Do not denounce the foreigner, or lament anyone but us.
> This is the heart of the matter—our affliction came from us.

How true, thought Fardusi. *How very, very true.*

His gaze returned to Jessica. He studied her for a long moment.

Amazing. Her eyes—they are so green. Like two flashing emeralds.

The only one in my family to have such green eyes, like my own, was Shana.

TWENTY-FIVE

Outside the open doorway to the second room on Madeline's duty list, she heard footsteps in the hall. There were voices too, conversing in low but angry tones. Across the hall, she heard the door open and close. A moment later, a woman entered the room where Madeline continued her cleaning. Without so much as a word, she pulled the dark scarf away from her hair and threw it onto the bed. Madeline glanced up. The woman was unusually attractive, beautiful even, but obviously upset.

I've not seen her here before.

Madeline busied herself with the feather duster, attempting to brush away the particles of dust that seemed bent on resettling in the same area. There was no closet in the room, only an open nook with wall hooks and a bar stretched across the opening, containing several wooden hangers where some clothes had been carelessly hung. In the corner under the clothes, an ugly black semiautomatic rifle leaned against the wall.

The ornately carved bed had been used the night before, and Madeline made short work of straightening the covers. She had already cleaned the room in which the other two occupants were staying and gathered up her things to carry across the hall to the last room. As she walked past the woman there was still no conversation.

Outside, she was surprised to see one of the other women sitting in front of the last door.

"I beg your pardon," Madeline said to the woman, taking note of the handgun strapped to her waist. She was reading a copy of *Mahjubah*, a popular Islamic women's magazine published in Tehran by the Islamic Thought Foundation. The guard looked up as she approached.

"Please, I need to go inside and take care of the room."

The woman's gaze dropped to the cloths, towels, feather duster, damp mop, and pail on the pushcart. Madeline decided to try one of the few conversational phrases she had so far learned in Farsi.

"Bebakhshid: Fårsi ballad ni stam." *I'm sorry: I don't speak Persian.* "Shomå Engelisi baladid?" *Do you know English?*

"I speak it well enough to understand what you are saying, and far better than you speak my language. Who are you?"

"My name is Madeline. I have been assigned to care for these three rooms during your stay here. I understand that one of your group requires food brought in. Is this the room?"

The guard nodded.

"Is your associate ill?"

"She is not my 'associate,'" the guard replied. "She is our prisoner. You will need to bring her meals because she cannot be released to eat with others."

Madeline felt her skin crawl. She had not been told about any prisoner.

"Is she dangerous? Will I be safe inside?"

The guard's face broke into a gradual smile. "Yes, I assure you that you are safe, but while you are inside, you must not speak with her. She is to talk to no one. That includes you."

Madeline nodded. "I understand."

The guard got up from the chair and stepped aside.

Madeline knocked and waited. No response from behind the door. She knocked again. Nothing.

"Go on. Go inside and do your work. Be quick about it."

Nervously, Madeline opened the door.

JESSICA HEARD THE USUAL DULL SOUND of the latch. She looked up from her cot, the only piece of furniture in the room.

A young woman entered the room, leaving a metal pushcart of cleaning supplies in the doorway. The woman had dark hair and brown skin, a maid, obviously, in her uniform of brown pants and smock, high to the neck and buttoned at the wrists. She stepped into the room hesitantly, looking around quickly, though Jessica did not know what she hoped to find.

"Hello," said Jessica, sitting up on the edge of the cot.

The maid stared at her for a long moment, but said nothing.

"My name is Jessica. Jessica Cain."

The young servant dipped her mop into the pail and began working on the floor.

"I am an American. Do you speak English?"

The servant continued the mopping stroke, push and pull, back and forth. Jessica caught her eye movement and an almost imperceptible nod of the head. Just then, the guard's face appeared in the doorway.

"Be quiet. You must not speak unless spoken to."

"It can't hurt to be a little sociable."

"You must be quiet or I will tape your mouth."

A feeling of anger rose inside her as she remembered the painful discomfort of being gagged. She decided not to press her luck.

Back and forth.

The maid came nearer, bent slightly over her dreary task. Jessica lifted her feet as she watched the mop make wet designs on the tiles.

"Madeline."

Jessica's heart stopped for an instant. The servant continued pushing the mop back and forth, under the edge of the cot. Her back was toward the guard.

"My name is Madeline," she whispered again.

Jessica strained to hear more, but that was all. As soon as she finished, she moved away from that corner of the room, without looking again at Jessica. Minutes later, she was at the door, putting her cleaning tools on the cart. She did not look back and the guard closed the door.

Jessica heard the lock turn. Once again she was alone, but a new factor had just been introduced into her dilemma.

Madeline. She speaks English. She works for them, but apparently she is not one of them.

Jessica stared at the door for a long time.

SUNSET WAS REZA FARDUSI'S favorite time of the day to be in the enclosed garden that his ancestors would have called a pairidaeza. The extreme heat was starting to be tempered by breezes coming off the Gulf. Shadows grew longer under the olive and fig palms. The elaborate drip irrigation system measured out the necessary amount of water to thirsty herbs, flowers, and vegetables. The silence was disturbed only by one of the gardeners carefully raking up weeds and leaves around an area of green shrubbery.

Fardusi's white shirt was open at the collar. Though the sea breezes were doing their best to refresh the stale afternoon air, sweat beads lined his forehead and perspiration formed damp circles underneath his arms. Today had been unusually warm for this time of year. Swatting at a pesky fly, he hoped that tomorrow would be cooler.

At the end of the path, he turned and faced the great house. His heart swelled with pride as he viewed it and as much of the surrounding compound as he could take in from where he stood.

The biruni and the andarun were places of ceaseless activity. Servants traveled back and forth, bearing messages from Fardusi to his wives or from one wife to another. Iranian and foreign guests still came to visit this man whose business acumen had made him a formidable force in the shipping industry. Although he was now retired, his counsel and connections were still sought by those who succeeded him. He was powerful, respected for both honesty and shrewdness, and more than a little feared by those who had tried to diminish his influence.

However, his power had been reduced during the past decade, and he, more than anyone else, knew it. Since the revolution, the influence of the mullahs had risen, throwing the nation into a blinding battle of piety over politics.

The fanatical determination of the mullahs to turn Iran into a religious state, scrupulously adhering to the ancient codes and beliefs of Islam, had removed the spotlight from the nation's desperately shaky economy. By the time the spotlight of concern had refocused, it was almost too late. Those now in leadership were woefully lacking in the art of governing and almost totally ignorant in the ways of commerce and enterprise. World distrust of the new leaders had sharply affected the availability of investment capital, both foreign and domestic.

Trade embargoes, a falling petroleum output, a slump in world prices, the punitive cost of an eight-year war, and official indifference to the state of the economy all left their heavy mark. There were, perhaps, a dozen business leaders left in the country whose connections were crucial in maintaining Iran's position as a key player in the world marketplace. Eventually, the new political leaders had come to the realization that without them, the economic viability of the country would disintegrate overnight. Thus, while official Iran neither trusted nor approved of them, these men were tolerated out of sheer necessity.

And imposed upon at will, Fardusi thought, as he looked up at the windows of the two rooms in which Iran's female warriors were residing. He thought, as well, of the young American hostage, alone in her room across the hall. He did not like it. Not at all. Having these women in his house ran against his grain. He was of the old school and saw Iran's new women of war as a sign of the nation's weakening status, both at home and around the world.

These new female warriors were fanatical, thoroughly committed to the concept of Jihad as interpreted by their leaders. Fardusi considered himself to be a dedicated Muslim. He was also well educated, an avid reader with a special fondness for Persian poetry, and a serious student of Islamic history. It was from this latter discipline that his questions had surfaced regarding Jihad. Sooner or later, the Muslim community would have to deal with these issues.

The sun had almost disappeared behind the compound wall. He sat down on a bench and watched as two bees energetically sought the pollen from a bed of narcissus. Here was another reason that Reza loved this land. A little water, a dab of fertilizer, and anything seemed willing to grow twelve months out of the year. One of the bees bumped the other in a territorial dispute over a particular blossom. The second bee would not be denied its rights and returned to drive away the first one. Back and forth they scrambled and bumped and circled, with defiant moves that showed their determination to dominate.

Reza watched and then smiled ruefully. The two bees had totally lost perspective. There were dozens of other blossoms ready to honor the renowned work ethic of the bees. It appeared likely, however, that these two would return to the hive spent and without any produce. Their only harvest would be animosity between the two of them and disfavor among the many who were counting on their contribution to the society of which they were all a part.

"You two must be Muslim bees," he chuckled, then followed their flight as they disappeared into the garden. "You have your own little Jihad."

Fardusi thought back over what he knew of Jihad's outworking among the Muslim nations. Its initial formulation centered on a charter drawn up by Mohammed himself, centuries ago in Medina. It declared that the brotherhood of Islam took precedence over all other ties and relationships, so much so that a believing father might have to slay an unbelieving son. This brotherhood bound all Muslims together and guaranteed them the protection of the community. Various Jewish tribes were also included as "a community along with the Muslims," while retaining their own religion. They were guaranteed the same privileges and were under identical financial and community obligations as the Muslims.

From the beginning, Mohammed had dedicated himself to the conversion of Arabs to Islam, particularly those of his hometown. Above all, he desired to see the Ka'ba purified from heathen practices and given to Allah. Peaceful efforts had proven ineffective, and soon the time for forceful action came.

The first stage was the most difficult. Mohammed had to persuade the Medinians to attack their old friends in Mecca. These were people they knew by both marriage and commerce. Now they were being called upon to take up arms against their "heathen" brothers. Blood relationship is a sacred tie between all Arabs and it was not easy to turn brother against brother. However, by preaching war as a sacred duty, Jihad, Mohammed gradually incited his followers to attack the Meccans.

The attack actually consisted of only three small skirmishes. The first raid was carried out in the sacred month when war was banned throughout Arabia. Mohammed justified the action in the Koranic Sura 2:214:

> They will question you [O, Mohammed] with regard to warfare in the sacred month; say: "Warfare therein is a serious matter; but to turn [men] from the way of God and to disbelieve in Him and in the sacred temple and to drive his people from it is more serious with God, and infidelity is more serious than killing."

To break a truce that had bound all Arabs was no light matter, but such scruples could not override the necessity of bringing idolatry to an end.

From this event, others moved swiftly. Mohammed himself led three hundred Muslims against a thousand Meccans at Badr. Then, a series of operations ended with the expulsion of all Jews from the Hijâz, because they refused to acknowledge Mohammed as a prophet. At his instigation, a couple of Jews were murdered and no blood money was offered to their surviving kin.

With several smaller victories under his belt, Mohammed continued to incite his followers to liberate the countryside of infidels and idolatry through implementing his new doctrine of religious war. Eventually, Medina was taken and the Jews, who after a short siege surrendered unconditionally, were brought to Mohammed. Their old friends, the Aus, pleaded on their behalf. Mohammed asked the Jews whether they would accept the verdict of one of the chief Aus, to which they agreed. He appointed a man who was suffering from a deadly wound to pass final judgment. He declared that the men should be put to death and the women and children taken as slaves.

The sentence was carried out. Prisoners were led out to the edge of a trench that had been dug in the marketplace, where they were beheaded and thrown into the mass grave. The execution of over eight hundred men occupied the entire day and went on into the night. Only one Jew converted to Islam. The rest, after prayer and reading the Scriptures, went calmly to their deaths.

Mohammed subsequently began a systematic encirclement of Mecca and eventually forced an armistice with the Meccans, removing the barrier which had kept the Bedouin from joining the Muslims. From then on, though Mohammed lived only four more years, great victories were enjoined and the shape of the Middle East was settled for centuries to come.

Still, it does not seem to ever be enough. Jihad has become a way of life . . . and death . . . to millions. To my own children. Surely this is not the way in which the Prophet intended for us to walk. When will it end?

Dusk was turning to darkness when Reza Fardusi walked back to the house. The garden was quiet. Beyond the pairidaeza wall, a truck could be heard making its way up the hill. Reza opened the door and went inside. As he did, his thoughts turned once again to the unwelcome women upstairs, and to the child they were guarding.

He called for a cup of hot tea and went to his favorite chair. When the tea arrived, he dismissed the servant and settled back, clenching a chunk of ghand, a crudely broken sugar, between his front teeth while sipping the brew. It was the traditional Persian way of drinking tea, and tonight Fardusi was feeling very traditional.

Not until the cup of tea was finished did the last of the sugar lump disappear. By that time, he had decided what he would do about his little guest with the green eyes.

MADELINE LOOKED AT HER WATCH. It was later than usual when she took the Bible from under her pillow. She ran her fingers over the worn cover, at the same time looking at a small photograph of her mother and little sister. Her thoughts were jumbled together: her mother and sister, her dream of becoming a nurse, her beloved homeland . . . and the girl.

It had been impossible to get Jessica Cain out of her mind. Madeline had been taken by surprise, expecting a dangerous adult on the other side of the guarded door. Instead, she had found a young girl. It had to be the one they had spoken of earlier, when they said that three women and a girl were guests of Reza Fardusi.

But this girl is not a guest. She is a prisoner. Apparently, these three women are assigned to guard her. What could a child like that have possibly done? She is certainly not a native. She said she was . . . an American. And she sounds like one too.

Later in the day, Madeline spoke with one of her friends about the new guests, only to discover that this matter was already an item of speculation among the other servants. Madeline's contact with the American girl simply added more fuel to the hallway gossip.

One rumor had it that Reza Fardusi was adopting a young girl who was the same age Shana had been when she died. Another was that he had chosen her as a child-bride. Still another was that she was to be wed to Roshan's oldest son, Ali. Madeline pitied the girl if this was to be her fate. She did not like Ali at all. None of the rumors rang true to Madeline, however. She could not forget the three guards.

It doesn't make sense. Who is she? Why is she here?

Madeline opened her Bible, took out the bookmark, and began reading where she had left off the night before. Barely into Psalm 82, she stopped and stared at the verses. Then, she read them again.

> Defend the cause of the weak and fatherless;
> maintain the rights of the poor and oppressed.
> Rescue the weak and needy;
> deliver them from the hand of the wicked.

Madeline stared at the wall, the Bible open on her lap. Finally, weary, she replaced the bookmark and laid the Bible on the floor. Turning out the light, she settled back onto her pillow and looked up at the darkness. Her lips moved in prayer for her mother and Tamara back home. She started to say "Amen," and then faltered.

The American girl.

She said her name was Jessica Cain.

She looked at me as though I might know her.

But how could that be? I've never seen her before.

Madeline scooted further down under the lightweight cover and closed her eyes.

"Rescue the weak and needy, Madeline; deliver them from the hand of the wicked!"

What?

Madeline sat up straight, her hands gripping the sides of her bed.

She turned on the light and looked around. Throwing back the cover, she got out of bed and went to the door. It was still shut tightly. Opening it, she looked both ways up and down the hall. No one was about. Puzzled, she closed the door again and returned to bed.

I could have sworn . . .

She turned the light out and slipped between the covers again. It was getting late and she had to be up early in the morning. Her eyes closed and she felt herself drifting off to sleep.

"Rescue the weak and needy, Madeline; deliver them from the hand of the wicked!"

This time she did not move. Her body tingled as she stared wide-eyed into the darkness. This voice was different than any other she had ever heard. Was it coming from somewhere inside the room? Or, was it only in her mind?

Is that You, God?

Silence.

Nothing else—only the face of the little prisoner locked away in the biruni.

Is this about the little girl?

More silence. And . . . a Presence!

Are You trying to say something to me about her?

I've heard others say that You talk to them.

Even my mother used to say it.

But, I've never heard You, have I?

"Is this really You, God?" she said aloud to the darkness.

Madeline lay there for a very long time before drifting off to sleep.

TWENTY-SIX

John laid the comics aside and thumbed idly through the sports pages. The Forty-Niners were playing in Kansas City today. The Golden State Warriors were at the Coliseum for an afternoon NBA game against the Phoenix Suns. And the San Jose Sharks NHL team didn't seem to be anywhere, as far as he could tell. He tossed the paper onto the floor and stood up.

What difference does it make? Who cares?

There had been a time, a few months ago, when John would have taped the Niners game, in order to watch it later.

Months? More like a few years ago!

He picked up his coffee and walked to the window. The day was overcast, and the weather report offered a sixty percent chance of rain in the North Bay. Afternoon clearing. Patchy clouds and cooler. High temperatures in the low sixties along the coast and mid-seventies inland. Esther emerged from the back of the house, swishing back a renegade lock of hair with her hand. "Some days, it just doesn't pay to have hair," she stated emphatically, kissing John and reaching for the steaming cup resting on the counter, all in the same move.

A tentative sampling was followed by a smile and a satisfied sigh. "You are such a coffee maker, love," she said.

"I know," John answered. "It's a gift."

"Now that's one that I've never heard of before. Did Paul decide that after preaching to the Gentiles?"

"No, it was in some ancient manuscripts found in an old coffee can near the site of the Dead Sea Scrolls."

Esther laughed and they hugged and kissed again.

"You're silly. Anything in the newspaper?"

"The Niners are in Kansas City this morning. The Warriors are facing off the Suns. The price of housing is up, and so are interest rates. The stock market was down last week, and so was the dollar. And Snoopy went to sleep while typing the great novel. Fell off his doghouse. Took a nose dive right into his food dish."

"Did he hurt himself?"

"Guess not. He just can't smell to write anything."

"Oh, that's bad, John!"

"What do you expect for a Sunday morning without a pulpit?"

Esther walked over to the sofa and sat down. "It does seem strange to not be at the church when we're right here in town."

"You can say that again!"

"It does seem strange . . ."

"Okay, okay. Enough already."

Esther leaned back, never taking her eyes off John. She watched him tap his foot to some internal beat that no one else could hear. He touched the tips of his fingers together, released, then touched again.

"Want to talk about it?" Her voice had a warm lilt that suggested curiosity. "Feeling guilty about being at home instead of in church?"

John stopped his foot-tapping and grinned sheepishly.

"No, nothing like that," he answered. "But you're right about one thing—I want to talk about it. Do you want to listen?"

"I'm here for you."

"Just like always. You know how much I love you?"

"How much?"

"About this much." John held up his fingers, a small fraction of an inch apart in measurement. It was something they had done with each other all their married lives.

"That much? I'm so impressed." Esther smiled and swallowed the last of her coffee. "It sounds like this could take a while. How about letting me get us another cup?"

A moment later, she returned and handed him his fresh cup as she sat down. "Okay, friend and lover and father of my kids, tell me what's on your mind."

There was a long silence, while John deliberated as to how to begin.

"Okay. It has to do with Jessica."

Esther waited, tracing the rim of her cup with a finger.

"Actually, I guess it has to do mostly with me. I'm wondering about . . . about whether or not what I'm doing is morally right? I'm learning how to fire a gun so that I can go get her back. Carla says that I should never point the muzzle of a gun at something or someone I am not ready to destroy. Honey, sometimes there is so much anger inside me at the people who have taken her that I could kill them all. Yet, when I get a gun in my hands on the firing range, and I actually begin thinking about doing it, I don't know. Is it right for a Christian to kill someone?"

Esther did not answer. She held back, sensing he wasn't through yet.

"Actually, I guess it goes deeper than that. Is it right for a pastor, a shepherd of God's flock, to kill someone? To actually be the aggressor, even if it's necessary to get Jessica back? Part of me says, 'Why do you even ask the question? Of course, you have the right and the duty. Do whatever it takes. Lie, cheat, steal, kill. Just get her back!' But another part of me asks what sort of example I am supposed to be to the family of God. I tell them that God answers prayer. Do I really believe that? I think my answer is yes. But if that's true, why doesn't He tell us where she is? Why doesn't He just deposit her on our doorstep? On any doorstep, for that matter, where someone will have compassion and see to it that she gets home."

John paused and took a deep breath.

"And what if all this is just an internal ruse? What if I'm too scared to do it? Too frightened to face whatever odds are out there between Jessica and us?"

Esther put her cup down and moved closer to John. She took his hand and began weaving her fingers together with his.

"John, look at me." He hesitated at first, then turned, his troubled eyes caught up in her steady gaze. "First of all, get this straight. One thing you are not is a coward. Trust me. You have proven that beyond all shadow of doubt. Are you frightened? I hope so. If you have a lick of sense left in you, you should be scared beyond belief. I know I am. But you can use that fear to hone your senses. It can either rob you of your courage or put the final edge on your survival skills.

"I know a little about how you feel regarding the use of a weapon against another human being. I'm frightened to death of guns, but if it were a life or death matter where you were concerned, I would use a gun to save your life. You can count on that, John."

His eyes never left her.

"If a burglar came into our home, entered our bedroom, and started to stab me, and you had a gun on the night stand, would you use it to defend me?"

"Of course, but that is different. In that situation, the burglar is the aggressor."

"And doesn't the biblical ideal dictate that you are to be my protector?"

"Of course."

"Then, what is the difference in this circumstance? You are Jessica's father. She's counting on you to be her protector, just like I am."

John sat absolutely still, pondering what he was hearing. Finally, he looked up.

"Remember what David wrote in Psalm 20? 'Some trust in chariots and some in horses, but we trust in the name of the Lord our God.' Am I putting my trust in man's ability instead of God's?"

"I'll answer you with Psalm 147. 'His pleasure is not in the strength of the horse, nor His delight in the legs of a man; the Lord delights in those who fear Him, who put their hope in His unfailing love.' Let me ask you, darling, do you fear Him? Is your hope in His unfailing love?"

"You already know the answer to that."

"I know I do, but say it anyway."

"Yes. I fear God. I hold Him in great awe. I don't want to do anything that will displease Him. And I do hope in His unfailing love. What else do I have to hope in?"

"Then, my dear, relax. His good pleasure is upon you. He sees your situation. The very fact that you wrestle over this issue, when both God and I know that you want Jessica back more than life itself, is proof enough that you are not relying on your strength or ability. Even if you learn to shoot like the Lone Ranger, how will you ever know where to go to find her or what to do when you get there? We have a situation that is so impossible that, unless God intervenes, we will surely fail. Agreed?"

John nodded, finding it hard to believe that Esther was talking like this, with such confident and outspoken faith.

Esther squeezed his hand in hers. "Besides, how well do you shoot?"

"Carla considers me lucky that I haven't seriously wounded myself yet."

"See what I mean?"

John reached out, pulled Esther over onto his chest and

wrapped his arms around her. They remained that way for a long time.

In the distance, they could hear the bells at St. Mark's Lutheran Church, releasing the faithful for another week.

"Come on, dear," said Esther, pulling loose from John's embrace. "Let's get some breakfast and smell the roses and think about how nice it is that you don't have to preach this morning."

0800 LOCAL TIME
BANDAR-É ABBÁS, IRAN

AT EIGHT O'CLOCK, REZA FARDUSI was at his dining table spreading goat's cheese on lavâsh bread, a thin bread folded twice into a square. The servant had also placed yogurt, jam, and honey on the table in case the master of the house desired them. He washed every third bite down with tea. Occasionally, he liked a bowl of cornflakes, even though such luxuries were expensive, but not this morning. He had other things on his mind.

At eight-twenty, he scribbled a message on paper, folded it once and called for the servant. He handed the message to her, with instructions to deliver it to the person occupying the first room on the left, at the head of the stairs. She curtsied, stepped back, and turned to leave.

"Wait!"

The servant stopped in midstride.

"You are new here, aren't you? I've not seen you serving in this house before."

"Yesterday was my first day in the biruni, sir," she answered, a touch of nervousness in her voice. "My name is Madeline. I have been in your employ for four months now."

"Where is Theresa?"

"She is sick today, sir. It's nothing serious, but Madame thought she should stay in bed. She may be well by tomorrow."

"What was it that you did yesterday? I did not see you here."

"My assignment is to clean the rooms on the second floor. The ones in which your guests are staying. I am also to provide them with food and anything else they require. My only reason for being in this room is Theresa's illness. I hope I have not displeased you?"

"You've done quite well, thank you. You are serving all three people upstairs?"

"Four actually. There is a young girl in the room opposite the others."

"You have seen her?"

"Yes."

"Have you spoken to her?"

Madeline hesitated. Was she about to get into trouble with her employer? Then, she decided to heed her mother's advice: *Tell the truth always. Then you never have to remember what you said.*

"She spoke to me first. When I started to respond, one of the women told me not to say anything. If I did, she promised that I would be in trouble."

"What did the girl say?"

"She told me her name."

"And does she know yours?"

Again, Madeline paused before she confessed.

"I whispered it to her when my back was turned to the other woman. I am sorry if it makes you unhappy."

Fardusi smiled and motioned with his hand. "You acted well, Madeline. Just what I would have done in your place. Now, go with this message. You will be serving lunch today, yes?"

"Yes, sir."

"I am inviting the Azari woman to join me. Ask the cook to prepare a light lunch."

"Yes, sir. At once."

"Before you do anything else, please deliver the message. First door on the left. And, be careful."

She shot a questioning look over her shoulder.

" . . . of the stairs, Madeline. Be careful of the stairs."

She started up the steps, still shaking inside from having actually carried on a conversation with the great Aghå-yé Reza Fardusi, and paying little attention to the stairs as she went up. They were well constructed and not at all dangerous. As she ascended, it dawned on Madeline that the old man had something else in mind when he cautioned her to be careful.

"WHAT YOU PROPOSE IS ENTIRELY out of the question. It is simply not possible." Leila pushed back from the table and poured the remainder of the Coca Cola from the bottle into her glass.

"Why is such a thing impossible? Where will she go? She is a little girl, thousands of miles from her home."

"No, I am sorry. It cannot be permitted." Her tone was adamant. So was the scowl on her face.

"But, when will this Marwan Dosha arrive?" Fardusi continued to press.

"We do not know. It could be tomorrow."

"And it could be a month from tomorrow, or even longer. When was the last time anyone heard from him?"

Leila was silent. She didn't really know.

"Do you consider it wise to keep the child locked up indefinitely?"

"Those are my orders."

"To keep her under lock and key?"

"To keep her secure here in this compound."

"It is no problem, then. You can release her into the compound. Keep a guard with her if you like, though I seriously doubt that she can climb ten-foot walls with her bare hands. See it from this point of view. The girl needs some socialization. Look at her. She is too thin. I'm told she hardly eats. She's been locked up in a room of some type since Septåmbr. Soon it will be Desåmbr. She needs to play with other children. She can continue her training here. It will break up the monotony for her. She is not dangerous. Keeping her in that room alone is cruel. What has she done? She was born to an American father who has embarrassed the great Marwan Dosha."

"Cain did not simply embarrass Aghå-yé Marwan," Leila shot back. "This man aligned himself against The Cause. He foiled a critical part of the Holy War effort to recover the land of Palestine for its rightful citizens. He must be punished and the work we have started must go on."

"But the girl did nothing, did she? Don't you see? She is an innocent. Perhaps you are right. Perhaps the incident originally planned for Jerusalem would have been a benchmark victory that is still needed in order to show the world just how serious our people are. On the other hand, we could be enmeshed right now in a deadly all-out war with Israel, if Dosha's scheme had been successful. A war our nation would be sorely pressed to carry out successfully. It is not for me to say."

"Perhaps the girl is needed as a pawn in some larger scheme that will move our Cause forward," Leila countered lamely.

Fardusi folded his arms over his chest. "That still is not reason enough to deprive her of the basic human rights deserved by any child. It is not the Iranian way."

Leila stood and began pacing back and forth.

"It is not the Iranian way? What right do you have to judge whether or not this or that is 'the Iranian way'?" she snapped back in indignation. "You were obviously born to a privileged class, under the Shah. Otherwise, you would not live in all this . . . this opulence. If you had grown up on the streets in Tehran, you would see things differently."

She pulled out a pack of cigarettes, shook one out and placed it between her lips. She was reaching into her pocket for a book of matches when Fardusi spoke up. "Please, don't light that here in the house. I am one of the few left in our country who do not smoke. I apologize for inconveniencing you, but you must smoke outside. And please remind your two friends to do the same. I will die soon enough as it is, and I intend to do so without your help or anyone else's."

Frustrated, Leila replaced the cigarette and dropped the pack into her shirt pocket. "Why are you so interested in this girl?"

Fardusi shrugged. "Why not? I believe she is the focus of a worldwide search, is she not? And now I find that you have brought her to me for safekeeping. If our roles were reversed, would you not find that an interesting circumstance?"

"You want her to be taught by a private tutor, here in the compound?"

"Yes. It will be easy. I have such people in my employ for the benefit of my own children."

"And you want to allow her to mingle with your children as well? I find that very strange. Aren't you at all concerned about her influence and the immoral ideas that she might foist off on your children? What about her Christian ideals?"

"What about them?"

"Well, what if she draws one of your children away from the faith?"

"I thank you for your great concern over the spiritual welfare of my children. But are you truly worried about a twelve-year-old American girl proselytizing my children and inciting them to renounce their faith? You can't be serious."

Leila did not respond. She moved slowly across to the far side of the room and then turned to face him.

"I have thought about it and my answer is still no. It is inconsistent with my orders. Furthermore, it smacks of giving privilege to the enemy that is unwarranted and undeserved. They did not give my mother and baby brother any special consideration," she added vehemently. "Nor my father. They shot them down in cold blood. My only other brother died at the front for all the people, not for the privileged class alone!"

Fardusi was standing now, facing Leila. He smiled, but his face was hard and cold, like chiseled steel, his eyes passionless and restrained.

"Forgive me if I have been presumptuous in all this. You have suffered much, of course, and your family has given the ultimate gift of devotion to The Cause. I apologize for not adequately appreciating your feelings in this matter.

"There is something I wish to make clear, however," he continued, matter-of-factly. "I was born into a family of seven children, in the poorest section of Sir Jån. I too grew up on the streets. I polished shoes, sold cheap socks and T-shirts, and toted a samovar on my back around the marketplace each day, in order to sell hot tea and make a few rials to help support our family. I was not born into privilege. Nor am I just an old, aberrant leftover of the Shah's fallen regime. Though I may not see things to be quite as black and white as you seem to, I assure you that I am as devoted a Muslim as you are, and my love for Iran is unconditional."

"I too apologize if my words or their tone have been offensive in any way." Leila turned toward the staircase. "We are grateful for your cooperation in the use of your compound and for your kind hospitality."

"You are most welcome," responded Fardusi, with a slight bow. *No sense in upsetting you more, at least not for now. Even though you and your kind are eating away the very core of our nation's pride and heritage by your attitudes and actions.*

TWENTY-SEVEN

When Madeline and her friend Alisha arrived ten minutes early, several of the other "regulars" were there already. Madeline excused herself while Alisha talked with two of her Filipino friends and waited until the leader, Arun, a slim, gentle, former Hindu from Calcutta, finished speaking to one of the group's young members.

"Excuse me," she began, with nervous politeness. "We have not met until now, but my name is Madeline."

"I know. I have seen you here, off and on, over the last couple of months. What can I do for you?"

Glancing at her wristwatch, and aware that the service was to begin in a matter of minutes, Madeline spoke quickly and in low tones. Arun's eyes narrowed as he listened to her story of the American girl in the upstairs room at Reza Fardusi's residence. Partway through, he stopped her and motioned to another young man to join them. She continued as they both listened intently.

"You're sure the name was Jessica? Jessica Cain?"

"Yes," she replied. "I am sure."

"It is time to begin the service," Arun said, "but when we have finished, I want to talk with you further. Okay?"

Madeline nodded and moved away to join the others.

Ninety minutes later, the meeting broke up and, in twos or threes, the participants departed for their homes. Alisha stayed behind with Madeline, but kept checking her watch, worried that she might be late returning to her room. At last, Arun and the other young man came over to where they were sitting and immediately resumed talking as though there had been no interruption of their earlier conversation.

"Can you describe what the girl looks like?"

Madeline nodded, while Alisha listened with an ever-increasing curiosity, as her friend gave a detailed description. When she had finished, Arun went over to a corner in which old newspapers were stacked three feet high. His hands shuffled through the pile, occasionally pulling out a copy, then dropping it to one side. Finally, he stopped and returned with a section of the *Emirates News*, a small English daily published in the UAE.

"I bought this in Abu Dhabi two weeks ago," he stated, handing Madeline the paper. "Is this the girl?"

Madeline stared at Jessica's picture, underneath the headline caption:

AMERICAN GIRL STILL MISSING

The article briefly restated the story of her disappearance. It highlighted the belief that she was alive and being held hostage somewhere in the Middle East, possibly Saudi, the UAE, or Iran. The governments of all three countries denied any involvement in her abduction or any knowledge as to her whereabouts, and all pledged to do everything in their power to assist in her recovery. A telephone and telex number of the American Embassy in Abu Dhabi, UAE was included.

"It's her!" Madeline looked up at Arun. "It's the same girl!"

"You are certain of this?"

"There's no question. This is the girl! She is at the Fardusi compound where I am employed. I take care of her room and bring her food. She is under twenty-four-hour guard."

Alisha was reading the article now, her eyes wide with excitement.

Arun introduced Madeline to Rashad, a fellow believer and Arun's best friend. Rashad was an Arab, a five-year convert to Christianity, and an official representative of the phosphate mining industry at Wadi al-Hesa in Jordan. They had met three years before, introduced by a mutual friend while drinking tea at a sidewalk cafe. Once they discovered their common faith in Jesus Christ, they had become inseparable in fellowship.

Arun explained that Rashad came to Iran every month or so and always managed to include an extra New Testament, a paperback Christian book, or a Bible commentary among his personal things. If the book or a magazine looked too obviously "Christian," in order to make certain that it would not be confiscated when entering Iran, he simply removed the cover and glued another in its place. So far, he had been successful in his efforts to increase his friend's Christian library resources.

"We must do something," Arun exclaimed, looking at Rashad. Rashad nodded in agreement. "But what?"

Ten minutes of animated discussion passed by, until Alisha pulled on Madeline's sleeve. "We've got to go. If we are late, it will mean trouble!"

Madeline nodded and started walking to the door with the others.

"All right," Arun rehearsed the plan. "Rashad is leaving for Jordan on Tuesday. As soon as he arrives there, he will contact the American Embassy."

"Will they believe me?" asked Rashad. "And, even if they do, will they do anything? You know how the Americans are. Most of them are well-intentioned, but sometimes I think they don't have any idea how to deal with us."

"Just a minute." The excitement was electric in Arun's voice. "Madeline, we'll need something from the girl as proof that she is here."

"Like what? I can't walk in with a camera and take her picture. Anything I do will be very dangerous, both for her and for me."

"She is one of us, don't you see?" said Arun. "Her father is the pastor of a church in California. This girl must be a Christian too, and in great trouble because of what her father has done. Now that we know where she is, we have to do everything we can to help her."

Madeline traced an invisible pattern on the floor with the toe of her sandal. Finally, she looked up at Arun. "You are right, of course, but I am frightened. If something happens, those women who are guarding her are not above killing us both!"

The others were silent in the knowledge that what Madeline said was undoubtedly true.

"Will you pray for me?" she whispered.

They formed a tiny circle and joined their hands together. Arun led in prayer, asking God for wisdom and protection to be upon each of them.

As soon as he said, "Amen," the girls rushed through the doorway and ran toward their Bandar home.

HOW LONG HAD IT BEEN since she had slept through the Adhan?

Maybe the tape broke and there wasn't any call to prayer this morning. Jessica smiled mischievously at the thought of slipping into the minaret and cutting up the magnetically taped prayer. She tried to stretch. It was a halfhearted try, at best. Jessica knew that she was getting weaker from lack of exercise and her recent refusal to eat. She was too depressed to eat. Since her arrival, she mostly lay on the cot and stared at the ceiling. The feeling of despondency was deep, like a pain in her belly. How long had it been? Months? She had lost track. It had to be sometime in November. Even the realization that she couldn't remember the exact date depressed her.

Thanksgiving! It's probably getting close. Turkey and all the trimmings. The whole family together. I wonder if Papa and Gramma Stevens and Papa and Gramma Cain will come to California this year. Jeremy. Wouldn't it be great to wrestle together on the living room floor until Mother yelled at us to stop it? Mom and Dad. We would all be holding hands around our beautiful dining room table, filled with corn on the cob, stuffing, a fruit salad. Cranberries. Sparkling cider. And pumpkin pie with whipped cream!

Jessica turned onto her side and faced the wall. She stretched out her arm and, with the other hand, began moving the tips of her fingers back and forth, barely touching the skin, creating a pleasant, tingling sensation. *Daddy used to do this all the time when I was little. I would sit in his lap and he would read or watch cartoons with me and I'd stretch out my arm like this . . .*

She closed her eyes to shut out that memory. It was too painful to think about home and family and Thanksgiving this year.

This would be a good time to pray. That is, if I thought God really cared . . . I've been praying for an awfully long time and . . . nothing has happened . . .

Jessica started at the sound of the door being unlocked.

She rubbed her eyes in the realization that she must have dozed off again. Her arm was asleep from the circulation being cut off by the position she was in. She moved it slowly, dreading the moment that the blood would return in full force.

It was the servant again, the one named Madeline.

The guard stood in the doorway, watching as she placed Jessica's food tray on the cot. There was no other place for it, except the floor. Jessica looked up in time to see her wink one eye, then look down at the tray. Reaching over, she took the pillow from under Jessica's head and proceeded to fluff it up. Next, she bent down and lifted Jessica's head, placing the pillow underneath her once again.

"Write something to your father."

Jessica stiffened with surprise, as she looked up at the young woman serving her. *Did she just whisper to me? Or am I starting to lose my mind?*

Again, the servant winked.

Then she turned, walked across the room and disappeared through the doorway. The door closed after her, and Jessica heard the familiar sound of the lock tumblers falling into place.

What was that all about?

Jessica lifted her feet and legs over the food tray and sat up on the edge of the cot, her weakened condition causing the room to swirl. She closed her eyes until things began to settle down, then slowly opened them again.

The tray was still there. Bread. Cucumbers. Tomatoes. Yogurt. And some kind of mush in a bowl. Jessica put the tip of her finger into the mush to see if it was warm. Surprise. It was. She picked up the spoon and lifted the bowl from the tray.

What's this?

Underneath was a piece of plain white paper.

She set the bowl down and picked up the paper that had been folded under it. As she opened the fold, another paper fell out. This one had something on it. She picked it up, disbelievingly. It was a page from the Bible!

THE GOSPEL ACCORDING TO ST. MARK

Chapter 1. The beginning of the Gospel of Jesus Christ, the Son of God; As it is written in the prophets, Behold, I send My messenger before Thy face, which shall prepare Thy way before Thee.

And, on and on and on! She turned it over. There was more on the back. It went all the way to verse 43 of the first chapter of Mark. Unbelievable! She felt of the paper, turning it over again. Something dropped onto its surface. A tear.

She must be a Christian too!

The realization was almost too wonderful to comprehend. Jessica put the leaf from the Bible on the bed and looked at the door.

That guard could come in at any moment.

The thought caused her to roll up the page and secure it between the mattress and the metal frame, under her pillow. She could hardly wait to read it. It had been weeks since she had read anything at all. Now, to have a page out of the Bible ... *Oh, thank You, God!*

Picking up the bread, she took a bite. It was fresh and tasted good. She bit into it again. Next, she took the spoon and dipped into the mush.

What's this?

There was something in her mush!

Yuk! Wouldn't you know it?

Gingerly, she reached into the pastelike substance and pulled it out.

Hey!

It was a small pencil.

She licked it with her tongue and wiped it dry on the thin, lumpy mattress. The piece of blank paper she had dropped in her excitement caught her eye again.

"Write something to your father!"

Jessica's hand shook as fear and exhilaration ran together inside her mind.

What is this? Could it be some kind of trick? No. Surely not. This isn't the sort of thing these goofballs would do. That girl is telling me that she is a Christian. That's why she's put the Scripture here under the bowl. She must know who I am. She's read about what Daddy did in Israel and knows that I've been kidnapped. She's trying to help me.

Suddenly she was hungry. She began eating the mush with fresh enthusiasm. It didn't taste as bad as it looked, though she wondered how much lead might be left in it from the pencil.

She dabbled her spoon in the small side dish filled with creamy white yogurt before putting it down and moving the tray to one side.

Jessica picked up the pencil and paper, checking the door at the same time to be certain it was still closed. For a while, she thought about what to write. Then, setting the bowl and the yogurt on the floor, she put a carrot stick in her mouth and used the food tray as a writing table.

The piece of paper was very small.

What can I say that will let them know I'm here? Where is here? I can't tell them where I am, because I don't know myself ...but that girl knows. She can tell them. Okay, then. "Write

*something to your father." Put something down on paper that will
let him know it's really me writing.*

For a long moment, she pondered. Then, in her best handwriting, she wrote three words and a capital letter.

Underneath, she signed her name.

Painstakingly, Jessica folded the tiny missal and placed it on the tray. Next she put the empty bowl over it, checking to be sure nothing was sticking out from under the edges. She added the container of uneaten yogurt to the bowl for extra weight, to keep it from slipping off the hidden message that would assure the world Jessica Cain was still alive.

Finally, she stuffed the last of the bread in her mouth and sat back with the carrot stick in hand. And waited. Waiting was something she was getting good at.

MADELINE PLACED THE GUARD'S food tray on top of the others before opening the door. She carried them into the room, placed them on the edge of the girl's cot, and began rearranging the dishes to make them easier to carry. She felt the guard watching her every move.

Be careful.

That's what Reza Fardusi had said yesterday as she prepared to go upstairs and attend to the three female warriors and their hostage.

If he only knew the half of it.

She desperately wanted to see if the girl had hidden a message, but she was afraid to look now. Her hand shook slightly as she placed the girl's tray on top of the others. Then, as she turned toward the door, her ankle gave way and she stumbled.

Jessica's tray slid forward. Madeline tried to regain her balance as she dropped to her knees. She was able to keep all of the trays together—except for one.

From her kneeling position, Madeline watched in horror as the contents of Jessica's tray scattered onto the tile floor.

TWENTY-EIGHT

The large bowl pitched over the tray's edge, sending the container of yogurt flying toward the guard who was standing in the doorway. She tried to avoid being hit, but it was too late.

"Watch what you are doing!" she yelled, as the upside down container landed on her foot. Yogurt spilled out over her toes and onto the floor.

Madeline let out an involuntary groan as she put the remaining trays down. She saw the small piece of paper directly in front of her, halfway between where she was kneeling and the guard, but the guard's attention was focused on her foot, from which she was angrily wiping the spilled yogurt. Seeing her chance, while still on both knees, Madeline reached for the large bowl and scooped in the piece of paper with the same motion.

Getting to her feet, she dropped the paper into the bodice of her uniform and quickly began gathering up the wayward utensils.

"I'm so very sorry," she pled, in a suitably penitent tone. "It was an accident."

"You should have been more careful. I need a damp towel."

"Wait just a moment and I'll get one for you."

"Be quick about it!" the guard snapped, now glaring at Madeline with yogurt on her fingers as well as her foot.

Madeline gathered up the contents of the trays and hurried down the stairs to the kitchen. Moments later, she returned with a towel. The guard wiped her hands and feet with the cloth and then handed it to Madeline. Without a word of thanks, she closed and locked the door to Jessica's room, and sat down on the nearby chair.

"I am truly sorry for the inconvenience," apologized Madeline. "Can I get you anything now before I go?"

"No. Just get away from me!" The woman shook her head, still upset, then picked up her magazine and began reading.

Madeline retraced her steps down the staircase and across the great room. Alone in the kitchen, she washed the dishes and trays, putting them in the storage area. Looking around to be sure no one had come in, she released the top two buttons of her uniform and retrieved the paper. She was glad to see that it had escaped any damage from "yogurt fallout." Madeline could not keep from smiling as she thought about what had happened. It could have been a disaster; instead, it turned out to be rather humorous.

Anxiously, Madeline opened the tiny missive and, reading its message, frowned in puzzlement. It was definitely written and signed by Jessica's hand, but what could it mean?

Shaking her head, she refolded the paper and slipped out the back door.

TUESDAY, 08 NOVEMBER, 1710 LOCAL TIME
AMMAN, JORDAN

RASHAD RAUFBAR'S FLIGHT DESCENDED into Queen Alia International Airport, thirty-five kilometers south of the city, a little after five o'clock. Rashad's frustration had been building for the last three hours. Equipment problems had delayed takeoff and now he wondered if the American Embassy would be closed.

Clearing customs was swift. Rashad had only his carry-on luggage. He was used to traveling light and had no purchases to declare. No one noticed that he was lighter than when he had departed this same airport by one Bible, two New Testaments, and a commentary on the Gospel of Mark. Pausing at a public phone near the main exit of the ultramodern terminal, he looked through the phone book. Finally, he found what he wanted and dialed the six-digit number. Once, twice, three times the phone rang. Four, five, six. *Great. I've missed them. They're gone for the day. Now what shall I . . .*

"Hello," the voice was low and clear, a male voice. "You've reached the American Embassy. Our offices are closed. We are open Monday through Friday, from 0900 to 1600 hours. If this is an emergency, and you are at a touch-tone phone, press zero and then pound. Someone will answer your call as quickly as possible. Thank you and have a good day."

Rashad hesitated, then pressed the two keys. It was ringing, but the sounds of human beings, moving in all directions through the terminal, made hearing difficult. He was about to hang up when he heard a voice say, "Hello, how may I help you?"

"Hello," Rashad shouted into the telephone. "My name is Raufbar. Rashad Raufbar. I would like to speak to someone concerning a missing person."

"A missing person?" repeated the voice.

"Yes, thank you."

"All personnel who can assist you have gone home for the day. If you will call again tomorrow after nine o'clock . . ."

"Please. I have information concerning the whereabouts of an American child named Jessica Cain. She has been missing for several weeks. I know where she is."

"I am sorry, sir. I am unable to help you. You will need to call again in the morning, after nine o'clock."

"But it is very important that I speak with someone now. My plane was late getting in or I would have called sooner."

"I am sorry, sir. There is no one here to . . ."

"Thank you," said Rashad, by this time thoroughly exasperated by the bureaucratic dunderhead on the other end of the line. "May I have your name, please?"

His only response was the sound of the phone disconnecting.

Frustrated, Rashad gathered up his carry-on and pushed his way through the terminal door. People were jostling one another for taxis in the usual confusion for which Amman's airport is renowned. Seeing a city bus pull up to the curb across from him, Rashad made his decision. He would call his office tonight and leave word that he would not be in for work until after noon. That would give him time to personally go to the embassy and talk with someone in the morning. Tonight, he would stay with friends in the city.

As he boarded the bus, he thought how ironic it was that he, a Jordanian, seemed more concerned about the missing American child than were the Americans.

THE FOLLOWING MORNING, RASHAD'S friend dropped him off at the American Embassy, between Second and Third Circles. Rashad walked up the steps where he explained the nature of his visit to a man in military uniform guarding the entrance. He waited while the "uniform" spoke into an intercom with someone inside. A moment later, he unlocked the door and motioned for Rashad to go in.

Upon entering, he saw another security person, a woman who motioned him through a metal detector. He emptied his pockets of keys and coins and passed through successfully the first time. A male member of the embassy's security staff did a cursory body search, then stepped back and nodded to the woman.

"Come with me," she said, with a winning smile. "Over here. Please fill out this form and specify the nature of your visit. When you are finished, I'll be over there. Bring it to me."

"Thank you," said Rashad, not knowing whether or not he was simply impressed by the security measures or grateful at the feeling of finally getting somewhere.

For the next few minutes, he busied himself filling out the form. Then he walked to where the woman sat talking with someone on the telephone, and handed her the paper. She glanced over it quickly, with a practiced eye, then looked up at him as she put down the receiver.

"You say here that you have knowledge of an American citizen who has been declared a missing person? May I have the name, please?"

"Jessica Cain."

The woman started to write the name, then looked up again, quizzically. "Did you say Jessica Cain?"

"Yes, that's correct."

"One moment, please."

The woman turned and dialed a number on the phone. "There is a gentleman here, a Mr. Rashad Raufbar, who says that he knows the whereabouts of a missing American citizen, Ms. Jessica Cain. . . . Yes, that is correct. . . . No, I'm not certain of that. He says he called after hours yesterday. He has taken off work this morning in order to speak with someone personally. . . . Yes, I'll tell him. Thank you, sir."

She put the phone down and turned to Rashad.

"Mr. Johnson will see you in a few minutes, Mr. Raufbar."

"What is his position here in the embassy?"

"He is an assistant to the ambassador."

Rashad checked his watch. "I need to be in my office before noon."

"He'll only be a few minutes. May I get you some tea or coffee?"

"No thanks."

"Have a seat please. I'll call you when he's free."

Rashad sat down and started thumbing through a recent *National Geographic.* There was also an international edition of *Time* and a copy of this month's *New Yorker* on the table. By the time thirty-five minutes had passed, he had thumbed his way through them all. Then, just as he put the *Time* back on the table, he saw the security agent wave to him. He got up and walked over to her desk.

"Mr. Johnson is ready to see you now. This gentleman will show you to his office."

A man in a lightweight business suit smiled and held out his hand. "My name is Ryker. Ken Ryker. Please, come this way."

Rashad followed him along a corridor, past some open door-ways that revealed people working in cubicles cluttered with the usual telephones, computers, file cabinets, and a great deal of quiet chaos.

Ryker stopped at one of the doorways and motioned for him to enter.

"Mr. Johnson, this is Mr. Raufbar. He wishes to talk to you about a missing person named Jessica Cain."

Assistant to the Ambassador Roy Johnson stood to his feet and came around the corner of the desk. The office was small and the furnishings plain. A steel desk and two vinyl-covered, steel-frame chairs opposite. Two metal file cabinets, a picture of the President on the wall. A framed montage of pictures featuring a rather plain-looking woman and three children was on a small table under a window with a view of the parking lot. By the looks of things, Rashad knew he still had a way to go to get to the top man.

"Mornin'," Johnson drawled, his accent heavy with southeast Texas. He grasped Rashad in a firm handshake. "How ya doin'? Here. Sit down and make yourself at home. It's a little close in here, but we're tight on space. Worse yet, I'm long on paper but short on secretary. Can I offer you some coffee? Tea?"

At least he's not a pretentious bore.

"No, thank you."

"Will that be all, Roy?"

"You got a minute, Ken? Why don't you stick around?"

Ryker nodded. He pulled back one of the vinyl chairs and motioned for Rashad to sit down. He then proceeded to claim the other one for himself, stretching his legs out full length and fold-ing his hands over his stomach. Johnson pushed some papers back and sat on the edge of his desk.

"Now, what is it you have for us, Mr. Raufbar? Mr. Ryker here tells me you've got some news about one of our numerous missing citizens'.'"

Rashad noticed that Johnson had not taken his eyes off him since he stepped into the room. His first impression of the man had been one of mayhem and low-ladder status. Now he wondered if he might have misjudged. Tall, lanky, leather-looking face with high cheekbones. Tie, loose at the neck, top collar button undone. Suit jacket pushed back by his hand, casually tucked into a pants pocket. He looked like a cowboy dressed in city clothes, but Rashad guessed the man knew his way around. CIA even?

"Yes, sir." said Rashad. "I know where Jessica Cain is located."

Johnson's eyes never flickered as they bored into the Jordanian sitting before him. "Jessica Cain?" he repeated slowly.

"Yes, sir. The young girl who was kidnapped in Israel back in September. She's the daughter of the pastor whose group was held hostage and who . . ."

"I know who she is, Mr. Raufbar. And I know that there have been hundreds of 'Jessica sightings' around the world these last two months. None of them panned out. What makes you think that you've seen her?" Johnson got to his feet and walked toward the window.

"Well, actually, sir, I haven't seen her. . . ."

Johnson whirled around, his long, bony finger suddenly inches away from Rashad. "Now, you look here, son. I've got a ton of things to get done today. I personally have handled a dozen of these blasted sightings, and I'm gettin' mighty tired of it. If you haven't seen her, then what are you doing here sayin' that you have seen her?"

Rashad sat calmly, but his heart had kicked into high gear. The man could really be intimidating. "I understand your frustration, Mr. Johnson. While it is true that I have not seen her, I am acquainted with a maid who works in the home where she is being held prisoner."

"What's her name?"

"Madeline."

"Madeline what?"

"I'm sorry. I was introduced to her on Sunday evening and didn't think to ask her last name. I met her at a house church gathering that a friend of mine leads."

"How do you know that she has found Jessica Cain?"

"She identified her from a picture in the *Emirates News*."

"The *Emirates News*? Just where is this maid who thinks she knows Jessica Cain? Are you sayin' she's in the UAE?"

"No, sir, she is not."

"Well, then, where is she?"

"In Iran."

Johnson stared at Rashad, then looked over at Ryker.

"In Iran," he repeated, his voice suddenly flat. "And just where in Iran is she supposed to be?"

"She is being held in the house of Reza Fardusi, a well-to-do businessman who lives in Bandar-é Abbås. She has been there under twenty-four-hour guard for several days."

Johnson glanced over at Ryker who was writing on a yellow pad. Johnson walked back around the desk and dropped into his chair. He folded his hands and looked hard at Rashad.

"You sayin' you're just comin' in from Iran?"

"Yes, I do business there on a regular basis. I work for this company." Rashad laid his business card on the desk. "We're located at Wadi al-Hesa. Phosphate mining. We also have offices here in Amman."

"How do you know the maid is tellin' the truth?" asked Johnson, looking at the card, then tossing it onto the desktop. "Maybe she's just makin' this up. Maybe she's a plant or somethin.' Could be she wants some fame and fortune. Or maybe she's hopin' to lead us on another wild goose chase."

"Goose chase?" asked Rashad, puzzled. "What is goose chase?"

"Never mind," Johnson brushed his question aside with a wave of his hand. "You got the address of this place?"

"Yes, and I have something more."

"Something more? What?"

"This." Rashad reached into his wallet, withdrew a small piece of paper, and handed it to Johnson.

"What's this supposed to be?" asked Johnson, taking it from Rashad.

"It is a note by Jessica's own hand. See? She signed it."

Johnson stared at the crude, penciled message.

"What's it supposed to mean?" he asked, handing it to Ryker.

"We do not know. The maid asked her to write something to her father. We wanted to get something that would clearly identify her beyond any doubt. That is what she wrote. Three words and the letter 'F'. Plus her name."

"You got no idea what it means?"

"None," answered Rashad.

Ryker shrugged. "Could be some kind of coded message. The

maid asked her to write something specifically to her father?"

"Yes."

"Well, then," Johnson said, reaching for the phone. "Ken, let's get a copy of this off to Washington for a handwriting check. They can contact the father and find out if he makes any sense out of this message. Mr. Raufbar, I'd like for you to meet the Ambassador before you leave. I'm sure he'll want to thank you for your help."

With a mumbled, "Good to have met you, Mr. Raufbar," Ryker scooped up Rashad's business card, the yellow pad, and the piece of white paper with its mysterious penciled message and disappeared through the doorway.

Johnson dialed the ambassador's extension and sat back in his chair, listening as it rang.

Rashad glanced at his watch. He was happy for the chance to meet an ambassador of the United States, but he was also anxious about the time. He needed to get to work.

Johnson noticed Rashad's nervous time check and read between the lines. "I'd like to send a letter of appreciation, on embassy stationery, to your employer for what you have done here. I can't actually give him the details, of course. In fact, if this turns out to be Jessica Cain, it will be critical to this young girl's safety that you keep quiet about this. I'm sure you understand?"

Rashad nodded.

"Good. Now, can you give me a name?"

Gratefully, Rashad wrote down the name of his supervisor and handed it to the cowboy in a business suit, busy doing embassy work and who knows what else.

No doubt about it, thought Rashad. *I missed totally on the first impression. He's very sharp indeed.*

TWENTY-NINE

When the phone rang, Esther breathed a sigh of relief and politely excused herself from the two young men at her front door dressed in white shirts and dark ties, explaining that she was not able to spend time today discussing their religious ideas. She closed the door and hurried to pick up the phone.

"Hello?"

"Hello. Is this Mrs. Cain?" The feminine voice at the other end of the line was familiar.

"Yes."

"Mrs. Cain, I'm calling from the State Department in Washington, DC on behalf of Mr. Charles Rodeway. He would like to speak with you and your husband."

"John is not here right now."

"Mrs. Cain, I apologize for this, but I must have verification of your identity. We've been through this routine before."

"Yes, I know. All right."

The questions, now familiar from their last phone conversation with Rodeway, were asked and answered again.

"Thank you for your patience, Mrs. Cain. I'll transfer you to Mr. Rodeway now."

Esther's heart was pounding as she waited and wondered what had prompted this latest call from the State Department.

"Hello, Mrs. Cain. Charles Rodeway here, at the State Department."

"Good morning, Mr. Rodeway."

"Reverend Cain is not available?"

"No, I'm sorry. He's away at the moment and I don't expect him back for at least an hour."

"Okay if we talk for a few minutes?"

"Yes, of course. Have you some new word about our daughter?"

"Actually, that's why I am calling. We do have something and need your help in determining just how authentic this may be. As you know, we've had innumerable 'Jessica sightings' these last few weeks. She's been seen all over the globe and, of course, all the follow-up has proven negative. This one, however, appears to have some possibilities. I hesitate to get your hopes up unduly, Mrs. Cain, but this is something that only you or your husband can verify."

Esther's heart was pounding. Her mouth was dry. Her legs felt suddenly weak and she looked around for a chair to sit on.

"Well, it seems that a young businessman visited our embassy in Amman, Jordan yesterday. He had been to some sort of house church meeting where he was introduced to a maid by his friend who is the leader of the group."

"A Christian church group?" Esther interrupted.

"Yes, I believe so. It seems the maid is working at the home of a well-to-do businessman and thinks that your daughter is being held there against her will."

Esther's head was pounding now. She clenched her fists, resisting the temptation to break down and cry over the news that someone had actually seen Jessica alive.

"Are you sure that it's Jessica?" asked Esther, her voice quivering with excitement.

"No, we're not absolutely sure. The maid apparently identified your daughter from a newspaper picture. This Jordanian businessman, the church leader, and the maid decided to try to get something from the girl that would verify to us that it is really your daughter. The maid managed to slip her some paper, and a pencil hidden in a bowl of breakfast food. Supposedly, she asked the girl to write something to her father. What they got back is a small piece of paper with three words and the letter 'F' written with a pencil."

"What words?"

"The words are, 'I remember Anne F.' That's A-n-n-e. Do they mean anything to you?"

I remember . . .

Esther's mind suddenly froze on the memory of a conversation with John one evening last month out by the pool.

"Mrs. Cain, are you still there? Do those words mean something?"

"Yes, yes, they mean something! When John and Jessica were in Amsterdam, they visited the Anne Frank Haus. That has never been in any of the media coverage. It was unimportant. John told me about their visit and how much it moved Jessica to be there where that poor little girl . . ." Her voice broke.

"I understand, Mrs. Cain. That's terrific. Anne Frank. Isn't that something. That daughter of yours is quite a girl to have so much presence of mind that she could come up with an item she knew only her father would remember. That's what we needed to be certain that this person really is your daughter. I'd also like a handwriting comparison check to be done. Do you have something there that you could fax to me?"

Esther thought for a moment. "There are some papers in her desk from the opening of school this year."

"Good. Send me a couple of sheets that have a sample of her handwriting. Even though we don't have much here, I think there is enough to be able to corroborate that this is your daughter. And we have her signature. That was written out, not printed. Our experts will be able to tell."

"If she is in Jordan, will their government help us get her back?"

There was a pause on the other end of the line. Then, Esther heard Rodeway clear his throat.

"Mrs. Cain, I'm sorry if I've misled you. What I said was that a Jordanian businessman reported this to our embassy in that country. But this man had been traveling. Your daughter is not in Jordan."

Esther's throat began to constrict as she tried pushing back the sudden apprehension. "Then where is she?"

"This man was on a trip to a city called Bandar-é Abbås when this encounter took place."

"Bandar-é Abbås? Where in the world is that?"

"Iran, Mrs. Cain. It would appear that your daughter is definitely in Iran."

NINETY MINUTES LATER, John came in from parking the car in the garage.

"Honey?" he called out.

"In here."

John followed the sound of Esther's voice until he stood in the doorway to Jessica's room. Esther was sitting on the bed, legs folded yoga-style, and a family album of pictures open on her lap. He could tell that she had been crying.

"What's up?" he asked, his senses suddenly spiked with alarm.

"They think they've found Jessica."

"Is she . . ."

"She's alive, and I'm almost certain that it is her."

"Fantastic!" John clapped his hands together. "So why the tears? What's the situation?"

John hastily pulled the chair out from the desk where Jessica most often did her homework. For the next hour they talked excitedly back and forth, their emotions running alternately between dismay and relief. John laughed, wiping his eyes, as he heard about the message, "I remember Anne F."

"Can you believe that?" His voice choked with emotion. "She knew that we would surmise it was her! At least she's still alert. I wonder if they're treating her okay?"

"It sounds as though she's in some wealthy Iranian's home. The maid who brings her food said she is in a locked room, under twenty-four-hour guard. Why don't they just let her go, John? What do they want with a twelve-year-old?"

John did not answer. He did not want to say what had been in the back of his mind during this whole ordeal.

"Does Rodeway know the exact location where she is?"

"I'm not sure. I didn't have presence of mind enough to ask that question. He does want us to send him a sample of Jessica's handwriting. He said that would definitely confirm whether or not it is her."

"I'll give him a call, hon. Don't worry about it. We'll find out. Have you found something she's written?"

Esther nodded. "It's on the desk behind you. Oh, I just know that this is her. What will they do to get her back?"

"I'm not sure. That's something else we'll ask. Where is Rodeway's number?"

"On the counter in the kitchen. By the phone."

"Okay. Let's give him a call."

FRIDAY, 11 NOVEMBER, 1130 LOCAL TIME
WASHINGTON, DC

CHARLES RODEWAY TAPPED his fingers on the arm of the chair. The two men with whom he had been speaking for the last fifteen minutes sat directly across the desk from him.

Donald Furlong was a Washington fixture, with slightly pudgy features, a gray three-piece suit, and a burgundy tie that seemed to be perpetually out of line with the rest of his body. Wire-rimmed glasses sat perched on his nose, the thick lenses reinforcing his waning eyesight. He had spent his entire career at the State Department. There was no finer analyzer of handwriting in the country.

Frank Galinger was also a career man at State and had seen it all at posts in Saudi Arabia, Egypt, Jordan, and before the Revolution, in Iran. He was thin, about six feet, receding hairline with touches of gray, and a face that his friends said could make him Clint Eastwood's brother. In addition to other assignments with the Department, he had been, for most of his diplomatic career, an undercover agent for the CIA.

"That's it then. It really is the girl?" Rodeway looked across the desk at Furlong. "There's no doubt about it?"

"Absolutely none," Furlong answered. "I'm ninety-nine, point nine percent sure on this one. It would have helped to have a little more from the subject to compare with the samples her parents sent, but I'm positive as it is. It's the girl."

Rodeway pressed his fingers together, back and forth, like a spider doing pushups on a mirror. "What's to be done, then?"

Galinger popped some gum in his mouth. He hated the no smoking rule that had been adopted throughout the State Department Building. He was an inveterate smoker, with a habit that was longer in tenure than his diplomatic career. He supposed all the warnings were accurate, but life was too intense not to have some form of nervous release. Since the ban on smoking had gone into effect, however, he'd been thinking about giving it up. Again. That's about as far as it ever went with Galinger.

"Well, Charlie, we've got no diplomatic relations. No embassy. Everything we do in there has to go through the Austrians or the Australians. We don't know the exact relationship that exists between 'official' Iran and these misbegotten malcontents, but we have to assume some sort of connection. The group that took her claims to be the Palestinian Islamic Jihad. We know that they have financial aid coming in from Hizballah sources. They've been trained in terrorist tactics by the Iranian Revolutionary Guards, up in the Bekaa Valley in Lebanon. The whole thing is a rat's nest. No, it's worse than that. It's a hive of killer bees, and if we get involved, our chances of being stung really bad are higher than the boss is going to want to take."

"You don't think he'll want to take action then?" asked Rodeway.

"Oh, sure, he'll *want* to take action, but will he approve our sending in Special Forces to get her out? Come on, Charlie. I know it's been a big deal in the media and all, but what we've got here is one little kid. Do you think he's going to chance another Desert Storm showdown for one child? You've seen the polls. So has the boss. He's hoping things bottom out soon or his chances of a second term are nil. You think he'll risk another Iran-Contra scandal by dealing under the table with that bunch of bandits? Forget it."

"Then what?"

"You've got two choices. One, send in a team of our best 'players' to pull her out. That is, if you're sure you know where she is. It'll take a chunk of money to pull it off. We could drop the boys from one of our carriers. I don't know who's out there, but it's easy to find out. When you're ready, put them in small boats, run them up to shore, arrange transportation to get them from the beach to the target, be willing to take out all opposition, get the girl and drive back to the beach, hope the boats haven't been discovered and scuttled, jump in, run back out to sea, and get picked up by the Navy. A simple life and death operation with very little chance of succeeding, and only a dozen or so of our best men at risk.

"Or, two, you do the prudent thing and quietly walk away."

"Walk away? You can't be serious. We can't just leave her there!"

"You got another idea?"

The room grew heavy with silence.

Galinger pushed himself up out of the chair and moved to the door. "You've got my recommendations, and you know the one I favor. You can quote me on that."

Rodeway did not respond.

Galinger opened the door and disappeared down the hall.

Furlong sighed and got to his feet.

"If there's nothing else, Charlie, I'll be going."

Rodeway waved him off with a hand motion.

"Thanks, Don. As usual, you've been a big help."

Furlong paused at the door and looked back.

"Sorry, man. Hate to leave you with it looking like it does."

"Goes with the turf," Rodeway smiled briefly. "See you around."

Furlong stepped into the hall and disappeared in the opposite direction from Galinger.

Alone, Rodeway turned his chair around so that he could look out the window. He could feel a little girl's future slipping through his fingers. Galinger was right. This was a political football that had much too much risk attached to it. Politics aside, the international community would erupt in protest if such a raid were approved by the President. The options would be presented to the Secretary, but he already knew what answer would be forthcoming.

Rodeway began laying out the way this could be handled with the Cain family, as well as anyone else who might eventually become involved. He had to develop a plan to cover the decision with the appearance that "we're doing everything possible to find and rescue Jessica Cain from her captors."

It wouldn't be easy, but it had been done before. The hardest part would be looking his own kid in the face after determining to waste someone else's child for "the nation's good."

It's a terrible way to run a country!

"It's nice to be able to share some good news with you, since you've both been through such a great deal these last couple of months." Charles Rodeway's voice carried a mollifying tone, as though he were trying to soothe a delicate situation. "The handwriting on the note definitely matches the samples that you sent to us. I'm sorry it has taken so long to get back to you, but we wanted to be sure."

"Thank you," John answered. "We were already positive that it was Jessica who wrote that note, but we're very grateful for this extra confirmation."

John could hear muffled sounds over the extension phone in their bedroom. He knew it was Esther, softly crying. His own eyes were puddling over the emotional news that Jessica really was out there somewhere, trying to communicate to her parents that she was still alive.

"So what happens now?" he asked.

"Well, Reverend Cain, it's Monday. Some of the key people we need to confer with have been outside the Beltway for the weekend. Once they get back, we'll bring them up to date and go from there. It's possible we won't know what option is best until sometime later in the week."

An alarm went off inside John's head.

"Wait a minute, Mr. Rodeway. Are you saying that no one is going to work on this until later in the week? This is our daughter we're talking about. This is a helpless, twelve-year-old American who's being held against her will by some international thugs. Who knows what's going on with her right now?"

"Of course, of course," Rodeway's appeasing tone continued. "You are absolutely right. I didn't mean to imply that we would not be working on this every single day. I've already been in touch with some key people in the Department, and beyond. The Secretary has been informed, but it will take some time to determine the proper course of action."

"How much time?" John persisted.

"As I said a moment ago, we should have determined our best options and have a strategy in place, I would think, by Friday, if not before."

"Will you be in touch with the Iranian government before then?"

A slight pause was noticeable.

"That's one of the problems in this case," Rodeway answered. "We're unsure as to whether or not there are any direct or indirect connections here between your daughter's abduction and 'official' Iran."

"You mean that Iran's leaders may be behind this?" John asked incredulously. "I can't believe that rational people would do such a thing as this."

"As you say, the emphasis should be on the word 'may,' " Rodeway answered. "The Iranians are a difficult crowd to deal with on a good day, and we have no way of knowing what their connection may be. Furthermore, we certainly don't want to do anything to jeopardize your daughter's situation. If their government is involved, as soon as they realize that we know her whereabouts, they'll deny any knowledge, quietly move her, and we'll be back to square one."

A chill gripped John at the thought. What Rodeway was saying made sense. It would be devastating to know where she was being held, only to have her disappear once again.

"Okay," he said, finally. "Honey, do you have any questions for Mr. Rodeway?"

"No," her voice was husky. "We appreciate all that you are doing. It's just this feeling of helplessness. I want my baby back."

"We're working very hard to make that happen, Mrs. Cain. I will be back to you later in the week, just as soon as I have something further to report. In the meantime, it is imperative that this be kept confidential. If the media gets hold of what we know, then all bets are off."

"We understand," replied John.

"Well, that's it for now, folks. I'll be in touch."

"Thanks again, Mr. Rodeway. We are deeply grateful to you and all who are working with you to get Jessica back home."

"I speak for all of us, Reverend and Mrs. Cain, when I say, 'You are most welcome.' "

"Good-bye, then."

"Good-bye. Send up a prayer for us."

"We will."

RODEWAY PUNCHED THE SPEAKER BUTTON on the desk phone. It was suddenly very quiet in his office. Leaning back in his chair, he looked at the picture of his wife and son on his desk, and tried to imagine how the Cains must be feeling right now. What if it were Samuel Charles Rodeway, Jr. out there somewhere, instead of Jessica Cain? He rubbed the back of his neck to relieve the tension.

With a heavy sigh, he put the red folder marked CAIN, JESSICA into the file drawer and locked it. Knowing what he knew was depressing. Trying to assuage the parents in this situation was unsatisfying, to say the least. He'd been given his assignment the day before, but, having completed the first stage still did not make it any better.

"Tell the parents whatever you have to in order to give them hope and keep them quiet. They will need to believe that we're on top of this and that we're going to get her back. Buy a few days of time. Meanwhile, contact the Australians over there and see if they can help, even though we already know the answer they will give us. Beyond that, there's not much. It's probably a lost cause and we've got too many other things on our plate right now to start World War III over a kid who was in the wrong place at the wrong time. But, do what you can."

Rodeway knew what all that meant.

"It's an impossible situation and too far down the list of world events in terms of importance. Cover our backsides on this one, Rodeway. Do all the right things and document what you do. If anyone takes a fall on this, it better be the Iranians, not us."

Simply put, the girl is expendable.

ESTHER DABBED AT HER EYES with a tissue as she came out of the bedroom. John put his arms around her and held her close, gathering strength from feeling her there. His thoughts were leapfrogging over dirt paths, stone walls, rooftops, and walls with chains attached.

What has our little girl been through? What is happening to her right now? Is it anything like I went through in Jerusalem? These people are killers. They will stop at nothing to reach their objectives. They must have taken her on the spur of the moment, so why are they going to such great lengths to keep her? Why didn't they just do away with her?

"What, honey?"

"What?" John looked down at Esther.

"What did you say?"

John had been so deep in thought that he suddenly realized he must have spoken out loud. "I guess I was just . . . wondering about Jessica . . . and what they hope to gain by holding her hostage."

Esther was silent as she slipped out of John's arms and walked over to the window. He was surprised to hear her ask the same question that was in his mind. "Do you really think the State Department is going to do anything to help get her back?"

Now, it was John's turn to be silent. He moved next to Esther and placed his arm over her shoulder.

"I don't know," he answered. "I wish I could be sure, but I don't know. Rodeway sounded evasive, didn't he? Did you pick up on his conciliatory tone? I began to feel as though he was trying to give us hope, without committing to anything else. Did he come across to you that way?"

Esther nodded her head and then turned to look up at John.

"We've got to do something," she exclaimed, the strain of her emotions seeping through the spoken words.

The phone started ringing again.

John went to answer it, thinking perhaps Rodeway was calling back.

"Hello."

"Hello there, Reverend Cain. I know you told me to call you John, and I'm workin' on that. Maybe I could call you Father John or Pope John for starters and work my way up from there."

"Hello, Jim," John responded, recognizing the adopted Mainer accent of Jim Brainard. "Where in the world are you?"

"The only place in the world that anyone should ever be, of course. Down here in God's country, listenin' to the wind blow and watchin' the clouds roll in over the bay. I tell you, the white-caps are sittin' up on a deep blue sea and the sky is dark and ominous. As long as I can watch it all from my window, without havin' to venture outdoors too much, it's as cozy as a corner in heaven."

Esther looked at John questioningly. John mouthed back the words, "Jim Brainard, Booth Bay."

"So, anyway, I got to thinkin' about you folk out there in sunny California, and thought I'd give you a call." John listened as the tone of his voice changed to one of concern. "Any word on Jessica yet?"

"Well, nothing I can say over the phone, Jim, but we're optimistic."

There was a long pause and John could sense the man on the other end of the line trying to interpret what had been said as well as what was being left unspoken.

"Well . . . that's good, Reverend Cain."

"The name is John, and, if you don't start using it, I'm going to quit thinking of you as my favorite Roman Catholic friend."

"All right, *John*, I can probably get used to callin' the Reverend Cain by his first name 'bout as quick as I can get used to bein' around my first Protestant pastor. Although, if it wasn't for that beautiful young thing you married, I don't know if I'd waste my time on you."

In September Jim Brainard had come out to California, while John was still in Israel, in order to be with the Cain family. He had done it, he said, having sensed that it was what "God wanted me to do," a kind of spiritual leading that this Roman Catholic layman found both strange and exhilarating. His follow-through on that "leading" had resulted in a strong, mutual admiration between the two men.

Though Esther had been in the hospital during his visit, she too had grown fond of this crusty, yet warmhearted New England transplant from Philadelphia. His unabashed openness about himself and his late wife, Middie, was a gift wrapped in candor. He confessed to them both that he had not been able to talk about things so personal to anyone else since Middie's death.

Jeremy had hit it off with Jim Brainard almost immediately. He accepted him as another grandfather figure in his life. Jim took him on, as he had so many others in his lifetime, just as he would his own flesh-and-blood grandson.

And, now, this phone call.

"Well, I'm looking at her right now, Jim, and I can tell you that she's just as pretty as ever. Before I forget it, thanks for the card and letter too."

Since Jim's return to the East, a card and a letter had followed up his California visit.

"It was good to hear from you and I apologize for not writing. I've been sending out lots of letters, but not so many to my friends, I guess."

"I'm sure. I see Jessica's picture on TV all the way back here. I know that this thing is runnin' you both ragged. That's part of the reason I felt led to call."

"I guess I don't quite follow," answered John.

"What I mean is that in a few days, Thanksgivin' is comin' around again. Have you thought of that? No. I didn't think so. Look, how's about you and the family jumpin' on a plane and flyin' back to Boston? I'll come get you and we can spend Thanksgivin' at my place in Booth Bay. What do you say?"

"I'd say that was a very kind offer, Jim. To be honest, we haven't given Thanksgiving a lot of thought. Just a minute." John put his hand over the phone.

"Jim Brainard wants to know if we will spend Thanksgiving at his guest house in Booth Bay."

"What? Oh, goodness, how can we possibly . . . I mean . . . there's so many loose ends . . . what about . . ."

"Listen, Jim, as you can imagine, we're standing here in total shock over the idea. We'd be honored to come spend Thanksgiving with you, but we've been so focused on getting Jessica back that we've thought of little else."

"All the more reason for you to come. You need a respite. It ain't Florida, mind you, but there's somethin' about walkin' in a Coastal Maine breeze that clears the mind and soul. Just sorta gets in under your jacket and makes you glad to be alive. You folks need a few days of that kind of livin' so's you can get on with whatever you're doin' and bring that little gal of yours back home."

John stood there, listening, not knowing exactly what to say.

"I take that silence to be a resounding yes to my invitation," Jim went on. "I knew you'd want to do this, so I've already made reservations on United from San Francisco to Boston. You know, Thanksgiving is the busiest time of the year for travel, so I didn't think we could wait for you to make up your mind. I've got the seats, three of 'em. You can pick your tickets up at SFO. They're all paid for. Room and board is on me."

"No, Jim, wait. You can't possibly do that."

"Don't need no preacher tellin' me what I can or can't do, now, do I? I've already gone and done it anyway, so pack up some duds and I'll see you on Wednesday evening in Boston. Your plane leaves at ten-thirty that morning."

"Jim, I don't know quite what to say. . . ."

"Good. It's nice to know a preacher who's at a loss for words. Aren't many around these days. Well, I can't sit here and jaw with you all day. See you next week."

"Okay, Jim, we'll see you. And, thanks," John said, belatedly, as he heard the phone line go dead.

John hung up the phone and turned to Esther.

"How can we just up and leave?" Esther questioned, arms folded across her chest. "What if there is further word about Jessica?"

"We'll let Rodeway know the number. The church too. Hon, I think it's a good idea. We've been at this nonstop since the day I got home from Israel. Here's an opportunity for our first break. He has already bought the tickets and intends to meet us in Boston."

"When will we come back?"

"I didn't think to ask, but we can probably come back on Sunday or Monday, depending on traffic. Maybe he's already taken care of that too."

Esther let her arms fall to her sides and she smiled weakly. "I guess I'm outnumbered. Actually, it does sound pretty good. I've never been to Maine. It sounds sort of 'lobster and clam bake-ish,' doesn't it?"

"It does, and that makes three of us who've not been to Maine. Besides," he added, his voice pensive, "we'll be that much closer to Jessica, five or six hours in fact."

Esther nodded as she began thinking about what they would need to pack for the trip.

FROM THE SITTING ROOM WINDOW, his hand still resting on the phone, Grandpa Brainard looked south and east across the bay. The whitecaps were in earnest now, and no vessels of any shape or size could be seen plying the harbor's rough waters. Autumn colors were all but gone, with only a few faded specks of red and gold dotting the landscape along the far shoreline.

Winter is coming. In more ways than one.

He was one of the strange ones who lived along this wild stretch of New England coastline. He didn't mind the rain, wind, sleet, and snow that came with the extended winters of Maine. Of course, he didn't have to work outside in the elements, either.

Sitting here, however, high atop McKnown Hill, he was in the best of all worlds. One that he and Middie had made for themselves. The tourist season was over. Hill House was empty, except for himself. Memories of Thanksgivings that had come and gone since Middie died were conspicuous with the bleakness that followed her death. Last year had been better. Rosa and Manuel Posadas had invited him to join them and their two boys for Thanksgiving dinner. He had accepted and it was still a warm recollection. Rosa had served a traditional American Thanksgiving dinner with special Puerto Rican and Mexican touches that revealed pride in their native heritages.

Yet, even with the memory of that cheery interval, a deep-seated hurt churned inside Grandpa Brainard over what those evil men had done to Rosa. He pressed his eyes shut to drive away the dark thoughts. She did not deserve to die like that. No one did. And to think that the same ruthless man who had carried out this ghastly deed now had John and Esther Cain's little daughter was an anguish almost more than he could bear. He would give anything to get his hands on the one who had masterminded it all. A man, strangely enough, whom he knew.

Marwan Dosha.

His eyes grew moist and he quickly blinked away the tears.

As soon as he had confirmed that the Cains were coming, he telephoned Manuel and invited him and the boys to join them. Manuel thanked him profusely, but said that he was taking the boys back to New York City to visit his and Rosa's parents.

So, it would be the Cain family, or what remained of it, who would join him for the holiday. The more he thought about it, the more he let himself gain energy from the idea that he was not merely filling in his own emotional void. With a rush of new-found gladness, he was giving what he could to a family that was needier than many, and doing it in a most unique way. He imagined that the Cains had given themselves to others in ways past counting, without ever hoping to receive anything in return. Now, God was permitting him to be part of a payback plan to these faithful shepherds who were living with an overwhelming loss. He hadn't felt this good about Thanksgiving since . . . well, since Middie was here.

Three months ago, Grandpa Brainard and the Cains had not known of one another. Yet, both had suffered through deep depression over the loss of loved ones. Independent of each other they had struggled and, for the most part, had overcome. Their victories were clearly orchestrated by a Bigger Hand than any of them possessed. He saw that so very clearly. Wouldn't it be wonderful if Middie could be here now to appreciate how much he had grown in his faith these last few months?

Every day, he read his Bible, actually Middie's. Jim thought back to the passage he had read two days earlier from the twelfth chapter of Romans. He smiled, thinking that he had never before gotten that far in reading the New Testament. In late September after returning home from California, he had begun in Matthew and was now in Paul's first letter to the Corinthians. It had been on Saturday, however, that he paused at one of the "holy places," as he liked to call them. It had the touch of Middie's telltale yellow marker on it, with two separate phrases further underlined with a pen:

> Love must be sincere. Hate what is evil; cling to what is good. <u>Be devoted to one another in brotherly love.</u> . . . Be joyful in hope, patient in affliction, faithful in prayer. <u>Share with God's people who are in need. Practice hospitality.</u>

He found great pleasure in turning a page and finding a verse that she had marked with her own hand, as something especially precious to her. Wherever Middie had added an "underline" emphasis, Jim figured it must really have been important to her. He would linger over such "holy places" in an attempt to discover what it might have been that had made that verse so special.

Sometimes, he knew. Like this past Saturday, when he read about hospitality. He knew he was supposed to invite the Cains for the Thanksgiving holiday and take care of their round-trip flight expense. The idea had hit him full force. Just like the time he knew that he was supposed to fly to California to be with Esther Cain, a stranger hovering between life and death in a hospital. Another victim of Marwan Dosha.

Sometimes, he knew. At other times, he could only wonder at what a specific Bible verse might have meant to Middie.

To a handful of such passages, Jim had attached bright yellow flags on the pages to remind him to ask his new preacher friend about them. But, even though he didn't fully understand their meaning, he always found those "holy places" to be special points of meeting with God.

And, strangely enough, with Middie too.

Jim reached over and picked up the Bible from the lamp table by his chair. He opened it to First Corinthians and settled back to see what other wonders he might discover before Thanksgiving rolled around.

THURSDAY, 17 NOVEMBER, 0835 LOCAL TIME
BANDAR-E ABBÁS, IRAN

THE SILENCE WAS BECOMING INTOLERABLE. Several days had come and gone since anyone had spoken to her.

Not since that old man talked with me. The guards don't say anything. They won't let me talk to the maid. I can't leave the room except to go down the hall to the bathroom. I have nothing to read . . . except this.

Jessica reached under the mattress and pulled out the tiny roll of paper containing the first forty-three verses of Mark's Gospel. These verses had become a pathway to the familiar for her. She had read them over and over so many times that she could quote large sections by heart.

The ministry of John the Baptist. The first eight verses. She tried to imagine what he must have looked and sounded like. *I'll bet the people back home would have a hard time relating to this guy, if he showed up to preach.*

The baptism of Jesus, verses nine through eleven. Jessica didn't really understand why Jesus had been baptized. *We are baptized to show our faith in Jesus and that He has forgiven our sins. So, why baptize the Son of God? I remember Daddy saying that He wanted to be an example for all His followers.*

Jessica thought about her baptism. She remembered being both nervous and excited as she donned the white robe worn by all baptism candidates at Calvary Church. Then, when she walked down the steps and into the tepid water, there was her dad waiting for her. He had this really big smile. He was obviously happy that she was there. She'd been happy he was there too. There was something comforting, reassuring, about having her father there. She forgot about in the congregation witnessing this significant moment.

She could always count on her dad being there. That is, until now. Now, there was no way for him to rescue her. Unless . . .

Unless that maid managed to get my note out.

After the yogurt incident, the guard had insisted that the Azari woman arrange for a maid other than the one whose "stupid incompetence is intolerable." Jessica's heart sank as she overheard them arguing in the hall. The conversation was in Farsi, making it impossible for her to understand what they were saying. At first, she was fearful they might have found the note, but it was soon apparent that that was not the case. That evening, however, a different maid served her meal.

How did the first one know who I was? If only I could talk to someone!

The temptation of Jesus. Just two verses, but Jessica remembered the whole story from Sunday School. *He was tested three times by Satan. It seems strange to imagine Jesus being tempted. After all, He is God, isn't He? I mean, if He had given in to temptation and become discouraged, He'd never have been able to forgive my sins, or anybody else's for that matter. Daddy said Jesus was tempted in every possible way. In fact, he made me memorize Hebrews 4:15: "For we do not have a high priest who is unable to sympathize with our weaknesses, but we have One who has been tempted in every way, just as we are, yet was without sin." I used to think memorizing was such a pain. Now, I wish I'd done more.*

I wonder if Jesus was ever this lonely and this far away from home? Jessica stared at the bare wall. *Of course, He was. How far is earth from heaven?*

The call of Peter and Andrew. Five more verses. *It happened right there in Capernaum. We were at Peter's house. These guys seem more real than ever since our visit to Galilee. They left their fishing business and followed Him. Being there in person really makes a big difference. I can actually picture Jesus calling them, and I can see them leaving their nets and everything.*

Jesus cast out demons in Capernaum. Verses twenty-one through twenty-eight. *I'll bet that was a sight. It would have been neat to watch! There's one outside my door right now that I'd like to see Him take care of.*

Simon's mother-in-law healed of sickness. Three more verses. *All it took was for Jesus to touch her and, before you knew it, she was up and serving them. Awesome. Totally.*

More demons and devils. *I wonder if there's any difference, or if they're all the same.* A preaching tour in Galilee. *Verse thirty-five is interesting—kind of where I'm at right now. "And in the morning, rising up a great while before day, He went out, and departed into a solitary place, and there prayed." I guess I'm learning about solitary places, huh? Being alone this much is no fun.*

A leper healed, verses forty through forty-three. That's where her precious page ended . . . *"And He straitly charged him, and forthwith sent him away; . . . " I wonder what the "charge" was?*

She felt a growing skepticism about whether she would ever find out. Those verses were on the next page, that she didn't have. Her mysterious friend had not been back. *Where is she? I wish I could see her . . . talk to her . . . O God, I wish I could talk to her.*

Suddenly furious and angry with the whole circumstance, she picked up her shoe and threw it at the door. It hit with a thud.

A moment later, the door was opened and the head of the guard poked through the opening. Seeing the shoe, she grinned and shut the door again.

Jessica was certain that the woman believed they were getting to her.

Well, she's right!

THIRTY-ONE

Line upon line of city lights danced with seductive brilliance against the dark earth backdrop, announcing the star of the show as it dropped out of the sky. The crescendo sound of rubber crushing against cement marked the grand finale of another mysterious tale of human beings in flight. The press of bodies against safety belts as the huge jet slowed confirmed that the lights would go up any moment and the doors would open, permitting the audience to leave. The show was over.

This morning, fog had shrouded San Francisco in a gossamer illusion of make-believe, permitting only the tips of the tallest buildings and the twin towers of the Golden Gate Bridge to poke their way through. This evening, however, the rain that fell on Boston was cold, wet reality.

Minutes later, in the terminal, John and Jeremy shook hands and hugged Jim Brainard as they waited at the restroom door for Esther. When she reappeared, Jim greeted her with polite tenderness.

"How are you, Mrs. Cain?" he asked, taking her gently by the hand.

"I'm fine, Jim." She smiled and stepped up to him with a warm hug.

"Your wounds are all healed?" he asked, concern in his voice. There was a twinkle in his eye as he stood back to look at her.

"Completely."

"Oh, that's wonderful. You really do look ravishing."

"Well, thank you," Esther responded laughingly. "I feel anything but ravishing after flying for the last five hours, but I believe your compliment is removing my travel creases even as we speak."

"Splendid," said Jim, putting his arm around Jeremy's shoulder. "Come on, Jeremy. Let's go gather up your luggage and get on the road. We've got about two and a half hours of driving ahead, maybe a little longer in this weather, and then we'll be home."

"Great," Jeremy said enthusiastically.

"Ever been here before?"

"No, it's my first time."

"Well, this is God's country, son. Not like that swarming gaggle of surfers and freeway fanatics you put up with in California."

"Wait a minute," Jeremy protested. "California's not so bad."

"Ah, you've been brainwashed, son. You've got sand between your ears. Right here is the best place for livin' in the whole world. Just wait'll you see it tomorrow. You won't want to go home. Fact is, I been thinkin' 'bout you, after you get out of school next spring. If you don't have a job, I could use some help durin' tourist season."

"Really?"

"Yup. Ever painted much?"

"I helped Dad do our house the summer before last. I've painted my room too."

"Great. With that kind of experience and a couple of good references, I might be able to keep you busy. That is, if your mom and dad approved."

Jeremy glanced back at John with boyish enthusiasm. The possibility of spending an entire summer in New England before starting college was great! New people. New places. It appealed to his adventurous spirit.

"That's a nice prospect, son," John said, winking at Esther. "Let's give it some thought."

Twenty minutes later, luggage stored safely in the trunk of Jim's Buick, they drove out of the parking area and made their way toward Interstate 95.

ONCE ON I-95, JIM DROVE AT the speed limit most of the time, though a sudden heavy downpour caused him to slow considerably as they crossed from Massachusetts into New Hampshire.

"Welcome to winter's eve in New England, folks," Jim chuckled, as he turned the windshield wipers to full speed. "Just be thankful that this is rain and not snow."

Another severe squall hammered their vehicle between Portland and Freeport. Eventually, they left the turnpike and crossed over the Kennebec River. Turning onto US 1, they made their way through Wiscasset and the dark countryside beyond.

In the backseat, Esther's head rested on John's shoulder. Small talk had lapsed while Jim concentrated on the road and the others dozed, weary from the day's travel. At last, leaving Highway 1, the Buick turned onto Route 27 for the final leg.

Two hours and twenty minutes after leaving Logan Airport, Jim eased the Buick along Booth Bay's dark, narrow streets. There were few lights in the windows at this hour, and even fewer traffic lights. His passengers were awake and peering out the side windows, trying to glimpse some of the character of this historic fishing village. The darkness held its secrets well, however, revealing little of its mystical seaside charm.

Five minutes later, collars up and shoulders hunched over, the three men lifted luggage from the car's trunk while Esther ran for the cover of the front porch. The others followed after her, as Jim fumbled for the key and then pressed it into the lock. As the door opened, wind chimes signaled their entrance. Reaching in, he flipped on a light switch. Eager to get out of the chilly wind and rain, the four pushed their way inside.

Slipping out of her coat, Esther looked around the spacious parlor, its hardwood floors spreading out beneath a large oriental rug. At the near side, a rosewood grandfather clock stood like a sentinel at the bottom of the staircase. Across the room a large, cherrywood desk served as the place for registering guests during the season. In between was a fireplace, together with two high-back leather chairs and a coffee table covered with magazines. A lamp and breakfast table surrounded with padded straight-back chairs occupied a place in front of the double windows. Pictures of fishing boats and quaint villages accented the walls.

"What a lovely home, Jim," exclaimed Esther, a look of delight on her face. "It is truly exquisite."

Jim smiled as he walked across the room to the kitchen. "The credit goes to Middie. I've just tried to keep it pretty well like she left it. Added a couple of pictures, but that's about it. Let me put on some tea water, and then I'll show you to your rooms. We're the only ones here, so you've got the run of the place. A cup of hot tea and then a good night's rest. Sleep in tomorrow, if you like. I'll set a few things out and make some coffee in the morning. You can get up when you want to."

"Please, Jim," Esther replied, "there's no need for you to wait on us. It's enough that we're here to enjoy this weekend with you."

"It's what I do, my dear," Jim said, leading the way to the stairs. "Come on, now, let me show you where you'll be makin' your bed for the next few nights."

ESTHER WAS THE FIRST TO AWAKEN. The comforter had been a welcome sight the night before, and had made the large bed cozy and warm. Rising up far enough to see out the window, she realized that the dawning of a new day had already come and gone. She had slept soundly and felt amazingly rested.

New England must agree with me.

Outside, the rain had stopped and dark clouds pushed along by the wind moved swiftly across the horizon. Quietly, she got out of bed, pulled an emerald green silk robe over her pajamas, and went to the window. The view was breathtaking.

Several boats were tied up at the docks near the bottom of the hill. A man was walking across the deck of a single-masted sailboat, evidently making last-minute preparations for winter. Straightaway, a deep blue sea wearing hundreds of whitecaps stretched toward the horizon. On either side of the harbor, the rocky, tree-lined, coastal rim furnished a protective barrier from the open sea.

Minutes passed as Esther stood quietly, her thoughts suspended somewhere beyond the clouds. Hearing a sound behind her, she turned to see that John was awake. Hands behind his head, he was looking across to where she stood at the window.

"It's beautiful, John," she announced with relish. "Come here and see."

"You're beautiful," he answered with a sleepy smile, "and I can see from here just fine."

"You've got a one-track mind."

"And you've got the cutest caboose on the track."

Esther moved around to the opposite side of the bed, picked up a pillow, and threw it at John.

"You're bad," she said, with a flirtatious look.

He stopped its flight in mid-air with one hand and, with the other, reached out and pulled her down on the bed. They wrestled playfully, laughing as the bed covers flew. John ducked as Esther flung the pillow at him again. An instant later, he was pinned on his back, with Esther extended above him, looking down. The sounds of their laughter quieted. Her expression was one of confident assurance, a tempting brew of coyness and innocence, seductiveness and desire. Slowly, she lowered herself toward him.

Their lips brushed lightly, then again, more passionately.

"I love you, my darling."

"I love you too."

Another kiss. Even the room's early morning chill felt provocative. Breathlessly, they kissed again, delighting themselves in the stirring, the delicious yearning and desire they were feeling for each other.

JIM WAS BUSY PREPARING VEGETABLES in the kitchen sink when Esther appeared in the doorway.

"Good mornin'," he called out, observing the pleasing blush on her cheeks. "You're lookin' mighty pert and healthy this mornin', dear lady."

Esther felt her face warm as she stood there, thinking back over the last hour, but Jim's attention was already back with the vegetables.

"Sleep well?"

"Like a stone," she replied. "That bed is so comfortable and the room is absolutely marvelous. Middie's decorating abilities, I presume?"

"Naturally. You don't think an old codger like me could do decoratin' like that, do you? My Middie made it an art form."

"She must have been quite a woman."

"Yup, that she was. A lot like you, I imagine. She was a beauty. Brains too. Everybody who knew her loved her," he said, a bit wistfully, as he looked up from his task. "Especially me."

An unforeseen vulnerableness bared something between them.

Esther felt it and was surprised. The satisfying glow of love still lay warm on her body. Somehow, Jim could feel it in her, and it had awakened in him a wistful longing for his lover.

There was much about this man that surprised her. He could have been her father. At first look, he appeared gruff and distant. His silver-gray hair poked unruly strands in all directions. His big, well scrubbed hands made the carrots he was peeling look tiny by comparison. Jim's face had been lined by the years and his brown eyes were the sleepy, sad eyes of an old dog. But when he smiled, she knew why he was called "Grandpa." Everything about him lit up. His gruffness was a big ruse. This was a face for children to trust and to play and to laugh with. Adults too, for that matter.

"I wish I could have known her."

Jim moved the carrots to one side and looked up.

"She would have liked you."

Esther walked over next to the sink.

"I'll bet that if she were here, she'd be telling me what to do next to help get dinner going."

Jim smiled.

"Right you are. Well, how good are you at turkey stuffin'?"

"If you've got the stuff, I'm great at it."

"Good, because the first and last time I tried it, it tasted an awful lot like wet sawdust."

THE TABLE NORMALLY USED FOR B&B GUESTS at breakfast was opened up and extra leaves put in place. A beautiful tablecloth with matching napkins was from Jim and Middie's one trip to Europe. Plates, glasses, cups, forks. The perfectly browned turkey was presented at the center of the table, surrounded by mashed potatoes, brown gravy, carrots and beans, cranberries, and apple cider. Pumpkin pie cooled on the cherrywood desk. More than enough. The smell of wood burning in the fireplace. Curtains pulled back to present a yard that was still green and a glorious seascape stretching to the horizon. The perfect Thanksgiving dinner.

Jim helped Esther with her chair. Then, the men sat down, John to her right and Jeremy, a table's width away.

"Let's hold hands and pray," said Jim, reaching out for Esther and Jeremy. "I know it's usually your job to do the prayin', John, but I guess I'd like to do it today, if that's all right."

"It's not just 'all right.' I was hoping you would lead us."

The others bowed their heads, while Jim tilted his slightly upward and closed his eyes. "God, we're mighty grateful that You've let us be here today, thanks to those good pilgrim folk that got this whole great land of ours goin'. We're mighty appreciative of their sacrifices, and we're askin' for Your help in keepin' this country strong.

"I'd have to say, too, that it feels awfully good havin' my new friends here with me. God, You know these folks have been through a lot lately. We admire 'em for it, but it's got to take its toll and so my prayer is that You will bless this good family. Refresh their spirits. And, wherever their precious daughter is right now, I want You to watch over her. Keep her safe, and make some plans for gettin' her home soon.

"We're thinkin' 'bout little Jenny and my Middie today too. 'Course we know they're up there with You, but we'd still appreciate Your checkin' in on 'em today, this bein' Thanksgivin' and all. And we'll thank You for that favor in advance. Now, please, bless this food to the nourishment of our bodies. Amen."

A murmur of "Amens" could be heard as Jim opened his eyes and glanced around the table. Esther had produced a tissue to wipe the tears that ran freely down her cheeks. John continued to stare at his plate, apparently not trusting himself to speak. Even Jeremy looked as though he was swallowing back a wave of emotion that kept trying to break out.

"Now, I want to make somethin' clear," Jim said, waiting until each of the others were looking his way. "You all have every right to shed tears while you're here. I hope you can cry out all the bitterness and the anger that you must be feelin'. In fact, I even do a little cryin' once in a while. We've all suffered some powerful blows lately. You lost your little Jenny in the accident. Now your other girl is bein' held captive somewhere. You've been through a lot.

"My Middie's gone. I've got no family close by. We couldn't have children, which means no grandchildren, so I've just up and adopted whoever looked like they needed a grandpa. Still, it seems like my lonely times get to be pretty long stretches. God is good, though. That's one thing I'm findin' out for sure lately. It may not look like He's workin' much, but He is. So, let's be thankful for all the good things we have goin' for us and stop dwellin' on the bad."

"A good idea," John agreed.

Esther smiled and patted Jim's big hand. "You're not just good *to* us, Jim. You are good *for* us."

Jim's face lit up as he cleared his throat.

"Jeremy!"

Jim "Grandpa" Brainard glowered at him, his countenance full of mock sternness. "Are you goin' to start passin' somethin' before it freezes over? Or are you just plannin' to sit there and starve to death?"

Laughter filled the air as food began circling the table.

Esther's gaze went to the window. It was starting to rain.

THOUSANDS OF MILES EAST of Booth Bay, the darkness of night had settled outside the small window with the narrow crack. A bowl and a spoon rested on a tray, on the floor beside the cot.

Thanksgiving Day's dinner had consisted of åbgusht, a thick brew of potato chunks, fatty meat, and lentils mashed in a bowl, served with some thick, oval-shaped sangak bread, and a glass of strong tea. It had barely been touched.

There was no laughter in this room. Its sole occupant lay curled in fetal fashion, facing a blank wall.

No pumpkin pie cooled nearby. Such delicacies were too painful to even think about.

This room was drenched in emptiness. So was the motionless form huddled on the bed.

No homey smell of logs burning in a fireplace here. Nothing at all. The last flicker of hope had gone out.

Jessica Lee Cain had given up.

The grandfather clock finished striking five just as the last dish was put away. While they were cleaning up, Esther had discovered an espresso maker in the kitchen. Her offer to make lattés all around had received resounding affirmation from the male contingent who were now seated contentedly in front of the fireplace.

After serving the hot drinks, she dropped onto the rug and leaned back against John's legs, watching the fire's warm glow.

A low-pitched moan reverberated through the house as nature's forces tugged unremittingly at the eves, while rain pelted the window directly behind them. Esther turned far enough to see transparent pearls of water aglow in the window's reflection of the fireplace.

"What did you say?" John asked.

"What? Oh, I must have been thinking out loud. I was listening to the storm and being mesmerized by the fire at the same time." Esther sipped at the latté before setting it on the stone hearth. "I said, 'A shelter in the time of storm.' That's what this place reminds me of."

She looked over at Jim.

Sitting back in his chair, he had stretched his shoeless feet toward the fire. With his heavy gray socks, dark pants held up by navy blue suspenders over a red and black plaid shirt that was open at the neck, Esther thought he was a living, breathing stereotype of the Maine woodsman. And there was more. Firelight had softened the old man's face, releasing the residue of a little boy.

"You're borin' holes through me, young lady," Jim growled good-naturedly. "You got somethin' on your mind? Out with it."

Esther laughed as she reached for her cup. "I'm seeing in you a mischievous lad who is not yet done playing, and I'll bet he comes out in all sorts of situations. He's the part of you that the kids love so much. I know this will sound a little silly, but if you don't mind, I'm going to call you 'Grandpa' rather than Jim. It fits you much better."

"Humph," Jim snorted, a twinkle appearing in his eyes. "You see the 'kid' in me and it makes you want to call me 'Grandpa.' Here I was hopin' I reminded you of Robert Redford or maybe even Harrison Ford. Instead, I'll bet you look at me and think of oatmeal!"

For a moment, Esther couldn't imagine what he was talking about.

"You know," he went on, "the old geezer in the commercial. That's the guy I remind you of. Right?"

Everyone laughed.

"I hope you don't mind what I just said, Jim. I guess it was a bit personal."

"Of course, I don't mind. 'Grandpa' it is. Right now, I kinda feel like family anyway."

"Hey, if Mom can call you 'Grandpa,' then so can I," said Jeremy. "A young guy needs a few good men in his life to go to for advice. Dad and my real grandparents are that way, and it's beginning to mean a lot to me. More than it ever did before. I'd sure like it if you and I could have that kind of relationship too, Mr. Brainard."

"Oh, you would, would you? Well, if it's okay with your mom and dad, then I'd consider that sort of friendship to be a great honor, Jeremy."

"It's more than okay, Jim," said John, putting a hand on his arm. "We'd consider your being part of our family a real honor. In the midst of our personal crises, it seems as though God has brought us together. I think we need each other, don't you?"

"There's no doubt about it." Jim's voice was husky as he placed his big hand over John's. His eyes grew moist. "I think we need each other very much!"

"I just wish that Jessica . . ." Jeremy paused, his features alight with the reddish glow of the fire. "I wish that she was here with us right now. Wouldn't she love this?"

Everyone stared straight ahead, alone with their thoughts. The moment was far too fragile for words. A small pocket of wood pitch broke the silence by suddenly sputtering and sending a shower of sparks upward into the chimney. Grandpa Brainard, newest member in the Cain family, shifted his position in the chair, throwing one leg up over the other.

"Has the government made any headway toward findin' out where she is?" he asked.

When there was no immediate response, he glanced around and saw his guests looking at each other. It was John who finally spoke.

"Jim, since you're a member of our family now, that makes Jessica another one of your adopted grandchildren. You have a right to know what we know. In fact, I intended to talk this over with you anyway, because you served in the military."

"In Korea," Jim confirmed. Esther saw his eyes take on the distant look of someone who was remembering.

I suppose the thoughts of war are never far from those who've been there.

Her attention began to drift as John shared the confirmed "Jessica sightings" that had led searchers out of Israel to Jordan, then to Saudi Arabia and the United Arab Emirates. Esther was in a faraway place where a part of her was being held hostage in another war that she did not understand.

Are any wars understandable? How did we ever become involved in this? We are ordinary people who were living ordinary lives, at least until Jenny died . . . and the terrorists came. It seems like years ago, but it's been exactly sixty-eight days since the September Strike weekend. Sixty-eight days since the world was held hostage by those terrible people. Sixty-eight days . . . since they took you from us. O sweetheart, I pray that God is watching over you right now!

Esther came back into the conversation as John rehearsed what had been learned, confirming her present location to be a city in Iran called Bandar-é Abbås.

Jim got up from his chair and went to a small bookcase near the grandfather clock. He ran his hand over the book spines on the top row, then pulled out a large volume and returned to his chair. "This atlas is three or four years old, but maybe we can locate it on the map."

"I know exactly where it is," John said. "We've plotted it at home from the first day we found out."

Grandpa Brainard flipped through the pages, finally coming to a stop.

"Here's Iran."

They circled in close together to look.

"And there is Bandar-é Abbás," John said, putting his index finger on the tiny spot. I found out that 'Bandar' means 'Port' in Farsi. It's a city of about 200,000. Do you know anything about it?"

"I don't know much about Iran, period. Nothing about this 'Bandar' place."

"Most of us know very little about Iran, but I've been reading up on it these last couple of weeks. It's in the Old Testament, you know."

"Really? Fill me in."

"Well, Cyrus the Great was the first Persian ruler of note. He shows up during the sixth century B.C., in the Old Testament books of Ezra and Nehemiah. The Achaemenian Empire which he founded lasted from . . . I think it was 558 to 330 B.C. That's close anyway. Darius I and Xerxes are also prominent in the biblical account. These two expanded the Babylonian Kingdom, as it is also known, all the way to India in the east and the Aegean Sea in the west. Even Egypt came under Persian rule for a while. From that period, a dynasty was carried forward until the last Shah, Mohammed Reza Pahlavi, celebrated the 2500th anniversary of the Persian Empire in 1971. Of course, the influence of the kingdom surged and waned all throughout that time, until coming into its present form.

"In the early twentieth century, oil became a major factor. When WW II rolled around, the country was officially declared neutral. In reality, it became a buffer zone between Nazi Turkey and the Allied USSR. After the war, the Russian forces were persuaded to withdraw. Mohammed Reza Shah assumed absolute power and aligned Iran with the West. Under his rather repressive, but in some ways very forward-looking regime, the nation modernized rapidly. Illiteracy was reduced, women emancipated, land holdings redistributed, health services improved, and a great deal of industrialization took place."

"So why did they kick the Shah out, dad?" asked Jeremy.

"From what I can gather, an oil price revolution in 1974 was his undoing. US arms merchants talked him into squandering the nation's new wealth on arsenals of useless weapons. Huge fortunes were wasted. In the end, the flood of petro-dollars was stuffed into the pockets of a select few. Meanwhile, inflation soared and the majority of people were worse off than before."

"No wonder they hate the West today," remarked Esther.

"Yes, the Shah made some serious mistakes in his relationship with the West. For example, he tried to break religious and cultural differences by such edicts as a ban on women wearing the chador. You know what happens in America when a dress code is imposed in the workplace or at school."

Jeremy smiled. "A revolt!"

"Yes, and there was a revolt in Iran, as well. Resentment made the devout Muslim women stay indoors rather than appear in public dressed in a manner they considered to be immodest. Students were the first to resort to violence. They wanted faster reform, while devout Muslims wanted reforms rolled back. But there was one point on which everyone was united—they hated the Shah's conspicuous consumption. Unrest continued until, by the late seventies, the economy was spiraling downward and the Shah's regime was beginning to falter. He finally fled on January 16, 1979. That date is now a national holiday celebrating his demise."

"And then comes the Ayatollah," Jeremy injected.

"That's right. Khomeini was the leading Shia cleric, a man thoroughly opposed to the Shah's policies. He had been banished to Turkey for many years, and was in exile in Paris by the time the Shah fled the country."

"Not a bad place to be exiled, I'd say," Jim commented with a chuckle.

"I guess not. Anyway, Khomeini returned to Iran in February 1979 and found his constituents waiting. He instituted his fiery brand of nationalism and Muslim fundamentalism and, once in control, he became known as Imam, the Leader. He set up a clergy-dominated Islamic republic. It's the world's first true Islamic state since the time of the caliphs. In so doing, he pitted Iran against the rest of the human race, with the USA being specifically pinpointed as the 'Great Satan,' although he threw in the USSR as a 'Great Satan understudy,' for good measure."

"Didn't the American Embassy crisis in Iran take place that same year?" asked Grandpa Brainard.

"Yes, in October," John answered. "They were held without any justification for 444 days and this, for all practical purposes, destroyed Jimmy Carter's presidency. Since then, various Iranian-backed terrorist groups have been responsible for taking hostages in Lebanon, killing those US marines in a truck bombing in Beirut, and scores of other actions. They sponsor an Iranian Revolutionary Guard training camp for terrorists in Lebanon's Bekaa Valley. No doubt there are other camps around as well."

"Not the kind of people you want to see move into the neighborhood," commented Jeremy.

"That's true when it comes to any terrorist, regardless of national background, son. The fact is, there are many wonderful Iranians. Thousands of them live in America today, and make a real contribution to this patchwork quilt of a society you are growing up in. They could be your neighbors and you would respect and appreciate them. Being Iranian doesn't make people bad, Jeremy, any more than being Japanese or German does.

"The actions of these Islamic radicals deserve the censure of civilized mankind; but don't ever fall into the trap of hating an entire class or a race because of a minority that acts irresponsibly. Evaluate what people are on the inside by what they do, not by how they look."

Jeremy nodded with understanding.

"It's hard though, isn't it?"

"Sometimes, yes," John answered simply. "Like right now. Whatever happens, however, I don't want to watch you grow up with bitterness and hatred in your heart. God wants more from us than that. Our fellow human beings deserve more than that. Jesus came to make a difference."

"Have you been able to gather how it is there since Khomeini died?" asked Esther.

"The Iran-Iraq War has taken a terrific human and economic toll on the nation. Iran's neutrality throughout Desert Storm restored some of her lost credit in the West. The top leaders seem to want normalcy and progress, but it's going to come very slowly, especially if the Islamic fundamentalists have their way."

"Do you think this can have anything to do with Jessica?" asked Esther, repeating a question she had asked herself hundreds of times already. "I simply can't figure it."

"Authorities have confirmed that September Strike was carried out under the banner of the Palestinian Islamic Jihad. The PIJ is a radical core group under the umbrella of Hamas, and Hamas is far to the right of the PLO, if that gives you any perspective at all. Hamas rejects the right of the Jews to live in Israel; now that Arafat and the PLO are settling differences with Israel by carving out the beginnings of a new Palestinian State, Hamas opposes them as well."

"I still don't understand the connection," Grandpa muttered.

"The Palestinian Islamic Jihad is a terrorist group that receives much of its financial backing and tactical training from the Iranians. They must be planning to do something with her. I'm sure she's only a pawn, but Marwan Dosha has got a plan for using her. You can count on it. The guy is evil personified."

Esther shivered involuntarily.

"He's gotten his people to move her to Iran," John concluded, "because it's safe to hold her there."

"Okay," Grandpa mused, rubbing his chin, "it all begins to make some sense. There's the thread that ties it up all right. So, back to my original question. What's the government doin' to get her back?"

John reached for the poker and prodded the logs, causing another shower of sparks as he revived the low-burning flame. Then, he settled back in his chair.

"That's the question of the hour, Jim. At first, the State Department said they were thinking about the best way to approach the problem. They needed a few days, or so we were told. We expected to hear from them every day. Nothing. I finally called Rodeway to see what was happening. He said there were some behind-the-scenes contacts being made, but that they had to be careful, because no one knows what level of involvement there may be in the Iranian government itself."

"Hmm, makes sense," Jim said thoughtfully. "It could also be a stalling tactic by a bunch of bureaucrats who don't want to admit that they're afraid of another Jimmy Carter scenario."

"That's exactly what we have been thinking. It's been two weeks now and nothing has happened. It's the reason I want to talk about Korea."

"What's Korea got to do with this?"

"What I need right now is someone who is retired from Special Forces, somebody experienced in covert military tactics."

"Guys I knew back in the Korean conflict are too old, if you're thinkin' what I think you're thinkin'."

"There's got to be somebody out there who can help me. I . . . we've made a decision this past week."

"And what might that be?"

"I'm not waiting any longer for something to happen. If they get wind that we know where she's being held, they'll move her. When is the last time our government carried out a successful hostage exchange with these people? She could be there for years; or worse, they might decide they have no further use for her. I'm going in to get her, Jim. I'm going to bring her home."

Grandpa Brainard watched John's determined face. Esther looked down, anxiously twisting the corner of her blouse. Jeremy watched his father, a look of admiration clearly visible.

"You ever have any military duty?" Grandpa's question broke the stillness.

"No, unfortunately. That's another reason why I need someone to go with me. I have been learning how to fire a handgun, though," he added.

"Think you could shoot somebody?"

"That's the big question I've been wrestling with ever since taking my first lesson. The conclusion I've come to is that in order to protect my family, I can do it. I'll fire only in self-defense, but I will do it if necessary."

"Hmm," Grandpa mumbled, as though he was not at all convinced. "Are you good?"

"Good?"

"Yes, at shootin' your handgun."

"Not the greatest, but good enough. I've worked hard at it the last few weeks, and I've had a good instructor."

"Does he know what you're up to?"

"He's a 'she,' and, yes, she guessed it."

"Does she think you're a good enough shot?"

John paused before answering. For some reason, he was uncomfortable talking about his shooting prowess in front of Esther and Jeremy. Especially Jeremy.

"You know, Jim," he said, finally, "I'm not the least bit comfortable with any of this. I'm a peacemaker, not a warrior, but these people have kidnapped my own flesh and blood. I could never live with myself, now that I know where Jessica is being held, if I didn't go in after her. I hope that I don't have to point my gun at anyone; but, in order to protect and recover Jessica, I will shoot."

Once again, Grandpa Brainard was silent, his mood seeming to take him out of the intimate circle they had become.

Where is he? Esther watched his response to her husband's daring proposal. *What is he thinking?*

Grandpa Brainard scooted to the edge of his chair, reached down and picked up another piece of firewood. Pulling back the screen that covered the fireplace, he tossed the log expertly onto the embers. Then he turned to John and smiled.

"I've got to hand it to you," he said, placing his hand on John's arm. "You've got more guts than I ever thought a preacher could muster up. I'm concerned about the 'brains' department, but maybe you'll surprise me there too. When I think of you sneakin' into Iran, rescuin' our girl, and gettin' back out again successfully, well, it's about as far-fetched an idea as the Virgin

Birth. But somehow God managed to pull that one off, so I reckon He can do the same with you."

He looked again at the map. "You sure about this? That she's really at this Bandar place?"

"I know she was a week ago. That's the last time I spoke with Rodeway. How much longer she'll be there is another question," John answered. "Maybe the fellow who gave the information to our embassy in Jordan can confirm that she is still at the same location. We can see if they'll give us his name. I could say that I want to thank him for what he has done."

"Well, then, I guess we'd better get goin' on this. It's too late tonight, but first thing in the mornin', I'll call a friend I've kept in touch with over the years. We served in Korea together. He's not the one you want, 'cause he's been missin' a leg ever since the war. Got a medal for it too. Not the best kind of exchange, but several of his buddies are still livin' today on account of that leg. You're lookin' at one of 'em. This fella's got a son that retired from the SEALS about three years ago. I believe he's workin' for some kind of private security organization now. If anybody can give us a hand here, he may be the one. Let's just hope we can reach him okay."

"Thanks, Jim." John let out a heavy sigh. "Thanks for helping, instead of knocking my plan. I know it's a long shot, but it's all we've got."

"Don't thank me," snorted Grandpa Brainard. "I think you're nuts and should have your head examined. I also think it wouldn't do any good, because you're gonna do it anyway. I just need to find someone who's crazy enough to go in with you and get you back safely to your family. For what it's worth, though, I'll tell you this much. If the situation were reversed, I'd be doin' exactly what you're doin'!"

"Maybe if we pray about this together, it will go smoothly." It was Esther who spoke up, a worried look on her face. "Truth is, I'm scared. Scared to death."

She glanced up at John and then at Jeremy and Jim.

"My insides are in knots just thinking about this. I don't know whether I'm supposed to fall apart or be the brave warrior's wife. The thought of losing one more member of my family is . . . well, it's too much. It's just too much. I can't chance losing the man I love. We've suffered more than enough already without that. But I want my Jessica back too, and I can't fault John for wanting to go after her. There doesn't seem to be any other way. We can't simply abandon her. She's our baby."

"The only alternative is to wait and see if the State Department can work things out," answered Jim. "From the sound of things, they may be shinin' you on in order to cover their bureaucratic buns. Could be they've already decided she is expendable. I guess it boils down to who you trust. You know what they say . . . 'the Lord works in mysterious ways.' "

Grandpa Brainard turned to Jeremy.

"You've got one great dad here, young fella. Here's somethin' else to put under your hat. If you were out there, instead of Jessica, just think about it . . . he'd be layin' plans to come and get you."

Jeremy blinked, surprised at what was a new thought.

"Same is true for you, Esther. I guess the question you have to answer is, would you want him to act any other way if things were different and you were the hostage?"

Esther walked over to the window and stared into the stormy darkness. Then she turned to face the others.

"No," she said quietly. "John, do what you have to do. Go get her and bring her home where she belongs."

Esther walked back to where the others were standing and put her face in John's chest, circling his waist with her arms. She held him tightly while the others watched. Then she looked up, her eyes moist and filled with concern.

"And if you don't come back alive, I am going to kill you!" The incongruity of her statement caused everyone to break out in laughter.

"How about leading us in a prayer, son?" John asked. "Grandpa is right. I would be coming for you. And, if your mom and I were there, you'd be figuring out some way to do the same. Hey, we're family. We're responsible for each other, and God is going to give us success if we trust Him for it."

Jeremy swallowed back his emotions, then held out his hands. A circle of prayer formed for the second time that day, as Mom, Dad, and Grandpa Brainard listened to Jeremy pray for his sister's safe return.

THIRTY-THREE

Grandpa Brainard hung up the phone and looked at John.

"Well, that's it. Harry tells me that his boy is out in the Seattle area. Lives in Bellevue, just across Lake Washington."

"That's my old 'stomping ground,' " John noted. "I pastored near there before going to Baytown. My parents still live in Kirkland."

"I've never been out that way, but I hear it's pretty nice. Anyhow, he's workin' for a big computer software company. Name is Herschel Towner. Widower already and he's only thirty-five. Wife was killed by a drunk driver. No kids. From what Harry said, I don't think his boy has gotten over losin' her."

He paused for a second, his mind flashing back over his own painful loss. Then he continued.

"Happened two years ago. Since then, he's been headin' up the security for the whole enterprise and particularly for their top level people. Harry said he'd give him a call and get back to us as soon as he reaches him. Maybe today, if we're lucky. You heard me tell him that we're in a bit of a hurry, so let's just sit tight. Interested in some breakfast?"

"Sure," said John and headed for the kitchen. "We'll let Esther and Jeremy make their own when they get back." The two of them had been gone nearly an hour now. Jeremy wanted to get out of the house and look around, now that the rain had stopped. He had talked a reluctant Esther into bundling up and going with him.

John and Grandpa sat at the table that had been the scene of their Thanksgiving dinner the afternoon before. They ate toast with peanut butter and jam and drank fresh ground Costa Rican coffee.

"I pay a great price for this jam, so eat hearty, lad. Alice Conklin makes this stuff. She lives just two doors away," Grandpa commented, waving his hand toward the homes located immediately behind Hill House. "Been a widow for 'bout five years and thinks I ought to be a bit more attentive. She comes over 'bout every other day. Says she wants to make sure everything is okay."

"I see," John grinned as he reached for his cup. "All this time, you've been holding out on us, eh?"

"Get out. Nice lady, but not my type."

"Is that so? And just what is 'your type'?"

"I like 'em svelte, more like your Esther. Although you really do need to feed that woman, lad, 'cause she's too thin, don't you know?"

"Too thin?" echoed John questioningly. "Hey, I've got news for you. I like her just the way she is . . . slender, sleek, and sexy!"

"She is all of that, for sure. I thought all preachers' wives were supposed to be plain and dowdy. That is, unless they're on TV. Then, they're supposed to be super-stylish and have hairdos that look like mattress factory explosions. Your wife can hold her own with the best of 'em, and that's the truth."

"She's special, all right," John said with a smile.

"And don't you forget it, either," said Grandpa Brainard. "Anyway, you know the old sayin', 'Once you've been to Paris, there ain't no goin' back to the farm.' Right?"

John chuckled as he sipped the hot coffee.

"I've been there with Middie," Grandpa continued. "She was everything a woman should be. The way I see it, a woman needs to be able to talk 'bout somethin' else besides roses, weather, and jam. Alice has spent her whole life here on this hill. Took over the home from her parents when they died. She's a fine person and has done well too, but doesn't seem to care much about anything beyond the city limits. I'm used to somebody who's interested in the world, know what I mean?"

John nodded. He certainly did know.

"I'm happy the way I am. Probably too old and too set in my ways to include anybody else in my life anyhow. Middie and I, we knew each other the way . . . well, you know, the way you and Esther seem to. When you've been lucky enough to have had a person like that in your life, anything else is bound to be second best."

John nodded again.

"I get lonely," he said wistfully. "It's mighty quiet here in the winter time, but I'm still doin' okay."

"I can see that you are, Jim. Of course, now that we've agreed to adopt each other, you're going to have to come and spend part of these winters with us."

"In California?"

"That's where we live."

"Oh, I don't know. Too many freeways, tons of people and . . ."

"Don't give me excuses. Just make up your mind. We aren't going to take no for an answer."

"You're beginnin' to sound like a stubborn Mainer and you've barely been here twenty-four hours," Grandpa retorted good-naturedly. "Here, have some more coffee."

IT WAS TEN AFTER THREE THAT AFTERNOON when the call came.

Grandpa took the phone.

"Hello." He listened for a moment, then motioned to John. "He's right here. I'll let you talk to him."

"Hello, this is John Cain."

"Hello, Reverend," said a voice resonating in John's ear, reminding him of someone talking from inside a barrel. "I got a call from my dad saying you've got some cockamamie idea about going to Iran to rescue your kidnapped daughter."

"Yes, sir, that's it in a nutshell," John replied.

"You've gotta be nuts!" the voice boomed into John's ear.

"You'll get little argument from anyone on that score."

"It's crazy. Insane. Forget it, Reverend. It'll never work."

"I can't forget it, Mr. Towner. They've got my daughter."

"Let the diplomats work it out."

"I don't have any confidence that they're able or even willing to put our country at risk to achieve my daughter's release."

There was silence on the other end of the line, broken only by the sound of heavy breathing.

"Well, that's the first sensible thing I've heard since my dad called. You're right on that. There is very little they can do, short of starting a war. Maybe nothing."

"They tell me that they are working on all the different options."

Towner swore into the phone. "Oops. Sorry, but, that's what it is. Just a big crock of . . ."

"I get the picture," John broke in, "and I agree with you. That's why I've decided to go get her myself. We know where she is."

"You're absolutely sure about her location?"

"Ninety-nine percent. Unless they move her before we get there." John casually threw the "we" pronoun into his sentence. He desperately needed to hook Towner and reel him in. "But I can't do it by myself," he concluded.

"You can't do it at all," bellowed Towner. "There's no way. Who do you think you are? You can't just walk in and say, 'Come on, sweetheart, get your things and let's go home.' Surely you understand that."

John paused, a feeling of anger quickly overtaking his emotions. *Careful, careful. You need this guy. Or someone like him.*

"You know, Mr. Towner, you are right on all points. I'm crazy for even thinking about this mission. I can't just walk in and take her out. I know that. But I can't simply stay here and do nothing either. Forgive me for tossing your own words back, but surely *you* understand *that*. I'm told that you can help us, that if anyone has the skills needed for getting in and out safely, it's you. It has even been suggested to me that you may have been inside Iran at one time or another. The truth is, I don't believe we're going to get my daughter out of there by conventional means. So, here I am, asking if you are willing to help me. If it's money, I'll do my best to make it worth your while."

John could hear the man breathing. Then, he swore softly.

"I must be crazy. Dad explained your situation to me. Actually, I followed your escapades in the media back in September. Pretty impressive stuff." His tone had become grudgingly respectful. "You may not have any sense, but you've got guts!"

"So I've been hearing. I'll accept that as a compliment, coming from someone like you. Now, what do you say, Mr. Towner?"

"The name is Hersch. Give me a day to transfer my duties over to my assistant—if I can find him, that is. It's a holiday, you know."

"I know" John smiled as he nodded to Grandpa Brainard. Grandpa smiled and gave the "thumbs up" signal.

"Can you be out here Monday morning?"

"I can try. It's the highest air traffic weekend of the year. We've got tickets back to San Francisco for Monday morning. I'll see if I can do a destination change."

"Okay. Get out here and I'll see what I can do. Let me know your ETA and I'll pick you up at SeaTac."

"Thanks, Mr. . . . Hersch. And, my name is John."

"Is the last name spelled with a K or a C?"

"With a C."

"Okay. Just make sure the undertaker can spell it right. I'll not kid you—we stand a good chance of getting killed." Towner's voice sounded flat, without emotion.

"I know," John replied.

HERSCHEL WINSLOW TOWNER III PUT DOWN the telephone and pushed away from the huge oak desk. Getting to his feet, he walked across the plush carpet to the window. Steel-gray eyes looked out over the huge employee parking lot. Cars of all colors and descriptions usually filled every available space, but the long holiday weekend had left it virtually empty. His big hand brushed across the dark, gray-flecked hair that still remained above a receding hairline. Even this had been cut short, military-style. His well-muscled, six-foot frame rocked back and forth on the balls of his feet.

The area nearest his building was reserved for executives, his bread and butter. Usually, a quick glance at the rows of Mercedes and BMWs reminded him of the megabucks that flowed like water through this place. There were probably more millionaires per capita here than in any other comparable business on the West Coast. His own six-figure salary and benefits would have him on easy street in a few years. That was because he plowed most of his earnings back into the corporation's stock plan for employees.

A lot of his friends thought he had it made. He knew better. His life was as empty as the parking lot outside his window.

He still lived in the two-bedroom condominium that Sharon had picked out the first week after they arrived. They had been married by one of the naval base chaplains in San Diego. A week later, he signed his final release papers and concluded a twelve-year stint as a member of the elite SEALs branch of the Navy.

Until Sharon, being an integral part of a SEAL unit had been his whole life. They had introduced themselves after Hersch's speech at the San Diego Downtown Rotary Club. Until that day, he had thought all Rotarians were bald and overweight. To his surprise, he had seen her talking with two other female Rotarians during the lunch hour. Afterward, she came forward and shook his hand, thanking him for his talk. That had been the beginning for them both.

In that rarest of human occurrences, they found themselves instantly smitten by the other's presence. He invited her to dinner on the following Saturday. She accepted. Four months later, he watched as she approached him in a simple beige dress, edged with lace. Ten minutes later, they were husband and wife.

He had left the SEAL's organization without a second thought. Life had bloomed with a love he had never dreamed possible, as Sharon Parker-Towner became his new life. His job as Director of Security for OCEANS, an upstart software manufacturing company that was rapidly overtaking a highly competitive marketplace with startling new innovations in voice-activated word processing, had brought them to the attractive mini-metropolis of Bellevue, spreading out to the east of Lake Washington.

Sharon had been the one to find the condominium that faced out over the lake. Along the water's edge, tall evergreens stretched into the sky, their ample trunks surrounded by generous expanses of green. The grassy expanse framed colorful rhododendrons in full bloom like pieces of natural art. They both agreed this must be the last stop before heaven. By nightfall, papers had been signed and the 1,700-square-foot unit that would soon be their home was in escrow.

Four months later, Sharon announced that she was pregnant.

Hersch was ecstatic.

Two months after that, the doctor pronounced Sharon and their unborn baby dead.

Hersch went wild!

Killed at an intersection by a drunk driver who ran a red light and plowed into the driver's side of her vehicle at sixty miles per hour. Rescue workers had to use the "jaws of life" to extricate her broken body from what was left of her car. They rushed her to Bellevue's Overlake Hospital, where she was pronounced dead on arrival. The drunk driver had no license, no insurance, and suffered no injuries beyond a few cuts and bruises.

It had been two years since the police officers had walked into his office and informed him of the *accidental death* of his Whole World. He didn't view it as accidental. As far as he was concerned, it was out-and-out murder. From that moment, the shocking reality of his loss killed something inside him. He still lived in the same condo and worked in the same office for the same company, but he was not the same. He was a hollow man. All reason for living had died.

At first, he had been totally consumed with hatred toward the man whose irresponsible act had taken Sharon from him. He wanted to kill him, slowly, with his own hands. Instead, a liberal judge gave the man five to seven years for manslaughter. He was due for a parole hearing soon. Hersch was resigned to the fact that the man would soon be given his miserable life back by some paranoid do-gooders, probably just long enough to kill someone else. Meanwhile, Sharon was gone forever. The scales of justice were pitifully unbalanced.

He thought of ways to kill himself. He could leap off the Aurora Bridge or dive from a ferryboat into the Puget Sound's frigid waters. His never-ending pain would finally cease. Overdosing on sleeping pills was not an option. That was not the same as smashing his car into a tree or shooting himself. The violence somehow seemed necessary in order to equal the grim death of his beloved. It was easy to think of ways to die, much harder to find a way to go on living. He thought back over the call from this Cain character. Who knows? Maybe he had just found the way. Heroic. Violent. It fit.

Everyone has a breaking point. Hersch always thought this rule did not apply to him. He had watched others die, but he had never really understood the meaning of death until now. It had crashed in upon him all of a sudden, and with unexpected ferocity. Ever since, memories had been breaking his heart.

The only thing that kept him from The Deed, as he called it, was his one unspoken fear. The fear of the unknown.

Neither he nor Sharon had been regular churchgoers. During their first month in Bellevue, however, a neighbor invited Sharon to join her and a small group of friends in a weekly Bible study. Sharon had been reluctant at first to discuss the invitation with Hersch, but he had encouraged her. She had no friends as yet in Bellevue and, besides, what could it hurt? After all, she was a college graduate with an above-average intellect. "If the group is too weird," he had laughed, "just don't bother going back. No harm done."

The night after her first meeting, she returned home with a glowing report. They were all young married women about her age, and they took turns as group facilitator. They attended the same church and invited her and Hersch to join them some Sunday in worship and afterward for brunch. Sharon's initial wariness quickly disappeared when she found them all to be really "normal" people. She already had decided to go back the following week, though Hersch quickly declined the offer to visit their church.

He still remembered his childhood days in the little hellfire-and-brimstone country church where his parents had been Sunday School teachers. The preacher wore a white shirt and a shiny, black suit. He wiped at his sweaty face with a white handkerchief and then waved it at the little group of the faithful, while bellowing about the evils of sin and the pits of hell. For Hersch, the result had been a feeling of nonreality when it came to religion. He disliked all preachers on the basis of his experience with one. Much too otherworldly for him. If something was real, he ought to be able to feel it, taste it, smell it. He could do that with Sharon. She was real. He couldn't do it with God. He wasn't real.

Still, since Sharon's untimely death, a lurking uncertainty had melded with large doses of guilt and self-pity, darkening his soul with its ever-present shadow. That last month of her life, Sharon had begun to talk more and more about God and Jesus. She even went to church on a couple of occasions, though she had been careful not to press Hersch to join her. Looking back, however, he was certain that a definite change had overtaken Sharon. One that he liked. Her eyes sparkled more than ever. Her laughter lit up the room. The ardor of her love for him continued to soften his military bearing.

Then suddenly, it was over. She was gone.

The object of his worship was no more. Heaven had turned into hell after all. Maybe that old, sweaty preacher had been right all along.

Hersch suddenly smashed his fist against the wall, near the window where he knew it would not punch through.

His hand came away bloody. As usual.

Slowly, he walked back to his desk, reached for the phone, and dialed his assistant.

THIRTY-FOUR

SeaTac International's main terminal was crowded, though not as wall-to-wall as it had been the day before. Holiday celebrants, with that all-important extra day to get home, were now saying their good-byes.

John saw it as a fabrication of fleshly tapestry seen every day along the edge of these concrete highways that led to the sky. People were making progress, going somewhere, living out today's destiny in the heady environment of a modern airport, preparing to enter a long, slender tube similar to the one from which he had just extricated himself. John took little comfort in the thought that every jet was shaped and powered by 280,000 moving parts, each one manufactured by the lowest bidder. These flying culverts constantly hurtled their human cargo through the sky without any regard for the fact that the only other intelligent beings known to fly with wings were angels.

Having successfully completed his cross-country flight from Boston, he was still rehearsing all the reasons why he hated to fly when he saw him. Looking self-assured and relaxed in jeans, sport shirt open at the collar, and a gray tweed jacket, the prematurely balding man was holding a small sign with J. CAIN scrawled across it. The man remained immobile, permitting John to close the gap between them. As he approached, John shifted his carry-on and shook the man's hand.

"Hello. I'm John Cain."

"Herschel Towner." John felt his gaze and sensed that he was taking measure of a preacher with a strange mission. "You check anything?"

"No. This is it."

"Good. Come along. My car is this way."

They moved into the steady flow of people headed toward the exits, careful to avoid colliding with those coming from the opposite direction.

"A busy place," John commented, in an effort to strike up conversation.

Towner nodded.

"I appreciate you meeting me."

"No problem," Towner answered, matter-of-factly.

They excused themselves as they stepped around a group of Japanese tourists near a restroom door, apparently waiting for someone to emerge from inside. Moments later, they were in the multilevel parking lot. An elevator took them to the third floor and, as they stepped out, Towner pointed toward a dark green 1992 Mercedes.

"That's it," he said. "Hop in and let's get out of here."

As they sped away from the parking lot toll booth, John noted that while it was not raining, the roadway was wet, causing an arc of recently deposited rainwater to rise and fall on either side of the automobile.

"You hungry?" asked Towner, looking over at John as if he was still sizing up this stranger alongside him.

"I had breakfast on the plane, but I could eat something light," John replied.

"There's a restaurant in the Marriott that's pretty good. We'll go there." The hotel was not far from the airport and soon they were inside ordering.

John had expected Towner to say, *"Okay, I'm running this show so listen up and do what I say. Here's the plan."* Instead, he began by asking questions and listened attentively as John spoke. He wanted to know about Jessica—her age, physical condition, emotional maturity, everything. How did John think she might be holding up? Was there any word as to whether she had been abused or otherwise treated inhumanely? John responded with what he knew, becoming more aware than ever as he spoke that he really knew precious little. It was mostly conjecture.

What did John know about Bandar-é Abbás? Where else in the Middle East had he traveled? Had he been told anything about the place where Jessica was being held? The traffic, what the buildings were made of, the number of people in the streets, how many policemen or guards, how were they armed? Before long, John realized clearly just how ill-prepared he was.

"I'm afraid there's little else I can contribute," John said, finally. "Now that I'm sitting here with someone who knows the score in matters like this, I appreciate more than ever what we're up against."

"Good," said Towner. "I'd hate to think that, in addition to being completely unprepared for what's ahead, you were also stupid. For what it's worth, just sitting here listening, I've been able to discern that much."

"That much what?"

"That whatever else you may be, Reverend, you're not stupid. Touched, balmy, and completely loony perhaps, but not stupid." Towner smiled for the first time, as John laughed out loud in response.

"Okay, then. Assuming you are right, let's get a couple of other things squared away. My name is not 'Reverend.' It's John." Towner half-smiled again, nodding as John continued. "And, since I'm asking for the privilege of putting my life and the life of my daughter into your hands, I'd like to know up front why you don't like me very much."

Towner's eyebrows lifted in surprise. "What makes you think I don't like you?"

"Hey, I've been in the people business all my life. I know when I'm being accepted and when I'm being put off. So far, you've put me in the latter category. Now, I'm not suggesting that we have to be bosom pals, but I need to know where I stand and just how much you can be counted on when things get a little rougher than they are right now. So, the question stands."

Towner stared into his cup while the waitress delivered their food. "There you are, fellas. Anything else I can get you?"

"Maybe a little coffee, when you have the chance," John answered, smiling up at her. "And some milk to go with it. Two percent, if you have it."

"You got it," she said pleasantly. "And here's your check. I'll be your cashier when you are ready. Enjoy your meal."

As the waitress moved on to the next table, John looked across at Towner. "Mind if I ask a blessing?"

He caught another flicker of surprise before Towner motioned with his hand, as if to say, *"Be my guest."*

John bowed his head. "Thanks, Lord, for bringing us here safely. Thanks for the food that has been prepared for us. And, thanks for Mr. Towner. Let our relationship be good and our efforts successful. Continue to watch over Jessica until we can bring her home again. Amen."

John opened his eyes in time to see Towner still staring at his cup. Slowly, he looked up.

"The name is Hersch, to you," he began, leaning forward until both elbows rested on the table and his hands were folded in fists under his chin. "Although I'm not sure that God remembers either name. The only time I think He ever heard it before today was at Sharon's—my wife's—funeral. I've not been in church since I was a kid and I don't know what I think about God. I guess I think that if He really exists, He's doing a mighty poor job of things, what with my wife and your daughter being the way they are. On top of that, I've never liked preachers much. Not since being harangued to death in church as a kid. Now, does that answer your question?"

"How many preachers have you known, Hersch?"

"I've watched some of those TV preachers."

"Do you know any of them?"

"No, not personally. Actually, I've only known one preacher personally. When I was a kid."

"And?"

"And I didn't like him. Too much hellfire for my tastes."

"So, on the basis of what you remember about a preacher you knew when you were a kid, you've wiped out the whole category. Is that about it?"

Towner went on eating without responding.

"Come on, Hersch," John continued, "you can't put us all in the same box with one person you didn't like. I'm sorry that your experience with religion appears to have been so negative. You need to lighten up a bit. There's a lot of good stuff about God and the way He works in our lives. You just have to be a little more open and cut Him a little slack."

"You are a lot different than I pictured you would be," Towner admitted.

"Thanks, I think," John smiled back. "If I wasn't a preacher, I just might be a regular fellow, the kind of guy you could learn to like, right?"

"Okay, okay." Towner put down his fork and extended his hand across the table. "I hear you and I accept you. You're the second preacher I've known personally. You don't seem that bad, so I think we'll get along. What I've read about you in the papers makes me think that you're more of a man than I might have given you credit for. Besides, you're right—if we're going to pull this off, we've got to get along. More than that, we've got to trust each other with our lives."

John reached out and gripped Towner's hand firmly.

"Are you prepared to die doing this?" asked Towner.

"No."

"Good. I wouldn't take anyone with me who was planning on dying. Let's go out by the pool and get started. We can sit out there the rest of the day without being bothered by anybody. You can see through the window from here that the whole area is covered by a sunroof so the rain can't get us." He chuckled at the juxtaposition of those two concepts. "I've done a little research and made a few phone calls since we talked last week. I'm going to give you my thoughts on this operation. You jump in any time with questions or ideas. Okay?"

John nodded his agreement.

BY THE END OF THE DAY, John had developed a healthy admiration for Herschel Winslow Towner III. He knew his stuff, and his attention to detail was impressive. His matter-of-fact attitude toward the whole project was actually a bit intimidating.

Together they hammered out a plan. It was predicated on ample amounts of courage, surprise, and sheer audaciousness. Towner drove John back to the airport and they shook hands a final time.

"It's been . . . 'interesting' is the word, I guess . . . getting to know you, John. I'll see you on Wednesday at JFK in New York. We'll meet at the British Airways ticket counter at two o'clock to join up with the tour group. Then, on to London and Tehran. Once we're in Iran, we'll put the next phase of the plan into motion. Twenty-four hours later we'll be toasting our success in Sharjah."

John's heart beat rapidly with excitement. Impulsively, he grabbed Towner in a bear hug. At first, he could feel Towner resist in surprise, then finally give in. He hugged John in return.

"One more thing," said John, releasing his hold on Towner. "We've talked about the money needed for expenses, but we've not discussed your fee. I've been so excited about the rest of our plans that I forgot to ask about that. I apologize. Can you give me an idea so that I can start getting ready?"

Towner was quiet as he stared into John's eyes.

"Tell you what, partner. Before I met you, I had a figure in mind. Since I've spent the day with you, I'll need to revise it somewhat. From what I gather, it doesn't make any difference. We're going to get your girl, whatever the cost. Right?"

"That's right."

"Okay. Let's not worry about it. You can't afford me anyhow. Besides, I was getting bored on the job. This will give me a little break."

He waved as he turned to walk away.

"Wednesday at two," John repeated. Then he headed for Gate 27 and his United flight on to San Francisco.

The flight from New York to London was uneventful. The same could be said for the final leg from London to Tehran. British Airways. Long, boring hours. Modest meals. Poor movies. Crowded seats and aisles. The usual international flight experience in tourist class. He knew that Towner preferred traveling in business or first class, but was relieved at his unspoken sympathy for John's lack of ready cash.

Upon returning home on Monday, John had emptied the special bank account of the funds raised to seek Jessica's whereabouts and ultimate release. It had totaled $33,479 US, which he now had strapped to his leg and around his waist in two currency pouches. In addition, he carried a telephone credit card and his ticket from SFO to JFK. The thought of carrying all that ready cash made him nervous, but he knew it would spend very rapidly in the underworld of international terrorism and counter-terrorism into which he was being immersed once again. And the people he was dealing with didn't accept Mastercard or American Express.

In JFK's International Flight section, John and Hersch shook hands with Ms. Langford, the group leader for Blue Planet tours. She had two married couples and four other singles in tow. A few hours from now, this all-American contingent would meet a group of twelve British citizens, rounding out another out-of-the-ordinary tour group, just the sort of thing for which Blue Planet was famous.

One of Hersch's old SEAL team friends was a founding partner of Blue Planet. They had worked together in Southeast Asia while in the military. The first year after Sharon's death, Hersch had taken time off his regular job to work as an assistant tour leader with a BP group traveling to northern Thailand. Anything to get away from reality.

After Herschel's initial telephone conversation with John, he had contacted his friend on the chance that he might want to help, perhaps even join them himself. When the situation was described, his friend mentioned the BP group already scheduled for Iran right after the holiday. It was a relatively easy matter to add the two men to the list.

The visas were the biggest hurdle, with such late notice. Technically, anyone applying for a tourist visa has to wait for the forms to be sent to the Ministry of Foreign Affairs in Tehran for approval. This can sometimes mean two or three months. But Iranians are not great lovers of rules, and several well-placed phone calls, numerous forms and photos, two new passports that didn't look new, and an inordinate amount of John's dollars, resulted in two transit visas valid for up to two weeks.

After takeoff, the two men exchanged small talk with their fellow tour members, careful to keep their true identities hidden. John felt foolish at first, but eventually slipped into his new role like an actor on stage.

In New York, adjacent to the control area, Hersch had handed the new passport to John.

"You are now Dr. John Castle, professor of religious studies at Union Seminary, Berkeley," Hersch informed him. "I am Harold Trent, a dealer in oriental rugs. I have a business in Seattle. We're two bachelors who've known one another since college days. You okay with that? You've got no problems masquerading as someone else? No moral dilemma or anything?"

It was the first time John had ever passed himself off as someone other than who he really was. Did he have problems carrying a passport that was not his own, in effect, lying about his identity? He wasn't terribly comfortable with the deception, but he couldn't come up with a better solution.

"I'll manage," he grinned.

Towner chuckled at that.

Early on, a couple of the single ladies appeared particularly interested in the two bachelors who, they decided, were good-looking and available. After the obligatory conversation, however, the men moved to the back of the plane near the restrooms, and remained there until the ladies had had time to strike up conversations with two businessmen sitting in the row ahead of them.

Hersch and John talked through the plan over a chicken dinner, complete with vegetable, salad, a hard roll, and a layered cake dessert. Towner washed it down with a small bottle of white wine, while John contented himself with mineral water. Satisfied that they understood what they were doing, they settled back to watch the movie. Exhausted, John dozed through most of it.

It was nearly noon on Thursday when they left London. By this time, attention was focused more on the Brits than the Americans. That was fine as far as John and Hersch were concerned. The less conspicuous they were, the better they liked it.

Hours later, the plane began its final descent. This was no ordinary, white-knuckle approach for John, however. This was the real thing. It was time to step on stage and take the leading role. He looked at Hersch, who smiled and nodded. A moment later, John began experiencing pain in his left ear. As they dropped lower in altitude, the 'pain' increased.

Ms. Langford was eventually summoned by one of the other tour passengers. From the look on John's face, she could see that the pain was intense. He said he felt like throwing up and reached for a sick bag, just to emphasize the point. He chewed gum, yawned, moved his head back and forth, all to no avail.

By the time they landed at Mehrabad airport, John was what the youngest of the single ladies sympathetically referred to as "one sick dude." They managed to get him through customs after convincing the not-so-friendly agent that he was not a worthy candidate for quarantine. It was simply the case of an ear that needed to pop open.

It was clear to John, just by looking at the airport, that they were in a different world. The place was full of large photographs of Khomeini, his successor Ayatollah Ali Khomenei, and President Hashemi Rafsanjani. After waiting at length in the baggage claim area, Ms. Langford returned to inform the group that their bus was not going to be available until the next day. This was not a problem, however. They would simply take taxis to their hotel.

John, Hersch, and one of the married couples made the long ride into Tehran's central district in a dilapidated Iranian-made Peykan. It coughed and sputtered the entire distance, its leaded gas and archaic engine typical of most vehicles on the road. The combination of ancient engines and low-grade fuel made worthy contributions to the city's notorious reputation for having the third-highest level of sulfur dioxide of any city in the world.

Hersch informed them that on many days during the year, the pollution levels were so high that the government warned the elderly and people with respiratory problems not to leave their homes.

"Kind of like L.A., only worse," he noted dryly.

On this day, however, the air was clear and snow could be seen on the Elburz mountain range at the city's northern edge. Hersch went on to say that in the foothills were private villas with high walls, barred windows, and swimming pools, renting for at least $2,000 a month. Homes here could easily cost over $2 million. Iran's highest peak, Mount Demavend, towered into the sky at 18,300 feet, northeast of Tehran. The mountain range was obviously the glory of an otherwise dilapidated and depressingly grimy urban sprawl.

As they came closer to the city center, the female passenger asked the question that had been tweaking John's mind as well.

"What do you suppose this decal is about?" she asked of no one in particular. The driver had already pled "No English," and the others believed it to be true. On the inside of the taxi's passenger door, where one might expect to find a "No smoking" sign in America, was a decal that they later realized was widespread. It presented the silhouette of a woman's covered head and the words, "For the respect of Islam, Hijab is mandatory."

It was Hersch who knew the answer.

"It means that they will not serve you unless you wear a proper hijab. I saw a decal just like this back in the airport, only it said, 'Bad hijab is prostitution.' That's really kind of funny, since Iran's prostitutes tend to be more covered than ordinary women. They even veil their faces."

The man's wife looked curiously at Hersch.

"You seem to know a great deal about this place, Mr. Trent. Have you been here before?"

"I read a lot," he replied.

The group eventually arrived at Hotel-é Bozorg-é Ferdosî, the area's only three-star hotel. John and Hersch were assigned their room first and quickly disappeared into the elevator.

Later at dinner, Hersch reported that John was too sick to come down, but promised to take some food up to their room in case his roommate felt up to eating later.

THURSDAY, 01 DECEMBER, 1830 LOCAL TIME
BANDAR-E ABBÂS, IRAN

THE TAXI STOPPED DIRECTLY in front of the compound entrance. Rolling down the rear window, he handed the requisite identification papers to the armed guard. The man looked at the picture and then at the occupant before nodding imperceptibly and motioning the car forward.

"You are expected at the main house, the second building on the right, straight ahead."

Dosha nodded as his driver started the car forward. A servant was standing at the door to the main house as they drove up. He opened the passenger door and stood back as Dosha got out, paid the fare, and handed the driver four 2000-rial notes for the tip.

"Kheilî mamnünam," he smiled, taking the money. *Thank you very much.*

"Ghâbel nabüd," *Don't mention it.*

"Salâm aleikom, Aghâ-ye. In taraf." The servant greeted him with a slight bow as the taxi pulled away. *Peace be upon you, sir. This way.*

Dosha followed him inside the house until they stood in the entry area.

"Wait here, please." The servant disappeared through a door-way. A moment later, he was back.

"Aghâ-yé Reza will see you now."

As Dosha entered the room, he was immediately greeted by an old man with a well-trimmed beard and emerald green eyes.

"We've been waiting for you for some time. At last, you are here. I am honored." Fardusi motioned toward a dark leather chair, partially covered with a wool afghan. "Please, make your-self at home."

"It is good to finally be here. I had hoped to arrive a couple of weeks earlier, but other matters detained me." Dosha reached into his pocket and pulled out a cigarette. "May I offer you one?"

"Thank you, no. If it is not too much to ask of my guest, I will join you in the garden, while you smoke. It is not permitted within these walls." Fardusi raised his palms in an openhanded signal of apology.

"That's all right. I will wait until later, thank you," Dosha responded.

At that moment a young Filipino woman appeared, bearing a pot of tea and several glass cups, which she placed between them on a small table.

"Thank you, Madeline," acknowledged Fardusi.

For the next few minutes the men exchanged polite pleasant-ries, for the most part in English, sounding for all purposes like two partners preparing to close a business deal. At last there was a lull in the conversation. Dosha shifted around in the chair.

"You have the girl?" he asked.

"Of course."

"Is she in this house?"

"Up the stairs."

"I would like to see her."

"I assumed as much. First, let me introduce you to the individual selected by our friends in Tehran to be the girl's official guardian." Fardusi called out, "Madeline?"

The maid reappeared from the kitchen.

"Would you ask Khånom Azari to join us?"

"Baleh, Aghå-yé." *Yes sir.* Even though he had spoken to her in English, Madeline always tried to answer in Farsi whenever possible, with some of the few phrases that she had learned since her arrival. Fardusi liked that. She walked rapidly across the room and up the stairs, disappearing beyond the visibility of the landing. A minute later, she reappeared, followed down the staircase by Leila Azari.

Leila was dressed in denim jeans, a long white shirt buttoned at the wrists, her head covered with an embroidered scarf. As Madeline returned to the kitchen, Leila moved easily and confidently across the room on bare feet to where the two men rose to greet her.

"Khånom Azari, this is Aghå-yé Marwan Dosha," Fardusi acknowledged politely.

"I have heard your name many times," she said demurely. "It is a pleasure to have this privilege of meeting."

"And I have heard of your exploits also," Dosha responded. "You have a well-deserved reputation for some of the work you have done in Lebanon and Germany. Will you join us in some tea?"

"Thank you," Leila said, waiting as Dosha moved a third chair over from the dining table while Fardusi attended to the tea. The three of them sat down.

"I have inquired about the girl and Aghå-yé Reza Fardusi has informed me that you have been overseeing her stay. Is she well?"

"Yes. However, she is weaker than at the beginning. The last several days, she eats very little. Her despondency is increasing. I do not think she will last another month."

"Fortunately, that will be unnecessary," said Dosha. "Everything will be finished, as far as she is concerned, by tomorrow night."

"Oh?" queried Fardusi, eyebrows lifted. "Will you be moving

her to a new location?"

"No. May I see her?"

"Of course," answered Leila, standing quickly to her feet. "I will take you to her at once."

"Please," Fardusi interjected, as he and Dosha stood. "If you do not plan to move her, then what?"

Leila was impatient to guide Dosha away from Fardusi's questions. Her dislike for this testy old man had increased with each passing day in his house. She hated the way he held his ground with her, refusing to fully yield to her right to be in charge. Besides, this was a moment in which to look "important" in the eyes of a man whose reputation she admired. And, now that she had seen him, her pulse rose at the thought of being alone with him, even for a short while.

Dosha paused, however, and turned back to Fardusi.

"Tomorrow night, the members of the local Council will be joining us, is that not true?"

"It is as you say. I have arranged it."

"You have a camera and an operator?"

"Yes. This has been arranged, as you requested."

"Good. As soon as everyone has arrived, we shall enjoy dinner together. Then, we film the girl reading a prepared statement outlining our demands. Afterwards, thanks to your kind hospitality, we shall enjoy some dessert."

"It will all be the finest Persian cuisine. My chef is the best. Will there be anything else?"

"That is all we need. After dessert we will return to her room and film Miss Cain one last time, as she is being shot to death."

The matter-of-factness of the man's tone added to the coldness to his statement. Fardusi stopped midstride to stare at him. Even Leila was obviously stunned.

"It is an essential part of the plan," Dosha assured them with a smile. "A symbolic sacrifice is needed to give credibility to our threats, should the world try to push aside our demands. There can be no better sacrifice than Jessica Cain. She is known around the world. Her demise will assure people everywhere that we are not to be denied. Now, may we continue? I want to see her before I go to my hotel."

Leila Azari turned and silently ascended the stairs, closely followed by Dosha. Fardusi turned away and walked to the glass door looking out on the illuminated garden. Its low-lit beauty did not give him the normal rush of pleasure. Not tonight. Not after what he had just heard.

IN THE KITCHEN, MADELINE stepped back from pressing her ear to the door. Her mouth was dry and her heart pounded twice as fast as usual. What she had just heard was unbelievably evil! Rushing to the sink, she wretched a suddenly upset stomach, then reached for a glass of water to rinse out the awful taste.

That poor girl. O dear God, that poor little girl. She could be my little sister! Madeline closed her eyes as she leaned against the counter and tried to rein in her emotions. *Lord, how could I ever bear it if something like this were to happen to Tamara? It would be too terrible. Jessica Cain is Your child too, Lord. Something must be done. This cannot be permitted to happen. But, what, Lord? What can I do? What can anyone do to help her?*

FRIDAY, 02 DECEMBER, 0800 LOCAL TIME
TEHRAN, IRAN

THE MORNING FOLLOWING John's "illness," Hersch reported to Ms. Langford that Dr. Castle had spent a restless night, was feeling somewhat better, but had decided to remain in their room in order to be ready for the next day's journey into the countryside. Though he would enjoy the day tour of Tehran, Hersch said that he had decided to stay with his friend. Ms. Langford offered to request the services of a physician through the hotel management, but Hersch declined. Dr. Castle looked better, he said, and with rest, he ought to be fine for the next day's travel plans.

Hersch stood in the hotel doorway and waved good-bye to the group as they boarded the sightseeing bus in what promised to be a smog-drenched day in Tehran. As they rounded the corner and disappeared from sight, he stood for a moment, watching the flow of foot-traffic moving by. It looked too much like a funeral, he decided, the predominant color being black. The only vivid color he noticed came from the dresses of little girls, with bare arms and legs, a symbol of freedom soon to be lost. They would need to don the chador by nine, the age Khomeini had declared girls mature enough to be married.

Hersch walked back into the lobby and waited for the elevator to take him to the fifth floor where he would spend the day caring for his "sick" companion.

Six months after the Iranian Revolution, Khomeini had declared on national radio, "There is no fun in Islam. There can be no enjoyment in whatever is serious." As the elevator door opened, a dour-looking man stepped out, glaring at Hersch as he brushed past. Behind him were two women completely covered with black chadors. A third woman stepped out in an ankle-length coat that Tehran residents call a manteau. It was dark green in color and buttoned up the front, making it less likely to fall open and expose the wearer, a crime punishable by flogging or even imprisonment.

He shook his head. *Khomeini was right. There is no joy in Mudville.*

Hersch was alone in the elevator when the door closed behind him. He looked forward to a few hours of relaxation, then remembered that the mullahs controlled the television for much of the day, with readings from the Koran, prayers, and pretaped sermons.

How did I ever let myself get talked into this?

AT THREE O'CLOCK, AN HOUR before their group was scheduled to return, Mr. Harold Trent and Dr. John Castle stepped out of the elevator and made their way across the hotel lobby.

The desk clerk, who was aware of his sick American resident, nodded at them both. Dr. Castle looked much better. What was the expression he had learned while studying at Arizona State University? The picture of health? Yes, that was it. Dr. Castle certainly looked to be the picture of health.

The two Americans paused long enough to leave their key at the desk and a message in Ms. Langford's box. Dr. Castle was feeling so much better that the two of them had decided to see what they could of Tehran on their own. They might not be back in time for dinner, but would be ready to rejoin the group tomorrow morning. The clerk watched as the men climbed into a Peugeot taxi and were quickly lost in the never-ending river of old metal, treadless rubber, and carbon monoxide.

AT TEHRAN'S MEHRABAD AIRPORT, Trent and Castle presented their tickets for the Havåpeimå'î-yé Jomhürî-yé Eslåmî-yé Irån flight to Bandar-é Abbås. Its full Persian name is a mouthful, even for locals, and many of them refer to it simply as Homå, after the mythical bird used as the airline's symbol. The rest of the world knows it as Iran Air.

There had been no problem getting domestic tickets through a downtown agency, even though Iran Air's own ticketing personnel had pronounced the flight completely booked. A friend back home, who had spent considerable time in Iran on behalf of the State Department, had told Hersch that the airline usually reserved a certain number of seats on every flight for special customers, until a few hours before boarding time. Foreigners often counted as "special customers," especially if the foreigner could offer the agent a handsome amount of rials above the regular purchase price. This had proven to be the case for Mr. Trent and Dr. Castle.

A few minutes before six o'clock, the Iran Air Boeing 737 lifted off the runway and began its journey by banking away from the teeming metropolis below and settling on a south, southeast heading. Approximately two uneventful hours later, the plane touched down gently, a few miles east of Bandar-é Abbås.

As Mr. Trent and Dr. Castle disembarked with the other passengers, they immediately sensed the difference in weather conditions. The air felt much warmer and more muggy than in Tehran. They carried no luggage, nor had they checked any. It was all still in a closet in the hotel in Tehran. If anyone looked in on them this evening, they would be reassured that the men had simply not as yet returned from going out on the town.

They had no return tickets. There were no flights out until the next day anyway. By that time, if everything went as planned, they would be knocking at the doors of the US Embassy in Dubai, UAE, slapping one another on the back, and holding tightly onto the twelve-year-old package they had come halfway around the world to claim.

Mr. Trent, the rug merchant, and Dr. Castle, the professor of religion, had never been more serious about their reason for being anywhere than they were about being in Bandar-é Abbås tonight.

THIRTY-SIX

"Are we ready?" Paul Heilbrun called out to the eleven other men.

"You bet." "Yes." "Ready, boss." The response was enthusiastic, in spite of the fact that at twelve-thirty at night it was a chilly forty-two degrees and falling.

"Okay, Buddy, let's ride."

Lights on, the truck slowly moved forward into the tunnel.

"I get a kick out of this run every time we do it," Buddy Ryan commented to his boss, as he guided the battery-powered, electric industrial truck along the tunnel floor.

"You always were a bit of a mole," commented Heilbrun.

"It's an amazing piece of work—I can't help but admire it."

"How many times have you been through?"

"This makes five . . . no, six for me. And you?"

"I've lost track, maybe ten or eleven. I'm not sure."

As the men talked, their eyes never left the appointed task of inspecting the Coast Range Tunnel superstructure, between the Tesla and Irvington Portals. Though no structural problem was anticipated, the vehicle carried enough tools and supplies to take care of any minor difficulty encountered in the Bay Area's primary water source. To ensure its viability, however, water was periodically shut off and a crew sent through for an official check of the 29-mile tunnel under the rolling hills south of the burgeoning cities of Pleasanton and Livermore. It was a bumpy ride, with lots of dampness and chill, but it was essential to keeping the promise that had been made to the people seventy years earlier.

The Coast Range Tunnel served as an important link in the Hetch Hetchy Aqueduct system, bringing precious water from the Hetch Hetchy Reservoir, nestled high in the Sierra Mountains east of the San Francisco Bay, to residents living along the coastlands.

What was at the time of its construction the longest underground construction project in the world, the Coast Range Tunnel extended from Tesla Portal at the end of San Joaquin Pipeline, westerly to Irvington Portal near Mission San Jose. Starting at elevation 399, it dropped 83 feet, finishing at 316, and consisted of three basic parts: a 25-mile tunnel, a 3½-mile tunnel, and a half-mile pipeline joining the two tunnels across a valley at Alameda Creek. Having been constructed in softer and more treacherous ground than its connecting mountain tunnels to the east, it had been lined with concrete in circular form for the entire distance.

It was a critical part of the amazing 149-mile-long network that culminated in spilling its precious cargo out from under the Pulgas Water Temple and into the Peninsula's Spring Valley Reservoirs. These man-made lakes provided pure mountain water every day to the citizens of San Francisco, Santa Clara, Alameda, and San Mateo counties.

Paul looked at his watch. One-ten. The trip, at an average speed of approximately six miles per hour, could be accomplished in five or six hours. With the occasional stop to check and repair any suspicious-looking area, the inspection was normally an all-day ordeal for the men.

Heilbrun felt a sudden chill run up his back. He buttoned the top of his coat and slipped his hands into a pair of waterproof gloves. Buddy glanced over at his boss and smiled.

LESS THAN A MILE BEHIND THE INSPECTION CREW, four dark-clad figures moved swiftly and silently, headlamps their only source of light. Two of the intruders made certain that each small waterproof package was securely attached to one side or the other of the tunnel. The remaining two followed, connecting each package with a small insulated wire. Once in place, they were concealed well enough so as not to be noticed unless someone were to carefully inspect the hidden crevasses for suspicious material. That was highly unlikely. And, once the water was running again, it would be too late.

They had worked without conversation for almost an hour

before pausing over the nearly completed task.

"This place looks very solid," one of the dark-clad figures commented. "Do you think this will actually work?"

The lead man patted the most recently installed package. "With this stuff, there will be no problem. It is little but powerful. No problem so long as you have wired it correctly."

"Each one is securely connected. When the button is pushed . . . boom!"

They laughed.

"Come on, let's finish and get out of here. I'm dying for a cigarette."

FRIDAY, 02 DECEMBER 1730 LOCAL TIME
BANDAR-E ABBÁS, IRAN

THOUGH NONE OF THE MEN had been inside before, over the years they had driven by and verbalized their curiosity about what lay beyond the walls of the Fardusi compound. Tonight, they were about to find out.

They reached the main gate on foot, at the predetermined hour, and waited while the guard checked their identification and called ahead to announce their arrival.

It was even more magnificent than any of them had thought possible. White buildings surrounded the compound, separated occasionally by well-tended trees and gardens that framed the entire setting in understated loveliness. Shadows of evening fell across the gravel drive that curved gracefully through fountains and still more gardens, bestowing the additional reality of function and architectural symmetry to the scene. Low lights flickered along the drive and throughout the gardens. The setting was a reminder of a grand and glorious Persian past that, inwardly, each man valued with secret pride, while outwardly criticizing it as pretentious and garish.

A servant stepped out of the main house and came toward them. A few steps away, he paused and bowed his head politely, waiting for the men to make the next move. Walking slowly, they followed him into the house. This evening would be the stuff of many stories, most bearing little resemblance to the actual event, the telling of which would become theater for their children and grandchildren in years to come. Stories about the night their father or grandfather ate dinner at the house of Reza Fardusi. Stories of the important work they had done on behalf of Hizballah, the Party of God. This was a night to feel one's importance.

Just before eight-thirty, the last guest arrived at the security gate in a taxi. Rolling down the rear window, he showed his face to the guard, but offered no papers this time.

"Shab bekheir, Aghå-yé." *Good evening, sir.* The guard was respectfully cordial as he gave instructions to the driver. A moment later, the car moved slowly up the driveway to the entrance of the main house.

The passenger opened the car door and paused to present a generous tip to the driver. As the taxi pulled away, the man stood for a moment, taking in the surroundings.

This is, indeed, a place of beauty. And beautiful things will happen here tonight.

This would be the preacher's daughter's last night on earth. The very thought brought a quick rush of satisfaction. And, then there was Leila Azari. After the tasks of the evening were over, perhaps . . . well, there would be time for that later. He walked up the steps as the servant came forward to greet him.

Once inside, he was ushered into the dining room where the others had already helped themselves to generous portions of chelo kabåb and jüjé kabab, long thin strips of lamb and chicken, that had been marinated overnight in seasoned yogurt. Just before serving, it had been grilled and was now presented with mounds of chelo rice. The entire main dish was accompanied by a raw onion, a pat of butter, and a bowl of yogurt to stir into each portion of rice. The usual nuts and fruits were attractively placed, and empty bowls were stacked nearby, ready to be filled later on with the deliciously refreshing pålüdé, a sorbet with rosewater, ground pistachios, and sultanas.

Reza Fardusi rose to greet his last guest. Kissing first one cheek and then the other, he was conscious of the scar that ran across an otherwise flawless face, disappearing into the man's beard.

"Khosh åmadîd." *"Welcome."*

"Motashakkeram, shomå kheilî mehrabün hastîd." *"Thank you. You are very kind."*

"Let me introduce you to the others who have preceded your arrival." Fardusi led Dosha to each of the others. "Aghå-yé Marwan, this is . . ." and so it went around the table. Marwan Dosha mentally noted that only one man stood when introduced. It was evident that not everyone was pleased at his presence.

He was mindful that his recent failure had evoked strong criticism in Hizballah circles; there were subtle ways to express these feelings without saying a word. He had used them quite effectively on others, and now, Dosha had just experienced one of those subtleties. His jaw tightened as he moved around the table. Then, he proceeded to help himself to the food.

The meal continued in relative quiet, the guests following their familiar custom of sparse mealtime conversation. Upon finishing, they moved to another part of the room and reclined on pillows surrounding an elaborately woven oriental rug, while hot tea was served.

"Thank you, Madeline, that will be all. Perhaps a bit more tea later on with dessert," Fardusi said, as he watched her finish pouring the last glass cup.

Dosha, with his never-ending penchant for details, registered that it was the same Filipino servant who had been on duty the previous evening. He then dismissed the detail as unimportant, while the girl nodded to Fardusi and backed several steps away from the men before disappearing into the kitchen.

IT WAS MADELINE'S SECOND DAY in the main house since her banishment on the occasion of the Great Spill. For the most part, her friend and fellow Filipino, Alisha, had taken her place, alternating with Theresa who was still not completely recovered from her recent illness. At first, Madeline had thought this might be God's way of covering for her clumsiness. She viewed Alisha as a much more mature Christian than she could claim herself to be. After all, it was Alisha who had taken her to the little church she had since come to love. And so, she had told her more about the girl in the room upstairs.

To Madeline's chagrin, Alisha refused to serve as a go-between. She would carry no messages or do anything else that might jeopardize her job or her life. She was sympathetic to the little girl's plight, but was frightened and refused to help her.

Two days ago, however, something had taken Alisha out of the lineup. She had gone to bed with a virus. When this was reported to Reza Fardusi, he specifically asked for Madeline to replace her. Mrs. Muños chuckled when she told her and said she thought it was partly because he genuinely liked Madeline and respected her efficiency, and, partly because he felt the need to assert his authority. On this night especially.

When Madeline asked why this was so, Mrs. Muños replied that the soldier woman, Leila, and her cohorts, would not like it, and that made their employer's decision seem all the more delicious to her. An unspoken power struggle clearly existed between Aghå-yé Reza and Leila Azari. While animosity was rarely openly displayed, those who served them sensed what was under the surface. Mrs. Muños did not like Azari, and she could not comprehend why they were holding a child hostage in the upstairs room. The Azari woman was up to no good, and somehow, she had drawn her employer into this dubious scheme.

Mrs. Muños went on to say that Reza Fardusi had recently confirmed her belief regarding his resentment of these female warriors who had, for all practical purposes, taken over the second floor of his home. Madeline thought Mrs. Muños to be quite proud of the confidence that had been shared with her, for it confirmed her position as the staff member closest to Fardusi. Furthermore, Mrs. Muños did not mind at all that Madeline was able to appreciate the glory and honor that had been bestowed upon her.

When Madeline asked about this evening's guests, she was told that they were important officials, but the purpose of their meeting remained a mystery. For Mrs. Muños, it was enough that tonight the great Fardusi was determined to reclaim his authority, and that one of her own workers was to be a symbol of that determination.

Unable to shake the apprehension she felt, Madeline stood in the kitchen, stacking dishes to one side of the stainless steel sink. The only other person present was the chef, busily concluding her cleanup up of the food preparation area.

"Make sure the dishes are washed and put away before you leave tonight," the chef said, without looking up.

"Of course."

"I'll be going in a few minutes. You can handle the rest of the evening?" It was more of an order than a question.

"I will be fine, thank you," Madeline replied. The sooner the chef left, the better. She was desperate to know more about what the men in the next room were up to. She still could think of no way to help the young American girl.

While serving them this evening, she had overheard little. The talk around the table was confined to the banal interchange one usually hears while waiting on men during dinner. Then, one brief exchange had focused her attention.

It was the man who had casually declared the night before that he was going to kill the girl. Tonight, he sat next to Reza Fardusi. As she poured hot tea into a glass cup near his plate, he turned to Fardusi and asked, "Where is the girl?"

Fardusi motioned toward the staircase as he bit into a generous portion of chelo kabåb. "Up there. The women are guarding her."

"I would like to see her again."

"And you will, of course," said Fardusi, wiping his mouth with the back of his hand. "But first, you must have some pålüdé. It is delicious. Madeline? Please."

Madeline set the teapot to one side, moving with smooth efficiency as she placed a small bowl of pålüdé in front of the stranger. He did not look up or acknowledge her presence. His mind was obviously on other things.

Those "things" undoubtedly include the helpless hostage upstairs. . . .

Madeline was sure of it. Her heart pounded anxiously.

These men are all here about Jessica Cain!

Her mind was racing now, as she busied herself at the sink. The frightening knowledge that this evil man's threat of murder was soon to be carried out set off an inner panic that bordered on desperation.

At the opposite end of the counter from Madeline, the chef was gathering up a small basket of leftover fruit. She knew this would be taken back to the servants' quarters to be shared with the others. The basket would be left by the door in the entryway leading to the tiny rooms where the contract employees lived. This small act of thoughtfulness had long endeared the otherwise stoic chef to her compatriots.

The outer door had barely closed when Madeline rushed to the door leading into the great room, where the men were finishing their meal. She pressed her ear against it, but could hear only a jumble of voices.

Bravely deciding on a more direct approach, she opened the door and stepped unobtrusively into the room, waiting quietly as though prepared to respond to any command. She gathered that Farsi was not the first language of the man with the scar. For that reason, they spoke in English, with only occasional lapses into Farsi.

" . . . it is extremely dangerous," one of the men was arguing, shaking his head vehemently.

"I agree," affirmed his table companion. "Once the world realizes that we have her, the outcry will be great."

"The world need not ever know where she is," said the man with the scar. "They know the Palestinian Islamic Jihad are responsible for taking her. That is enough. We will remain silent as to her whereabouts."

Madeline noted the discontented murmur that followed as the men debated the plan being proposed by Dosha. She had the distinct feeling that what the others thought really didn't matter. He had already decided what he was going to do. The heated discussion around the table would ultimately be of little importance in determining the final outcome.

Reza Fardusi appeared to have been more an observer than a participant. When finally he saw her standing there, he lifted his eyes questioningly in her direction. Responding to Fardusi's movement, the men quickly quieted and looked in her direction, surprised to see her there.

Madeline stepped forward.

"May I bring you anything else?" she asked, making a conscious effort to keep her voice calm, free of the terror she felt inside.

Fardusi waved her off. "No, Madeline, but please, stay nearby. We may wish to have some refreshments later."

Madeline backed away, then turned and reentered the kitchen. Once by herself, she leaned against the counter and released a deep breath. Fortunately, her presence in the other room had not been questioned. Unfortunately, she had learned very little, other than to confirm what she already knew, that something was about to happen to the girl upstairs.

Her mind raced, but she could think of nothing else to do. Just then, she heard the sound of a door shutting, and another voice. A woman's voice. It was Leila Azari. Chairs could be heard scraping on the tile floor. People were moving about.

Madeline pressed her ear against the door once again. She could barely make out what was taking place. Fardusi was introducing the woman. Their voices faded as the men began moving toward the staircase. Madeline carefully turned the doorknob until it released from the catch. She pushed it forward until a small crack permitted her to see and hear.

What came next caused her to catch her breath. The men were following Azari up the stairs. One carried a movie camera and tripod. She saw them pause at the head of the stairs while Azari unlocked the door to Jessica's room. Then they disappeared inside.

Madeline's heart sank.

Poor Jessica. O God, please help that little girl. I've done all I can, but it is not enough. Surely You can find it in your heart to watch over her. There are bad people in this house.

Madeline's eyes filled with tears as she stared up at the ceiling in desperation.

What else can I do?

Jessica was dozing fitfully on the cot. Two of her fingers moved back and forth, lightly touching her upper lip, a habitual motion acquired in early childhood.

At the sound of approaching voices and footsteps, she rolled over and faced the door. When the key entered the lock, she struggled to sit up. As the door opened, several shadowy figures stood in the entrance. One of them turned on the light, causing Jessica to shield her eyes with a hand.

Anticipating a guard or a servant, the only persons who had entered her prison in weeks, she was startled to see Leila Azari, followed by several men. As her eyes became accustomed to the light, she recognized two of them. One was the man who had stood in the doorway with Azari the night before and stared at her a long time. Behind him was Fardusi, the owner of the house. He was the last one to enter.

"This is the girl," Azari indicated, motioning toward Jessica with a wave of her hand. As she did, the men quieted, staring at her curiously. The one who had visited her cell earlier came toward her.

What is going on?

He stood in front of her now, unsmiling, his solemn look accentuated by the noticeable scar on his cheek. Jessica licked her lips in an effort to counter the sudden dryness in her mouth. She stared into his eyes, wanting to look away, but feeling helplessly drawn to him. They were not the eyes of a kind man. She ran her tongue across her lips again.

"Who are you?" asked Jessica, her voice small and quivering.

Before she could move, the man's hand reached out and grasped her chin, his fingers digging into the sides of her jaw. She tried pulling away, but he held her face like a steel vise gripping clay.

"Don't move," he said quietly. "I can easily snap your neck with this one hand."

Jessica clutched the edge of the cot, the man's face now only inches away from her own. He turned her head slightly to the left, then back to the right, before releasing his hold and stepping back. His eyes never left her face.

"You resemble your father, Jessica Cain, but perhaps your mother even more."

"You know my parents?" Jessica gasped in disbelief, rubbing the sides of her face with her hands.

"I know them all too well," he replied. Then he turned abruptly and spoke to one of the other men. "Set the camera up facing that wall."

For the first time, Jessica noticed the camera.

"You say you know my parents and you know my name. What's yours?" asked Jessica, recovering from her initial shock. The man turned to her once again.

"My name is Dosha. Marwan Dosha." Jessica caught the look of expectancy as he paused. Apparently he hoped that his name would mean something to her.

"I don't know you," she answered.

He blinked, as though in doubt that there was anyone in the world who did not know who he was. Then, he looked away to determine how the camera operator was coming along. The man said something that Jessica could not understand. Dosha nodded as he roughly grasped Jessica's shoulder. She winced in pain as he dragged her from the bed and pushed her against the wall. She was shaking, partly from having eaten very little during the last several days, but mostly from fear. The others in the room surrounded the cameraman, watching as Jessica bravely tried not to shake.

"Take this and read it," Dosha said, handing her several pieces of paper.

"What is it?"

"It's a message to your parents. Read it. Don't add anything to it, and don't leave anything out. Read exactly what is written."

Jessica looked down at the script and swallowed as she tried to hold it steady.

"Read! The camera is rolling."

Jessica glanced up into the round lens, a few short feet away. She could hear the whirring sound as her frightened countenance was being recorded. Brushing at her matted hair, she returned to the paper and began to read.

"My name is Jessica Cain. It is Friday, December 2." She paused and looked over at Dosha. *Is it really December? I've lost track.* She wanted to ask if this was the actual date, but he motioned for her to continue, and his grim look cautioned her about further questioning.

She focused her attention on the papers again and continued reading.

"I am a prisoner of war, held by the freedom fighters of the Palestinian Islamic Jihad. I have learned of their terrible plight since I was taken captive in Israel. They have been grossly abused and mistreated by the Jews and by the United Nations. The world has robbed them of their land and given it to the Jews who, in turn, have raped their wives and daughters, killed their fathers and sons, and destroyed their homes. Allah has called upon these freedom fighters to strike back. It will be a war to the death, if necessary. There is no other alternative until the Jews and their chief supporters, the Americans, agree to their terms.

"I, Jessica Cain, am the first of many children of the world who must pay for the sins of their parents. Unless the following terms are agreed to, others will follow me in death. They will be taken from the streets of their towns and cities. For every Palestinian home that has been destroyed by Jews, ten homes will be destroyed in Occupied Palestine and ten more in the United States, that Great Satan who fills the cruel hand of the Palestinian Islamic Jihad's sworn enemies. These are the Jews who, with weapons and money provided by that Great Satan, are able to continue their suppression of the Palestinian peoples. Schools will be blown up. Synagogues and churches will be burned down. Unless the following terms are met, one of America's cities has been chosen to feel the noose of persecution that the Palestinian peoples feel every day. It will tighten and cut off their very source of life.

"First, those under the judgment of Allah must at once agree to sit at the table of surrender and negotiate a just peace.

"Second, the United Nations must agree to rescind its 1948 decision to destroy the Palestinian people by taking from them their God-given right to the land of their fathers' fathers.

"Third, a new nation of Palestine must be at once recognized by the world community of nations, and it must encompass all of the territory now falsely known as the land of Israel.

"Be reminded of the recent deaths of the children in the city of Boston. Their martyrdom was necessary to demonstrate how easily the things that I have mentioned can be carried out within the borders of the United States. Israel is even more vulnerable. The true Palestinian peoples will not be denied their rightful inheritance. It has been promised them by Allah himself. Nothing you can do will change his divine will in this matter.

"As a symbol of your positive response to their demands, my release has been pledged, upon receipt of $100 million, or, approximately $1 for every boy and girl in Israel and the USA.

"This must be accomplished by the end of this year. If you are sincere, it will be easy for every man, woman, and child to give up $1 of their Christmas shopping money for the righteous cause of Islam's true followers. However, if the money is not deposited in a European bank of their choosing by December 31, I will be killed. Please help me come home. I forgive my father for abandoning me in Israel in order to do harm to the Palestinians. He . . . he did not know what he was doing. I want to come home safely. Please do everything they say."

Jessica looked up at the camera. It clearly recorded the fear in her eyes. And something else. What was it?

The whirring sound stopped. Dosha stepped forward and took the script from her hand. As he did, Jessica's knees gave way and she crumpled to the floor. No one offered to help her.

The cameraman folded up his gear while the others questioned Dosha regarding the message.

"How do you propose to carry out these attacks against churches, schools, and synagogues?"

"Our freedom fighters are already in place and prepared to act when the order comes," Dosha answered. "We will begin this month and continue unabated until the enemy says, 'Enough.'"

"They are in place already?"

"Yes."

"The targets have all been chosen?"

"They have, but we need added financial backing. The weapons and explosives are expensive. So also is the continued establishment of our commandos in places where they can strike terror into the hearts of Allah's enemies."

"How have you done this?"

"Some are in America under the guise of political asylum. A few are entrenched in corporations in major cities. A number are students on college campuses."

"And so you have come to ask us for additional funds beyond what is already allocated to Hamas and the Jihad? Exactly how much will you need?"

"Of course, the $100 million we are requesting from the enemy will be a major contribution," Dosha replied, with a sinister smile. "If they are foolish enough to provide even half that amount, it will supply us with the money we are spending for the centerpiece of our strike and more. Beyond this, an additional $10 million is required to complete funding of the preemptory attacks."

"The ones against their religious and educational institutions?"

"Yes."

"And to their homes as well?"

"In some cases, yes."

"Before we can agree to such a large amount as you are asking, you must tell us what you intend to do in the city of which you speak. What is meant exactly by the 'tightening of the noose'? We know you have been dealing with scientists in Libya and in the former Soviet Union. Have you acquired the bomb?"

"No, not the bomb, but something akin to its devastating power. We will not use anthrax either, though that is still a possibility at some future point. Libya has its scientists working on biological and chemical weapons and continues to refine them for future experimentation. All I am prepared to say now is that a major city in America has been chosen and our people are in place.

"In the days ahead, our 'weapon of choice,' which must remain a secret for now, will be placed in their hands. It is silent. It is simple. And, it is deadly. That which flows from under the temple will poison the earth. Tens of thousands will die in the short term and many more over time. The rest of the world will finally understand that they can resist us no longer. The result of our efforts should be breathtaking, indeed!"

The camera operator was standing by with the others, solemnly listening to Dosha's discourse on death.

"But, let us enjoy our dessert now and we can talk further," Dosha suggested, looking at Fardusi. Fardusi nodded, his countenance grim. The other men shuffled out first, followed by Fardusi and Dosha. Leila Azari was the last to leave. She paused at the door and looked back, checking the wilted figure of the world's best-known twelve-year-old. Then she stepped into the hall, closing the door behind her.

The room that had been prison for its child hostage fell captive to a silent mourning. Created with doors that opened to an alcove of hospitality, it was now a locked cell of suffering.

An innocent child lay helpless on a tile floor altar created by hell. Those who would rule the earth planned to kill her on it, as invisible demons danced with glee overhead at the mere thought. Spirits bent on evil rushed into the hallway and down the stairs, ready to incite the total ruination of Eden's tarnished crown.

It had happened before, that kings and cohorts sought to kill another Child. It should not have come as a surprise that evil men were still ready to kill the children.

The shadow of death's angel remained, seeking his prey, as the child's finger moved slowly back and forth, lightly touching her lip as she had done since childhood.

THIRTY-EIGHT

Madeline stood in the kitchen doorway as the parade marched down the stairs. Her employer kept a hand on the railing as he descended, a look of serious displeasure on his face. As he reached the main floor, he glanced up and saw her standing there.

"Madeline," he called, his voice stern and eyes snapping in anger. Madeline started, fearing that he was upset at seeing her waiting there.

"Madeline," he said again. "Take some bread and water up to the girl. She is not feeling well. And stay with her until she is better."

"Would it not be better to serve dessert before occupying your servant with other matters?" Leila's voice had an edge to it. Fardusi glared at her.

"You and I will do the honors of serving dessert, Khånom Azari. It will be a privilege, don't you think?"

Leila's eyes flashed resentment at being relegated to a servant's status, but she knew she had been trapped by the wily old man. "Of course," she replied smoothly.

Madeline's eyes moved rapidly across the rest of the entourage, but saw nothing that would indicate concern on their faces. The person with the camera equipment was talking to another who stood in front of him, and the man with the scar was smiling as he waited near the bottom of the stairs.

Quickly, she ran back into the kitchen. There had been the hint of urgency in Reza Fardusi's voice.

She withdrew a pitcher of water from the refrigerator and gathered half a loaf of bread from the evening's dinner.

As Madeline reentered the main room, Leila Azari was moving among the guests with a tray of glass cups, filled with hot tea taken from the serving bar. She paused to talk to the man with the scar. As unobtrusively as possible, Madeline made her way past the group and started up the stairs.

One of the female warriors stood at the head of the staircase, watching events unfold below. Madeline groaned inwardly. It was the woman who had demanded that she be taken off second floor duty in the first place. She braced herself for a confrontation, but the woman merely scowled and moved back into the hallway to unlock the door.

She must have overheard Aghâ-yé Reza's orders, Madeline thought, as she moved past, careful not to permit another accident.

Entering, she was shocked to see Jessica sprawled on the floor, opposite the doorway. She closed the door behind her, placed the pitcher on the floor, balanced the bread on top of it, and quickly went to the girl.

Her eyes were open, but she did not move.

"Jessica."

No response.

"Jessica!"

Jessica's eyes flickered, as she tried to concentrate on where the voice was coming from. Madeline could not believe it. She must have passed out in front of the people who were now downstairs eating dessert. They had walked away, leaving her alone in that condition.

"Here, Jessica. Take some water." In her haste, Madeline had forgotten to bring a glass. She knelt down on the floor and cradled Jessica with one arm while putting the pitcher to her lips. Water ran down her face and neck, spilling onto her blouse. The blouse was dirty and Madeline wondered when was the last time it had been washed. Jessica was focusing more now and reached up to push the pitcher away.

"Thank you," she said, weakly. Jessica squinted as she sought to identify her newfound benefactor. "You're the one . . . the message . . . Madeline?"

"Shh," Madeline warned, placing her fingers lightly on Jessica's lips. "Walls sometimes have ears. It is best to whisper, okay?"

Jessica nodded and offered a slight smile.

"Yes, I am Madeline," she said softly. "The message that you gave me was sent to your father. We have heard nothing, but we are certain that he has received it."

Jessica attempted to get up.

"Here, let me," Madeline said, as she helped her over to the bed.

"Lie down and rest," she urged, kneeling beside her again. "Eat some of this. It is fresh bread."

"I'm not hungry."

"Eat." Madeline's voice was low, but firm. "You need some food to regain your strength. What happened in here?"

"They . . . they put me in front of . . . a camera. A man said it was a message to my dad and made me . . . read from some papers." Jessica stopped and looked up. A tear spilled out onto her cheek. Madeline brushed it away with the tip of her finger.

"What did it say?"

"I don't remember everything. It was long . . . something about the Palestinians demanding their rights and stuff."

Madeline nodded. "What else?"

"That if they don't get what they want . . . they will kill me. They . . . they want money before they will let me go home."

Madeline waited, then said, "How much?"

"A hundred million dollars!"

"Are you sure? You can't be serious."

"That's what they made me read. It's supposed to be a dollar from every boy and girl in Israel and America. They said that they have to get it by the end of December. If they don't, they will kill me. And a lot of other children will die too, and keep on dying until they get what they want."

They fell silent as the impact of the message sank in. Madeline could hardly fathom the heartless reality of what was happening to this child nor could she comprehend what sort of evil mind could declare war on the children of the world.

"Rest here," she said, getting to her feet.

"Please, don't go," Jessica pleaded, clinging to her uniform.

"No. It's okay. I'm not going to leave you."

Madeline went to the door. She had not remembered hearing the lock set after she came in. Turning the knob slowly, testing it, she was careful not to make a sound. It opened. She paused, half expecting the guard to pull it open all the way and confront her. There was nothing. She cracked it further until she could see the guard, leaning on the rail at the landing, watching the people below in the main room. Turning, she touched her lips with a finger, urging Jessica to remain silent. Then mouthing the words, "I'll be right back," she stepped through the doorway.

Madeline crept, unnoticed, to within a few feet of the guard who remained engrossed in the proceedings below. Jessica was not close enough to see what was happening, but she could hear the voices, and they were conversing in English. She was struck by the tone of disbelief in the man now speaking. It was Reza Fardusi's voice.

"SURELY YOU DO NOT SERIOUSLY BELIEVE that the Jews and the Americans will give you this amount of money for the child."

"Perhaps. Perhaps not. If they do, it will go a long way toward financing The Cause. If they do not, we will continue with the plan anyway. It is a roll of the dice in either case. Not that I would ever roll the dice literally, you understand. I too am a Muslim. It's against my religion to gamble," Dosha concluded with a smile.

"Humph," Fardusi snorted with disdain. He had not cared for this man's reputation, even before they met, and he liked him even less now. He did not like the ostentatious attitudes of the other men. He did not like Leila Azari and her female warriors. In fact, he was beginning to think that there was nothing he did like about The Cause. "It appears to me that this whole operation is a gamble. And you seem to think you hold all the cards."

"Not all the cards," Dosha replied, his smile now replaced with a look of hard determination. "Just the trump card."

The others had grown silent, listening as the world's prime terrorist stood toe to toe with one of Iran's most feared citizens, a man hated by every person in the room. He was surely not one of them. Maybe he never had been. Reza Fardusi was always controversial, and yet, he survived. But, a growing contingent believed that it was only a matter of time. Perhaps this was the moment.

"You wager the future of your people and ours," accused Fardusi. "This plan of yours has too many pitfalls. How can we be expected to believe it will succeed when your most recent efforts have ended in failure?"

No one moved. All eyes were on the defiant old Iranian and the younger man with the scar. Fardusi's words hung between them like autumn leaves, tinged with flaming brilliance, yet so fragile that a thoughtless whisper might cause them to fall, leaving the old branch vulnerable to winter's final chill.

"I am your guest, Aghâ-yé Fardusi. As such, I will not respond to your indelicate words, though, under different circumstances and in a different place, you may be sure that I would be most happy to do so. My world is filled with dangerous tangles. The only order is that which I impose on it myself. With the help of Allah, of course," Dosha responded.

"Of course," murmured Fardusi, appearing not the least bit intimidated by the outlaw standing in front of him. "My apologies, as your host, for drawing attention to unpleasant memories. However, you have used my house for these past weeks as a prison for a child. Now, you want to ransom her in front of the world for an amount far in excess of any sane country's willingness to respond.

"Are you sure that it is the good of our Holy War that you envision? Do you have the Palestinian peoples and their future clearly in mind with this plan? Or, is it possible . . . forgive me for even mentioning it, but I must . . . is it possible that you have a personal agenda to which you wish to commit us? After all, the girl upstairs is merely an insignificant child. A pawn. Her father is the one who thwarted your assault on Jerusalem, is he not? How can we be assured that you are not merely meting out revenge through his child?"

Fardusi looked around. Score one. He saw that the other men were processing what he had just suggested. It was a possibility that had escaped many of them until now. As much as they disliked Fardusi, his logic did offer some serious questions.

Dosha felt it too. He wished that he and the old man were alone. He would make short work of him. A quick twist of the neck and Reza Fardusi would be a part of Iranian history.

"I believe The Cause is Allah's will and Aghå-yé Marwan is his chosen instrument. The plan is ingenious."

The spell of the standoff was broken between the two men by a strong, feminine voice. Leila Azari stood confidently at the center of the great room, a woman obviously comfortable with expressing her own views in a male world.

"This initiative will strike fear and trembling into the hearts of every Jewish and American family," she continued, hands on hips, feet spread apart. She was smiling, but a space opened around her as Fardusi's guests detected the authority in her voice. "A few synagogues, churches, and schools blown up will let them know that no one is safe. We must drive them out one way or another. You all know that. We must bring the oppressors to their knees."

Her voice rose slightly, carrying with it an edge of excitement.

"It is the only way that our Holy War can be waged successfully against the Great Satan. These agents of hell are responsible for the deaths of my mother and father and brothers. Am I not correct in assuming that they have killed some of your family members too? An eye for an eye. That is what the Prophet Moham-med, may the blessings and peace of God be upon him, has commanded."

Two of the men nodded their heads in agreement.

"And if the world does not acquiesce to your demands?" challenged Fardusi, his green eyes flashing in anger.

"It will not matter," injected Dosha. "A church, a school, a synagogue . . . each will serve as a graphic example. We will blow the infidels into bits and pieces and present them to the world as 'Happy Hanukkah' and 'Merry Christmas' gifts. We will celebrate their New Year's Eve parties with them. They will feel such terror as never before, in their hearts and on their lands. On the Christian holiday known as Good Friday, we will launch the ultimate weapon against the Great Satan. Tens of thousands will die. Millions will be scattered from their homes. We will break America's pride and glory. They will beg to come to the negotiation table.

"This time," he concluded grimly, staring coldly at Fardusi, "we will succeed."

MADELINE REMAINED MESMERIZED in the shadows. The guard, completely engrossed in the scene below, had still not surmised her presence by the time she slipped back through the door into Jessica's room.

Jessica sat on the edge of the cot, as with a desolate stare she watched the door. Madeline saw her countenance change from despair to one that probed for a strand of hope as she reentered the room.

"Did you find out anything?" Jessica asked, her voice a mere whisper.

Madeline vacillated, not sure of what to tell this child who was already on emotional overload.

"What is it?" Jessica's sensors were on a high pitch, picking up the least little hesitation. "What's happening?"

"It is not good," Madeline answered, measuring her words. "These people are very evil. They are talking about the message that you read."

"They said that they would kill me."

"I know."

"Would they really do that?" Jessica's plaintive tone caused Madeline to put her arms around her reassuringly.

"I wish I could say otherwise, Jessica, but I honestly believe that they might. Last night, I overheard them talking about you. The man with the scar, Dosha, said . . ." Madeline's voice broke.

"Said what?" Jessica demanded.

"He said that . . . he would kill you tonight, after the others have gone."

Jessica swallowed hard in disbelief.

"But why? Why would he want to do this?"

"I don't really know, but we have to get you out of here, and we have to do it now."

"How? Those women out there guard me twenty-four hours a day."

"I know," Madeline admitted. Her gaze took in the familiar simplicity of the room with its door to the hall, the pictureless walls, and the small window. Her scan of the room slowed for an instant, lingering on the window, before continuing on in hopeless perusal. Jessica watched, noting when her eyes fell on the window.

"It's not locked." Jessica's tone was subdued, matter-of-fact.

"What's not locked?" Madeline stared at her.

"The window. It's not locked. I can open it, but there is no balcony outside. I've looked before."

Madeline went to the door and cracked it open. The voices had quieted and the guard had returned to her place, occupied with another magazine. An M-16 was propped against the door-jamb. It would be impossible for Jessica to slip out this way now. She closed the door again and moved to the cot. Standing on the cot, Madeline pushed on the window. It did move.

She looked down and smiled.

"Turn out the light."

Jessica did as she was told and the room settled into darkness, except for the moonlight and the diffused glow emanating from windows in other buildings in the compound. Madeline pushed the window open and hoisted herself up with her elbows on the sill. She could see out and, looking down, caught a glimpse of a narrow protrusion, about four or five inches wide at the most. A few feet away was the window into the next room. It was open!

"There's a place about three feet or so below the windowsill, Jessica. It is very narrow, but it runs past an open window in the room next door. That's where the guards sleep. One of them is outside guarding the door now, and I overheard the Azari woman send the other one on an errand, so the room should be empty."

Madeline dropped back onto the cot and took Jessica's shoulders into her hands. They felt frail. For a moment, she wondered if the girl had strength enough left to do it, or if it was even possible on such a narrow ledge, but there was no other way. They had to act now or it would be too late.

"I'll run downstairs to the kitchen, go outside and come around to the back of the house. Do you understand so far, Jessica? Are you listening to me?"

Jessica nodded, her eyes staring down at the floor.

"When I leave, I'll tell the guard you have gone to sleep. Stay in bed until you're sure she's not going to look in on you any more, but don't wait long. As soon as you know the guard has settled down, go through that window. You can make it to the next room. It's only a few feet away, Jessica. Your only chance is to go out this window and back through the other one. I've been in there. It's a corner room with a second door that opens onto an outside staircase. You can slip out without being seen. All you have to do is get into that room."

"It sounds scary. I don't think I can do it."

"You must. It's your only chance. You've got to make your move as soon as possible after I've gone. I know it's scary, but it's the only way. I'll meet you at the bottom of the stairs. I can help you over the wall. We'll get you to some friends of mine who are Christians, the ones who sent the message to your father. I'm certain they will hide you until we can figure out how to get you out of the country."

Jessica nervously cracked her fingers. "I don't know ..."

Madeline stood to her feet. "I have to go. You can do it. You must!"

Jessica remained hunched on the edge of the cot, looking up at this stranger-become-friend. "I'm scared."

"I know." Madeline patted Jessica's shoulder. "So am I. Wait. Let's pray, and ask God to help us. Okay?"

"Yes," she whispered. Madeline reached over and grasped her hands.

"Lord," Madeline began, "we're holding hands with each other, but we need You to hold our hands too. We'll do our best and You must help us. Without You, we cannot do it; but with You, we can do all things. We are Your children. Help Jessica as she gets ready to leave this terrible room. Give her courage and strength. In Jesus' name, Amen."

"Amen," whispered Jessica.

"In a few minutes then?"

Jessica nodded slowly. "I guess."

HERSCH AND JOHN stood on the street corner opposite the Fardusi compound. John's hands were damp with nervous perspiration. Who would have believed, a couple of weeks ago, that he would be this close to taking Jessica home. He could hardly imagine they had come this far so easily. True, the most difficult part of their mission lay ahead, but still . . . He glanced over at Hersch. The man's eyes were riveted on the complex across the way. His nostrils flared slightly with each breath, and his concentration seemed total. John could see that the hound was close to the kill.

"I checked on this Fardusi fella, before we left the States," Hersch said at last. He spoke quietly, his gaze never leaving the compound gate, where the guard walked back and forth while surreptitiously sneaking a cigarette. "He's somewhat of a maverick, even for these parts. Survived the Shah and still manages to ingratiate himself with the powers that be. Nobody knows how he does it, but it has to be one delicate dance, that's for sure. He's envied, but not liked; feared, but not trusted. Most say he's survived by working both sides of the street. That's probably an understatement. Fundamentalists generally see him as not fully committed to The Cause, whatever that means. He's pretty much retired now, but obviously still keeps his hand in this Holy War business."

"What do you think is going on?" asked John. Two dark-colored Mercedes and a taxi were being waved through the gate at that moment.

"Hard to say. Wish we could see through that wall."

Just then, another taxi rolled past the guardhouse.

"A party maybe?" John asked of no one in particular.

"Doubtful." The response was tinged with cynicism. "These boys aren't the partying kind. Their idea of fun is to see how many people like us they can shoot with one bullet. Now that we're here, how are you doing?"

"I'm shaking in my boots, amazed that we've pulled it off so far."

"Ah, the easy part is over. This is the moment of truth. Getting in, getting your daughter, and getting out. Once we get out of there, the next hurdle is meeting up with the boat and leaving Iran in our wake. We show up in the UAE, and take a taxi to the American Embassy. By the way, did you remember to bring cab fare?"

"No problem," John grinned, checking the time on his watch and thinking of the remaining cash still strapped to his body. "It all sounds like a piece of cake."

"Just don't forget."

"Forget what?"

"Cake has a way of crumbling when you least expect it. Come on, let's fall back a few doors. We can still see what's happening. Hopefully, whoever's in there will be gone soon. We can wait until one-thirty. Two at the latest. Then, whatever the status, we hit the compound. We go in, grab Jessica, and get out. Not a minute longer than necessary. We know the room she's supposed to be in, so it should be easy. The boat is set to pick us up at four."

John nodded. They had rehearsed the plan several times since initially envisioning it.

"You mind if we pray?" he asked.

"Pray?"

"Yes. You know, ask God to enable us for what is ahead."

Hersch was quiet.

"Sure," he said at last. "Go ahead. I'm not certain He knows who I am, but you're probably no stranger."

"Trust me, Hersch," John smiled in the darkness. "God knows who you are. He knows when the sparrow falls. He counts the number of hairs on your head. He sees us standing here right now."

"Okay, okay. I get the point. So, pray already and, while you're at it, put in for a couple of angels long on courage and short on brains."

John continued smiling. It grew quiet with only the occasional sound of an automobile breaking the stillness. He put his hand on Hersch's shoulder and began asking God to watch over them.

THIRTY-NINE

Madeline opened the door and stepped into the hallway. The guard leaned forward in her chair and looked into the room as Madeline reached for the light switch. Jessica lay curled up on the bed in a fetal position, her face to the wall. The leftover bread and water was on the floor nearby. Madeline waited until the guard nodded, then turned out the light. The guard then closed the door and locked it.

As Madeline walked down the staircase, she saw that the men were standing up, preparing to leave. Leila Azari said something to the man with the scar, causing them both to break into laughter. Leila looked up as Madeline reached the bottom of the stairs, then quickly returned to her conversation. She noticed Fardusi staring her way, but passed to one side without a word and went into the kitchen.

As soon as the door closed behind her, she ran to the outside exit, pausing for a moment to catch her breath and steady her nerves. Then Madeline hurried around to the side of the house facing the driveway and looked up along the wall. The darkness partially hid the view, but not altogether. Madeline caught her breath and her hand went involuntarily to her mouth.

Jessica was almost out of the window!

Madeline glanced around. To her dismay, she could see the security guard standing at the entrance to the compound. Her eyes darted back to Jessica, then to the guard. She would be easy to spot if he turned in that direction. But, there was no turning back. Madeline's heart pounded madly. They were committed. Either it happened or it didn't.

JESSICA HAD REMAINED ON THE COT only as long as it took for the light to go out and the door to shut. Then, she was up on the bed, pushing at the cracked window until it swung open. By placing her elbows on the sill, as Madeline had done, she pulled herself up until her head and shoulders poked through the opening. Looking down, she saw the narrow ledge. It was not really a ledge at all. It wasn't even the width of her foot length.

"O Lord, I can't do this," she said out loud as her body sagged against the sill.

You must!

Jessica could hear Madeline's warning ringing in her ears.

It's your only chance!

Carefully, she edged out of the window until she could turn around to a sitting position on the sill. The narrowness of the opening made movement difficult, but by twisting and pulling, she finally managed to lift one leg across the sill and out along the wall, feeling with her foot to find the ledge. Then, she drew the other leg through and slid that foot down until it touched the ledge. Now she hung precariously, holding onto the sill with both hands. The muscles in her legs were tight like bowstrings as she clung to the side of the wall with her toes.

Jessica looked to her right once again. The open window was about six or eight feet away. Too far to hang on to the one she had just climbed out of, while reaching for the other. There was a span of two or three feet where she would have to let go.

Her breath came in short gasps now, and she realized again just how weak she was. In her mind, she heard again Madeline's stern warning — "*It's your only chance!*"

Slowly she edged along, ducking under the open frame. Then she straightened up, her body hugging the wall and one hand still on the window she had just come through. To move farther, she had to let go.

I can't keep my balance. I'm going to fall for sure! No. You've got to do it, Jessica. There's no other way.

Gingerly, Jessica slid her foot to the side, at the same time flattening her body against the wall. She closed her eyes.

Think tightrope. You're balancing on a tightrope. Stay perfectly upright. There's a net below to catch you, but you're not going to fall. The band is playing. The crowd is watching. Stay tight.

Both hands were flat against the stucco exterior, both feet jammed against the wall, heels hanging well over the edge.

A little farther. Come on, you're almost there. Easy . . . easy.

Her fingers felt the outer edge of the window casing. Her heart was banging away inside her chest. Another inch. And another.

One more step to the right.

Jessica's right hand reached over the windowsill. She opened her eyes.

Careful. Don't panic now.

Tension was so much in control of her body that it was hard to release enough air to make room for more. She pressed against the wall, inching her way over until both hands were on the windowsill. Hanging there for a moment, she forced herself to breathe normally. Then she tried heaving herself up, but missed getting all the way through the opening. She could feel herself sliding back. Her toe missed the ledge.

No!

She fought with her fingers to hold onto the sill. All her strength was focused now as her feet felt for the ledge. There! Once more, out of breath, she heaved her body up and through the opening. This time, her stomach landed on the windowsill. With one final push, she propelled herself through the opening and fell to the floor, inside the darkened room!

MADELINE TOOK A DEEP BREATH and whispered, "Yes! You did it, Jessica. I can't believe it, but you did it!"

Turning, she looked in the direction of the guardhouse. The guard was still there, but appeared to be reading. Obviously, he had not seen anything. She hurried past the front entrance to the main house and slipped quietly around the corner. Here she waited, her fingers drumming the railing impatiently as she watched for the door at the top of the stairs to open.

Come on, Jessica. Hurry. There isn't much time.

INSIDE THE ROOM, Jessica moved her hands along the tile floor. The shadow of a bed loomed nearby. On the opposite wall she made out the silhouette of a dresser, along with a table, chair, and another bed. Her heartbeat was almost back to normal, when a voice, in the distance, called out something in Farsi. She heard the doorknob turn and caught her breath as the voice that answered back came from right outside the door!

In the same instant that the door opened, Jessica rolled under a bed. She heard the click of the switch and froze as the room suddenly filled with light. She could see bare feet walking across the floor to the desk. Jessica wanted to push further back against the wall, but didn't dare to move, for fear of making a noise. She recognized both voices now, as belonging to her guards. The one who had called out to the guard at the door entered the room and sat down on the edge of the bed. Her feet were only inches from Jessica's face.

Both of them are in the room. I'm dead!

Their conversation, all in Farsi, continued for several minutes, until finally, the woman rose and moved away from the bed. Jessica's eyes followed her feet to the door, where they turned back into the room as the woman said something. Then the other guard joined her, flipping off the light as they went out. Jessica heard the door close and released a huge sigh of relief. She was damp with sweat as she rolled out from under the bed and stood up.

In the dark, the outline of the second door could barely be seen, but Jessica made her way to it quickly. Carefully, she turned the handle. It opened onto an outside landing that led to a fire escape with wooden steps. These were the stairs that Madeline had promised would be there. Jessica slipped through the door and shut it tightly behind her. She hurried down the steps, catching her breath for an instant, as a dark form emerged from the shadows at the bottom of the stairs.

"Oh, you scared me."

"Jessica! Oh, my goodness, you made it. You actually did it. You are so brave and I am so relieved and so proud of you. I can hardly believe it."

They hugged each other tightly, exorcising the tension that clutched at their throats.

"What do we do now?" Jessica asked.

"Come with me. We've got to get you over that wall. Beyond is a dirt walkway that leads to the street. It's too high to get over without help. I'll boost you up and you can drop over on the other side. It's about ten feet at the top."

"Then what?"

"Then, you must go in that direction," Madeline pointed off to the right. "You will cross four streets. When you have crossed over to the other side of the fourth street, turn left and go two more blocks. There is a house there. I know you can't read the street signs, but you will find it. It is brown with a blue door and has a small tree in front. You can knock. If it is locked and no one answers, hide across the street until morning. When you get inside, ask for Arun. He is Indian."

"Indian?" Jessica repeated, with surprise.

"Not like an American Indian," Madeline explained. "Arun is from India. He is the leader of the church that meets there. Tell him your name. He will know what to do. And remember, you are a fugitive. You must think like one until you are safely back to your family again. That means you can't trust anybody except Arun. When you reach him, do whatever he says."

"What about you, Madeline? What will you do now?"

"I must hurry back to the main house before I am missed. Now, do you remember your instructions?"

"Cross four streets. Turn left and go two more blocks. Brown house. Blue door. The man's name is Arun."

"Right. Now, hurry. Up you go."

"Wait! How can I just leave you like this? You've risked your life to save mine? Why?"

"We are sisters, Jessica. We will see each other again some day." Madeline put her arms around Jessica's frail body and kissed her on the forehead. Jessica held on tightly.

"Come, now. Up and over."

Jessica turned and stretched against the wall. Madeline cupped her hands together and guided Jessica's foot into the human stirrup that they formed.

Just then, shouts could be heard coming from the main house. Next came the fearsome sound of an automatic weapon from the opposite side of the building. Jessica looked at Madeline with alarm.

"Hurry," Madeline hissed.

Jessica felt herself propelled upward and fell hard against the top of the wall, momentarily knocking her breath away. There were pebbles and bird droppings along the ten-inch-wide surface, but no wires or broken glass to protect against intruders. Out of the corner of her eye, she saw Madeline hurry off into the darkness. Then she lowered herself down the other side and dropped onto the dirt path.

"SHE'S WHAT?" BELLOWED MARWAN DOSHA. He pushed Leila Azari to one side and rushed past her toward the stairs, taking them two at a time. One of the female guards was at the open door. The other was inside, standing on the cot in bare feet, looking out the window. She had fired an M-16 into the air to alert the staff that something was wrong.

"Where is she?" he screamed, his face livid with rage. "How could she get away?"

The woman on the bed turned back and stared helplessly.

"We don't know, Aghå-yé Marwan," said the one at the door. "We have both been here ever since the maid left the room. I saw her lying on the bed before the light was turned out. The door was locked. She could not have come this way. There is only the window . . ."

"Why was the window not locked?"

"It was," lied the woman in bare feet, not wanting to admit that they had failed to check it during all these weeks. "Besides, it is a twenty-foot drop to the pavement below. There was nothing she could have used to lower herself down, and it is too far to jump."

"Do you expect me to believe that she simply evaporated into thin air?"

"Perhaps the maid?" Leila had pushed her way into the room as the others now crowded in to see for themselves. "She was the last one in here. Get her at once."

The guard at the door rushed down the stairs.

"I saw her go into the kitchen," Leila shouted after her.

The guard bounded across the dining room and burst into the kitchen, sliding to a stop in front of the serving counter. Madeline looked up from where she was seated.

"What is happening? I heard gunfire and I was afraid to go out."

"Come with me!"

The guard pushed Madeline roughly out into the dining room. The others were rushing down the stairs, some shouting as they headed for the door, while the rest continued to mill about, all speaking at once to everyone and no one. Dosha was suddenly standing in front of Madeline.

"What do you know about this?" he roared, his eyes aflame with anger.

"I am sorry, sir," Madeline answered, looking anxiously up at Dosha. "I was in the kitchen and was afraid to come out. I heard gunfire and people shouting. I do not know what you are asking."

"You were the last to see the girl!"

"I left her in her room, yes. The guard looked in on her when I left. Aghå-yé Reza had asked me to take her bread and water. She was very weak and upset when I went to her."

"Did she speak?"

"Yes. She said that she had read a message to her father and that you had filmed it."

"Anything else?"

"Not that I remember, sir. She was very weak. I helped her to the bed. That is all."

Dosha swore and turned to Leila. "You let her escape. Get out there and find her! Where can she go? An American girl in this town can't go far without being noticed, can she? Do it now and don't return until she is found!"

Leila stood her ground. "How do you know this girl did not help her escape? What if she is not telling the truth?"

Dosha turned back to Madeline. He reached out and gripped her face in his hand. She flinched with pain, but did not move.

"If you are not telling everything you know, you had . . ."

"Stop it! Release her now!" Reza Fardusi moved in and put his hand on Dosha's wrist. "Now!"

Dosha let her go and stepped back, bristling with rage as he turned to face Fardusi.

"She is my servant, not yours," Fardusi declared emphatically. "If a servant of mine deserves punishment, I will see to it that it is done without any help from you. In fact, Madeline has obeyed everything that I have ever asked her to do. She is completely trustworthy, I assure you. She sometimes responds to my wishes before I have opportunity to ask."

"Besides," Fardusi continued, "I stepped into the kitchen a short while ago and I can assure you that Madeline was there, busy as usual, working at cleaning up the remains of this evening's meal."

Madeline looked at the old man with a start. If he had gone into the kitchen, then he knew that she had not been there.

He smiled reassuringly at her. "You may go to your room, Madeline. If there is further need, I will send for you later."

"As you wish, Aghå-yé Reza. Goodnight."

"Goodnight, Madeline. And thank you for everything you did for us tonight. You served us all very well."

"You are most welcome," she whispered, backing away and then disappearing through the kitchen door. For a few moments, Madeline leaned against the serving counter, her knees shaking and her heart beating at twice the normal pace. As she gathered herself together, the puzzling encounter with Reza Fardusi gradually became clear.

"... she sometimes responds to my wishes before I have opportunity to ask.... Madeline was there ... cleaning up ... this evening's meal. Thank you for everything you did for us tonight. You served us all very well."

Madeline clapped her hands together, stifling a sudden desire to laugh out loud. She had done exactly what Reza Fardusi wanted done, but could not accomplish without her help.

He wanted Jessica to escape! Amazing!

Madeline ran toward the servants' quarters, certain that she had seen a twinkle in the old man's green eyes when he last looked at her.

FORTY

At the sound of gunfire, Hersch and John looked at one another, startled, then scrambled to their feet and began running toward the compound.

"Wait a second." Hersch grabbed John's arm.

"Something's happening in there." John exclaimed, twisting away.

"Hold it, man. Use your head. You can't just go running in there and say, 'Hey, what's happening?' "

They watched anxiously as the security guard ran into the street. He had in hand what looked like an M-16 or an AK-47. Then another man came running out of the compound gate. They were shouting to each other, pointing first in this direction, then that. Obviously things were in a state of confusion.

"This is the time I wish I understood Farsi," Hersch growled under his breath. They were crouched between a garbage can and some bushes, three houses down the street. "Okay, get ready. It looks like God does answer prayer."

"What do you mean?"

"We need a weapon. Here it comes now."

A man carrying an automatic rifle was jogging in their direction. Abruptly, two houses away, he stopped and turned as someone shouted something. Then, he began running in the opposite direction.

Hersch swore, banging a fist against his leg.

"Sorry," he apologized.

"Me too," John said as he watched the man disappear around a corner.

"I meant . . . never mind."

A car roared out of the compound gate. Then another. The first car swung to the right, the second to the left. The sound of engines faded as their taillights disappeared into the night.

"What do you suppose happened?" John's voice was filled with anxiety.

"We'll find out."

"We will? How do you propose to do that?"

"Look, I know you want to run out there and grab someone and demand your daughter back, but there's nothing we can do while everyone is running around pointing guns. Good grief, it's a wonder they don't kill each other. We wait until it calms down."

"But Jessica . . ."

"No 'buts,' " Hersch whispered harshly, grabbing John by the shoulders. "We agreed before we left that I was in charge all the way. If something has happened to your daughter, there's not a thing we can do about it. Get that through your head. The chances are she's still okay. Whatever just happened in there may not even be about her. We'll cool it for a bit until things settle. Then we go in, just like we planned. Only maybe instead of over the wall . . . we'll just walk in through the front gate and knock on the door."

"Are you serious?"

"The element of surprise, my good man," Hersch's attempt to mimic an Englishman's accent wasn't half bad. "It's unlikely they're expecting Jessica's father to drop in for a social visit. Besides, there's been no more gunfire. Maybe someone accidentally shot his foot off. Who knows with this gang of thugs? We'll just sit back here in the shadows for a while and wait our turn at Mr. Fardusi and his crowd."

John glanced at his watch. Five after eleven. They moved back from the street into the shadows of a house that looked unoccupied, and settled down to wait.

It was after one o'clock before the lights in the compound began to dim and windows darkened. One of the cars that had left earlier returned, then left again. Two taxis entered and a few minutes later drove away. Whoever they were, the "extras" were leaving. That was good. The fewer the better. By ten minutes to two, it had been quiet for nearly an hour.

"Okay," Hersch said, getting up from the cement block he had been using for a chair, "it's time. Let's go. I'll lead the way. You stay out of the way. All right?"

John nodded.

"Don't mess me up now," Hersch cautioned. "Try to be a 'hero dad' and you'll get us both killed. They've got real bullets in those guns."

They moved out from the shadows and toward the gate.

INSIDE THE MAIN HOUSE, Reza Fardusi turned out the light in Jessica's room and walked down the stairs to the dining area. It was the first night in weeks that he was able to move through his house without Leila Azari and her female warriors being somewhere about. They had left the compound in a taxi, without so much as a word to their host.

A flick of another switch and lights in the dining room were dimmed, except for two small lamps at either end of the open area, casting warm shadows over what had, a few hours earlier, been a scene of complete pandemonium. His gaze went to the kitchen door and his thoughts to the maid named Madeline.

"How did she do it?" He spoke the words out loud, his emerald eyes emitting flashes of excitement at the thought of what had just happened. A small victory perhaps, but one carried off under the very noses of those who had chosen to deface his house.

Fardusi was weary of the turmoil and terror of the times. Whatever happened to peace on earth? The Holy War had given the world a generation that knew how to hate, not love. Even his own people spied on each other, brother against brother. He stared through the glass door at the softly lit patio garden.

Pairidaeza. The beauty of what our land once was has been reduced to postage stamps like this. Must the children of the world now be slaughtered to fertilize what there is left? When will enough blood have been spilt around the world to satisfy the anger of Allah? Was the price we paid not sufficient in the conflict with Iraq? Our children became fodder for the war machine. Their remains salt our earth with desolation. Surely Allah cannot be pleased with what is happening in our land. The people are poorer. The times are harder. And defective souls like Leila Azari and Marwan Dosha run rampant, killing the innocent with no remorse at all. My God, are we participating in our destiny or our punishment?

JOHN WINCED AS THE SECURITY GUARD FELL. He had watched from a few feet back as Hersch moved closer to the entrance. His slow, stealthy movement was capped by a sudden swiftness that surprised even John. The guard dropped, without a sound, under a hard chop to the back of his neck.

John helped drag him inside the small shelter where Hersch produced a roll of tape and proceeded to bind and gag the man. Then he commandeered an M-16 propped against the wall, while John lifted a handgun from the small leather holster on the guard's belt.

"Come on, let's get out of here."

Hersch began jogging through the shadows toward the largest of the buildings.

"This looks like the main house where the guy said your daughter was being held."

Just then, a light went out on the second floor. They waited and watched. Moments later, the main lights on the lower floor dimmed. Now, all was dark except for the normal outdoor lighting and what looked to be a small source of light on the first floor.

They walked up the steps to the front door. Hersch looked at John and smiled.

"This is it," he said softly and proceeded to knock.

John didn't know whether to laugh or gag. He could not believe they were standing at the enemy's front door, waiting for someone to open it.

Hersch knocked again, louder this time, the freshly confiscated weapon held loosely in his right hand. After witnessing his swift dispatch of the security guard, John had no doubt that the gun could be at ready status in a flash.

Suddenly the door opened.

"Balé . . . In chi-ye?" *Yes . . . what is this?* The old man's eyes widened in surprise as he saw the two men and the gun.

Hersch pushed him back into the house, the gun now pointed at his chest. John followed him in and closed the door, checking cautiously to see if others were about.

"Lottan." *Please.*

"Speak English," Hersch interrupted gruffly.

"No one else is here, please. I do not know you, but you may put your gun down. I'm an old man and quite harmless. You do not look like robbers, but this is a night of surprises. What is it that you wish from me?"

"Are you Reza Fardusi?" asked Hersch

"I am," the man replied.

John stepped forward.

"Where is my daughter?"

The old man started, his eyes blinking.

"You have been holding my daughter as a hostage. We've come to get her and take her home."

"I must say that I am surprised beyond words. You are the Reverend John Cain?"

John said nothing.

"And you?" the man asked, his hand nervously smoothing his mustache.

"Who I am is unimportant, and we haven't all day to visit." Hersch poked the barrel of the gun at the man's chest. "Where is she?"

"Ah, my friends, I regret to tell you that you are too late. She is not here."

John started forward, ready to pounce in outrage. Hersch pushed him back.

"She was here then? Where has she gone?"

"That, gentlemen, is something many people would like to know. She left a few hours ago, under her own power, for a destination known only to her." Fardusi smiled, carefully pushing the gun barrel to one side. "And to perhaps one other."

"How much do you know?"

Fardusi proceeded to tell what had happened in the earlier hours of the evening. John could hardly stand still as the story unfolded. The old man spoke softly, but rapidly and with authority. He was undoubtedly used to people answering his beck and call, not the other way around, as was the case at the moment.

John was hardly able to contain his emotions when the name of Marwan Dosha was mentioned. He had been here, intent on killing Jessica this very night, coming and going in one of the cars they had seen earlier.

John tried to take Fardusi's measure. The man had held his daughter hostage in his home for over a month. Yet, here he was, sounding like a concerned father himself, expressing relief that Jessica had escaped, admiring her courage and ingenuity. Gradually, John got the feeling that Fardusi had himself been a hostage of sorts. He should hate him, but he didn't. It was crazy. It was the Middle East.

"A moment ago, you said there might be one person who would know where Jessica has gone," John said, finally.

"Yes, permit me to make a call. She can be here in minutes."

"No funny stuff, Fardusi," Hersch growled.

"I assure you, there will be none. You have the upper hand, my friend."

"Speak only English."

Fardusi nodded as he picked up the phone and dialed.

"Mrs. Muños. My apologies for the lateness of the hour, but would you please send Madeline to the main house at once. It is urgent. Tell her not to waste time dressing, just to hurry. . . . No, there is not a problem. . . . Yes, I am fine. Now, attend to this quickly. . . . Yes, thank you. Goodnight." Fardusi put down the receiver.

"The young lady who most surely knows will be here momentarily."

"Who is she?"

"One of my staff, a young Filipino named Madeline. I believe she helped your daughter leave the premises."

"How did she do this?"

"We will ask her when she arrives. I will be most interested to know myself. If it is as I suspect, it was an act of great courage and valor. I hope it was arranged for the girl to meet someone on the outside. We will see. Meanwhile, may I offer you some tea?"

MADELINE THREW A HOUSECOAT over her nightgown and hurried barefoot to the house. Her heart felt as though it were in her throat.

She entered through the servants' door and turned on the light, before hastening across the kitchen. She stopped at the door, pausing to catch her breath. Then she entered the great room.

Aghá-yé Reza was alone, waiting by the two small lamps that illuminated the room. Then, suddenly she was jolted as two other persons appeared from the shadows, one on either side of her, each with a gun.

"It's all right, Madeline," Fardusi's voice sounded reassuring. "These men have come for Jessica."

Madeline went to Fardusi and stood beside him, facing the two strangers.

"Let me introduce you. I don't know that one's name, but this gentleman," Fardusi pointed to John, "is Jessica's father."

Madeline felt her heart skip a beat as she stared at John. She stepped forward slowly.

"You are the Reverend John Cain?" she asked incredulously.

"Yes. I am Jessica's father. I understand you may know where she is."

Madeline glanced over at Reza Fardusi. He smiled.

"It's all right, Madeline. I have the idea that you were key in

Jessica's timely disappearance tonight. You did the right thing. If you had not, she would have been dead before these men could have rescued her. We are curious, though. How did you do it? And where is the girl now?"

Madeline was at a loss for words. This meeting with Aghå-yé Reza could not possibly be happening. Add to it Jessica's own father. She stared back and forth at them both. Finally, she began.

For the next few minutes she told the sequence of events surrounding Jessica's escape.

"Where is she now?" asked John, finally, impatient to find her.

"I gave her directions to the house of my spiritual leader," she answered. Glancing at Fardusi, she continued. "A small group of Christians meet in the house of Arun. He is from India, a former Hindu. I worship with them when I can."

"Will you show us how to get there?" asked Hersch.

"Of course. If Aghå-yé Reza permits."

"Certainly. I will take you in my car," said Fardusi, smiling at Hersch. "I imagine that you will want to keep an eye on me until you leave, in any event, to be certain that I do not give away your presence here. You are planning to leave the country soon, I hope?"

Hersch smiled thinly, for the first time since entering the compound. "Right you are, Mr. Fardusi. Right you are."

John looked at his watch. "It's nearly two-thirty."

"I am not dressed appropriately to be out in the city, Aghå-yé Reza," Madeline said, hesitating.

"It is all right, my dear," Fardusi said reassuringly. "There is not time for you to change. Allah will forgive us this small indiscretion."

They went outside together and walked to where a creme-colored Mercedes was parked along the edge of the driveway.

"I will drive," said Fardusi, flourishing a set of keys, "though I will admit to it having been a while. We'll not bother my driver for this little excursion. He would not understand Madeline's attire, nor our reason for being out at this hour."

Fardusi proved surprisingly adequate behind the wheel and seemed to be taking genuine delight in the turn of events. They drove the short distance, directed by Madeline. Four streets. Turn left. Two more blocks. There it was. The brown house with a blue door. Fardusi parked two houses farther down the street, while John and Madeline ran back to the house and up the steps to knock on the door.

No response.

John pounded hard this time. A light went on inside. A moment later the door opened.

"Arun, it is Madeline. Is Jessica here?"

Arun rubbed the sleep from his eyes and stared at the woman in the housecoat and the man beside her.

"This is Reverend Cain, Jessica's father. We've come so that he can take her home."

"Come in, please," Arun invited, stepping back.

"I'm sorry," John responded. "There is no time. We are leaving the country in a matter of minutes. Where is she?"

"I'm sorry too," Arun answered, glancing first at Madeline, then back at John. "I do not know where your daughter is. I have not seen her. She did not come here!"

BACK IN THE CAR, THE MOOD was clouded over by the disappointment each person felt. So close. They had been so close. Where was she? Had she been recaptured? The most terrible thought of all . . . had they found her and killed her, disposing of her body only God knows where? So many questions and no answers.

The car moved slowly through the poorly lit streets as they retraced their path, discussing what to do now, hoping for some sign of Jessica's presence. There was nothing.

At this hour, the streets were empty of police. Nor did they come across any of the hated Komîté-yé Enghelâb-é Eslâmî, a combination of the Spanish Inquisition and the Gestapo, commonly known as the Revolutionary Guard. It was this group that each person in the Mercedes dreaded the most. Their primary role was to monitor internal security and enforce Islamic law, particularly in urban areas like Bandar. Residents did everything they could to avoid unnecessary contact.

As John stared out the side window, he heard Hersch outlining their next step to Reza Fardusi. A speedboat was coming in offshore. They were to be at the beach along the road, exactly one mile north of the Hotel-é Naghsh-é Jahân, at four o'clock. If they were late, and the boatman's presence went unchallenged, he was committed to waiting ten extra minutes. No longer.

John looked at his watch for the tenth time in the past half hour. Three-thirty five! His stomach felt hollow, empty. Then, a small, dark hand rested on his. He turned and looked into the eyes of Fardusi's maid. They were brimming with tears.

"I am sorry, Reverend Cain. I don't know what happened, but Jessica is a strong girl, and full of courage. I believe she got away;

if so, she will be all right. Perhaps she has to hide out for now and will come to Arun later. I wish I could do more."

"I'm sorry too. Madeline is your name?"

She nodded and smiled, looking down, as though intimidated by the company she was keeping.

"Madeline," John began, "if it were not for you, Jessica would be dead. You saved her life and did it at your own peril. How can I ever thank you?"

She looked up shyly as a single tear splashed onto her cheek.

"It was my privilege and duty as her Christian sister," she said simply.

A Muslim with connections to Hizballah. An American ex-SEAL who had lost what little faith he had possessed. A young Filipino Christian, barefoot, in nightgown and housecoat, who worshiped at the house of an East Indian convert from Hinduism. And an American pastor with a stolen .45 automatic tucked in his belt, riding around the deserted city streets of a seaport in Iran. John shook his head. It was crazy. It was the Middle East.

"Oh, oh."

Fardusi's hands tightened on the steering wheel, his eyes focusing on the rearview mirror.

"What?" demanded Hersch.

"The car that just passed. They have stopped and are turning around."

"So?"

"It is the Guard."

"Are you sure?"

"There is no question. They love driving around the city in their favorite brand of vehicle, the Nissan Patrol. I saw two of them for sure. There may be others. We recognize them easily. Their symbol is an arm with a bandaged hand clutching a rifle."

"And?"

"Their emblem is also on the license plate. I saw it as they went by."

"Do they have radio contact with their little friends?" asked Hersch, twisting around for a better look.

"Most likely, yes."

"So what's the normal procedure?"

"They will follow us until they decide what to do. Perhaps they will leave us alone. Or, they might pull alongside for a better look. Wait. Here they come now."

The Nissan pulled up alongside and kept pace, while the men inside checked out the passengers in the Mercedes. John could see three men now, all young and very serious. The driver was in plain clothes. The other two sported short stubbly beards and black collarless shirts. They were obviously curious about the car, its passengers, and the reason for their being out at this hour.

Again, John checked his watch. Three forty-five!

The Nissan dropped back and swung in behind them.

"What are they doing now?" asked Hersch.

"Perhaps they are calling ahead for help. They have seen a foreign woman in the car, her head uncovered, together with three men. We are probably going to be arrested."

"I have an idea. How far are we from your compound?"

"Five minutes at the most."

"Go quickly. And give John instructions for getting down to the road headed north. We've got a boat to catch."

"No. I left Israel without Jessica. I can't leave without her again!" John fairly shouted as he leaned forward, grasping Hersch's shoulder.

"You have no choice, buddy boy. We stay here, best case is we'll be tossed into the slammer. Worst case, they'll stand us up against a wall at dawn. Hey, if they've got her, then that's it. If they don't have her, she's obviously got friends who can hide her until we can do something else. But we've got to stay alive if we're going to do that girl of yours any good. And remember, you're with me. I give the orders!"

"He's right, Reverend Cain." Madeline's hand touched his once again. "You cannot help her tonight. If she has not been captured, she will be all right. We prayed, Jessica and I, before she escaped. I believe God has heard us and is watching out for her."

They could see the entrance to the compound about a block away. Hersch was giving instructions.

"When we get close, slam on the brakes. Open the door. I'll push you out. John, you shove Madeline out the other door and jump in behind the wheel. Madeline, fall on the pavement. Sorry if you get skinned up, but stay low. I'll fire over your heads and we'll drive off. Make up a story about being kidnapped. You should be pretty good at that by now. You can pick up your car at the beach."

Fardusi nodded. Moments later, he stepped hard on the brakes and skidded to a stop. His door flew open and he fell to the pavement. John leaned over Madeline and pushed the door open, virtually throwing her from the backseat. He followed her through the opening and slid in behind the steering wheel. Meanwhile, Hersch fired two rounds over their heads and then leaned out the window, getting off two additional rounds aimed at the Nissan sliding to a stop behind them.

John gunned the Mercedes with a force that slammed the open doors shut as they roared off into the night. In the mirror, he saw a confused and rattled Revolutionary Guard member stumble out of the vehicle. The Guardsman stopped first to stare at the two bullet holes in their windshield, then ran over to where Fardusi was helping Madeline to her feet.

John skidded around a corner and the scene disappeared from view.

"They'll be okay," Hersch announced, as though this sort of thing happened every day.

"I hope so."

"Do you remember the directions?"

"I think so," John repeated. "What time is it?"

"Almost four o'clock. Don't stop for red lights."

Their route was directly through downtown. No time to go around. John pushed the speedometer to eighty kilometers. Buildings flashed by. Thankfully, there was little traffic at this hour. John braked suddenly, the car skidding to one side, barely missing a car entering the intersection from the right. A block further down, a garbage truck moved out of the way as the surprised collectors gaped at the speeding car.

"Company," John called out, checking the mirror again.

Hersch looked over his shoulder.

One vehicle was being joined by another in pursuit of the Mercedes. John weaved in and out, narrowly avoiding a street maintenance crew, as they set up for the day's work. Past the NIOC Building on the right, the Mosåferkhüné-yé Iran on the left. John kept his foot on the gas pedal as they sped by the Iran Air and Valfajre-8 Shipping headquarters building. They slowed as the road made a sharp left bend, then a short way ahead another hard right.

"That's the ferry landing," Hersch commented. "You're doing great!"

Another hard right, then a left, as the Mercedes' tires squealed their protest, while trying to maintain a grip on the blacktop. The road straightened out at this point and John ran the speedometer up to 170 kilometers per hour.

"That's the hotel off to the left. Mark the odometer. We don't want to overrun the gangplank."

John looked down and checked the numbers as they rolled by.

"Almost there," he warned, looking out into the darkness. "I don't see anything."

"Well, it's show time, one way or the other. Our friends are getting close. Either our ride is there or it isn't. Wait. There it is. See it?"

The dark outline of a small craft could be seen in the water, a few feet off shore.

"Yes," John felt relief and excitement at the same moment.

He put the car into a slow slide, peeling away from the road and onto a stony stretch of hardpan that fell off toward the water. The boat was there all right, but so was the Revolutionary Guard!

John skidded the car to a stop about fifty feet from where the speedboat rocked gently in the shallows.

"Run for it," shouted Hersch as he scrambled from the car and dropped to his knees. The two pursuing vehicles had stopped about a hundred feet back. At least five or six men were getting out and running toward them. Hersch fired off a couple of rounds. The men stopped, then began returning fire.

The sound of automatic weapons and the thump of bullets in the sand and ricocheting off rocks was high motivation for John to run as fast as he ever had in his life. He heard the motor start up in the launch and saw it maneuvering away from the shore. At first, he thought they were being left behind, then realized that the boatman was simply turning for a fast getaway.

Can't be fast enough for me, he thought.

A sudden cry of pain! He stopped and turned to see Hersch thrashing on the ground.

For a brief instant, John hesitated, then started back toward Hersch.

"No, man, keep going."

"Not without you!"

"Keep going. That's an order."

"Shut up and give me that gun."

John grabbed up the M-16. "Is this the switch for fully automatic?"

"Yes."

He flipped it, pulled it up to his shoulder and sprayed bullets back and forth at will. In a matter of a couple of seconds the magazine was empty.

"Here." Hersch handed him another one. John remembered doing this at the Santa Clara shooting range. Carla Chin was beside him now as he ejected the empty magazine. *It's not a clip, John. The correct term for this is a magazine. Fully automatic you will probably not hit anything. But you might scare somebody to death.*

Right now, that was all John wanted to do. The full magazine went in smoothly. Hersch was trying to crawl, with one leg dangling helplessly and bleeding profusely.

Another bullet whizzed past.

This time John flipped it to bursts of three rounds each. The sporadic burp of the weapon felt scary to him as he fired in the general direction of their pursuers. He hoped they felt the same about it.

Then the gun was empty again. He threw it to one side and grabbed Hersch.

"Get out of here, man," Hersch grunted through clinched teeth.

"With you, not without you. So shut up."

Okay, God. I need Your help. It's time to do Your stuff again.

From somewhere, a strength came that surprised even John. Maybe it was the adrenaline pumping through as a result of the excitement and the danger. Maybe it was sheer desperation and fright. It felt to John like Someone Else had come alongside and helped him lift Hersch to his feet. Half carry, half drag. They staggered into the water.

"Here," a man's voice called out. "Let me have him."

The boatman dragged and John pushed as Hersch fell into the bottom of the boat. John scrambled over the side just as another hail of shots came from near the Mercedes. It was then that he remembered the handgun. Miraculously, it was still tucked in his belt. Pulling it out, he cocked it and fired.

Carla was there by his side again. *"Never point your gun at anything or anyone you don't intend to shoot."* John pointed in the direction of the gun flashes, steadying his one hand with the other as he crouched in the boat. He fired once. Then again. And again. *That's for Hersch. This is for Jessica.*

The boat continued moving back into deeper water, then suddenly roared to life and raced out to sea.

Away from the deadly hail of bullets.

Away from the guardsmen who had shot Hersch.

Away from enemies he did not know, who were determined to take his life.

Away from Madeline and Reza Fardusi.

And, away from Jessica!

John's face was wet with tears, the gun still pointed at the shore, his finger pressing the trigger again and again, though the magazine had long since been spent.

Hersch reached up and pried it from his hand.

John shook as he leaned over the side and cried for Jessica

FORTY-ONE

Dropping from the wall to the ground, Jessica lost her footing, falling backward onto the hard surface. She stifled a cry of pain as her shoulder banged against a loose rock. Rolling over and getting to her feet, Jessica looked around frantically. She could hear shouts coming from the other side.

She ran to the corner of the wall nearest the street. Just then, a man dashed out of the compound, waving a gun in the air and shouting at someone behind him. Another man emerged and ran in her direction. Jessica ducked back behind the corner.

I've got to get out of here.

Running back along the wall, Jessica passed the place where she had fallen, and sprinted into a narrow alleyway that stretched between two rows of single-story, cinder-block houses. She stumbled over a garbage can and fell forward, scrambling to her feet as it careened noisily across the alley. Gathering herself up, she ran on. Something dark scurried across her path. She hoped it was a cat, but her skin crawled—it was probably a rat.

Jogging across an empty street, she entered another dark alley. At the far end, she stopped to catch her breath and look around. It took only an instant for Jessica to realize that she was totally lost.

Which way did Madeline say?

The landmarks were unfamiliar. In her fright, she had lost all sense of direction. Should she go to the right or the left? Maybe it would be better to retrace and start over.

No. Not that. Not back to that place. I've got to keep going.

Jessica looked around, desperately trying to get her bearings. The street to the right sloped downward. She started walking, then picked up her pace. Down was easier than up and, by now, her breathing was raspy and her lungs felt on fire.

Soon she was stopping at every street corner, partly to see that the way was clear, partly to catch her breath. Jessica shrank back into the shadows as a creme-colored car went by. Then, she ran on. After what she guessed as having been a half mile or more, she dropped to the ground when another car approached. As it passed by, she could not be sure. It looked like a police car.

Policemen. Maybe they will help me.

She started to get up and call out.

No!

She froze.

No. I can't trust anyone. Everyone here is my enemy. Everyone, that is, except Madeline. I still can't believe it. She risked her life to get me out of there. But, I can't trust anyone. No one. If I am going to get out of here, I have to do it on my own. I can't ask anyone for help.

She stood to her feet and watched the taillights disappear around a corner.

Okay, if I am going to get out of here, how will I do it?

She continued jogging down the street, her lungs still burning for relief.

Lord, help me find the house that Madeline told me about. It's the only thing I can think of that sounds safe.

The landscape was leveling out now, and Jessica could smell the sea. Coming to another cross street, she looked to the left and, in the distance, made out the silhouette of a ship. Hesitating, she glanced around quickly, checking out the setting. She was surrounded by dilapidated buildings. About a block away, two men walked toward her. A car approached along the road from the opposite direction.

Jessica ran down the narrow street toward the docks. As she came closer, she saw the distinct outlines of not one but three large ships.

Maybe if I could get on a ferry like the one they brought me over on . . . no, that would be too dangerous. Customs. A ticket. Don't trust anybody. Besides, this doesn't even look like the same dock. And, I've got no money.

Jessica ran out to the edge of the dock and looked down into the water that lapped against the cement wall. It was dark and smelly. A short distance away, a giant crane materialized in the moonlight, resting on tracks that permitted it to move from one ship to another. Along the tracks the dock was covered with a thick, black dust.

Just then, she observed a man approaching and ducked underneath a smaller, nearby crane, crouching down behind a wheel. The man was dressed in dark, baggy trousers and wore a jacket pulled over a collarless shirt. He carried a flashlight.

Jessica held her breath as he stopped and turned on the light, flashing it back and forth in her direction.

He's seen me! What should I do?

After what seemed an eternity, he turned off the light and continued on past. Jessica let out a sigh of relief.

That time, I was lucky, but I've got to do something.

She started walking again, careful to stay in the shadows as much as possible. A little way farther, she paused alongside the biggest ship she had ever seen up close. From somewhere deep inside the steel hull, Jessica could hear the engine idling steadily, even though triple strands of dirty nylon mooring lines kept the vessel secure at the dock. She also noticed a series of numbers running vertically up the side of the vessel, indicating water level.

The vessel was painted black just below the 12-meter line and a greenish-blue above it. Signs of rust could be seen here and there and it looked as though a crew member had simply splashed paint over the worst spots without any thought as to how it might appear. She could make out the ship's name, by peering under the gangplank—M/V *EVVOIA*.

The gangplank! She drew back and looked at the long set of steel steps leading up to the ship's lower deck.

The motors are running. Maybe that means it is getting ready to leave. Where do you suppose it is going? Well, what does it matter. If I stay here, sooner or later I will be caught and taken back to that house. Or worse. If this ship is headed out to sea, wherever it is going has to be better than here.

She glanced over her shoulder. The man she had seen earlier must have been a watchman. He had disappeared and no one else seemed to be about. She looked up the ladder again. There didn't appear to be anyone around to stop her. Jessica took a deep breath and put her foot on the first step.

The ladder swayed slightly as she climbed, but a safety net had been tied to one handrail, pulled underneath, and secured to the railing on the opposite side. At least, if she fell, she wasn't going far.

Jessica looked back in the direction from which she had come and saw no sign of anyone. As quickly as possible, she reached the level of the deck and poked her head above for a look around. Then she climbed the last few steps until she was able to stand on the nonskid decking. There were enough lights along the deck to reveal signs of paint turning to powder and steel speckled with rust. All at once, voices sounded to her left.

Hide! Where?

Jessica ducked into a doorway and pressed against the wall as two men walked by. They were speaking a language she did not recognize. It was not like anything she had heard in recent months.

Once they were past, she stepped out onto the deck again and continued looking for a hiding place. Each doorway she came to looked foreboding. The walkways were narrow and she could not tell where most of them went.

I'll be found for sure if I stay out here. There must be a place to hide where they put the cargo . . . or maybe the engine room.

They sounded like good possibilities, if only she knew how to get there. She was thankful to still be wearing her sneakers from home. They enabled her to move quietly. Jessica was careful to stay away from the ship's rail where someone might see her more easily. Eventually, she came to a wooden ladder and looked up.

A lifeboat.

At that moment, voices rang out in laughter. She couldn't see them, but they sounded near enough and were getting closer. Quickly, she started up the ladder, iron pegs imbedded into a crude wood frame.

. . . three, four, five, six rungs!

Jessica scrambled over the side and dropped soundlessly into the bottom of the lifeboat just as the two men passed beneath her. A moment later they were gone. Letting out another sigh of relief . . . how many times had she done that tonight . . . she stretched out, exhausted.

And cold.

That watchman had been wearing a jacket. It was the first time she had considered the fact that, in these early morning hours before dawn, the temperature had dropped considerably. Her desperation to escape had forced every other thought from her mind. She shivered, wishing for the chador she had left behind. All she had were a pair of pants that reached her ankles, and a loose-fitting, long-sleeved shirt that had been given her after arriving at the compound. She hugged herself, briskly rubbing her arms, as she looked around for anything that might help.

The lifeboat was large, with space for several persons. There were benchlike seats wrapping completely around the outer edge, with oars lashed to one side, and four bench seats spanning the width of the boat. It looked as though it had been refurbished fairly recently, in a dark red. The faint odor of fresh paint was still present.

Several bundles, bound together and wrapped in waterproof canvas, were stored in the bottom of the boat. Jessica's fingers were stiff with cold and clumsy as she worked at untying knots. Finally, one of the bundles broke open. Inside, she found a blanket which she quickly pulled out and threw over her shoulders. To her surprise, she also discovered some crackers along with several tins of food. She managed to get the crackers open and ate a handful of them, suddenly aware of just how hungry she had become. And how exhausted.

She was thirsty too, but didn't see anything to drink. With a sigh, Jessica folded the canvas back over the food tins and laid her head on the pack. Pulling the blanket tightly around her shoulders, she looked up at the sky. The stars had disappeared as the blackness of night gave way to the slate gray of early dawn. As the warmth of the blanket eased her soreness and exhaustion, she closed her eyes. Soon, Jessica had fallen into a dreamless sleep.

SATURDAY, 03 DECEMBER
0835 LOCAL TIME

REZA'S WIVES HAD RETURNED to their residences, after being dismissed by the investigating authorities, the initial concern for their husband's welfare having been satisfied. They had been promised a family audience later in the morning, at which time the children would also be present.

Mrs. Muños bustled about the room, picking up empty tea cups and straightening chairs.

"How is your injury?"

"It is nothing, Aghâ-yé Reza," Madeline answered, stifling a yawn with the back of her hand. She sat on one of the dining table chairs, her left leg protruding stiffly from beneath Fardusi's afghan, which she had been given to wrap around her shoulders for the sake of modesty and to ease the morning chill.

"Ah, my dear, you are also weary, that I can see," smiled Reza Fardusi. He stood at the door, watching as the parade of official vehicles slowly wound their way around the fountain and out through the compound gate. Two cars carrying regular Bandar policemen, three more with the hated Revolutionary Guardsmen in tow.

"Do you think they really believed us?" asked Madeline, nursing the dark bruise and cut on her knee with a damp cloth.

Fardusi glanced in her direction, then let his gaze return to the last car as it bumped its way out onto the street and disappeared.

"Of course, they did," he answered, closing the door. "I . . . think we were very convincing, don't you?"

Madeline smiled. "I think you were convincing, Aghå-yé Reza. As for me, I am not sure. I was shaking too badly."

"It was your fright that gave a stamp of authenticity to your testimony. Those Komîté members are too dull to distinguish whether your fear was from being questioned or from being kidnapped. If they were more discerning, they would be doing something worthwhile with their time instead of merely intimidating the populace." His voice was filled with sarcasm, but his mind still marveled at the quick thinking that had saved them.

His being unceremoniously thrown from his own car in front of the compound had momentarily confused their pursuers. He remembered hearing shots fired, and later being shown two bullet holes in the windshield of the Guardsmen's Nissan. Unfortunately, none of the dolts following them had been hit, but were simply frightened out of whatever wits they had.

Fardusi had been suitably upset and profusely thanked the Guardsmen for saving his life and the life of his employee. They had stared disapprovingly at Madeline, even as she tried covering herself with her torn housecoat and the nightgown that had never been intended to reach to her knees in the first place. Her face and hair were inappropriately uncovered as well.

At first when they saw her in the car, they had thought she was a prostitute, or worse, some Persian man's wife or daughter caught in an act of immorality with three men. When the car's driver initially tried getting away, it had further served to confirm their suspicions.

Then, unexpectedly, the driver was thrown out on the ground, along with the woman. Shots had been fired as one of the criminals leaped from the back into the driver's seat and sped away. Recovering from their surprise, the Guardsmen called ahead for help. Reza Fardusi was informed later that his car had been recovered and was being impounded by the police.

"Did you catch our kidnappers as well?" Fardusi had inquired.

"Regretfully, no, though we think one of the criminals was wounded," the man officially in charge replied. "Two of our own were shot in a savage gun battle, about a mile north of Hotel-é Naghsh-é Jahan. An accomplice was waiting for them and they escaped in a speedboat. Shore patrols have been alerted, but it is believed that they made international waters and are no longer in Iran. Authorities have been alerted in our closest neighbor states; but, from the lack of assistance we have been given by the Arabs in the past, we do not hold out much hope that they will be apprehended."

"How could such a thing happen right here under your noses?" queried the angry and respected Bandar citizen. Fardusi suddenly changed from grateful rescued hostage to indignant Iranian country-man. "Can we no longer feel safe from kidnappers and bandits entering our own houses? What is our nation coming to? Is it not your responsibility to protect us from such reprehensible brigands?"

The Guardsmen were at once on the defensive and apologetic in their attempt to assure Reza Fardusi that they were doing all that was possible.

Was he certain as to their description?

Of course. He could never forget how they looked while boldly entering through his front door.

"Two men, dark complexions, dark hair. They spoke Farsi, so they most likely were Iranian citizens. One had a pistol, the other an M-16. They said they were taking me away for ransom money. Later, I found that they had overcome my gatekeeper and had taken the weapons that actually belonged here, in the compound. Just then, my maid came in. I had asked her to prepare a late snack for me after my guests had departed for the evening. She was told not to take time to dress in her uniform, since it was late and no one else was around. That's the reason she is not more suitably attired. Yes, I can give you the names of my guests as well.

"We were forced into the car at gunpoint. I was made to drive and, well, you know the rest. I do not know where they intended to take us because your men started to follow us before we had gotten very far."

"Is there anything else that you can think of?"

"No, I can give you no more assistance than that," Fardusi replied. "Can you add anything, Madeline?"

She shook her head and looked away, desperately wanting to laugh at the flustered Komîté members who now seemed very anxious to leave.

Finally, Mrs. Muños had disappeared into the kitchen to finish cleaning up after her employer's early morning visitors.

"Are you all right, Madeline?" Reza's voice was full of concern.

"Yes, Aghå-yé Reza," she replied. "I am starting to feel bruises and sore muscles, but they will soon go away."

"I will have one of my sons help you to your room and send for a doctor to look at your knee."

"Please," Madeline protested, not wanting to be near Reza's sons, especially in the manner in which she was dressed. "Mrs. Muños can help me to my room. And you must get some rest yourself. It has been a long night."

Reza Fardusi walked over to the glass door facing the inner garden. His thoughts ran back over the extraordinary events of the night, pausing finally to ponder the frightened green eyes of the young American who had been held hostage in his home during these past weeks.

As Madeline prepared to leave, Reza turned and smiled. "I am still amazed by what you did this evening."

Madeline stopped and looked at Reza, embarrassed to talk about her clandestine activities.

"I meant no disrespect for you, Aghå-yé Reza. I know you must have your reasons for having kept her here. But I could not stand by and let one of my sisters in Christ be executed for no good reason. I . . . I had to do something."

"No disrespect has been received, Madeline. Only shame on my part for not having had the courage to do the same as you. To begin with, I was not asked if I would permit her to be held here. I was told. At first, it seemed a little thing, one of the Guardsmen's many inconsequential games. Still, I was troubled when I saw how young she was. Such an attractive girl too. And so bright. Then, of course, there was that woman, Azari, and her female warriors. Never again!"

The old man shook his head sadly as he continued the unprecedented unburdening of his soul to a lowly Filipino servant.

"Do I understand that you did this because you are a Christian?"

Madeline nodded and smiled.

"I wish that I could say the same as a Muslim, without feeling shamed," he responded wistfully, his eyes still resting on the young woman standing before him. "We must speak further sometime about this God we serve. He has provided me with much sorrow and little peace in this life. You seem to have found a side to Him that I have missed."

"I have found Jesus Christ."

"Ah, yes, Jesus. He was a great prophet."

"He is more than just a prophet," Madeline spoke gently. "He is the Son of God."

Reza's piercing green eyes met hers, at first flint-hard, then slowly softening.

"The Son of God, eh?" he repeated thoughtfully. "That is where we differ when it comes to Jesus."

"I know."

"Then, we must talk further about Him. Perhaps I can straighten out your understanding on this matter," Reza taunted her gently.

"Perhaps, Aghå-yé Reza, but I doubt it." Madeline's smile met that of her employer. Both had acquired new feeling and respect for the other during the night just past. "I know too well just how much positive change Jesus Christ has brought to my life."

"I am certainly impressed, Madeline, and curious about how your faith has changed you. We will speak again. As for now, you must go and rest. I will ask Mrs. Muños to have something brought for you to eat. You will remain off duty until she assures me that you are sufficiently recovered. Understood?"

"Thank you, Aghå-yé Reza, for your kindness."

"Mrs. Muños?" Reza called out.

A moment later, Mrs. Muños entered the room.

"Take this young woman to her room, please, and see that she gets what she needs in order to be comfortable. I will send a physician to look at that knee. You can be very proud of Madeline, Mrs. Muños. She is a courageous young woman."

Reza Fardusi watched them disappear into the kitchen, Mrs. Muños with her arm around Madeline's waist, helping to keep her weight off of the injured knee. On the way to his bedroom, his mind wandered back to the green-eyed American girl and to the father and his friend who had come too late to rescue her.

I wonder what has happened to them? .

FORTY-TWO

In the early morning hours, while dawn was breaking, the speedboat raced through open waters, dodging cargo ships and offshore supertanker loading facilities, dhows, and fishing boats, finally slowing to move through extremely shallow seas, dotted with islands and coral reefs.

The sun lay low in the east but was already driving the chill from the night air. It would be warm again today, as it was every day, though at this time of year, the normally sweltering humidity would mercifully remain low.

They could make out the coastline now, outlined clearly by the sun rising at their backs. The seven United Arab Emirates extend for nearly four hundred miles from the frontier of the Sultanate of Oman to Khor al-Odaid, on the Qatar peninsula in the Persian Gulf. They are interrupted only by an isolated outcrop of the Sultanate of Oman, on the coast of the Persian Gulf to the west, and the Gulf of Oman to the east along the Strait of Hormuz. Six of the seven Emirates, the states of jurisdiction ruled by emirs, lie on the Persian Gulf coast. The seventh, Fujairah, is located on the eastern coast of the Qatar peninsula, and has direct access to the Gulf of Oman.

Now, the boatman painstakingly maneuvered through the shallows off Fujairah, all the while keeping an eye on the intricate pattern of sandbanks and small gulfs that shaped the coastline.

He finally saw what he was looking for and pointed, saying

something to the man seated behind him. The man nodded and looked down at the other passenger, checking him for the fiftieth time in the past three hours.

He was resting on some flotation gear, propped against the side of the boat with one leg stretched out, bare where his trousers had been cut away. An anchor rope tourniquet had been fashioned and tied around his upper thigh, to minimize blood loss. It was neither comfortable nor sanitary, but it had been the best that they could do. Fortunately, the bullet had gone completely through the leg, though it had left a large and hideous wound in its path.

The handler of the boat manipulated it expertly as they came near the sandy beach, cutting the engine at the last second. A car was parked along the highway above the beach, its driver waiting at the water's edge. He waded in, reaching for the side of the boat to hold it steady.

"We've got one wounded," the boatman said.

"So I see. How bad is he?"

"He needs care as quickly as possible. Took a round in the leg. Lost quite a bit of blood. My guess is that he's in shock."

"Help me get him up and over the side." It was John who spoke up, impatient to get Hersch to a hospital.

"Be careful, Rev. Don't get blood on your shirt. That stuff's hard to get out." Hersch attempted to joke, even though his words were slurred, each syllable shaped by pain, through gritted teeth.

"Shut up, Hersch," John said gruffly, patting his arm at the same time, grateful that the man who had become his friend under fire was talking, even if he wasn't making much sense.

Dragging the boat up onto the beach, the three of them worked to lift Hersch over the side and onto the sand. Then, with one at each end and the third placing his hands under Hersch's waist and thighs, they kept him as rigid as possible while making their way to the car. Once they had laid him in the backseat, the boatman shook John's hand.

"See you around, buddy," he said with a smile. Looking toward the car, he added, "Take care of ol' Hersch. I owed him one, so this makes us even. I've got to get out of here now, so I'll check on you guys later."

"Thanks so much for everything," John exclaimed. "We would be dead men back there if it weren't for you."

"Well, one thing's for sure, you gotta learn to stay away from that guy," he said, pointing toward the backseat. "He can get in and out of more trouble than any five people I know. Actually, things have been pretty slow around here lately. I guess a little excitement helps make life worthwhile. Besides, some guys will do anything to get out of Iran."

"Isn't that the truth!" John responded, with a grim smile.

"You know that you'll probably have a little explaining to do, once the powers that be catch up to you guys?"

"I know."

"Okay. Take care of our friend now, y'hear?"

"I promise."

John sat across from the driver, looking over his shoulder to check on Hersch again, as the car pulled out onto the highway and began picking up speed.

"If I'd known you guys were starting a war over there," the driver remarked, "I'd have brought an ambulance instead of this car. The first word we had on this operation was when Hersch called from London and said you needed some backup. I don't suppose you've got anybody at home who's authorized this little escapade?"

John shook his head.

"Passports? Visas? Wait. Do I even want to hear your answer?"

"Probably not."

"Figures. I guess that's why the boss was treating this with kid gloves. You two were trying to get somebody's daughter out of there, is that it?"

"Mine," John answered, staring out across the open sea.

"Sorry. No luck?"

"No luck. I'm sorry too."

"Couldn't find her?"

"Not soon enough. She escaped from where they were holding her a couple of hours before we hit the place." Lines of worry furrowed deeply into John's face. "She's out there though. And she's alive."

"She get busted for drugs or something?"

"She's twelve."

"Twelve!" exclaimed the driver, looking at John in disbelief. "Are you serious? A twelve-year-old?"

"Yeah."

"Wait a minute. Are we talking about that girl who was kidnapped in Israel a couple of months ago?"

"The same."

"I heard Hersch call you 'Rev' back there. Are you really a preacher?"

"In another life, my friend. In another life."

SHOUTS!

Sounds of someone running.

More shouts.

The noise forced her eyes open, as she struggled to awaken from a groggy stupor of exhaustion.

She lay still, afraid to move a muscle, trying to gather herself together.

What is happening? Where am I?

Her eyes slowly focused on a blue ceiling . . . no, it can't be a ceiling. It's something else. There was the distinct smell of new paint. Like the time she woke up that first morning after she and her mother painted her bedroom.

Finally, another shout jolted her, causing the unbalanced images floating in and out of her mind to vanish. She caught her breath at the cry of a seagull, and smiled as it swooped across her line of vision. The familiar gray and white scavenger bird looked as glorious as a noble eagle.

The sky. I'm looking at the sky!

Jessica turned her head to one side on the package-turned-pillow. Her movement released another odor, this one of canvas and something else she did not recognize, mingling with the paint that emanated from her wooden lifeboat surroundings.

And fresh air.

O dear Lord Jesus. I'm free. I really made it! I'm out of that horrible place at last!

For a moment, the full force of freedom actually took away her breath. Her excitement continued to build as she started to replay the events of the night before. Then, another shout broke into her reverie and Jessica struggled to her knees, lifting her head until she could see over the edge of the lifeboat.

Below, on the dock, two men were looking up at the ship. One called something out to a man on the deck who was standing a short distance from her lifeboat and leaning over the side. Farther forward, more men scurried about, unwrapping mooring lines as thick as a man's wrist, that had earlier stretched downward to the dock. Still others hauled cables and steam lines clear of connection boxes.

The engine was louder now and Jessica could feel its vibration. On the far side of the vessel a tugboat moved into position, sounding a loud horn as its powerful engines churned the sea. A narrow strip of dirty water became visible between the bow and the pier. Gradually the ship moved away from its moorings.

Yes!

Jessica's heart was pounding. She had guessed right.

We're moving. We're actually leaving this place!

She wanted to stand up and shout.

Don't trust anybody. These people may be just as bad as the others.

Her sudden rush of freedom deflated rapidly, replaced by mixed emotions of foreboding and reprieve, and a flashback to a television movie she had watched with Jeremy. The main character had been led to the death chamber and strapped into the electric chair. She could still see the look of hopelessness on his face, and the hand of the executioner resting on the switch that would end the man's life. At the last second, the telephone rang. The prison warden took the call. It was the governor, granting a stay of execution. They led the prisoner back to his cell. Jessica remembered asking Jeremy if he was free now. No, Jeremy had said, it's not over yet. It's just a "stay of execution."

A stay of execution.

Another loud blast erupted from the bowels of the tugboat.

It's not over yet.

Jessica peered cautiously over the outer edge of the lifeboat, watching the huge dock crane and waterfront buildings slowly recede from view.

"LET ME GET THIS STRAIGHT, Reverend Cain." The ambassador's face was stern as he glanced at the notes on his desk and shaped his mouth around each word. "You and this Herschel Winslow Towner the Third decided to take on the whole Hizballah terrorist crowd and the rest of the radical Muslim world all by yourselves?

"You entered the sovereign nation of Iran, using forged passports and counterfeit visas. Next, you feigned illness and left your tour group and its leader wondering what in the name of peace happened to their two missing male members. You flew to Bandar-é Abbás, broke into the home of an Iranian citizen named Reza Fardusi, shot up a contingent of Revolutionary Guardsmen, and then fled in a speedboat driven by somebody whose name I do not want to hear, entered the UAE illegally, without passports or any genuine identification papers whatsoever, and this morning . . . Herschel Winslow Towner the Third has been admitted into a local hospital here in Abu Dhabi, and is recovering from a bullet wound, a gift, I suppose, from the Iranian 'Welcome Wagon.' Now, here you are, sitting in my office requesting assistance in getting temporary passports. Is that it, Reverend Cain? Are there any details of which I am still unaware?"

John shook his head. "No, that pretty well covers it, sir."

The ambassador swore, just as a secretary walked into the office and handed him a fax. He scanned it briefly and stood to his feet.

"Excuse me. Just stay seated, Reverend Cain. Don't move a muscle."

Ambassador Geoffrey Carson, appointed by the President of the United States two years previously to the American Embassy serving the United Arab Emirates, disappeared into the next room.

In defiance of the ambassador's parting directive, John drummed his fingers impatiently on the arm of the chair while staring straight ahead, still trying to deal with the disappointment of the night before. At the same time, he reflected in amazement on where he was this morning.

After what he had seen in Tehran and Bandar, arriving in Dubai had been a little like walking out onto the surface of another planet.

The traffic was heavy, just like in Tehran. The difference here was that it appeared to consist wholly of BMWs, Ferraris, and Mercedes, sprinkled with a healthy number of Jeeps and Landcruisers. He had noticed an entire fleet of Toyota Cressida taxis in operation as well.

On the way to the embassy, wherever John looked there seemed to be suntanned female flesh on display under backless T-shirts, spaghetti-strapped mini-dresses, even shorts. In Palm Springs, no one would have looked twice; in Iran, the women would have been arrested. He had been informed by his driver that these women were all foreigners, but they still set the pace for the rest of the principality.

After arriving at the embassy, he was led to a small sitting room. The ambassador, he was informed, had someone in his office at the moment. Since John had no appointment, he would have to wait.

Meanwhile, an aid provided an excellent cup of coffee. She invited herself to sit down with him, obviously anxious to talk to someone who had just come from America. Her parents lived in Atlanta and she looked forward to visiting them next February. She then proceeded to fill in the blanks to his questions about this place where he and Hersch had landed. John was surprised to learn that eighty-five percent of the Emirates' population is expatriate, mostly Pakistanis, Indians, Sri Lankans, and Filipinos. They constitute the working class of house servants, drivers, and laborers. Americans and Europeans supply the know-how and managerial skills, as well as the money.

Ten minutes had come and gone before the ambassador returned, a handsomely carved pipe cupped in his hand. He sat on the edge of his desk and resumed his look of stern disapproval.

"Reverend Cain, there's something I'd like to be certain that you understand. During my tenure here, I have never heard of such audaciousness. You and your friend have broken most of the laws that anyone could be guilty of breaking in a forty-eight hour period. Do you realize that?"

"Yes, sir." John had begun to feel like a student who found himself in the principal's office for doing something bad.

"For goodness sake, man, do you think that your conduct is in keeping with the way someone from your calling and persuasion should be acting?"

"No, sir."

"Good, because you are right."

Ambassador Carson bit down on the pipe stem and stood to his feet.

"If we provide you with sanctuary and assistance toward your safe return to the States, you have to promise me that you will cease and desist from any future shenanigans of this nature. I can appreciate your parental motivation, but you've got to let your government handle this matter through normal channels. Agreed?"

"I'm sorry, sir," John said at last, "but no, I cannot agree to that."

Carson walked around to the other side of his desk. "And why not, Reverend Cain? Why do you, of all people, find it so difficult to submit to the authority of your government and follow the rules?"

"With all due respect, Mr. Ambassador, I have submitted to that authority. I have followed the rules and pressed the appropriate buttons for weeks. All to no avail."

"State informs me that they are working on this case."

"State has given up on this case, Mr. Ambassador. They've been stringing us along, sure, but there's really nothing that they've been able . . . or willing . . . to do. It finally came down to me trying to do something, or forget about my daughter. What would you have done, sir, if you were in my position?"

Carson fingered the bowl on his pipe as he came around to the side of the desk that faced John's chair. John did not move, but kept his eyes steadily focused on the ambassador, waiting for an answer.

"You and your friend Towner are a real pain, Cain." The ambassador chuckled at his own inadvertent rhyme and witticism, such as it was. John was too tired and frustrated by failure to express even a tacit acknowledgment of the ambassador's humor. His expression remained unchanged.

"Okay, you've made your point," Carson said, as he sat on the edge of the desk. "On an official level, I find your actions both foolish and reprehensible. You just can't go around doing what you have been doing."

He shifted his body and leaned forward. John was surprised to see traces of a slight smile crack the otherwise solemn facial veneer.

"On a personal level," he went on, "I admire your guts!"

Carson stood and smacked a fist into his hand. "I still can't believe you actually did it. You just got on a plane, flew in, and kicked butt the way we all wish we could. Incredible!"

Carson burst out in laughter. "Just incredible!" he said again.

"Begging your pardon, Mr. Ambassador," John interrupted. "I have to say that I'm not really proud of what we did. Breaking laws, like Hersch and I have done these past two days, is wrong. I know that. But, standing up against evil for the rights of oppressed people, in this case, my daughter . . . well, I think that is right. It's just hard to always know where the line runs and at what point a person should cross over. In my business, we have a saying that may sum up my being here in your office this morning. Sometimes it's a lot easier to get forgiveness than permission."

Carson laughed again. "When it comes to governmental red tape, I'm afraid you're right."

"My concern now is that I don't know where Jessica has gone. She must still be somewhere in Bandar. One of Fardusi's maids directed her to a small group of Christians who promised to keep an eye out for her. That's really my only hope now. I'm concerned too about Fardusi and his maid. Believe it or not, they were key to us getting out of there. Our escape may have left them in a dangerous position."

"My guess is that Fardusi will work his way out of it," responded Carson. "We know a little about that fellow. He's a wily one, that's for sure. Actually, I had my staff check the foreign news services in Iran, this morning, to see if there was anything of interest. There was."

"What?" John's voice was anxious as he sat up straight.

"Jacques Kandau is a correspondent with *Agence France-Presse*, who works out of Teheran. Yesterday, he reported two missing Americans. Their personal effects were found in the hotel room in which they were registered. A rug merchant named Trent, and a religion professor." Carson picked up one of the documents laying on the desk and flipped it open. "Dr. Castle, I presume?"

John smothered a grin and brushed at his rumpled suit trousers.

"Yes, well, it seems that we may have solved the mystery of the missing Americans," continued Carson, unfolding a piece of paper from his shirt pocket. "Now, about an hour ago, another story came over the wire from the TASS news agency. They report that bandits entered the Bandar-é Abbâs home of the highly respected Reza Fardusi, apparently with the intent of kidnapping him for ransom. A maid was also forced into Fardusi's stolen vehicle. . . . Good grief, did you guys actually kidnap these people and steal a car along with everything else? And the two hostages were being driven away when a Revolutionary Guard patrol became suspicious and stopped them.

"A furious gun battle ensued, leaving two wounded Guardsmen. It is believed that one of the bandits was also wounded. Both of the criminals escaped in a powerboat and remain at large, though an area-wide search is underway right now. Authorities in neighboring countries are being requested to be on the lookout for the kidnappers.

"Fortunately for you, from the descriptions, both appear to be from the Middle East, and are most likely Iranian in nationality. And, both men speak fluent Farsi." Carson looked up. "Would you like to regale me with your 'fluent Farsi,' Reverend Cain?"

John shook his head in wonder, as he rose from the chair. "I can't believe it. The man holds my daughter for over a month as a hostage in his house. Then, he helps us escape and bids us well in finding her."

"It sounds as though you helped him escape some local retribution as well. He was just being grateful by returning the favor."

The two men looked at each other for a long moment. Then, Ambassador Carson reached out and shook John's hand.

"That's life," he said, smiling. "And this is the Middle East."

He walked with John to the doorway.

"I'll have our staff work on arranging things for you and Mr. Towner. We'll get passport replacements for the ones you seem to have misplaced. You'll have tickets home. One-way, I might add. I can't promise you anything, but I'll do what I can to get State to become more active in locating your daughter. Especially now that we know she's really out here somewhere. Take heart, Reverend Cain. It sounds as though your Jessica is made of the same stuff as her old man."

"I appreciate whatever you can do, Ambassador Carson. I know I can't ask you for miracles, but I can ask Him," said John, glancing upward. "And I will."

"Remember, you're headed for home now, understand?" asked Carson. "We'll be in touch. Just as soon as your friend is ready to travel. From what I'm told, that may be a few days. Do you have a place to stay?"

"Not yet," John answered, "but I'll find something."

"I'll have Susan make a reservation for you. Come with me. She's at the front desk."

"Thank you. I'm sorry to have put you to this much trouble."

"Well, you have certainly livened up the day. I think we can take care of you and your friend without any difficulty. Then, as soon as he is able to travel, we'll arrange for you to head home."

"Thank you again, Mr. Ambassador," John said. *But, I'm not going home without Jessica. No matter what. Not on your life.*

FORTY-THREE

The M/V *Evvoia* was steaming steadily toward that imaginary line known as the Tropic of Cancer, the parallel of latitude that is approximately twenty-three and one-half degrees north of the equator, the northernmost latitude reached by the overhead sun. Captain George Callimachus strolled across the bridge, his dark eyes routinely checking instruments and gauges.

Evvoia's bridge was twenty-five feet wide and ten feet deep. It was crammed with radar consoles, helm, engine-order telegraph, and a plotting table. Two leather chairs were perched on pedestals to the left and right. Immediately above the instrument panel were large windows, permitting the captain a panoramic view of the forward section of the ship as well as the seas waiting to be traveled. Glancing at the overhead clock, he mused that they would reach the invisible parallel sometime after nightfall.

Fifty-three years old, George Callimachus had been making a living at sea for thirty-two years. His wife, Anne, and their three daughters lived in a suburb of Piraeus, Athens' bustling and somewhat seedy port city.

His early years were lived in Samos City, a small port community on the island of Samos. His elderly parents, both Greek, still lived in a small house at the edge of town. They were a proud pair . . . proud of being Greek and of having lived simple but honest lives. Proud of their two children. George's younger sister, Diana, was a schoolteacher in Athens, wife of an accountant who worked for Olympic Airlines, and the mother of two boys, eight and twelve. Jokingly, George would say to their friends that his parents were mostly proud of the fact that they could trace their ancestry all the way back to another Callimachus, the famous fourth-century scholar and librarian at Alexandria.

He had grown up working on the small family fishing boat, in the seas off Samos Island. Under the careful nurturing of his father, George developed a healthy respect and love for the sea. During his youthful years, he had been captivated by the romance of the grand ships that entered Samos harbor, disgorging vacationers and world travelers onto a community that was rapidly becoming reliant on tourism for its survival.

As soon as he was old enough to hire on, George began plying the Mediterranean on whatever ships were available. His dream was to one day captain one of the great ocean liners, put in at exotic ports throughout the world, and regale passengers with tall tales each evening around the captain's table. Like many boyhood dreams, it was fulfilled in part but not in whole. At age thirty-seven, he had finished the educational requirements, passed all the examinations with honors, and was hired as captain of a small cargo vessel owned by a wealthy London family. For the last five years, he had served as captain on the *Evvoia*, a large ship most often transporting grains and foodstuffs between Middle and Far East ports of call. In Bandar-é Abbâs, his vessel had taken on equal amounts of wheat and rice with the destination being the port city of Split, Croatia.

When in his normal shipboard routine, Captain Callimachus dressed casually, and the crew followed his example. He could most often be found roaming the decks in blue jeans and a white dress shirt, but no tie. Fair skinned, with a large, bulbous nose, and dark hair solidly streaked with gray, George Callimachus was likable but resolute. Strong and sure of himself, but quiet.

The entire rest of the ship's crew, including First Mate Paulo Morâles, were Filipino. Ranging in age from eighteen to thirty-five, each man had contracted to serve aboard the *Evvoia* for a specific time, with duties that ranged from the most menial to engineer status. They lived in private cabins sparsely outfitted with a bed, chair, writing table, and sea trunk for personal items. All meals were taken in the crew's mess.

Even the new chef, now only four weeks into his contract, was originally from Manila. It made sense to hire someone who knew how to cook for a crew possessing similar food tastes, but sometimes this was to Captain Callimachus' chagrin. He managed to eat most of what came out of the galley, but drew the line when it came to the coffee pot.

When he complained about the quality of his staple drink, the chef apologized, informing the captain that his galley assistant was in charge of making the coffee. Not completely sure who was actually in charge of what in the galley, the captain personally took the chef and his assistant aside to demonstrate how real coffee should be made. After several unsuccessful attempts, an adequate quality level had been reached about a week ago, and life had thus gone on.

Callimachus was pleased to be at sea once again. He particularly disliked Iranian ports of call. He had found Iranians, in general, to be a warmhearted and congenial people, shrewd but fair in business dealings. It was the religious right that had pulled the veil over their people's faces and over their hearts as well.

There was virtually nothing diversionary for his crew to do while in Iranian ports. All foreign seamen were suspect as to customs and morals and they were made to feel so unwelcome that most simply chose to stay on board. The "on board" environment of a ship can be extremely boring, however, and a crewman's ability to get away from the ship to tour a city or call home to his family is always an important part of the time spent in ports. Such opportunities for morale building were almost nonexistent when the *Evvoia* tied up somewhere in Iran.

The captain brushed an imaginary fleck from his white shirt. A refreshing breeze was coming through the open doors at each end of the bridge. The steady vibration of the engine tickled the soles of his feet. His hand rested briefly on the polished brass handrail that ran the full length of the instrument panel. He liked this handrail—it gave the bridge a certain appearance of distinction, found usually only in the best of ships.

First Mate Moråles was bent over the radarscope at the far side of the bridge, evaluating the distance between the *Evvoia* and nearby ships in the Gulf. Due to the amount of time required for their vessel to take evasive action or stop altogether, that information was essential while working in this heavily trafficked region.

Callimachus took a pitcher of water from the counter and poured himself a glass. He drank slowly, savoring both the taste and feel. In summer, the Gulf was invariably frying-pan hot, with temperatures regularly up to 45°C or even 50°C, and with an oppressive humidity. His casual albeit character-shaping relationship with the Greek Orthodox Church gave impetus to kidding around with other seagoing comrades about this region. "If you don't believe in hell," he would say, "wait until you sail the Gulf in summer!" Late November to early March, however, was generally pleasant, though today seemed a bit warmer than usual. It felt good to be inside and away from the sun's relentless rays.

SLIGHTLY ABOVE, AND ABOUT A HUNDRED feet back on the east side of the ship, Jessica stretched out in the bottom of the lifeboat. The sun's heat and clear blue skies, the throbbing of the engine and languid roll of the ship, tempered her spirit with a tranquillity she had not known in months. Occasionally, she sipped from the water bottle she had found in another package.

"Don't let yourself get dehydrated, sweetheart."

It was her father's voice again. How long since she had heard it? They were the last words she remembered him saying to her.

I wonder what he's doing. How is Mother handling this? Jeremy, I miss our wrestling matches. I even miss your teasing.

There appeared to be sufficient rations in the lifeboat for several people. Certainly more than enough for her needs, though the selection and taste left something to be desired. The carton of tootsie rolls was a surprise, and she downed several of those early on. She needed the quick energy that the candy provided.

Freedom!

It was hard to know just how to feel about it. For the first time in months, she felt totally free. No one guarded her door. No one even knew she was here.

I did it. Thank You, God. I'm free. I wonder where this ship is headed? And if the people on board are friendly?

She lifted the water bottle to her lips.

Don't trust anybody!

How would she get in touch with her parents? And what about all those children that the man named Dosha said he was going to kill? She needed to tell somebody. But who? Who would believe her anyway? She was just a little girl in a lifeboat on a big sea, too frightened to stand up and enjoy the breeze for fear that someone might see her and lock her in another room. There was one problem, however, that would have to be dealt with soon.

I need to go to the bathroom!

DINNER WAS FINISHED. DARKNESS HAD SETTLED over the ocean an hour ago. Angel Rameriz, chief engineer, was just leaving the TV lounge after watching two-thirds of *Shoot-out at*

Tombstone, an Italian video about Arizona cowboys. It was bad, but it helped to while away the time. English subtitles helped.

Rameriz worked two shifts each day, four daylight hours and then four more at night. Two others with his qualifications, together with three oilers, held forth with him below decks, in the bottom of the ship. They worked two at a time in the engine room, keeping watch over the monstrous Hitachi Sulzar, six-cylinder, 16,500-horsepower engine that drove the ship through the seas.

He pushed back the door, opening onto metal steps that dropped steeply into the caldron of heat and power that was his workplace. Suddenly, he stopped.

What was that?

Rameriz turned and looked up and down the narrow passageway.

Thought I heard something.

No one else was around. All doors were shut.

Guess it was nothing.

He stepped through the doorway and started down the steps into the world-painted-green that was his home away from home.

JESSICA'S HEART RACED as she reached up and locked the door to the head. Moments ago, she had crawled out of the lifeboat and climbed down the ladder to the deck. Her legs were stiff from inactivity and her bladder was so full that it hurt.

The first passageway was only a half-dozen feet beyond the ladder. She peeked around the corner. A dark-haired man in blue overalls was walking away from her. At the same time, she noticed that the doorway to one of the ship's restrooms was open. Jessica took one more look at the man and then slipped into the passage behind him and through the open door, closing it quickly.

Safe!

Minutes later, Jessica stood in front of the mirror and stared at her image. It was the first time she had seen herself in weeks. She was shocked at her reflection—hair matted and sweaty, face smudged with dirt and grease.

Spying a bar of soap, she washed her hands, then her face. It felt so good that she pulled off her clothes and indulged in a "sponge bath," finally rinsing off with handfuls of water scooped from the sink and poured over her body. Soaking wet and naked, she dried as best she could with paper towels, crushing each one tightly before dumping it into the trash basket. Reluctantly, she put her dirty clothes back on.

The floor was covered with soapy water and dirt. It wouldn't do to leave it in this condition. Someone might wonder how it got that way and become suspicious. Using more paper towels, Jessica bent down and wiped up as much as possible. It didn't look as good as it had, but with any luck, once the door was open and fresh air let in, it would dry before the next person came to use it.

Carefully, Jessica unlocked the door and peeked out. The passageway was clear. She scooted out, leaving the door ajar. Four short steps and she was at the exit to the deck. A quick look both ways. Then up the ladder and into the lifeboat. She arranged the flotation devices so that she could lie down on them like a mattress. Once situated, she gazed up at the stars.

Her body felt clean for the first time in weeks.

Her mind was as clear as the night sky.

Her last thoughts before sleep were of home.

1230 LOCAL TIME
ABU DHABI, UAE

HE COULD HEAR THE PHONE ringing. Once, twice, three times. He'd put off the inevitable as long as he could.

"Hello." The voice sounded drowsy at the other end. John glanced at his watch. In all that had transpired during the last few hours and days, he had lost complete track of time back home. Now, he realized that it was well past midnight in California.

"Hello, sweetheart."

"John?" He could almost see her throwing back the covers and raising up in bed. "John? Is that you?"

"Yes, hon. Sorry to get you out of bed. I forgot the time difference."

"Don't be silly." She was wide awake now. "Are you all right? Where are you?"

"Yes, I'm okay. We're in the United Arab Emirates. I'm calling from the US Embassy."

"Were you . . . were you . . ." he heard the catch in Esther's voice.

"We weren't able to get her out," he said huskily, "but we do know she is still alive."

There was a long silence. He heard Esther clear her throat. His eyes filled as he thought of the struggle she must be going through.

"What . . . what happened? What can you tell me over the phone?" Esther's presence of mind made him suddenly cautious. She was right. Who knows who else might be listening in?

Is this paranoia or what?

John recounted enough information, leaving out certain details, names, and places, to let Esther at least have some hope. It was not the phone call he had dreamed of making. It was simply the best he could do for now.

"Will you be coming home soon?"

"I'm not sure just when. Hersch is not feeling well."

"He's sick?"

"In a manner of speaking, yes. He has to spend a few days in the hospital here in Abu Dhabi. When he's better, we'll head back."

More silence.

"Is it serious?" Esther asked, her voice low.

"He's going to live, if that's what you're asking. It hit him suddenly, without any warning, but he'll be okay."

"Thank God."

"We are, believe me."

"And Jessica?"

"She's out on her own somewhere. I'm not quite sure where to look. She decided to get out and see some of the countryside, I guess."

"She's . . . by herself?"

"Yes. But, she has a number of Christian friends who are keeping an eye out for her. I'm sure we'll hear something soon. Honey, I hate to break this off, but I have to go. I'm going to visit Hersch."

"John . . ."

"Yes?"

"I love you."

"I love you too."

"Be careful."

"Count on it."

0245 LOCAL TIME
BAYTOWN, CALIFORNIA

ESTHER REPLACED THE PHONE and dropped back onto the bed, a feeling of hollowness inside.

They weren't able to get her. She's still alive and must have escaped. Jessica is still alive! But where are you, honey? What's happening to you now?

For a long time, Esther's eyes were closed, not in sleep, but in prayer.

She prayed for John.

He sounded so disappointed and lost, Lord. And he wants so desperately to bring our little girl home.

She prayed for Herschel too.

He's a good man, Lord, but John says that he's angry at You over the death of his wife. Now, something must have happened to him. Whatever it is, be with him in that hospital. And let him find Your peace.

Most of all, with feelings that fought for release from deep inside, she prayed for her baby.

"Mom?"

Her eyes opened with a start and she caught her breath.

"Mom, are you okay in there? I heard the phone ring."

Esther got up and felt her way around the edge of the bed in the dark. When she opened the door, Jeremy was standing there, in his shorts.

"I'm okay, son."

"It was so late . . . I thought maybe . . ."

"You thought right. It was your dad. Come on, let's go make a pot of coffee. I don't think I'll be able to get back to sleep, so why should you? Anyway, you want to know and I need some company. Okay?"

Jeremy followed his mother into the kitchen, reaching past her to turn on the light.

FORTY-FOUR

BOMB EXPLODES IN SYNAGOGUE

Dec. 4. CHICAGO, Illinois — A bomb blast shook central downtown Chicago yesterday, as worshipers gathered in a local synagogue for Sabbath day services. Three people were killed outright and thirty-two others sustained injuries, ranging from minor to critical. The injured included thirteen children, from nine to fourteen years of age.

Phone calls subsequent to the explosion credit the blast to the Palestinian Islamic Jihad, an extremist group attached to Hamas. The group has declared itself to be an avowed opponent to the Israeli-PLO Accord and demands that the UN rescind its 1948 affirmation of the State of Israel.

IS A "MYSTERY TAPE" BEING KEPT FROM THE PUBLIC?

Dec. 6. NEW YORK, New York — Unconfirmed reports indicate that a videotape has been received by CNN, and possibly several other networks, concerning the rash of recent terrorist attacks on public gathering places. The incidents have focused America's attention on its vulnerability to this sort of outrageous attack.

In the last five days, a Chicago synagogue, a Roman Catholic church in Baltimore, and a Baptist church in downtown Atlanta, along with schools in Racine, Wisconsin and Santa Fe, New Mexico have fallen victim to bombings by terrorists. In all, seven adults and twenty-three children are dead and fifty-two others have been injured. The Palestinian Islamic Jihad has claimed responsibility for these heinous crimes against American citizens.

....

....

JESSICA CAIN VIDEO RELEASED

Dec. 7. ATLANTA, Georgia—A videotape received two days ago, but withheld at government request until today, was aired on CNN as well as NBC, ABC, and CBS network news. CNN News revealed that each of the other networks had also received a copy of the tape featuring Jessica Cain, the missing twelve-year-old girl from Baytown, California. After conferring with State Department officials, the networks agreed not to release the video until now, due to its inflammatory nature.

Reading from a prepared script, an obviously shaken youngster indicated that her abductors were demanding the equivalent of one dollar for every boy and girl in America and Israel as a ransom for her life. In addition, a list of demands was read that included the abolition of the State of Israel and the repatriation of all political prisoners held by Israel and the US.

Young Jessica Cain has been missing since September 18, when her father and a group of Christians from California were abducted by terrorists connected with the Palestinian Islamic Jihad, the group now claiming responsibility for the current rash of terrorist incidents ravaging America and Israel. Officials in Washington expressed surprise that she was still alive, but offered regrets to the members of families that have recently experienced loss through acts of terrorism committed in cities throughout the country.

Demands for military intervention are being offered on the floor of Congress. The White House has ordered all National Guard units to report for duty, in cooperation with local police and the FBI. The President will make a special televised address to the nation at nine o'clock tonight, Eastern Time, to explain the Administration's nonnegotiation stance with regard to terrorist organizations.

Meanwhile, schools continue to close in many communities; malls have witnessed a sharp decline in sales due to shoppers staying away in large numbers this Christmas season, and during the past weekend, some places of worship indicated that as many as half of those normally in attendance during the Advent season have stayed away out of fear.

The whereabouts of Jessica Cain continues to be a mystery. Rumored sightings have been reported in various cities from Rio de Janeiro to Tehran. Sources have verified that the Reverend Cain flew to New York on November 30, but his present whereabouts are unknown and his family remains in seclusion, unavailable for comment.

....

SATURDAY, 10 DECEMBER, 1705 LOCAL TIME
THE GULF OF OMAN

IT HAD BEEN EIGHT DAYS since the *Evvoia* sailed from Bandar-é Abbås. Eight long and boring days for the ship's crew and for their young stowaway.

During the daytime, the temperature had been quite warm, though ocean breezes mitigated what otherwise would have been unbearable. Still, Jessica knew that she was burning under the intense sun. By the time she discovered the protective sun lotion in one of the survival packs, it was almost too late. Her face and arms were an angry red. As a counter-measure, Jessica spread out two of the waterproof covers from the foodstuffs, and laid them over the exposed parts of her body. It was hot and uncomfortable, but there was no other protection available.

After departing the Gulf of Oman, the port side of the ship faced out to sea in an east, southeasterly direction. From her lofty perch, all Jessica had been able to glimpse was the open sea. On one occasion, well off in the distance, she had seen another ship steaming in the opposite direction, but that was it, at least during daylight hours.

On the third night out, Jessica changed all that.

Up to then, her only excursions from the lifeboat consisted of nighttime visits to the ship's head. Always, well after dark, before she slept, and again just before dawn. As she grew more familiar with her surroundings, and the fact that often an hour or two could pass with no crew member in her vicinity, she made day-time forays as well, but only when absolutely necessary.

In the evening, putting cool water to her face was a luxury to look forward to as she removed the sweat and grime. However, the nights were cold, and Jessica often found herself shivering, even with the blanket around her. She tried wrapping the food parcel coverings as tightly as she could around her shoulders, and tucked her feet together under another package to stay warm, but this usually was not enough.

On the third night, after fruitless attempts to ward off the cold, Jessica decided to take a chance. Throwing off the wrappings, she slipped over the side and down the ladder. Once her feet hit the deck, she checked out the passageway where the head was located. No one was there. She glided past the entrance and continued along the deck, careful to stay away from the rail and in the shadows.

Seeing a set of steps to another deck, she glanced around and then started up. At the top she walked about twenty feet to another open doorway and peered into a room full of instruments, glowing in the dim light. She made out the figure of a man in a white shirt and blue jeans, standing by a console, talking into what looked like a telephone.

It must be a radio.

The man put the receiver back on its hook and turned toward her. She pulled away quickly, hoping he had not seen her, and ran back along the deck toward the steps, pausing in the shadows to check behind her. A minute passed . . . or was it an hour? When Jessica was certain no one was following, she took her time making her way back down the steps.

On the main deck again, she jogged back to the doorway behind her lifeboat. Pushing the door open, she discovered another empty passageway, with doors on the right side.

Maybe this is where the crew lives.

To the left was an open door, and beyond she could see stoves and a food preparation table. No one was about as she tiptoed in. A fluorescent light was on over the stove, and a cooking pot sat off to one side of the grill.

Evidently the restaurant is closed.

Jessica's stomach rumbled at the prospect of something to eat besides hardtack and tootsie rolls. She opened the refrigerator and saw two cartons of milk and some chicken, left over from the crew's evening meal. Lifting the milk carton to her mouth, she drank deeply. Then she stuffed two pieces of chicken into her pants pocket and continued drinking the milk.

Better leave some.

Milk running down both sides of her face, she replaced the nearly empty carton and closed the door. That's when she saw the pie. It had been cut and served, but three pieces remained. Jessica scooped up one of them.

Cherry pie. Hallelujah!

She made her way back to the ladder and, balancing the pie in one hand, pulled herself up with the other. It was awkward, but she didn't want to eat the pie until after devouring the chicken. This was, after all, a genuine feast.

After that first night, scavenging and wandering about the ship became Jessica's nighttime recreation. On a couple of occasions, she had near misses with crew members who seemed to appear out of nowhere; but most of the time, it was easy to stay out of sight.

She had no idea about the geography of the region through which they were sailing; a couple of times she thought she saw lights on the distant horizon, but they were soon gone. She had no way of knowing that her vessel was working its way along the coast of Oman and that she had spied the lights of the city of Aden, Yemen. Not long thereafter, the Gulf of Aden gave way to Bab al-Mandab, the Strait of Lamentations. Giving the island of Perim a wide berth, the *Evvoia* pushed on into the Red Sea.

In the early morning light, Jessica now saw land well off in the distance. She was curious as to their whereabouts, though she knew that it made little difference. Wherever the ship finally docked again would be better than Iran. She would get off and try to find help. She had no money and that would be a problem. What worried her even more was something that should have been simple enough.

How do I go about making an international phone call? I've got no money. No credit card. And what if the operator doesn't speak English?

These thoughts were troubling her as the *Evvoia* passed along the African coast of Somalia, eventually giving way to a tip of Ethiopia. Seeing land had given Jessica hope that they were nearing the ship's destination. When it faded from sight, her spirits fell.

Her face was beginning to peel from overexposure to sun and salt air. Even the tips of her ears had become tender to the touch. The sun had also worked its way through the matted strands of her long hair and singed the top of her head. She knew that she needed some lotion, in addition to the sunscreen she had finally discovered in the lifeboat supplies.

Oh, well. Better to be worried about this than to be back in that room with those awful people.

She suddenly shivered at the thought. It was a world she would like to forget.

Day turned into night and night into day. The monotony of ocean travel, accentuated by the discomfort and the tension surrounding her need to remain hidden, was wearing thin. Finally, late on her sixth night at sea, through an open door into the crew lounge, she spied several magazines and a paperback thrown carelessly on a table. On the top was an issue of *Time.* Seeing no one around, Jessica ventured into the room for a closer look.

The paperback didn't look like something she would be interested in, but the magazines were too good to pass up. And, in a corner of the room was a TV with a VCR!

How long has it been since . . .

Her thoughts ran nostalgically to Saturday morning cartoons and Christian music videos in the living room. Then, she heard voices coming from the other side of the closed door at the far end of the room. Unnerved, she ran back the way she had come, dashing into the passageway and out onto the deck. She was startled further still by lights not far from the ship. She ran to the ladder and was reaching for the first rung when she realized that she still held all three magazines in her hand.

Oh, no. What if they miss these? Will they come searching?

Knowing it was too late to return them, she quickly folded and tucked them at her waist and scurried up the ladder into the lifeboat.

"WHAT ARE YOU LOOKING FOR?"

Timothy Marcos, no relation to his homeland's former ruler, looked puzzled as he stood in front of the magazine rack.

"I was reading that *Newsweek* article on the Philippines. You know the one?"

"Yeah, Paulo mentioned it to me. Said it was pretty good."

"Well, now I don't see it. It was right there on the table last night, but now it's gone."

"Somebody probably took it to their cabin and forgot to return it. Ask around at lunch."

Marcos took a last look, moving some magazines that were stuffed in the front of the rack in order to check behind them, but it was not there. He shrugged his shoulders and headed for the galley. It was only thirty minutes until the lunch hour, and it was his responsibility, as assistant cook, to make sure the cabbage salad was ready and condiments in place for the crew's use.

During the meal, Tim asked about the magazine, but no one had taken it, or so they said. Every crew member knew that Timothy was a voracious reader. They kidded him about always having his nose in a book. He had graduated from high school last year and it was general knowledge that he was working as a cook's assistant in order to earn the money needed for higher education. What made it unusual was that Tim wanted to go to Bible school and train for the ministry. He dreamed of being a pastor one day.

Tim had become a committed Christian three years before, while attending a youth camp to which he had been invited by friends. His faith in Jesus was simple, direct, and life-changing. He was not pushy, but he was not afraid to talk to others about the changes he had experienced through knowing Christ as his Savior.

After starting to work on the *Evvoia*, he had been surprised one day by the visit of a man dressed in jeans and an open shirt. He came on board carrying bags of breakfast rolls, along with some Christian magazines, Bibles, and other literature. It turned out that the man was from the local Christian Seaman's Center, located not far from where his ship was berthed.

Tim had given him his name and, at the next port of call, he was amazed when a man from another Christian Seaman's Center looked him up to see how he was doing. He invited him and his fellow crew members to visit his tiny office, located near the docks. They were all permitted to call home on his phone, at rates substantially less than they would be charged elsewhere. The man had told them how churches from various denominations helped support his work through monthly or annual financial gifts, and how a network of similar centers stayed in touch with their seagoing contituents all around the world.

Impressed that local churches would be interested enough to reach out to people like himself, he accepted a Bible study course and the challenge of beginning a study group among his fellow crew members. There were three others who now met regularly with Tim to study the Bible. Two of them had committed their lives to Christ, while the third said he was "thinking about it."

Satisfied that no one knew the whereabouts of the *Newsweek*, Tim was surprised to see it on the table in the lounge the next morning, along with issues of *Time* and *People*.

Why would someone deny having something so unimportant and then secretly return it, without a word of explanation?

Tim decided it was too trivial to worry about. He picked up the magazine and sat down, flipping to the page at which he had stopped reading two evenings before.

THE FOLLOWING NIGHT, WHILE JESSICA was returning some magazines to the crew lounge, she noticed something she'd not seen on her previous visits. In a small box, between two wood-framed leather chairs, was a stack of *Reader's Digests*. Quickly, she pulled three from the bottom of the stack and carried these, together with a small section of cheese and bread confiscated from the galley, back to her hideaway.

She spent the entire day reading. As dusk settled that evening, she was engrossed in a story of an ongoing battle in Africa over elephant herds slaughtered for their ivory tusks. Jessica's inborn instincts toward the preservation of life had been well nurtured by her parents, teachers, and the church. This, together with her natural love for animals, brought feelings of loathing at the wholesale killing of these helpless creatures.

She was nearing the end of the story by the time she noticed a change in the ship's forward progress. They were slowing.

Putting the *Digest* down, she peeked over the edge of the raft. The scene that spread before her was breathtaking for anyone, but especially so to this pair of strikingly green, twelve-year-old eyes.

As far as she could see in any direction were the shadowy outlines of ships, like a city of watery skyscrapers, rising from the sea!

FORTY-FIVE

Captain Callimachus never tired of this. As far as he was concerned, this was what made being the captain of a ship worthwhile. The Suez Canal did not happen for him often enough.

Mindful that an armada of ships was already anchored in the area, at twelve miles out he ordered a decrease, first to three-quarter, then to half-speed. The three men on the ship's bridge were quietly busy now, as was the rest of the crew. The first mate and the captain had done this before. The helmsman was on his maiden voyage through the Canal, however, and both of the others were attentive to this fact. They knew what was expected and moved confidently in carrying out their tasks.

Earlier, the necessary documents had been gathered and laid on the captain's desk. Like most people, Captain Callimachus did not care for the seemingly endless paperwork, but he had long since given in to its inevitability. . . .

The last Classification Certificate issued to the *Evvoia* Four copies of the ship's crew list. The completed form declaring that the *Evvoia* complied with the Suez Canal Authority's double-bottom tanks requirement. Manifests covering each item and the exact amount of cargo on board, together with the names of every shipper and consignee. Four copies of the List of Passengers in Transit. This one was easy enough—there were no passengers on this trip.

He had checked over recent information sources for any

changes concerning vessels in transit through the canal that might have been made since the last time. Open on his desk was the *Guide to Port Entry* produced by Colin Pielow Shipping Guides Ltd. of England. It was the standard text for such a voyage.

Finally, there were the Deck Log Books, showing the date and place of their last call, completed up to the time of arrival at Suez Bay. Satisfied that everything was ready, he went out to the bridge to guide the *Evvoia* to its appointed place among the great ships.

At five miles, they spotted Separation Zone Buoy 1. Captain Callimachus spoke with Port of Suez officials on ship-to-shore radio, channel 16, informing them of their current latitude and longitude readings, the vessel's name and call sign, the draft of the ship, and the type of cargo being transported.

First Mate Moråles was paying close attention now to the position of the *Evvoia* relative to the many other vessels gathering in the Bay. All three men kept an eye out for the two light buoys marking the Canal South entrance. Callimachus saw them first, pointing to the eleven o'clock position. The buoys have a visible height of seven meters. Eastern, at Hm. 3.00 is black, cone-shaped, and shows one occulting green light every four seconds. Western, at Hm. 1.00 is red, similarly cone-shaped, and with a comparable occulting red light every four seconds.

"Engine back three-quarter."

"Engine back three-quarter, aye."

Moråles nodded and smiled. Reaching into his shirt pocket, he proceeded to ceremoniously lay a one hundred drachma note on the panel in front of the captain. The helmsman glanced over at the captain and grinned as he saw him pick it up, touch it to his lips, and stuff it in his pocket. It was a game they played between them, seeing who would make a particular sighting first. Moråles made sure the captain won more times than not. He knew that, at their next opportunity, the captain would take the note and combine it with some of his own for a bottle of wine to be consumed together.

"Steer two-one-zero," the captain ordered.

"Two-one-zero, aye."

The helmsman made the necessary course adjustments so that the *Evvoia* headed directly between the two entrance markers. Callimachus stepped back into his office to quickly review the instructions related to port plans and mooring diagrams in the *Guide to Port Entry*.

Minutes later he was back in the captain's chair observing

their progress. Finally he gave the order.

"Engine back full."

"Engine back full, aye!"

The ship eased into its appointed place and slowed to an all-stop. A short while later, the sound of the anchor could be heard as its massive bulk splashed into the sea and the *Evvoia* came to rest for the night.

Most of the crew members were out on deck after dinner, trying to count the number of ships waiting to enter the Canal. The moon looked cold and pale, the stars bright against the black velvet of the night. The lights of the ships in the Bay added a feeling of holiday festivity to the evening.

The scene provided fresh spirit and energy to the crew, a recognition that they were not alone in this business of sailing the high seas. Hundreds of others were nearby tonight. Their isolated life on board ship was tempered as they joked and laughed with each other.

The captain and first mate joined with the others in trading stories and answering questions about their transition through the Canal for those who had not been here before. That represented the majority gathered around the captain, and they were all curious to know what tomorrow held. It was a special moment, not only for information, but for a warm spirit of oneness and cama-raderie.

FROM HER HIDING PLACE Jessica listened to the men. They could have been boys on the play yard at school, only in grownup bodies. From her concealed perch, she luxuriated in one of the things she had missed most during the past months ... laughter.

Since Israel, she could not remember a time when she had heard people laughing. Everything had been so intense, so extreme. The sounds of frivolity and the occasional guffaws at the punch line of a joke washed over her like warm water.

More important, while staring at the lights of vessels too numerous for her to count, she overheard the captain's answers to questions posed by his crew. For the first time in eight days, she knew where she was. This was Egypt. They were on the Red Sea, the one Moses parted with his rod so that the Israelites could escape their bondage.

Bondage. I've heard the story of Moses so many times. I wish he were here right now. I could use some deliverance myself.

IT WAS NEARLY MIDNIGHT when the launch with the port officials finally arrived alongside the *Evvoia*. Captain Callimachus welcomed them on board and ushered the two men into his office. Within minutes, Tim Marcos entered, bearing a tray containing a pot of coffee, cups, and slices of cake from the galley. Callimachus nodded to Tim and continued answering questions as the young man served their Egyptian guests. One of the officials was going through the crew members' passports as Tim left.

Approximately thirty minutes after their arrival, the port officials returned to the launch and chugged off into the darkness.

THE *EVVOIA* WAS EIGHTH in line as it joined the convoy at 0600 hours in the early light of dawn. A crew member hoisted the Q flag, the International Quarantine Signal signifying a healthy ship.

Moråles had a radiophone in his hand and was talking ship-to-shore when the captain came onto the bridge. Northbound messages had to be repeated to agents at Suez. Otherwise, the *Evvoia* would not receive any advance information. Port Said agents passed messages to Suez agents, but the agents did not repeat them to the ships. It was one of those procedural idiosyncrasies that Captain Callimachus had suggested should be changed. Of course, nothing ever was.

The Canal proper runs from Km. 3.710 West Branch for vessels entering through Port Said Harbor, and from Km. 1.333 East Branch, for vessels entering East Approach Channel, to Hm. 3 at Suez, including the two channels of the Great Bitter Lake and all Canal bypasses. Today on Suez Bay, ships from many nations queued up to form a one-way parade to the north. The waterway was deemed so important that, even on Fridays and other religious holidays—including Ramadan, Islam's holiest fast which lasts for thirty days—Canal operations were permitted to continue at night.

As the Bay awakened, small boats with enterprising merchants selling fresh fish, poultry, cigarettes, candy, and well-worn paperbacks putt-putted about, dodging back and forth among the vessels. Lines, or flimsy ladders, were occasionally dropped over the side to permit the young entrepreneurs to come on board. Dickering and the transfer of cash and purchases took place on deck. Now and then, a ship's captain even permitted these Egyptian nationals to stay on board until the opposite end of the Canal was reached.

Convoy speed today was 14 km/hour. Progress remained steady and orderly as the awesome parade of ships passed El Shallufa and proceeded on into Little Bitter Lake. The flotilla then snaked through Kabret Bypass and the Great Bitter Lake before venturing along Deversoir Bypass into Lake Tinsal and finally exiting the Canal at Port Said. Often there was a wait of several hours in the Bitter Lakes area while ships traversed the Canal from the opposite direction. Today was no exception.

By nightfall, however, the *Evvoia* was churning through Mediterranean waters, the Suez Canal rapidly fading from view in the silvery wake of Captain Callimachus' vessel.

THE NIGHTS GREW COLDER as the *Evvoia* steamed northward. No amount of waterproof material from the remaining lifeboat provisions was able to keep the cold from numbing Jessica through and through. Her teeth chattered and she shook uncontrollably as she hunkered down in the bottom of the raft. On the third night came a chilling rain, complete with lightning and gale-force winds. Finally, out of desperation, and soaked to the skin, Jessica knew she had to get inside.

With hands so cold she could barely hang onto the ladder, Jessica climbed down to the slippery deck, leaning into the wind and rain as she fought her way to the passage entrance. The heavy door was closed tonight and it took all her strength to slide it open. A quick look assured her that no one was in sight. She stepped inside and let the door roll back in place.

At that same instant, halfway down the passageway, a cabin door opened and a man stepped out. His back was toward Jessica as he closed the door. Frightened, she sprinted the now familiar four steps she had taken so many times before on her way to the head. Then, just as she reached for the door, both feet slipped out from under her. Jessica fell with a hard thud that left her momentarily stunned. The man in the hall turned as she scrambled to her knees and tried to crawl into the head. It was too late. He was on top of her in a flash, pinning her helplessly to the floor.

Jessica struggled desperately, fear releasing a fresh flow of adrenaline. With an almost maniacal strength, she wriggled and kicked and tried to bite the man's arm, but to no avail. She heard him shout for help. Seconds later, three others were in the passageway.

"Hey, stop it, kid. Give it up!"

Jessica knew she had no chance. As suddenly and as totally as she had fought back, she now surrendered. Tears filled her eyes and spilled down her face, mixing with the dampness caused by the rain. The man who had yelled at her gradually released his grip from around her body. Jessica fell back in a wet heap, completely spent.

TIMOTHY MARCOS STARED at the child slumped in front of him. It all happened so fast. He had spotted her out of the corner of his eye. By the time he turned around, she had panicked and was scrambling to get out of the passageway. He was on top of her immediately.

"What did you catch there, Tim? Looks like you got yourself a stowaway," Angel Rameriz muttered. "Where do you suppose we got him, anyway? In the Suez?"

"It's not a 'him,' Angel," Tim responded, breathless from wrestling their uninvited stranger to the floor.

"What?"

"It's a 'her,' " Tim said, looking down at the sopping wet child, hair strewn across her face and clenched fists wiping at her eyes. "This is a girl."

"Are you serious?" Angel leaned down and lifted the stowaway's face so that he could see it. Green eyes blazed back and he quickly moved his hand away. "She's a feisty one, that's for sure. Be careful with her, though. She looks like she might have rabies."

The others laughed at Angel's joke.

Tim crouched down and spoke with a gentle tone. "Who are you?"

Jessica looked up, but said nothing.

"We aren't going to hurt you," he smiled reassuringly. "Do you speak English?"

JESSICA SHIVERED, WHETHER FROM FRIGHT or from the freezing cold rain, she couldn't tell. Her emotions were disordered by anger at having let this happen and the fear of being locked up again. The man who knelt down in front of her now was the one who had tackled her moments before.

His voice was soothing and kind. "Who are you?"

Jessica watched him through narrowed and hostile eyes, but did not answer.

"Hey, nobody is going to hurt you," the man repeated.

"Okay?"

He was young. His hair was jet black and straight. Bronze skin. Dark eyebrows and a mustache. No shoes. Faded blue jeans and a white T-shirt with the word Nike imprinted on the front.

He doesn't look like an Arab, but he's not an Iranian either. And he has a nice smile. Watch it, Jessica. You can't trust anybody.

"Just tell us your name."

His accent reminds me of ... someone ... Madeline! When he talks, he forms his words just like Madeline did.

The outside door opened and one of the crew led another man in out of the storm. He walked over to where she sat in a puddle of rainwater, shaking, wishing that she could stop, but finding it impossible. She looked up and recognized him immediately.

"Who is this?" asked Captain Callimachus. "Where did we get her?"

"I was just leaving my room, sir, and caught her by surprise," Tim answered the captain. "I think she was trying to get in out of the storm. She hasn't said anything yet. I asked if she understood English. I think she does, but she's not talking."

The captain stared at her for a long, disconcerting moment.

"She's cold. All right, Marcos, you caught her so you take charge for now. Get her a warm shower and some dry clothes." The captain glared at the sound of a snicker coming from one of the crew, now crowding around to see the spectacle. Word spreads fast on board ship. "You know what I mean. Guard the door until she's finished."

"I've got an extra shirt, Tim," one of the men volunteered and ran off to get it.

"I have an old pair of jeans she can wear."

"She'll need a rope to keep them up, Freddie."

"Nah, these have an elastic waist. They'll work. She's about my height."

"What about dry underclothes?"

There was an embarrassed silence, then raucous laughter filled the passageway.

"Hey, any of you guys wearing women's underclothes?"

More laughter.

"Actually, gentlemen," the captain spoke softly and the passageway became instantly quiet, "I do have some female undergarments in my cabin."

He looked around to see who might say something crude, but no one opened their mouth.

"They were left there when my daughters visited me just before school began. Jimmy, come with me and I'll get some things for you to take to the girl."

He turned back to Jessica.

"Get up and go with these men."

Jessica continued shivering, but made no move to respond.

"Do it now, young lady." The captain's voice was suddenly gruff, his eyes narrowing. "You're in a lot of trouble. See to it that you don't get into any more by pushing my patience too far."

The young man with the Nike shirt held out his hand to her. Slowly, still shaking from head to toe, Jessica reached out and let him help her to her feet.

"Rameriz, you go with him. See to it that she doesn't overpower Marcos here and try to escape."

More snickers could be heard as the crew parted to make way for Tim. Jessica followed after him shivering, sullen, and defeated. Rameriz brought up the rear.

"She looks hungry, Marcos," the captain called out after them. "When she's cleaned up, take her to the mess and give her something to eat. Let me know when she decides to talk and I'll join you later. Now, as you were, gentlemen. Clear this area. Paulo, get a mop and swab this down before someone gets hurt."

JESSICA STOOD IN THE DOORWAY and watched as the young crewman, whom the captain had called Marcos, entered the shower room ahead of her. He pulled a towel down from a nearby rack and placed it on the edge of a sink. Then, reaching into the nearest shower stall, he turned on the water, testing it with his hand until it felt warm.

"It's all yours," he said with a smile. "Get warm—and clean. There's soap in the dish. Oh, wait, here's the shampoo. Your hair looks as though it could use some. Come out when you are finished. If you're not out in fifteen minutes, I'm coming in to get you. Understand?"

Jessica didn't answer. Just then, two men came up and handed over the spare clothing she had heard them talking about. Her Nike-shirt guard took the things and handed them to Jessica. She looked at them and then at the young man.

"It's this or nothing," he said finally, in exasperation. "Take it or leave it. The wet stuff is coming off."

That was enough of a threat for Jessica. She snatched the clothes away from the young man and closed the door as fast as she could. She fumbled for a lock. There was none.

"There's no lock." The young man's voice could be heard clearly through the door. "Don't worry, you're safe. But, this door opens in fifteen minutes. I'll be coming in to get you if you're not out here. So, get busy!"

What choice do I have?

Without a word, still shivering and dripping water on the floor, she stripped off her clothes and stepped into the shower. That's when she made her second discovery. There were no shower curtains. But the water was warm and felt wonderful.

How long has it been?

Jessica couldn't remember. Eyes closed, she stood still, absorbing the warmth, as water cascaded over her body. Then, reaching for the shampoo, she soaped her hair and rinsed it. It still felt dirty and matted and so she shampooed again. For the first time in weeks her hair was beginning to feel clean. She lost track of time as she shampooed and rinsed her hair thoroughly for the third time.

"Two minutes and I'm coming in."

Jessica stopped, riveted with consternation as water continued to spray over her naked body.

"No!" she shouted back. "I'm not ready. Give me ten more minutes. Please!"

OUTSIDE THE DOOR, Timothy Marcos chuckled out loud. Angel Rameriz leaned against the opposite wall, arms folded, and grunted his amusement.

"I guess she does speak English after all. All she needed was a little motivation, Tim."

"Okay," Marcos called through the door. "You get ten more minutes. Then out you come."

Eight minutes later, the girl opened the shower room door and stood there, looking for all intents and purposes like the waif that she was. Her shirt was two or three sizes too big, but the pants fit surprisingly well. Her feet were still bare. She clutched her wet clothes in a bundle with one hand, while gripping her sodden shoes in the other. Her long hair was still damp.

"Feel better?"

She did not answer.

"Look," admonished Tim, "we've got to talk to one another sooner or later. It's only a matter of time. You can make it much more difficult by being uncooperative, but it won't do you any good. I'm not the enemy. I want to be your friend, okay?"

Still, the girl said nothing.

"You look hungry, so let's go find something to eat. If you promise not to give me a bad time, Angel will go back to his cabin. He's got to go to work in an hour. Will you promise?"

The girl shrugged and stepped through the door, then waited for Tim to lead on.

"You be okay?" Angel asked.

"I think we'll be fine."

"Okay. If you need help, just holler."

"Will do."

Angel walked away from them. Halfway along the passageway, he turned a corner and vanished from sight.

"Let's go . . . what did you say your name was?"

Still no answer.

At the end of the passage, they turned left and entered the seamen's lounge. The galley and mess hall were next door.

"This is the lounge. We come here to read and watch television when we're not on duty. Come on through here and I'll get you something to eat."

He led the girl through the small lounge and into the mess area, turning on the light as he entered. He stopped, but the girl moved up beside him, still holding her worldly goods in each hand.

"Let me take your things," Tim said, reaching out his hands. The girl shrank back.

"Hey, whatever-your-name-is, it's okay. Your clothes need to be washed and your shoes need to dry out. I will put them over here next to the heater and we'll turn it on. Before too long, these sneakers of yours will be warm and bone dry. All right?"

Her eyes never left his face as he spoke to her. Then, without a word, she held out her clothes and shoes. Tim took them and smiled again.

"Good. I'm glad that you're finally starting to trust me. I want to be your friend. It looks to me like you need one." Tim watched his charge out of the corner of his eye as he dropped her clothes on one of the tables and moved toward the wall heater with her shoes in hand. He was ready to drop them and catch her if she made a break, but she did not move. He flipped the heater switch and adjusted the thermostat. Bringing a chair around to face the heater, he turned over her shoes to check the bottoms. The tops were dirty and beat up, but the soles appeared relatively new.

"Hey, nice shoes," he said, grinning as he held them up next to the imprint on his shirt. "Nikes."

He placed them on the chair and walked around the table, opposite from the girl. If the kid was going to run, this was her chance, with the table between them. He saw her eyes flicker, but she made no move to attempt an escape.

Tim motioned for her to follow. "Let's see what we have to eat."

Her eyes are like emeralds. And when she called out from the shower . . . I wonder. . . .

They went into the galley. Tim moved past the range and opened the refrigerator.

"I've got some cold chicken. Here, you want some?" He held the plate of leftovers out to the girl.

She nodded and took two pieces, unconsciously licking her lips as she did.

"Here's a piece of watermelon too, straight from Egypt. Some bread. And a Coke to drink. Okay?"

The girl nodded again.

"Let's go back to the mess and sit at a table."

Tim grabbed another Coke and followed her through the door to the first table. He watched her hesitate for an instant, as though she didn't quite know what to do. Then she sat down, eyeing the food, but waiting. Tim was certain she was hungry. He started to say something, but checked himself just in time, dumbfounded at what she did next.

The girl closed her eyes and her lips moved.

What's this? Is she praying?

The moment passed. Then she opened her eyes and reached for a piece of the chicken. There was no doubt about her being hungry. She consumed it like there was no tomorrow. The chicken was interspersed with huge bites of bread and gulps from the bottle of Coke. Finally, she swooped down on the watermelon. It had no chance of surviving the attack.

Tim was amused at the sight of the hungry stowaway putting down her dinner.

What have you been living off of, kid? And where have you been hiding all this time?

There was one other question that needed to be asked first. He waited until the watermelon had disappeared. The girl carefully wiped her face clean with a paper napkin and finally looked up at Tim. Her gaze was steady, even defiant, as if she were thinking, *All right, I've eaten your food. Now what?*

"Hey, kid," asked Tim softly, watching carefully to see what her response would be. "Are you a Christian?"

Jessica stared at the man across the table.

Of all the questions he might have asked, that was absolutely the last one Jessica had expected. Her response was one that Timothy Marcos did not expect either.

FORTY-SIX

"Are you a Filipino?"

Tim's mouth fell open in surprise. He was glad that the girl had finally said something, but was caught off guard by her question.

"Yes, I am. Why?"

"Do you know Madeline?"

"Madeline who?"

"I don't know her last name, but she works in Iran as a maid. And she is from the Philippines."

"No, I don't know a Madeline. I'm sorry."

"Me too. She's nice."

"Is she? I'm glad."

"Are most Filipinos Christians?"

"Well, I don't know exactly how many. But, there are a lot of them back home."

"Is that where you're from? The Philippines?"

"Yes."

"Is it nice there?"

"Very."

"It's a bunch of islands, right?"

"Right."

"Are you a Christian?"

Tim hesitated. *When did I lose control of this conversation? Truth is, I probably never had it in the first place.*

He decided to go with the flow.

"Yes, I am."

"Have you been one very long?"

"For about three years."

"What's the fourth book in the New Testament?"

Tim chuckled. *She's checking me out.*

"It's the Gospel of John."

"That was easy. Anybody could know that."

"Oh? Well, then, what's the sixth book in the Old Testament?"

The girl thought for a moment. "Joshua."

"And the one after that?"

"Judges."

Tim had now regained the role of questioner.

"And the shortest verse in the Bible?"

" 'Jesus wept.' And do you know John 3:16?"

Getting the upper hand in this conversation was one thing. Keeping it, Tim decided, was proving to be quite another.

"Yes, I do. 'For God so loved the world that He gave His only begotten Son, that whosoever believeth in Him should not perish, but have everlasting life.' "

"That's from the King James Version, isn't it?"

This girl is full of surprises.

"Yes, it is," he replied.

"How come you know so much about the Bible?"

"We have a Bible study on board ship. Three other guys and me. And I read a lot. I'm working as a member of the crew in order to earn enough money to go to Bible college. Someday, I will be the pastor of a church."

He saw the girl's eyes blink with surprise as she leaned back in her chair. Her hands went down to her lap and she stared at them for a long time, biting her lip. When she looked up at him again, he could see that she was fighting back the tears.

"What's the matter, kid?"

Her lip quivered.

"Did I say something?"

She pushed her chair back from the table, but didn't get up. Tim was touched as he watched her. Not defiant any longer. Instead, she looked pathetically scared and alone.

"It's my dad."

"Your dad? What about him?"

"He's a pastor."

The answer stunned Tim and now he leaned back.

"Your dad is a pastor?"

The ship's prize stowaway nodded.

"Where?"

"California."

Once again, Tim was startled. He studied the youngster sitting in front of him. *Who are you anyway?*

"How old are you?"

"Twelve."

The girl did not look up, but continued watching her hands curl and uncurl in her lap.

"How did you get here anyway? You're a long way from home, aren't you?"

She remained silent while Tim realized that he'd asked two questions instead of only one. Was she deciding how to answer them? Or was she retreating into her earlier refusal to communicate? Just when he was beginning to wish someone else had been put in charge of this little ragamuffin, she looked up, her eyes darting about cautiously, as though she were inspecting the premises for unwelcome visitors. Then she looked straight at Tim.

"I was stolen," she answered finally, her voice subdued.

Startled by her response, Tim studied her carefully for some sign that would indicate she was lying.

"Stolen?"

"Yes. Kidnapped. By terrorists."

The girl's eyes remained steady, looking straight into his own.

"When were you kidnapped? And, where?"

"September 18. I was in Israel with my father."

Hmm. What is it about that date? It sounds so familiar....

"Hey, kid. I know you've got a name. Mine is Timothy Marcos. Do you think you can trust me enough to tell me what your name is? I want to help you, okay? And nobody on board this ship is going to hurt you. I can promise you that. So, what is it?"

The girl sat still now, her eyes fixed on the table.

"Your parents don't know where you are. Right?"

She nodded, pressing her lips together.

"Then, help me get you back together with them. I can't do anything unless I know your name."

"Jessica." She said it softly, but her hands were clenched into small, tight fists. Her body tensed. Tim saw that she was prepared to bolt. He remained quiet and did not move. Waiting. The moment passed, and girl seemed to relax slightly, though she had scooted to the edge of her chair. Her eyes were on him, searching to see what might happen next.

"Jessica Cain," she said at last. Her body was rigid once more, the earlier dullness in her green eyes now replaced with an uneasy look of apprehension.

"Jessica . . ." Tim suddenly sat up straight and leaned forward. *Cain. Green eyes. Long, reddish-brown hair. Twelve. Israel.* Even the date made sense. "You are . . ."

Before he could get the words out of his mouth, the door opened. At the sound, the girl leaped to her feet and whirled around.

"Wait, Jessica, it's okay. This is the captain."

She remained frozen in place, recognizing that there was nowhere to run. The captain had stopped in place as well, aware that his entrance had frightened the stowaway.

"Captain Callimachus, this is Jessica Cain," said Tim, introducing the wary child to his boss.

The man smiled, extended his hand toward the girl, who hesitated briefly, then grasped it with surprising firmness.

"And now, would you like to tell me what are you doing on my ship, Jessica?" he asked, smiling as he released her hand.

The girl did not answer.

"Jessica Cain," Tim repeated her name as he addressed the captain, "says she was kidnapped."

The captain glanced at Tim and then at the girl once again.

"Sir, she fits the description of that American girl who has been missing since September. She says that her father is the pastor of a church in California and that she was 'stolen' in Israel. It all fits, sir."

Captain Callimachus looked at the dismal face that peered back at him.

"Are you certain, Tim?" asked the captain, incredulously.

"I believe her. Look at her eyes, how green they are. The kidnapped girl has green eyes. Her features are the same. I remember seeing a picture of her, together with an article, in one of the issues of *Time* that we have on board. Just a minute. I think I can find it. . . ."

Tim started for the crew lounge.

"You won't find it."

He hesitated, then turned toward the voice that had spoken up so unexpectedly.

"It's not there," she said with assurance.

Both men were watching her curiously.

"It's in the lifeboat."

They looked at each other then and back at the girl. Suddenly, both the young man and the captain broke out into laughter.

"Young lady . . . Jessica . . . whoever you are," Captain Callim-achus chortled, "I think we had better have a nice, long chat. It seems you may have some stories to tell me about your passage on my ship. You have apparently made yourself at home . . . where? In one of our lifeboats? And you have even helped yourself to our library. I must admit that I am impressed."

The captain shook his head, still chuckling as he envisioned the pluck and courage of the young girl standing in front of him. He looked at Tim.

"Are you done here?"

"Yes, sir."

"Then, Jessica, gather up your things and come with me. I am taking you to my cabin. There is an extra cot that my daughter slept on while visiting me this summer. You must be tired. Tim, you come along too. You can prepare the cot while I get some more information from our passenger." Turning to Jessica he said, "I'll need your parents' names and address. Then, we'll call my company, the people who own this ship. They'll let your parents know that you are here and that you are safe. You *are* safe, you know. No one on board this ship will hurt you. We only want to get you home where you belong. In fact, you should be there for Christmas."

HOME. WHERE YOU BELONG. CHRISTMAS.

These men *were* different from the others. It was still too quick to be able to shed the distrust and the fear with which she had lived these past months, but at least the cloud was lifting. The young man who questioned her seemed nice enough, and he even claimed to be a Christian.

She followed the captain up the steps, but hung back as he opened a door and passed through.

"Come on," he urged, his voice not at all threatening as he waited for her to follow.

Cautiously, Jessica stepped into a large room. The walls were finished with panels of light oak. One held a calendar with a picture of beautiful white buildings clinging to the sides of cliffs rising serenely out of the sea. On another wall, near a curtained off area, were two pictures that appeared to be etched on wood. Each face depicted was that of a man, obviously from ancient times, and what looked like a cross rose from behind one of them.

A massive, wooden desk filled the center of the room and, on the side opposite where they stood, was the captain's leather chair.

In front of the desk, two steel-framed chairs without armrests. Underneath them was a rich-looking rug, its unfamiliar design woven with colors of beige, dark blue, and orange. The room had a warm feeling about it, Jessica decided, kind of like her father's office at the church.

Tim was busy setting up the cot, which the captain directed should be placed at the far side of the room. Clean sheets and a blanket were put in place as Jessica watched silently, her eyes recording all there was to know about this place. The curtained-off area, she concluded, must be where the captain slept.

"All right, Jessica," the captain said, pulling one of the steel chairs around so that it faced the other, "sit here, please."

Jessica sat down, nervously rubbing her fingers together.

The young man smiled and turned to go.

"Wait," she blurted out. Tim stopped and turned as she slumped back into the chair, embarrassed at having called out. The men looked at each other with a slight shaking of their heads. Tim walked back and knelt down on the rug beside her.

"Jessica," he said, his hand gently touching her arm, "we don't know where you've been or what has happened to you, but it's okay here. Captain Callimachus is a fine man and he will not hurt you. Take my word . . . as a Christian. Okay?"

Jessica sat still for a long moment, then nodded.

"Okay," she whispered, fighting to maintain the invisible barrier that held back a reservoir of tears.

Tim patted her arm as he rose. A moment later, she was alone with the captain. She looked up, her fingers now clasping at a corner of her recently acquired, oversized sweatshirt. The captain smiled.

"All right," the man said, "I must know some things about you. Your parents, where you live, how to reach them. I will let them know that they can pick you up at our next port. We will be at Split in approximately thirty hours, so we had better get to it."

For the next few minutes, the captain jotted down the information as Jessica responded to his questions.

"It is late now," Captain Callimachus concluded at last. "You should go to bed and to sleep. There is a toilet connected to my sleeping area, but perhaps you should use the one out on the passageway. I'm sure you know where it is?"

Jessica yawned as she nodded.

"Tim has placed a new toothbrush and some toothpaste on your pillow. There are soap and a towel there as well. You are free to come and go," the captain continued. "I'll be on the bridge for a while. If I am not here when you awaken, come out and I'll let you steer the ship."

Jessica's eyes widened at the prospect.

"Well, not really. This ship is steered in a manner different from a small boat like you may have taken out on the Bay in California. I have been there, you know. About a year and a half ago. Anyway, I'll show you how it is done after you have rested."

"Thank you, sir," Jessica said, as the captain turned to leave. "I'm sorry I've caused you so much trouble."

Pausing at the door, the captain looked at Jessica. "It is not necessary for you to apologize. In fact, your presence makes our journey just that much more interesting."

"Goodnight, sir."

"Goodnight, Jessica Cain."

"YES, THAT IS ALL THE INFORMATION that we have at the moment."

Captain Callimachus watched as raindrops pounded against the windows. The roll of the ship made him switch hands with the radiophone and grasp for a nearly empty coffee cup that began sliding away.

"That is all we know," he continued. "I think that you should contact the US State Department. She has no identification papers, but her personal knowledge and physical description seem to confirm that she is the missing girl. . . . That's right. No, let me give it to you again. It is "J" like in "John." The first name spelling is J-e-s-s-i-c-a. You have the last name. . . . Yes, that is the correct spelling. "C" as in "Christopher." . . . She says she boarded in Bandar-é Abbås. . . . No, I'm certain it could not have been the Canal. . . . That's right. It was purely by accident. She was trying to get in out of the weather when one of the crewmen spotted her. . . . No. . . . All right. I understand. . . . Yes. She will be ready when we arrive at Split. . . . You will let us know if you are successful in reaching the girl's parents? Yes, thank you. And you as well."

THE THIRD FLOOR OFFICES of G. Wellingham Ltd. faced London's beloved Thames River. On a bright summer's day, those who worked here thought there was no finer sight in the world. Tonight, however, it was cold and dark, with a heavy rain coming down steadily for the past twenty-four hours. It had been a routinely boring watch until the call came in from one of the company's four cargo vessels currently operating in the Middle and Far East.

The night communications officer excitedly turned away from the transmitter, running his finger down the list of home numbers taped to the desk in front of him as he reached for the phone. Five minutes later, he replaced the telephone receiver and checked his watch he knew that he had at least twenty minutes before G. Wellingham Ltd's chief administrator, Geoffrey Halerton, would arrive and place a call to the US State Department.

His reasons for coming out this late on such a miserable night were not entirely humanitarian, though the officer was sure Halerton was pleased that the child had been recovered. This promised to be a big story and that meant lots of publicity for the company.

Geoffrey Halerton was going to handle the matter personally.

SEVERAL HUNDRED MILES to the east, somewhere deep in Lebanon's Bekaa Valley, a dark-haired woman pulled the earphones away and placed them on a makeshift table by the radio receiver. Glancing over her hastily scribbled notes to be sure she had everything, she pushed back her chair and hurried from the warmth of the tiny room into the cold night air.

Her lungs felt the bite of each breath as she ran up the steep path. Regulations forbade the use of a light lest their location be discovered by an enemy whose military outposts were only a few miles away, and whose eyes never seemed to close in sleep. Her only illumination was a pale sliver of moonlight and pinpoints of distant stars. Stumbling on a stone, she reached down to catch herself. The papers dropped from her hand. With a curse, she ran her hands across the dirt and stone until she had recovered them all before hurrying on.

The path ended in front of a dilapidated wood and stone building sct against the side of the hill. Breathless, she pounded on the door until a man, still rubbing sleep from his eyes, opened and motioned her inside. The nineteen-year-old freedom fighter was not aware of the full importance of her information. Only that a very important and secret plan was at risk unless the American child-hostage, who had escaped in Iran eleven days earlier, was found and eliminated. She did know, however, that another otherwise boring night, spent monitoring the transmissions of vessels that had sailed from Bandar-é Abbås during the last eleven days, had finally paid off.

THE ROOM WAS DARK when Jessica awakened. There were no windows or portholes in the room, only a dim light from the captain's sleeping quarters. Jessica slid out of her bed and padded across the floor on bare feet until she could see that the captain's bed was empty. Then she made her way to the door and cracked it open, peeking out into the passageway. An open door at the far end revealed bright sunlight. Last night's storm had evidently passed through, leaving the seas calm and the decks washed clean.

She closed the door, turned on the light, and stifled a yawn while raising her arms and stretching out the muscles in her back and legs. She slipped into her borrowed "crewman's jeans" and pushed the socks she had been given the night before into her pocket. She would put them on later when she found her shoes.

Jessica left the room and, after stopping to wash up and brush her teeth, strode down the passageway toward the exit. Outside, the sun was bright and the sky clear, even though seas were running high enough to cause her to hold onto the door in order to maintain her balance. Carefully, she made her way to the bridge and stepped inside.

"Good morning, Ms. Cain." First Mate Moråles smiled his greeting.

"Good morning," she replied. She had seen this man before, but only at a distance from the lifeboat.

"Hello, Jessica," Captain Callimachus emerged from behind a bank of navigational and communication instruments. "You seem to have slept well, yes?"

"Yes sir," she replied, still intensely conscious of not being the centerpoint in a hostile environment. "Sir, do you know what happened to my shoes?"

Captain Callimachus looked at her feet and smiled. "I suppose the floor is pretty cold without them. You'll probably find them in the galley. I believe the seaman with whom you were talking last night may have left them there to dry."

"You mean Tim?"

"Yes. Why don't you run down and get them before you catch a cold?"

Jessica turned to go.

"By the way, I made contact with our ship's company headquarters last night. I explained to them who you are and instructed them to contact your State Department. They will notify your parents. I have suggested that we place you in the custody of an officer of our company or someone else who has the ability to care for you until your parents arrive. We'll be dropping anchor in Split tomorrow."

"Can't I stay on board until they come for me?"

"It is, unfortunately, not possible. We must anchor offshore overnight and wait for a berth to open for my ship. That may be the next day, but the docks are at capacity at the moment. It could be even longer. My orders are to take you off by tender as soon as we arrive. That's a small boat that will come out from the docks to pick you up. A representative from our company will come out to meet you. You'll be well cared for, I assure you, and your parents will be here soon. Okay?"

"Do I have a choice?"

"Not really. We're under company regulations with regard to stowaways. I'm sorry."

"All right, then. Thank you, Captain Callimachus. You've been very kind to me. I'll write to you when I get home."

"It has been a pleasure, Jessica. You remind me of my own daughters. God forbid that it would ever be, but I would wish that under similar circumstances, someone would help them in the same way I am able to do for you."

For a moment, Jessica was embarrassed as the captain, in the gallant fashion of European men, took her small hand in his and kissed it.

"Are you serious? I never thought it would happen."

Whenever he became excited, Charles Rodeway's unmistakably southern drawl became even more pronounced, causing each syllable to drift into the next like ocean waves rolling toward the beach. His words slowed, prolonging each vowel with lengthened tones. The door was open to the side office where his secretary usually worked. Under these circumstances, she could always tell when something was up by the way he spoke. But, she had called in sick this morning. Rodeway was alone.

He had been clearing security-sensitive papers from his desk and placing them in a small safe when the phone rang. He dropped the remaining folder on the edge of the desk as he listened to the news coming from his counterpart in London.

"Yes. . . . Yes. . . . Are we absolutely certain that it's the girl? No kidding. . . . Man, I'll tell you what, I can't believe it. First, that video. I figured she was a dead person before. . . . Yeah. . . . Now this. Okay, thanks, we'll get right on it. . . . No, nothing more for now, but I'll let you know how it goes. . . . Yeah. Thanks again. . . . What? . . . Yeah, well, I'll check with the boss. We should probably get somebody down there from Zagreb to pick her up. . . . Right. Okay, I'll be in touch."

Rodeway ran his finger down a list of frequently called numbers, copying several of them on a stray sheet of yellow paper. Then, he picked up the telephone and went to work.

THE PHONE BEGAN RINGING just as mother and son were sitting down to breakfast.

"Wouldn't you know it," Esther muttered under her breath.

"I'll get it," said Jeremy, stabbing a warm biscuit with his fork as he rose from the table. "Allison said she was going to call this morning."

"Ask her to call back, son. Breakfast is ready."

"Hello. This is Jeremy Cain. . . . Yes. . . . May I say who's calling?"

Esther looked up in time to see Jeremy's face grow serious. "Just a moment. She's right here."

Jeremy placed his hand over the phone and took a deep breath.

"It's Charles Rodeway . . . from Washington."

For one terrifying instant, Esther couldn't move. The normal ritual of preparing a meal had vanished. In its place a frightening jumble of disorder and confusion closed in.

"Yes?" Her voice shook while clearing her throat. "This is Mrs. Cain."

"Mrs. Cain, this is Charles Rodeway at the State Department. I have good news. We believe we've located your daughter."

Esther's hand was shaking so that she gripped the receiver with both hands. "Are you . . . is she . . . is she all right?"

"Yes, she is. A young girl who fits your daughter's description was found stowed away on a cargo ship bound from Iran to Croatia. She has no passport, but we are certain that it is Jessica."

Tears streamed down Esther's face as she looked over at Jeremy.

"It's Jessica. They've found her," Esther whispered.

"Is she okay?"

Esther nodded, suddenly unable to speak.

"Oh, thank You, Jesus," Jeremy breathed, as he began to cry along with his mother. He stood behind her, arms encircling her waist and buried his face in her shoulder as she turned her attention back to the telephone.

"I'm sorry, Mr. Rodeway. You'll have to forgive us, but your news is more than overwhelming. We're trying to get it together here."

"No apologies are necessary, Mrs. Cain. You've been through a terrible ordeal and now you're on your way back. I understand that Reverend Cain is still out there somewhere. Last I heard, he and a companion were recovering from an unofficial visit to some of our friends. Do you know how to reach him?"

"I certainly do. As soon as we are finished talking, I'll call him at his hotel."

"Is he still in the UAE?"

"Yes. The embassy has informed him that they will issue temporary passports, but will only approve travel back to the States. He's not very happy with that arrangement, I can tell you."

"Well, we can change all that now, Mrs. Cain. State just didn't want those two single-handedly declaring war on an entire nation."

"Where can we go to get her?"

"That will not be necessary. I've been authorized by the Head of Consular Affairs to take her off the ship at its next port of call and repatriate her as rapidly as possible. We'll have her home in three or four days, maybe sooner."

"Wait a minute, Mr. Rodeway." Esther was wiping away tears with a napkin from the table. Breakfast had grown cold, having been all but forgotten in the excitement. "That's our daughter you are talking about. Of course we are going to meet her. Where will she disembark?"

"She'll be taken off the ship at the port in Split."

"Split? I don't know where that is."

She thought she noted a slight hesitation. Then, she heard him clear his throat.

"Split is a port city in Croatia, along the Dalmatian coast."

"Croatia? You mean Yugoslavia? Or, at least that's what it used to be called. O Mr. Rodeway, she can't be getting off there. Won't that be too dangerous?"

"Not really, Mrs. Cain. It's been weeks since even one shell has been fired into that locale. It's very calm right now. There is a large port there that is visited by ships from many nations, including the United States. Lots of loading and unloading of goods and supplies for the Bosnian-Herzegovinian people. There's a strong United Nations presence there as well. I assure you it will be perfectly safe. Besides, we really have little choice. She has to be taken off the ship at its next port of call. We'll send someone down from our embassy in Zagreb to pick her up and bring her out."

"When will she arrive there?" Esther asked, calmer now as she sat down on the chair that Jeremy had pulled over for her.

"The *Evvoia*, that's the ship she is traveling on, is scheduled to get in sometime early tomorrow evening. Around five o'clock their time. That's about eight tomorrow morning, on the West Coast."

"Mr. Rodeway, I intend to meet my daughter." Esther's tone changed, resoluteness permeating her voice. "I know that as soon as I contact John, nothing you can say will stop him either. Now, you can help us get there or make it that much more difficult, but John and I will not sit and wait for her to come to us. We've worked too hard and it's been too long for that. Am I making myself clear?"

There was a long silence at the other end of the line.

"Mr. Rodeway?"

"Yes, I'm still here. Just thinking. I'm a parent too, Mrs. Cain, and I understand. It's not what I think best, as a State Department official, but I figured this would be your reaction. Actually, it would be mine too. That's why I've already checked the airlines to see what might be available. United has a flight to New York out of SFO at eleven o'clock. I was able to get you a seat in tourist. From there you take Alitalia to Rome."

"I'd like to take Jeremy too."

"Sorry, no can do. I had to pull some strings just to get one seat. It's full to New York. Besides, we don't need any more citizens in there than necessary."

"But you just said it was safe."

Rodeway's voice changed and became very businesslike.

"I know what I said, Mrs. Cain. Now, please. We don't have much time. If you are determined to go through with this, you will have to take what I'm offering. It's the best I can do. You need to call your husband and get to the airport. Have your son drive you. Are you okay with that?"

"Yes," she answered, realizing that she might have pushed him a little too far. "We can do that."

"Tell you what. Have your husband meet you in Zagreb if he can make connections in time. Tell him that Rome or Zurich are probably the best entry points. He should be able to get to one of those. I'll pass the word to our embassy in the UAE, asking them to provide whatever assistance they can. Your connecting schedule is tight in New York, but you should be fine. In Rome, it's even tighter and I'll make arrangements for them to hold for you, in case your plane is delayed. Here is your flight info."

Rodeway called off the numbers and departure times of each flight as Esther scribbled them down on the note pad.

"All right," she said, after repeating the flight information back to him. "I'm on my way."

"Be careful, Mrs. Cain. Don't forget your passport. And good luck."

"Thanks for your help, Mr. Rodeway. I hope we will be able to meet one day."

"It will be my pleasure. Sorry to rush now, but I've got to go."

She heard the phone click as she put the receiver back and turned to Jeremy. They hugged each other and laughed as Jeremy lifted his mom and whirled her around the room. Esther answered Jeremy's questions, filling in parts of the conversation with Rodeway that he had not put together. His face dropped a little at the realization that she was going without him, but the disappointment quickly passed.

"Jeremy, I'm giving you the day off from school. I'll write a note for you on the way to the airport. And, I need you to get your dad on the phone while I throw some things into a carry-on. After you get back from the airport, I want you to call your grandparents too."

"Okay."

"Ask them not to say anything to anyone until we have her."

Esther started for the bedroom, then stopped and turned back.

"Honey?"

He paused, phone in hand.

"When you reach him . . . let me tell him. Please?"

"You got it," Jeremy smiled, as he reached for the directory containing the numerical sequence for international dialing.

WEDNESDAY, 15 DECEMBER 1750 LOCAL TIME
ABU DHABI, UAE

JOHN COULD HEAR THE TELEPHONE ringing as he hurried to unlock the door to his room. He had been down in the hotel lobby, catching up on the world with a day-old edition of the *International Herald*. Now, he willed the phone to keep ringing as he fumbled to get the key in the lock. This far from home, every call was important. The key was left dangling in the door as he rushed to lift the receiver.

"Hello?"

"Hello. Dad?"

"Hey. Is that you, Jeremy?"

"In living color. Say, this is a really good connection. You sound like you're right next door. Are you okay?"

"I'm fine. How about you and Mom?"

"We're doing just great. I'm really glad I got you. It must be tonight where you are, right? What time is it there, anyway?"

"It's nearly six. I just walked in from the lobby. It's good to hear your voice, son. I miss you."

"Miss you too. Wait a minute. Here's Mom."

"Nice talking to you," John replied, not knowing if Jeremy had heard.

"Hello, sweetheart." Esther's voice sounded fresh and warm. "Are you okay?"

"I'm fine. Hersch is on crutches, but doing good. We're about ready to bail out of here."

"Good. Listen, I've just talked with Mr. Rodeway from State."

John's hand tightened on the receiver with a sudden apprehension, as he waited to hear what came next.

"He said that they've found Jessica! Honey, she's alive. On a ship somewhere in the Mediterranean. Can you believe it?"

John felt with his hand for the bed and sat down.

"Are they sure?" he asked, his voice hoarse with emotion that threatened to break out from some unknown, subterranean place. John wanted desperately to believe, but was unprepared to weave his way through one more disappointment, unwilling to face one more near miss. "Are they really sure?"

"Mr. Rodeway says that it's her. She stowed away on a ship that will be in port by tomorrow night. I'm going to meet her. Can you join me?"

"Where?"

"She's going to be taken off at Split."

"Split. Isn't that in what used to be Yugoslavia?"

"Yes. Now, I guess it is part of Croatia. I am flying New York to Rome to Zagreb, Croatia's capital city. Mr. Rodeway says that we have an embassy there and that they will take us to Jessica. Can you do it?"

"Can I do it? Of course, I can do it. I'll meet you there tomorrow at the airport. I can hardly believe it. After all of this . . . she must have sneaked onto a ship at Bandar and slipped out of the country on her own. What a kid!"

"You said it! What a kid! Oh, and Mr. Rodeway said that he would contact the embassy there and ask them to help you. By the way, what will Hersch do?"

"I'll find out, but my guess is that he'll want to head for home. He's been gone from his job longer than he'd planned. He's out of the hospital though, as of yesterday. I managed to get him a room next door to mine."

Esther proceeded to give John the flight numbers that Rodeway had left with her.

"Okay, darling," she said at last. "I've got to run to catch a plane."

"Wait," John said, a note of sharp tension in his voice. He closed his eyes, then opened them again.

"What is it?"

An invisible hand had suddenly swept away the elation over news about Jessica. It was gone. Vanished. All that was left was a feeling of hollowness in the pit of his stomach. He stared at his hand. It was shaking, and he forced himself to concentrate on stopping it.

"John, are you all right?"

"Yes . . . but . . ."

"Something's the matter, I can tell. What is it?"

"Listen, have Jeremy contact Jim Brainard. See if he can join you in New York."

"What?" Esther sounded perplexed. "Are you serious?"

"Never more so, hon."

"I can't imagine that he could get a ticket at this late date. My plane is full from San Francisco. I'm sure it will be the same in New York."

"I understand. Look, I'm not sure why, but all at once I've got this strange feeling. I think Jim is supposed to come too. No questions. Just get going. If I'm right, Jim will be there. If not, well, we'll chalk it up to too much time in the Arabian sun."

"Okay, if you're sure."

"I'm sure."

"All right, I've got to run now. I still have a plane to catch." John could hear the excitement in her voice.

"See you in Zagreb tomorrow," he said. "Be careful, sweetheart. I love you."

1055 LOCAL TIME
WASHINGTON, DC

"READY ON YOUR CALL to Mr. James and Mr. Henderson."

"Thank you," Rodeway responded, picking up the phone. "Hello, gentlemen."

"Good morning, Charles. Why don't you hang it up for a day and go home to your wife and kid? That way you'd give the rest of us a break and we could catch up on our work." Harold Henderson, head of Consular Affairs in Washington, DC, laughed as he spoke.

"What's up, Charlie?" The clipped New England intonation of Deputy Undersecretary of State Roland James always brought a smile to Rodeway, who swore jokingly to others that he was the only one at State who *didn't* possess a regional accent.

"Some good news for a change. I might have waited, but I need some direction here."

For the next few minutes, the Political and Diplomatic Security Section's senior officer updated the other two on the Jessica Cain case. Both men were surprised and enthusiastic over the news that the girl had been found; they had privately written her off weeks ago. They listened as Rodeway pointed out the concerns over what her return home might mean in relation to recent terrorist threats and the subsequent rash of bombings, attributable to the Palestinian Islamic Jihad.

"I think we should keep her under wraps until we catch this Dosha fella, or until the FBI runs these misbegotten fanatics back into their holes," Henderson declared emphatically. "No publicity."

"Do you seriously think we can keep her recovery a secret, Harry?" queried James, his raspy voice ending in a high, squeaky pitch, causing Rodeway to pull the receiver away from his ear.

"Well, at least there should be no publicity until she is safe," Henderson insisted. "They're dropping her off in a red area."

There was a moment of silence as each man mused over the truth in this added ingredient of caution.

On a quarterly basis, the State Department distributed a travel report on one hundred sixty-seven countries to its staff members. Each country was listed under one of four designations: *status green* = modest risks; *status yellow* = some precautions warranted; *status orange* = essential travel only and with rigorous precautions; and, *status red*. This month *status red* included twelve countries around the world declared "highly volatile," in which "travel is strongly discouraged." Croatia, with the exception of Zagreb, was *status red*.

"Is there any other place to get her out?"

"Not really," answered Rodeway. "Not unless we run a chopper in and pick her right off the ship's deck. She's on a cargo vessel bound for that port. It's headed for Marseilles after that, with no stops in between."

"Why don't we take a different tack?" asked James. "This thing has had so much publicity, let's go ahead and grab some of it for ourselves. God knows the State Department could use a few kudos for a change."

"I say no press," Henderson proclaimed adamantly. "The rule is, be prudent. Play it safe. Deal with publicity like the enemy it usually is. We all know publicity is a fickle friend, even on a good day. What if something goes wrong?"

"What could possibly go wrong?" James exclaimed, his voice

taking on that irritating nasal sound that Rodeway detested. "We send someone down to meet her. She gets off the boat, into a car, and onto an airplane. Look, we could even send the CG himself to pick her up, along with, maybe, a consular officer and a CNN reporter. Get the parents and take them too. Make a party out of it. Give her a heroine's welcome home and all that. Americans love this sort of thing. The world will love it too. It's so 'Rockwellian,' what with shots of the family being reunited and all. State will look as though we're doing our job for a change. Maybe we can turn it into such a setback for Dosha and his crowd that they'll back off. At least for a while. What do you think, Charlie?"

"There are always risks attached to any operation, but I tend to agree with you, sir," Rodeway answered. "The level of risk here seems minimal, and this could well be the year's biggest story. Better to feed on the publicity than be eaten by it."

"I still disagree," growled Henderson, "but if you both think it is the best thing, I'll go along. Just keep a lid on it, Charles, until you've got her. No pictures released until she's out of the red area and home where she belongs. Good grief, think of what that kid must have been through. How old is she?"

"Twelve," responded Rodeway.

"Twelve," Henderson muttered. "She should be home packing away her dolls and thinking about boys."

"That's where she'll be in a couple of days, sir."

"Okay, Charlie," said James. "Make it happen. See you in the papers."

"Thank you both for your time." Rodeway began moving to wrap up the conference call. He had covered his backside, always an important thing to do in this business, and gained approval of what he had already started. That had been the main purpose for calling his boss and the undersecretary. Now he needed to get the rest of the pieces in place. "I've got an hour's work ahead of me, and my assistant is sick today, so I'd best get to it."

"Give my love to that wife of yours, Charlie," said James. "Maybe when this is done you could come over for dinner."

"Thank you, sir. We will look forward to it."

"Good luck, Charles," echoed Henderson.

"Thank you, sir. I can always use a truckload of that."

2015 LOCAL TIME
JOHN F. KENNEDY INTERNATIONAL AIRPORT, NEW YORK

ESTHER HAD STOLEN JUST ENOUGH sleep time to be miserable. Her eyes were burning so much that she stepped into a restroom to wash them with drops of Visine for relief. Then she hurried out of domestic and onto the bus. There was enough time between connecting flights, but none to spare. She was amazed at the amount of traffic pushing its way through what seemed to be perpetual gridlock.

This driver needs a medal or something. How in the world does she manage to get this big bus through these narrow places? Maybe God, in His infinite wisdom, had known from the beginning that some New Yorkers would need the "gift of driving" in order for the rest of us to survive the experience. Esther smiled at the thought.

She stepped down from the bus at the JFK International Terminal, her only piece of luggage a carry-on thrown over her shoulder, and walked toward the sign marked *Alitalia.* A uniformed female inspected her bag at the door and, in answer to her question regarding directions, pointed "up that way." Esther was about halfway to the next door when Jim "Grandpa" Brainard fell in beside her.

"What's a pretty thing like you doin' in a place like this?" he said, rolling his eyes around the stark room through which they were walking.

"Lookin' for an older man," Esther answered teasingly, in her finest Brainard banter.

"Well, look no further, lady. Just hand me your bag and give me a hug and let's find out where we queue up. Hey, now, isn't this somethin'? Our little girl is comin' home at last. I tell you for sure, I'm lookin' forward to meetin' her. I think we're over this way, Esther. Through that door, it looks like."

"I'm so glad Jeremy managed to reach you in time, but I still can't believe you are here. Say, do you suppose there's a place to get some mineral water around here?" Esther asked. "I'm desperate for a drink. During the last few hours, I seem to have acquired a first-class case of traveler's indigestion. I think the water and a couple of Anacin might help."

"We'll keep a lookout. They just announced boardin' will begin in about fifteen minutes, so we have to keep movin', but . . . there. I think I see somethin' down that way. Follow me." Grandpa Brainard led the way past people standing around in sleepy-eyed groups of twos or threes, along with others who sprawled uncomfortably in chairs, heads back, mouths open, eyes closed.

Grandpa purchased a bottle of Evian for Esther and eventually found a chair where she could sit and rest. He sat across from her, listening as she told him of her conversation with Mr. Rodeway and what she knew of the plans for Jessica's recovery, reiterating

John's request for Grandpa to come with her.

"John will be so glad. He seemed to think that your being here is very important. I can't believe you got a seat with no more notice than this."

"A friend in high places," Jim answered simply.

Esther shook her head. Weariness, and the gradual release of tension, was catching up to her. Just then, a woman's voice came over the loudspeaker, announcing boarding for their flight.

"Time to go," he smiled sympathetically. "Once we're on the plane, you need to get some shuteye."

At exactly three minutes past ten, Alitalia's DC-10 bound for Rome backed away from the terminal and slowly turned toward the runway. Rodeway had made a reservation for Esther in first class, a giant step up from tourist, she thought, as she entered the cabin and sank down into the soft leather seat. Esther had never flown in first class before. Unfortunately, all that had been available to Jim was an inside seat halfway back in tourist. She had tried to exchange with him, but he would not hear of it.

After they were off the ground, Esther pointed out Grandpa Brainard to a flight attendant. She nodded understandingly, and, in a few minutes, returned, saying that she had found one open seat in business class. Moments later, Esther had offered her first class seat to the man next to the empty one in business. He spoke only Italian, but, with the help of the flight attendant, quickly realized his good fortune and was delighted to trade up. With the transaction accomplished, the flight attendant disappeared into the tourist section. Minutes later, a surprised and very pleased Jim Brainard was seated next to Esther, giving instructions for changing their watches to "Italy time," and enjoying the orange juice that was being poured into real glasses.

THURSDAY, 15 DECEMBER, 1250 LOCAL TIME
ZAGREB, CROATIA

MILTON CRESTON HAD BEEN busy making arrangements ever since arriving for work this morning at the embassy. Creston was young and a little nervous about all this. It wasn't the complexity of the assignment that worried him or even any potential danger. On the surface, it was a very simple operation. Fly to Split, get the girl, fly back. A piece of cake, really.

The conundrum for Creston centered on the realization that there would be international publicity surrounding the journey. Not that he minded what that might do for his career. Throughout the morning, he had grown increasingly excited about the prospect of seeing himself on television for the first time, as would his new bride, his parents and friends back home, even the Secretary of State and, probably, the President. Factor in too the millions of others who were bound to be supremely interested in this unusual outcome of an event that had gained world-wide notoriety.

None of that troubled him. He was elated. His frustration had come at eleven-thirty when word was passed down that he, together with a two-person crew from CNN and the girl's parents, would now be joined by his boss, the Consul General. Not that Daniel Banks was a bad guy. In fact, he was well liked by the embassy staff and had the approval of the Croatian community, at least, as much as might be expected under such stressful times.

It was this very popularity that caused Creston to see the handwriting on the wall. His personal moment of glory would be neutralized by his boss, who must have realized the career implications of this event and decided to take advantage of the situation. His presence would relegate Creston to the level of an assistant, which, in fact, was exactly what he had signed on to be. All morning, he had been touching a dream that was certain to lift his diplomatic career out of obscurity and place him on the fast track. Lack of life experience and professional seasoning notwithstanding, he knew that his "moment" would be stolen by the CG, and that knowledge birthed a wintry resentment.

Creston pushed back from his desk, opening an attaché case as he did, and stuffed a handful of papers inside. Mostly official forms to be passed along to the appropriate people, authorizing CNN's team and the girl's parents, along with himself, and now the CG, to board this afternoon's C-130, UN supply flight to Split.

On any other day, Milt would have looked forward to getting out of the gray-grimness of a winter day in Zagreb. There was no snow on the ground, but the frost had already permeated the topsoil. It was overcoat time in Croatia. Had he taken a moment to consider things, he would have realized just how skewed his thinking was. Instead, he waited dejectedly in the doorway to the Consular General's office, listening as Banks gave last-minute instructions to his administrative assistant.

It was an opportune time to rehearse the details of the journey, to make certain in his mind that nothing had been overlooked. That was what he was trained to do. That was what he was paid to do. His usual alertness, however, had given way to feelings of rancor and depression.

It was clearly overcoat time, in more ways than one. It was also time to get the CG in tow and head for the airport.

"That's right, sir, everyone is in place. The CG and an attaché named Creston are personally handling the matter. Both her mother and father are flying into Zagreb. CNN has a news team on site and ready as well. . . . Yes, sir, the mission should be completed and the family back in Zagreb tonight. . . . Not a hotel. They've been invited to stay with the CG and his wife. . . . I look for them to be in Frankfurt sometime Friday afternoon. . . . Well, we want to debrief the child and check her out medically and psychologically there, before they come home. . . . Okay. Thank you, sir. I'll keep you apprised . . . Yes . . . Good-bye."

Rodeway hung up the phone and turned his chair to face the window. An icy rain was falling on the nation's chief municipality, but a good feeling warmed his "father" nature. Otherwise, this would have been a truly miserable day.

JOHN'S CONNECTING FLIGHT from the UAE had taken them through Zurich. After a four-hour layover they were headed south again, proving once more, according to Hersch, that "the shortest distance between two points is not necessarily a straight line."

"Zurich. Zagreb. Isn't it odd that each city we land in today begins with the letter Z?

Hersch pushed his crutches farther down until they were

jammed against the bulkhead. The embassy had thoughtfully requested this seating so that he could stretch his leg and be as comfortable as possible. He eyed John quizzically. "Are you okay, Cain?"

"I think about things like that," John chuckled. "I mean, how many cities can you think of that begin with the letter "Z?"

"Zonguldak."

"Get out of here."

"It's a port city in Turkey."

"Really? Are you pulling my leg?"

"I don't do legs right now," Hersch grimaced, shifting his own to a more comfortable position.

"Are you sure you feel up to this?" asked John, concern furrowed in his brow as he watched Towner trying to ease his discomfort. "I still think you should have gone straight home."

"I wouldn't miss this reunion for anything. It's payback for the pain."

Just then, the flight attendant brushed against John's shoulder on his way forward with the drinks cart.

"Zhdanov."

"Zhdanov?"

"In the Ukraine on the Azov Sea."

"Okay, okay," John exclaimed in mock exasperation. "You've made your point."

Towner gave a satisfied smirk, leaned back, and closed his eyes.

"The only other one that I can think of is Zion."

Towner peered at John out of the corner of one eye. "Illinois?"

"Jerusalem."

"Doesn't begin with Z."

"In ancient times, it was the site of the temple. It's now a hill in East Jerusalem. The most important hill in the world," said John, letting his mind drift back over the events that had recently occurred there . . . events in which he had been directly involved.

"I know a few senators who might not agree with you on that," Towner bantered back.

"That's true," John chuckled, "but when was the last time you felt confident that our nation's leaders knew what was really important?"

"Get some sleep, Cain. You're starting to sound too much like me. You need to catch some Zs so you'll be sharp when you see your daughter."

"I don't usually sleep and fly at the same time."

"No? You mean I have finally discovered something that puts a little fear in you?"

"Flying is worse than Iran, Hersch, and I was scared to death there most of the time!"

"You shouldn't let a little plane ride get you down," Hersch chided.

"Isn't that the idea?"

"What?"

"After you get up here, don't you want the plane to get you down again? Gently?"

"Rev, you're okay . . . for a preacher. A little fear never really hurts. In fact, it sharpens us up. There's a huge difference between fear and cowardice. And a coward you ain't, John. After what we've been through, I'd go with you anywhere. And there aren't many guys I'd say that to."

"Thanks," John answered, taking momentary pleasure from Hersch's extravagant compliment. Just then, he felt the plane start its gradual descent. Instinctively, he closed his eyes and his hand tightened on the armrest.

Towner shook his head and settled back, turning his attention out the window where one frozen field after another kept disappearing under the wing.

1435 LOCAL TIME
ZAGREB, CROATIA

JOHN AND HERSCH were the final passengers to exit. John led the way down the steps to the tarmac, looking back once to check on Hersch. He saw Esther standing to one side, hands tucked inside her coat pockets, protectively surrounded by two strangers in overcoats and two uniformed UN soldiers, each with an M-16 cradled in his arm. He guessed that the overcoats were from the embassy. And there was Jim Brainard. John waved as Esther came forward to meet him. They embraced, then looked at each other and began to laugh.

"Your eyes are red," said John. She closed them as his lips touched first one, then the other. "When did you get in?"

"You've lost weight," she replied, running her hand over the stubble that was sprouting on his chin. "Less than twenty minutes ago."

"Arabic food has been very good to me," he answered with a thick accent. "In and out. Doesn't stick to the ribs. Very tasty on its way through, though."

They laughed and hugged again. Then Esther pulled away and

moved toward Hersch. He paused and smiled as she hugged him and kissed his cheek.

"Herschel Towner, I am so pleased to finally meet you. We will never forget what you have gone through to help us," she said, standing back at arm's length, eyeing his crutches. Her words became husky with emotion. "John was careful in what he told me on the phone, but I was certain that you'd been wounded. Thank you for all you've done. And for bringing John back to me, like you said you would."

"Hey, it was nothing," he said feigning brusqueness. "The Iranians took one look at John and decided to throw him back. The rest was easy."

Herschel grinned as the others laughed.

"Truth be said, it was your husband who got us out of there. He's quite a guy, Mrs. Cain."

"Esther," she corrected, glancing over at John, a look of pride on her face. "Yes, actually, he *is* quite a guy."

She took John's arm and wrapped hers around it tightly.

"Let me introduce you both to our friends. This, of course, is your father's old soldier buddy, Jim Brainard, referred to in our family as Grandpa." She turned to acknowledge the two strangers. "And this is Consul General Banks and Mr. Creston, an attaché from our local embassy. Gentlemen, my husband and Mr. Herschel Towner, a dear friend from Seattle who has been helping us try to find our daughter."

"It's a pleasure to meet you," Banks responded, as the men shook hands. "I regret that we don't have time to offer you our local hospitality, but that will come later."

"Dear, these gentlemen have indicated to me that Jim's presence, and now, I suppose yours as well, Herschel, is a problem for them," Esther interrupted. "We are flying to Split by special dispensation from the UN, but they are not prepared for extra passengers."

"Yes, if we had known, Creston might have arranged for it," Banks explained. "Unfortunately, we had no knowledge that you two were joining us here. Our flight is warming up over there even as we speak."

All eyes followed in the direction Banks was pointing. The motors on a gigantic, olive-green C-130 were just beginning to turn over. It was then that John first noticed the warmly clad figure of a man with a television camera balanced on his shoulder, film obviously rolling. To one side stood an attractive woman dressed in ski pants, boots, and a heavy wool jacket. She was saying something into a hand-held microphone.

Hersch started to speak when John suddenly interrupted. "I appreciate the imposition, Mr. Banks, but you must understand our circumstance. These two have been deeply involved in getting Jessica back, and in fighting against the acts of terrorism that are now being directed at our country." He spoke loud enough for the news team to be able to pick up his words. "I regret that we were unable to inform you that they would be here, but I assure you that their presence with us is essential. We cannot go on without them."

"But Mr. . . . . Reverend Cain," protested Creston. "This sort of thing takes advance preparation. We'll be flying into a dangerous area."

"Mr. Rodeway at the State Department said it would be quite safe," responded Esther sweetly, picking up on what John was doing. "That's a big plane over there, Mr. Creston. Don't you think we could manage to squeeze these two in with the rest of us?"

Creston looked over at Banks, helplessly. The CG shrugged his shoulders and, with a telling glance at the whirring camera, nodded. Without a word, Creston turned and jogged off toward the airplane to talk to the man in charge. They had not even gotten off the ground and, already, he was being called upon to smooth things over so that the CG could look good on camera.

1615 LOCAL TIME
SPLIT, CROATIA

AS JESSICA EMERGED from the passageway, she was surprised to see the crew of the *Evvoia* standing single-file, shoulder to shoulder, along the deck. Captain Callimachus was at her side and behind her, Mr. Hatzimustafovic, the shipping company's local representative in Split, who had come aboard a short while earlier. His shirt was open at the collar and Jessica noticed that his pants showed signs of wear, as did the navy-blue suit jacket that he wore underneath a raincoat. The man seemed okay. Besides, what choice did she really have? She had come to trust the crew of the M/V *Evvoia*. Why not Mr. Hatzimus . . . whatever?

The sky was dark and overcast, hiding the sun's final attempt at providing some cheer for what had been an otherwise dreary day. She felt raindrops and, with them, a biting breeze whipped across the deck. It was cold enough to make her pull the wool jacket, that the captain had insisted she take from his closet, up under her chin. The jacket was several sizes too large, but she was glad to have it on as raindrops stung her face.

In fact, everything she was wearing had been given to her by the captain or by members of the crew. Fresh underclothes, thanks to the captain's daughters. The jeans and pullover that she had been given the night before were "officially" hers now. Their rightful owners had insisted. Only the Nikes she wore on her feet were originally hers before last night.

As she started past the line, the first crew member reached out and took her hand.

"Have a safe trip," he smiled.

Jessica suddenly felt embarrassed, but there was no time to recover. The next sailor had his hand out now.

"Godspeed," he said, shaking her hand firmly.

The tiny procession moved on slowly, each man shaking her hand and wishing her well, until she reached the end of the line. The last person, standing next to the steps leading down to the waiting transfer boat, was Timothy Marcos. He held out his hand.

"God bless you, Jessica," he said smiling broadly. "I hope to see you again someday."

Jessica's eyes filled with emotion that she could no longer contain. She brushed past his hand and threw her arms around the young man, holding onto him as tightly as she could. The other crewmen shuffled around them, several brushing at imaginary "specks" in their eyes. These men of the sea had been touched by this girl-child who seemed so vulnerable and unprotected, and yet who had survived terrors they could only imagine with a braveness that commanded their sincere respect.

"Thank you for everything, Timothy Marcos," Jessica wept, her face buried in his chest. Then, she looked up. "I will never forget you. Never. I will tell my father about you, that you want to be a pastor someday. Maybe he'll be able to help you."

Now it was Tim's turn to be embarrassed. He glanced up at the crew's faces, but they were all nodding or smiling their approval. He looked at Captain Callimachus. The captain reached over and touched her shoulder.

"It's time to go, Jessica."

She released her hold on the young man who had watched out for her the night before and all during the day that had followed.

"Perhaps," said the captain, looking at Tim, "we could offer up a prayer for Jessica?"

"Yes, sir, that would be wonderful. May I?"

The captain nodded, motioning to the crew with his hand. Those with hats snatched at them respectfully as they bowed their heads. The stiff breeze had let up, at least for the moment, but large drops of cold rain began falling in earnest as Tim cleared his throat.

"Lord Jesus," he began, "we want to thank You for our captain and the ship's crew. We thank You for our families back home, our health, and our jobs. But, most of all, today we are here to thank You for Jessica Cain. You chose us, out of all the ships' crews in the world, to be the ones to carry her back to her family, where she belongs. Keep her safe now, as she leaves us. Watch over her and help her always to know how much she is loved. In Jesus' name we pray, Amen."

A chorus of "Amens" echoed from the crew.

"Thank you again for everything," said Jessica, smiling appreciatively at the crew. With Mr. Hatzimustafovic following her, she waved her hand and started down the same steps on which she had surreptitiously boarded the *Evvoia*, some thirteen days before in Bandar-é Abbås.

"Goodbye, Jessica," the crewmen shouted down as she stepped over into the chunky-looking, wooden tender that waited below.

"Bye," she called out happily, waving again. "Thank you."

The motor chugged into action and the tender moved out from under the *Evvoia's* long shadow. She glanced over at the shipping company's representative. He was talking to the boatman in a language that Jessica did not understand. *So what else is new?* she thought, turning her attention to the direction in which they were headed.

It was a big harbor. Bigger, at least, than the one at Bandar. Now, as they churned along through the sea, past several cargo vessels anchored offshore, she could see others lining the docks. Small fishing boats, trawlers, a barge, even two ominous-looking warships were scattered about, some in motion, most patiently waiting their turn for whatever attention was deemed appropriate. It was part of a world and a life that now seemed both familiar and foreign to her.

Huddled against the cold wind, she tried to guess which dock they were headed to. Captain Callimachus said that her parents had left earlier from wherever they had been, some city to the north with a funny name. He was certain that they would be at the dock when she arrived. If they were delayed, Mr. Hatzimustafovic had promised to stay with her until they came.

Even though they were still too far out, Jessica kept peering over the edge of the boat, scanning the docks as they came closer, in hopes of seeing some sign of them.

It's been so long. How many weeks?
She couldn't remember for certain.
A million years. At least!

1620 LOCAL TIME
SPLIT, CROATIA

THE NEWS TEAM WAS on the ground first.

A smiling Milton Creston was caught by the camera as he led the way out of the airplane and down the steps to the tarmac, followed by the Consul General, then Esther, John, and Jim Brainard. Herschel Towner was last, and the others waited as a crew member tried to assist him. He was having none of it, however, exercising his independence by carrying his crutches in one hand, while limping down each step and balancing with his other hand on the railing.

He grinned sheepishly upon arriving at the bottom step.

"Ain't life grand?" he grimaced ruefully. The others laughed, huddled under umbrellas in the drizzling rain.

Two mud-spattered jeeps roared around the corner of the terminal and headed in their direction.

"Methinks that yon chariots are ours, my dear," John whispered in Esther's ear.

"I'll go in a wheelbarrow, just so long as there's room in it for one more," she answered, watching as the vehicles came to a stop in front of them. Each one was clearly marked with the letters UN across the hood.

"Hop in, folks," invited Daniel Banks. "And hang on. We're a few miles away yet. Our drivers will take us straight to the harbor. We'll pick up your daughter and come right back here. By that time, they'll have the plane unloaded and be ready to take us back to Zagreb."

Esther wasted no time climbing into the nearest jeep.

"Which dock do we go to, sir?" asked the first driver.

Banks looked at his attaché, waiting for the answer.

"Pier 12," Creston answered, fumbling through the sheaf of official-looking documents in his hands. He looked up. "Take us to Pier 12."

Both drivers nodded as the others finished settling into the confines of the jeeps. The camera crew was the last to climb in.

Where was that fax with the pier number? As unobtrusively as possible, he sorted through the file once again, in case he had passed over it by mistake. No. It still was not there among the other papers. The cold rain stung his face as they bounced along the two-lane highway toward Split's harbor. He thought back to when he had left his office, frowning at the realization that it must still be on his desk. No problem. He remembered clearly.

Pier 12.

1645 LOCAL TIME

THE BOATMAN HELD THE TENDER steady while Jessica climbed over the side and onto the small platform. Hatzimusta-fovic joined her and pointed up the narrow, wooden steps to the top of the dock. Jessica nodded and began climbing. Nearing the top, she paused to look around. There was no sign of her parents. She continued to the top of the steps and waited for Hatzimusta-fovic to join her.

"Your parents are not here yet?" he asked in heavily accented English.

"No." She couldn't keep the disappointment out of her voice.

"Do not worry." He patted her shoulder and then pointed toward the opposite end of the dock. "They will be along any minute. Come, let us go over there and wait."

The rain had let up for the moment, although a chilling breeze was back again, whipping at the collar of Jessica's jacket as they walked toward a long row of warehouses situated along the shore. Just beyond the dock, a loading crane squatted like some giant *Jurassic Park* insect, waiting to gobble up its prey. Not far from the crane, several dock workers huddled in front of a large building to get away from the wind. Jessica's eyes darted back and forth, sharp with excitement and anticipation.

Where are they?

1645 LOCAL TIME

ESTHER GLANCED IMPATIENTLY at her watch.
Where is she?

They stood together at the pier's edge, staring out into the harbor, surprised at the amount of shipping traffic in this sup-posed war zone.

"Split has served for some time as a major loading and un-loading point for goods and supplies bound for Bosnia," explained Banks to anyone listening. "Many of the units attached to the UN Protective Forces have landed their heavy equipment here. Their most important logistics line runs to the interior from this loca-tion."

Five more minutes passed and small talk decreased as the cold dampness and the feeling that nothing was happening set in.

"Are you sure we're in the right place?" Esther asked, concern growing the longer they waited.

"This is Pier 12," Creston answered. "The fax we received from the *Evvoia*'s home office said they would deliver her to Pier 12." As soon as he mentioned the fax, he wished he had not.

"May I see it?" asked Banks, holding out his hand as he stared into the distance.

"Sir?"

"The fax. May I see it, please?"

Creston hesitated, desperately wishing he was somewhere . . . anywhere . . . but here. But he stubbornly bucked up and decided to make the best of it.

"I'm sorry, sir. I didn't think it was necessary to bring it."

Banks gave him a sharp look.

"She should be here by now," Esther said, looking first at John, then at Daniel Banks.

"I'm sure they were just delayed a bit," said Banks. "Still, it won't hurt for us to double-check. Right, Milt? In case there was a last-minute change that we don't know about?"

Creston felt the edge in his boss's tone. *I should have brought the fax. He knows it. I'm sure, though. . . .*

But Creston no longer was as sure as he had been.

"Yes, sir. I can contact the embassy from the jeep."

Esther felt John's arm around her, drawing her close. She watched as Creston hurried away, then turned her gaze back to the sea. *Please, God. Let her come quickly.* She closed her eyes to ward off the apprehension gnawing at her stomach.

Minutes seemed like hours. She watched as the attaché put the phone pack on the jeep's front seat, and hesitated for a moment. Was that uncertainty she saw on his face? He jogged back and pulled the CG aside. She observed Banks' hand grip the attaché's arm. Then quickly, it fell back to his side. Banks turned and walked toward them, a look of concern and apology on his face.

"I must ask you to get back into the jeeps. It seems that we have a small hitch in things," Banks said, his voice calm and reassuring.

"What's the matter," John asked guardedly.

"It's nothing really. We've just been waiting at the wrong pier. It appears that she is coming into Pier 21, not Pier 12."

"What?" Esther's tone was anxious and tinged with frustration. "We've been standing here waiting for our daughter at the wrong dock?"

"So it seems, Mrs. Cain," Banks answered, conscious that CNN's faithful reporters were filming away. "I'm truly sorry for the mix-up. Let's be off—Pier 21 is only a short distance and we can be there in five minutes."

Esther glanced up at John. His face glowed with unvoiced emotion as they ran to the jeeps. As soon as everyone was in, they roared off into the growing darkness. A short distance farther, they noticed lights coming on, apparently automatically, along the docking area. Ships tied up for loading and unloading dwarfed the jeeps and their occupants as they sped by.

All Esther could think about was the need to hurry.

1655 LOCAL TIME

JESSICA DROPPED A STEP behind the Croatian, letting his body shield her from the cold breeze. As they neared the land's end of the dock, she looked again at the men standing close to the building. She assumed that it must be a warehouse. There were four. No, there were five. She had not seen the one squatting in the shadows until he stood up.

"Over here, Jessica," the Croatian said, as he pointed away from the men, toward a stack of large wooden crates. She breathed a sigh of relief. She didn't like the idea of being here, outnumbered by five strangers.

Remember, Jessica, you can't trust anybody.

The familiar sound of that inner voice surprised her, coming as it did from a past that already seemed ancient, not simply hours old. The past thirty-plus hours on board the *Evvoia* had dulled her need for universal distrust and the animal alertness so essential for survival. The closer they came to the workmen huddled near the building, however, the more her cautionary instincts surfaced. Now they were moving laterally, away from the men, and Jessica's tenseness gradually eased.

The crates provided shelter from the wind while still keeping the scene in full vision. Jessica backed against the crates, hands in her jacket pockets, as the two stood waiting.

A sudden chill sent a shiver through her body. *Come on, Mom and Dad. Hurry.*

As they waited in the growing darkness, lights along the dock were automatically activated by some invisible timer. They were not powerful enough to illuminate the area with bright light, but it was better than waiting in complete darkness.

Across the way she watched as a man tried to light a cigarette for one of his friends. The match blew out and he lit another. Then they started to walk away.

Two other figures suddenly appeared out of the shadows, from a narrow opening at the opposite end of the same building, and walked swiftly toward the place where Hatzimustafovic and Jessica stood waiting. She felt Hatzimustafovic's hand on her shoulder and glanced up. He was looking at her and smiling.

"Your parents?" he asked.

Jessica's face lit up with excitement as she looked toward the approaching couple. She began jumping up and down. Then, as quickly as she had started, she stopped her dance of joy. Not more than twenty feet away, the approaching couple walked beneath a dock light.

She saw them clearly now. Inside, something crumbled as longing gave way to shocked disbelief.

They were not her parents, but she knew who they were. From deep inside came a cry of terror.

The next five seconds ran like a movie in slow-motion.

The man and woman paused as he withdrew his hand from his coat pocket. Without a word, he pointed it. Jessica saw the flash a millisecond before the silencer's muffled popping sound reached her ear. In the same instant, Hatzimustafovic groaned, falling back against the crates. Another flash. She heard the sickening impact of the second bullet finding its mark, and, out of the corner of her eye, saw the Croatian slide to a grotesque sitting position on the pavement beside her.

Frozen with fear, Jessica watched the handgun swing ever so slightly until it pointed directly at her. Behind the dark barrel, the man with the scar was smiling. Leila Azari's face was a mixture of dark fury and hatred. Her hands never left the pockets of her coat.

What happened next left Jessica dazed and bewildered.

The force of the explosion threw her backward, slamming her body against the stack of crates!

FORTY-NINE

John, Esther, and the others had just passed Pier 19 when they heard the explosion. Dead ahead, a flash of flames shot upward into the sky, then disappeared, only to be replaced by an eerie glow.

"What was that?" exclaimed Esther.

"I don't know," John replied, instinctively tightening his grip on her shoulder.

Cars and trucks were parked haphazardly along this section, partially blocking the narrow street and causing the drivers to slow as they weaved their way through. The street continued to narrow until it was completely blocked by an ancient Volkswagen that acted like the cork in the neck of a bottle.

"Come on," said John, scrambling out of the jeep.

"Wait, let's stay together," admonished Banks, looking around to check the quality of their position. He didn't like it. There was not room enough to turn their jeeps around without backing up for at least a block or more. "Be careful, everyone. We don't know what's happening. It could be just an accident. A gas explosion. It might also be shelling or a bomb, so stay close. Remember, people, we're in a war zone."

The cameraman from CNN stood by, ready with his gear, chewing gum and looking like he did this every day. For all that John knew, maybe he did, although he noted that the reporter appeared a little more anxious. Grandpa and Milton Creston stood quietly nearby. Towner was the last to join the circle.

"Mr. Towner, you wait here. You'll only be in the way. I would suggest Mrs. Cain and Mr. Brainard do the same. I'll leave a driver. He's well armed. The other one goes with Reverend Cain, Creston, and me, for a look around."

"In a pig's eye," Herschel grunted.

"I'm serious," Banks said firmly.

"So are we," Grandpa retorted emphatically. "Now, son, you can waste your time and everyone else's by standin' here arguin.' It ain't goin' to change a thing. We're stickin' together. You all go on ahead, and I'll be along with Hersch here. Take these boys who've been drivin' us with you. They look like they can handle themselves okay. We'll catch up."

Without waiting for orders, the drivers had placed themselves at the front and rear of the small contingent, facing out, M-16s at ready. They listened to the discussion, even smiled to themselves as the old man put the CG in his place, but their eyes never stopped searching out the darkened rooftops, windows, and alleyways.

Banks knew he was not completely in control. The circumstances he had started out with a few hours earlier were not the same as those facing him now. It was time to reconnoiter and make the best of it.

"Okay," Banks sighed in resignation. "Let's go. But stay together."

"Sir," one of the drivers touched Grandpa's arm.

Grandpa looked up questioningly.

"Take this. You may need it."

The soldier held out a handgun that had been strapped to his waist. Grandpa took it gratefully, turned it over in his hand, and smiled. "Thank you."

The others struck out with Grandpa walking behind Herschel Towner III, who limped along after them.

"You want to stick that thing in my belt before you hurt one of us with it?" Hersch asked.

Grandpa chuckled.

"Son, I was shootin' these things before you were even a gleam in your daddy's eye. But yes, I don't mind if I do stick this in your belt. I'm a senior citizen with enough weight to carry around all by myself. I don't need extra."

He reached over and pushed it through Hersch's belt and they walked on, with Hersch trying to move faster. The others had disappeared on ahead. The two of them were alone.

THE FORCE OF THE EXPLOSION threw Leila and Dosha forward onto the pavement. Jessica had fallen backward against the crates as the shock wave of invisible energy slammed against her with enough power to crush the breath from her body. Her ears felt as though they would burst. And then it was over.

Stunned and breathless, ears still ringing painfully, a dazed Jessica tried to focus her eyes. Less than a dozen feet away, she saw Leila Azari lying facedown, not moving. Dosha had pushed himself to his knees and was shaking his head. He looked behind him in the direction of the blast. The old building at the end of the pier was a blazing inferno. Broken timbers were still falling; shattered pieces of glass littered the roadway and the end of the pier.

Jessica raised her head at the same moment that Dosha looked back at her. She saw him glance over at Leila. He was looking for something.

The gun.

The explosion and his fall had knocked the gun out of his hand.

Jessica saw it at the same time Dosha did. It was far enough out of reach that he had to stand up or crawl for it. He chose to stand. At the same time, Jessica forced herself up from the pavement. Dosha was moving to his left to pick up the weapon. Jessica started to run in the opposite direction, away from the pier. Her entire body throbbed from having been thrown backward onto the crates. Still, she managed a few quick steps before darting behind a stack of large wooden boxes that had survived the blast. As she did, she heard the first bullet tear into one of the boxes, just above her head. A second shot buried itself deep into whatever the boxes contained.

She could hear footsteps behind her now. A curse and the sound of a crate falling. The man with the scar had given chase. The sounds ignited adrenaline from a reservoir that Jessica thought had long since been depleted, and she ran faster than she could ever remember. Faster than any race on the school track back home. She ran for her life!

Past the huge crane. Across the steel tracks. Along a brick building. Running under one of the pier's lights she felt, as much as heard, the sound of another bullet ricochet off the bricks above and in front of her. It was too close and a chip from one of the bricks stung her cheek, creating a small, stinging cut just below her eye. She winced in pain. Then, she was around the corner and facing a decision—take the street that stretched out along the waterfront or one of two alleyways close at hand.

She chose the nearest alley. It was narrow and dark, but clear of debris. She ran as fast as she could, fueled by the fear of what was behind her. Then, a jog in the alley appeared so suddenly that Jessica bounced off the wall and fell backward to the ground. Scrambling to her feet, she dodged around the corner and ran on. Her hand was bleeding from having scraped against the wall. No matter. She ran on, desperate to put distance between her and the man with the scar and the evil woman who had kept her a prisoner. How had they known where to find her?

And where are Mom and Dad?

1717 LOCAL TIME

SIRENS BLARED AS JOHN and the others ran out of the narrow street and stopped to stare at the scene. A sign on the side of the building nearest them indicated that this was Pier 21, or what was left of it. The main warehouse at the end of the pier was a total loss.

They heard shouting as men rushed down the gangplank of the nearest large ship toward the blaze, but there was nothing they could do. For the moment confusion and bedlam were sovereign rulers of this scene.

A short distance away John saw a man helping a woman to her feet. She looked smaller in stature and, at first, he thought it might be Jessica. He started toward them, but, a second look made him hesitate. It was a grown woman. He could see her clearly now, in the firelight. She seemed dazed, but was walking and appeared to be okay. Besides, there was someone helping her already. He turned his attention away from them and back to the question foremost on everyone's mind.

Where is Jessica?

1722 LOCAL TIME

LEILA AZARI WALKED UNSTEADILY with Dosha's help, badly shaken from the effects of the blast. It was a clear case of the left hand not knowing what the right hand was up to.

After three fruitless days of looking for Jessica in Bandar-é Abbås, Dosha had left Leila with instructions to continue the search while he flew to Istanbul. There, over the next few days, he was able to negotiate the purchase of several Soviet-made rocket launchers, and meet with local PKK leaders to plan further violent disruption of Turkey's profitable tourist trade. From there, he had flown to Cairo for a meeting with two representatives of the Palestinian Islamic Jihad. They had been fresh with news regarding ongoing acts of terrorism in Israel, nurtured and carried out by underground cells headquartered in the Gaza Strip.

It was on his last day in Cairo that Leila had contacted him with the news.

A relatively unsophisticated but effective network had set about monitoring the radio transmissions of the M/V *Evvoia* and three other vessels known to have sailed from Bandar-é Abbås during the first forty-eight hours following Jessica's escape. An extensive search was also made of ships still remaining in the harbor. But it was the radio station at a Revolutionary Guard training base in Lebanon that finally broken the mystery of Jessica Cain's disappearance.

Upon receiving word of the *Evvoia*'s location and her next port of call, Dosha instructed Leila to meet him in Ancona on Italy's central Adriatic coast. From there it was a simple thing to ferry across to Split, well ahead of the *Evvoia*, and prepare to meet the girl. Dosha had voiced his hope of finding her father there as well. After his interference with the plan for Jerusalem, Dosha had decided that the Reverend Cain was a man deserving "special and permanent attention."

Now, hurrying to get away from this scene of devastation, he was furious with himself. Yet, how could he have known that Serbian sympathizers would blow up a warehouse right where he would be doing business? No matter. He had chosen to first take out the man standing next to the girl. That decision was his mistake. It had given her a chance to run.

Certainly Jessica Cain was no match for his much-heralded skills. She should have accepted her place as a useful pawn in the greater scheme of things, and yet she had not given up easily. That had surprised him, especially from a twelve-year-old. People's passivity was always important to his success; it made his work so much easier. If only she had acted the way most other people did, all of this would have been unnecessary.

It also gnawed at the back of his mind that she was doubly dangerous because of yet another mistake, born out of his own self-assured arrogance. He had enlightened her regarding the goal of his mission. In retrospect, that had been a grievous error. If she somehow managed to get to safety before he caught up to her, she knew enough to jeopardize the plan.

But for now, Dosha could concentrate only on escaping. He had to get them both away from this place. He guided Leila toward the narrow street that led back to their rental car.

"What happened?" Leila's first words came as she stumbled along beside Dosha.

"An explosion," Dosha growled in reply. "Some stupid Serbs."

Just then another boom was heard in the distance.

"They must be firing on the city now," said Dosha, as he half carried, half dragged Leila out of the lighted area. "Too bad we weren't warned about it. They picked a fine time to declare war on this place."

"I'll be okay," Leila declared, pushing away from his grasp around her waist. "Are we going back to the car?"

"Yes."

"And the girl?"

Dosha's silence was her answer.

They were almost to the street, when two men emerged from the shadows, headed toward the fire. One was on crutches. The other one was older . . . he looked . . . familiar? But that was impossible. Dosha glanced over his shoulder. The old man had stopped and turned, staring back after them. He pushed Leila forward. *Hurry.*

"Wait!"

The voice was familiar too. Where . . . ?

1725 LOCAL TIME

"YOU DOIN' OKAY, SON?" Grandpa Brainard asked, glancing back at Herschel.

"I'm fine," Towner grunted in response.

They came to the end of the street and started out into the open area ahead. About a hundred feet away, they saw John and the others standing together, watching as men ran from one of the nearby ships toward the fire. The sirens were getting closer and, at last the first fire engine rounded the corner, headed in their direction.

A man and woman were coming their way also. The woman appeared dazed, maybe even injured. Grandpa started to call out at the precise moment the man glanced up. His mouth fell open and he remained speechless, as the man and the woman hurried past Grandpa and Hersch.

"It's him," Grandpa whispered finally.

"What?"

"It's him," Grandpa said again, his voice low. "I'd recognize that face anywhere."

"Whose face?"

"It's Dosha. Give me that gun, Hersch."

"Wait . . ."

"The gun. Give it to me."

Grandpa fumbled with Hersch's belt as he groped for the handgun, never taking his eyes off the man and woman.

"Are you sure?"

"Positive. He lived at my house for a week."

Now it was Herschel's turn to gape.

Grandpa took the gun. He stepped forward, uncertain what he should do about the two figures receding in the darkness.

"Wait!" he called out earnestly.

"STOP!"

Dosha hesitated, uncertain whether to obey or run. *The man's voice . . .*

"Can you run, Leila?" he whispered.

Leila nodded.

"I know who you are, Marwan Dosha, and I have you covered with a gun. Don't move or I'll shoot."

Dosha was paused in stunned disbelief. That someone would actually call out his name was the last thing he expected. *How could that old man possibly . . . wait . . . of course. Now I remember. It was Booth Bay. The inn on the hill. The old man ran the inn. But how did he get here? No time for that now. He's here, that's all that matters. And he knows who I am.*

"Run, Leila," he ordered in a low voice, pulling a P14●45 from the belt holster hidden under his jacket. Without another word, he turned and fired.

The bullet missed, but it was close enough to send Grandpa and Hersch diving for cover. Dosha fired again. Grandpa threw himself down behind a garbage barrel and got off a round in return. Towner had been scrambling for cover at the first sign of gunfire. Looking around to see if Grandpa was all right, he noticed one of his crutches lying in the middle of the roadway, between them. The second bullet zinged as it glanced off the stone wall right above him.

Grandpa was peering out from behind the barrel. The street looked empty. There was no one there. Where could they have gone so fast? He stood to his feet, the gun dangling from his hand.

"Here, give me that," Hersch limped over to where Grandpa was standing and reached around, taking the gun.

"What happened?" One of the jeep drivers ran up to them. The news team was right behind them.

"Mr. Brainard here thinks he saw a man that he knows."

"Do you always shoot at people you know, sir?" the young soldier asked dubiously.

"What's going on? Are you both okay?" John was out of breath as he ran up to the others.

"It was Dosha," answered Grandpa.

John stared at Grandpa. "Are you certain?"

"I said I'd never forget that face. And I didn't."

"When he called out to him," added Herschel, "the guy fired at us and took off. There was a woman with him."

"A woman?" John repeated. "Dark hair? Jeans and a jacket?"

Herschel and Grandpa both nodded.

"Then I saw them too. There was a man, over that direction," John continued, pointing excitedly. "He was helping a woman to her feet. She looked dazed. At first, I thought she might have been injured by the blast, but then they began walking away. Anyway, he was helping her, so I didn't pay any more attention."

"Sounds like the same people that came through here," Hersch commented dryly. "Then Doc Brainard went after the guy. Called him out by name and told him not to move. Just like the OK Corral. Only this fellow didn't listen very well. The woman ran and the guy got off a couple of near misses. Doc fired back. Me, I dove for cover. Nearly broke my neck on these crutches doing it too."

Hersch's half-serious, half-lighthearted description failed to elicit any chuckles.

"I'm sorry, John. I don't think I hit him. Now, they're gone."

"It's okay," John consoled his friend. By this time, they had been joined by the others as firefighters continued to crowd onto the pier and into the open area between the dock and the burning warehouse. Horns blowing, sirens wailing, and people shouting had drawn most of the attention away from the small cluster of Americans. A policeman started toward them, only to be intercepted by another officer and sent in the opposite direction.

"This is all starting to make some sense," John said grimly. "Let's get back to the jeeps and drive around."

"Why?" queried Banks. "What good will that do?"

"Stop and think," said John. "If that was Dosha . . ."

"It was," Grandpa interrupted emphatically.

"Then, he was here for the same reason we are. Jessica. Somehow, he found out that she was coming here and he wants his hostage back. Or worse." He glanced over at Esther, noting her ashen look. "As long as he has her, she's worth millions if the world comes up with the ransom he's demanding. Or it could be that he thinks she knows something. At any rate, she is important enough to Dosha that he came here tonight to find her."

Another artillery boom echoed in the distance. Everyone was listening now. Even Creston, whose name could well have been "Crestfallen," listened as he stared gloomily at the pavement in front of him, both hands jammed into his coat. He looked miserable, and John understood why.

"All right, we've searched and she's not here. However, there is a man over there by those crates, where that policeman is now. He's dead, but not from the blast. I found him just a couple of minutes ago. He's been shot." Exclamations of surprise and horror were cut short as John continued, "But there was no sign of Jessica. Now, if she was not with Dosha when you saw them, and she's not around here, that must mean that somehow, in all the confusion, she managed to get away."

John looked next at the attaché.

"Creston, I know you feel terrible," he continued. "Perhaps if we hadn't waited at the wrong pier, we would have been in time to get her. Maybe. But, it's also possible that we could have shown up just in time to get us all killed. Either by the blast or by Dosha. Maybe the Lord had a hand in delaying us this way."

Creston glanced over at Banks. Banks said nothing.

"Okay, let's get out of here. We have to assume that Jessica is close by. She hasn't seen us, but she probably has seen Dosha. That means she'll be hiding, trying to get as far from here as possible, without giving herself away."

"Do you really think a twelve-year-old will do all that?" asked Banks, with a look of disbelief.

John turned to Banks, controlling his emotions now with great difficulty. "Sir, with all due respect, last September I left my daughter in Israel in the hands of terrorist killers. That was three months ago. Since then she's made it all the way to Iran and from there to here and she's still alive. I don't know how, but with God's help, she's done it. Don't doubt for one minute that this twelve-year-old will do all that. Dosha believes it too. That's why he's here. So, let's get busy. We've got to find her before he does."

John strode off down the narrow street, the others hurrying to catch up. Banks was still the Consul General. Creston was still his attaché. The two UN soldiers still carried their automatic weapons. But, it was clear to everyone who had taken charge.

FIFTY

Jessica pressed against the building, trying to stay under the narrow overhang and out of the rain. It was not coming down as hard as it had earlier, but she was still soaked through and shivering from the cold. Directly beneath her, she could hear the past hour's runoff coursing through one of the city's ancient drainage channels that carried excess water to the sea. She could not stop shaking. Was it from the cold rain? Or was it from fear? She wasn't certain and it really didn't matter. How long had it been? Three hours? Four? Too long, anyway.

If I stay here, I'll freeze to death. Got to keep moving.

She walked on to the end of the alley.

Be careful, Jessica.

Another big gun boom sounded in the mountains somewhere above the city. This time, she felt the ground shudder as the shell hit less than a block away.

This is unbelievable. In the movies, yes, but, this is real life and those are real guns.

Jessica huddled against the building.

What kind of place is this? Why is everyone bent on killing?

She winced as she thought back to the shipping company's Croatian representative.

He died standing right there next to me, and I can't even remember his name. "Hats . . . something." The poor man . . .

Jessica came around the corner, climbed three low steps, and began walking along the sidewalk, making sure to stay close to the buildings. The street was empty of traffic. She automatically tried each door she came to. They were all locked. Some windows had glass and she thought about breaking one in order to get inside. Others were already broken and long since boarded up. She shied away from the idea of breaking and entering, not so much because she felt it would be wrong, as from a sudden sense of claustrophobia at the thought of being trapped inside one of those buildings. As long as Dosha and Leila Azari were around, she wanted to be free to run.

She came upon a large hole and stared at the muddy water that had been captured in it. It seemed out of place. No construction barriers around it. All at once, amid the incessant pounding of artillery fire echoing from the mountains behind the city, she knew what had caused it and hurried on, suddenly anxious to get away.

As Jessica continued walking, she saw the spires of an old cathedral straight ahead, facing onto a small city square. Coming closer, she saw that it was one of the few buildings in the area that had not suffered the wounds of war.

Jessica started toward it when she heard something behind her. Glancing back, she saw a small, dark-colored car come around the corner, moving slowly in her direction.

Maybe it is the police. Or, Mom and Dad looking for me.

Jessica halted, bone weary from the constant tension of running and hiding, desperately wanting this car to be the answer to all her prayers. Her emotional resources spent, she leaned against the nearby building. She knew she was not thinking clearly, and it no longer seemed to matter.

This has to be a policeman. Who else would be out here tonight? But, what if they're like the policemen in Iran? Oh, dear. What if it's not a policeman? What if it is . . .

The car suddenly sped up and headed toward her. Something snapped inside.

Run, Jessica, run. You can't trust anybody!

Fantasy gave way to reality. She was back on the streets again, running for her life, and she knew it. Jessica sprinted to the next opening between buildings, about half the distance to the corner. It was another narrow alley and she dashed into it, feet splashing in the mud and water. A car door slammed.

Someone has gotten out.

As the car sped off she knew instinctively that whoever had gotten out would follow her on foot. And, whoever was inside the car was turning at the corner. She heard tires squealing in the distance. The driver was racing around to where this alley opened onto the next street. Gauging the distance in her mind, she knew she was going to lose. The car and driver had the advantage. She was trapped!

Jessica ran with her left hand out, keeping her balance by feeling the wall. Otherwise, she would have missed it. For a brief instant, there was no building to touch. She stopped so fast that she slipped and fell. Quickly, she got up and investigated, feeling with her hands in the dark. There was a small opening between two buildings. She dodged into a space that turned out to be barely wide enough to stand in without twisting around. Pausing for a moment to catch her breath, she heard footsteps. She had been right. Someone was coming down the alley after her. Waiting silently, afraid to move, she watched through the narrow opening as a sinister shadow passed across her line of vision and disappeared out of sight.

Jessica let out a sigh and pushed on through the passage that was really nothing more than a place for stray cats to run. The farther she went, the tighter it became. Looking up, she could see nothing but walls that appeared as though they came together, high over where she stood. Ahead, however, she could see a narrow opening, outlined by a lighter shade of darkness than she was in. She pressed forward by turning sideways, hands at her sides, and sliding her body between the two cement block walls. Finally, not more than six feet from the end, the crevice became too tight even for her willowy figure. She pulled back, at the same time fighting off another wave of claustrophobia. In frustration, she pounded against the wall with her fist, fighting back tears that persisted in rolling out onto her already rain-dampened cheeks.

What was that?

Jessica looked back along the short distance over which she had managed to work her way. Her pursuers had not seen her come out. They must have surmised that she was still somewhere in the alley. She felt it. Someone was in the passage with her!

"Jessica," the voice called out softly.

A man's voice . . . one she would never forget. The man with the scar. Jessica froze. He couldn't see her if she didn't move. Could he?

"Jessica, I know you're in here."

He was getting closer. What to do? Frantically, Jessica looked back at the opening.

"Your jacket."

What?

"Take off your jacket."

The voice was real. Or was it? Jessica was so frightened that she wasn't sure what "real" was or wasn't anymore.

"Take off your jacket."

There it was again.

"Jessica . . ."

That voice is real enough. And he's closer than before!

Jessica slid her hand up and unbuttoned the jacket she had been given on board the *Evvoia*. She was almost out of it when . . . he was there!

"Come here, you little . . ."

Jessica screamed and pressed further into the narrow crack. The man's hand brushed against her shoulder and, all at once, the jacket was gone. Without its bulk, Jessica squeezed farther forward in the crevice.

"Come here," the voice snarled again.

He was close enough for her to see the shadowy outline of his face, even the scar that ran along his cheek. She screamed again.

"Give it up, kid," he growled, reaching in after her.

Jessica could hear his heavy breathing and the scraping of his feet in the mud, as he tried to push his way farther into the crack between the walls. She pressed forward again, her body scraping against the rough cement as she tried to stay away from him. His hand was there again. She felt him grasp at her arm.

"No!"

Desperately, she twisted forward, as hard as she could, smashing the man's hand against the cement. He cursed in surprise, as much as in pain, but it was enough. For a split second, his grip loosened.

And then, all at once, she was moving. A few inches. Just beyond his reach. A few more. And, suddenly, she stumbled out onto the street, falling against a lamppost to catch her breath. Her shirt was torn both in front and in back. Looking down, she saw scratches on her chest and supposed they were repeated on her back from having wedged through the cramped space.

She could hear the man cursing now and calling for Leila, his voice growing more distant with each shout, indicating a hasty retreat. Jessica looked around, knowing that she had to do something. But, what? Then, she spied the cathedral again . . . a sanctuary, a place of safety. The church had been that to her all her young life. Now she needed it more than ever. As fast as she could, Jessica ran toward the old building.

"YOU DIDN'T GET HER?" questioned Leila, standing by the open car door at the far end of the alley. "What happened?"

"Never mind. She's like a cat, that one, but her nine lives are about to end. Turn around and go back to the other street. Hurry, before she gets away again!"

While Leila threw the car in gear, Dosha reached into the glove compartment for a flashlight. With one foot on the brake and the other on the accelerator, she turned the wheel and skidded around until they were facing the opposite direction. An instant later, they slid around the corner and drove out into the open square.

"Easy, easy," Dosha motioned with his hand, not for one moment taking his eyes off the scene before him. Good news and bad. The good news, he thought, was the fact that the streets and the square were empty. People were inside tonight, protecting themselves as best they could from those crazy Serbs up in the hills. That meant they could move about in their search with relative ease. The bad news was the same. The streets and the square were empty. The girl had disappeared again.

"Where could she have gone so quickly? Would she retrace her steps into the alley?"

"No," Dosha answered. "She knows better than to go back into that alley. She's out here somewhere. The only question is where."

They drove around the square, returning finally to the spot where Jessica had escaped. Dosha cursed again as he stared at the tiny opening she had slipped through. Then his eyes darted around the square.

"She's here, Leila. I can feel it. She has got to be hiding here somewhere. Drive up to the corner. Then, you take that side and I'll take this one. Try all the doors. See if any are unlocked. If you find one, signal, and I will come to you. Watch me and I'll do the same."

Dosha got out and quietly closed the car door. Leila motored up to where the street entered the square, parked, and began walking back on the side opposite Dosha, testing doors as she went. Rain was coming down hard again, pelting them both until they were thoroughly drenched. Leila's dark hair glistened with dampness as she hurried up the steps of the church two at a time and pushed on the door. It opened.

She turned and waved at Dosha, on his way to the next doorway. When he saw her signal, he stopped what he was doing and ran the remaining distance across the square to join her on the steps.

"It's unlocked?"

"Yes."

"Then she's inside. She's got to be."

Dosha pushed the door open and they stepped inside.

"We need some light," Leila whispered quietly, as she felt along the wall for a switch.

"No!" Dosha put a hand on her arm. "We'll use my flashlight. Light up this place and we'll attract attention. Everything else has been blacked out since the shelling began, and we don't want anyone coming in while we are here. We certainly don't want to offer those artillery crews up in the mountains a real target. They probably even have SAMs . . . if they don't light them off in the wrong direction."

"You don't think much of the Serbs," Leila chuckled, in spite of the seriousness of the moment.

"I hate them," replied Dosha, oblivious to the shortcomings of his own self-styled morality. "I don't want to come back here until there is only one person left standing in the whole country. Then, I will gladly return and kill him, just to make certain that none are left to repopulate the earth. Now, let's find our little friend. You take the stairs up to the balcony. Wait at the top until I give you some illumination."

Dosha switched on the flashlight, grunting approval at its surprisingly powerful beam. It lit up the large, solid oak doors that, on Sunday, would open wide to welcome those parishioners daring enough to leave their homes and venture out to the house of God. He stepped forward into the center aisle, slowly moving the light back and forth between the well-worn pews.

Pausing at the center of the building, he turned abruptly and flashed the powerful beam toward the rear balcony. The light illuminated the cathedral organ and, above it, ranks of long, slender pipes. He moved the light across the balcony and then back again as Leila surveyed the area from her position at the top of the stairs. Finally, she shook her head and disappeared into the darkened staircase.

Dosha then trained the light on the wood-carved pulpit that towered above the empty pews. He climbed the steps until he was standing in the pulpit, moving the light in random, twisting patterns across the cavernous room, but revealing only an esoteric mix of stone gargoyles and radiant Madonnas. The beam passed across a large, circular rose window in the nave, above the baptismal font.

Standing at either side of the sanctuary, Dosha and Leila continued to check under each row; they tested the two side exits and found them locked. Then, stepping up to the chancel area, they examined the altar and two small rows of pews off to one side, facing three high-backed chairs on the other. Nothing.

Puzzled, Dosha motioned to Leila and they retreated from the chancel down the center aisle, until reaching the large doors through which they had entered. He switched the light off and, leaning toward Leila, whispered, "Stay here. Don't move."

Then, his voice cut through the darkness. "I must have been mistaken. She's not here. Let's go."

Opening the door, he glanced down at his wristwatch in the half light, then pushed the door shut. The sound of its closing reverberated through the sanctuary. They stood quietly, hardly breathing, listening for some sound of the girl as she emerged from a cleverly concealed hiding place, under the mistaken impression that her nemeses had given up. She had to come this way. It was the only available exit.

Five minutes

Ten.

At last, Dosha broke the stillness as he shuffled his feet. He switched on the flashlight, pointing it away from him while checking his wristwatch.

Seventeen minutes.

"She's not here," he said with a sigh, "or she would have shown herself by now. She must have hidden in some other place. Let's go back to the car."

Dosha returned the flashlight to a pocket, pulled the damp collar of his jacket up around his neck, and opened the door. Leila stepped through first, while Dosha took one final glance back into the darkened interior of the old church. Then, he walked out into the night. Quickly, they jogged across the square to where Leila had parked their auto. She slid in behind the wheel and looked inquiringly at Dosha. He said nothing, hands pushed deep in his jacket, a dispirited demeanor on his face as he stared at tiny rivulets of rain running down the window.

"Do you think that she might try returning to the docks?" Leila asked, breaking the silence at last.

Dosha's eyes closed for a moment, as though pushing the question away from his thoughts. When he finally looked at her, it was with a dark, smoldering rage that caused her to bite her lip and wish she had remained silent.

"It's too dangerous for us to go and see," he said at last. "You can count on policemen being there through the night, thanks to whoever blew away that warehouse. If she does go back, well, that's that."

There was resignation in his voice as he glared out the window.

"Maybe she'll die first from pneumonia," he spit the words out like bullets, suddenly banging his fist against the door.

People seldom outsmarted Marwan Dosha, and he detested those rare occasions when it happened. Always achieving his ghastly goals was one of the reasons the world had placed him at the top of its list of most-wanted terrorists. Remaining there was important to him. It was his raison d'etre.

Among his own kind, he was heralded as an Olympian of sorts, the Champion of Bad, the man looked up to by thousands of rock-throwing youth. His compatriots often joked that if he were an American, his face would be on Wheaties boxes at every breakfast table. They offered his ego the constant reassurance that he was indeed the most venerable and feared man in the world. Ultimately, the splendor of it all, the glory of being Marwan Dosha, had ignited the low flame of madness that causes every morally irrational being to boil over with diabolic acts.

There is a kind of insanity that slowly and indiscriminately overtakes rock stars and athletes, TV evangelists and politicians, successful professionals and world leaders, anyone who finally falls into the subtle trap of believing their own press releases and the praises of those who have something personal to gain. Without realizing it, Dosha had been overtaken and then completely enveloped by the flame. Now, it controlled him, fueling his passions, stoking his dreams and, more recently, blurring his instincts. Like some insidious and beguiling siren, its fervid voice called to him, urging him ever closer to the ruinous rock from which the mythical Lorelei beckoned.

To be outwitted by a twelve-year-old . . . and a girl at that! Dosha shivered. Was it the cold and the rain? Or something else? If his followers were to get wind of this . . . his eyes shifted back to Leila for an instant.

"When presented with an unexpected problem, as is often the case in my business, you learn to punt."

"Punt?"

"An American football term. It means that we are still in the game, but we must readjust our plan by playing defensively for a while, before taking over the ball once more and scoring the winning touchdown."

"How will we do that?" Leila asked, not at all sure that she understood what he was talking about.

"Instead of waiting until Easter, we're going to cut the time shorter. It will mean a loss in anticipated income," he continued, his words sounding like the evaluation of an investment downturn on Wall Street, "but no matter. I'll have my contact in Zurich arrange to gather up the gifts so graciously donated by our public thus far and then wish them all a Merry Christmas."

"A Merry Christmas?"

Dosha chuckled, the inner rage already stemmed and stored away, as thoughts of the next few days replaced it with a grim smile.

"Come. We need some rest. At daylight, we'll cross over to Italy. The ferry should be running. If not, we can hire a fishing trawler. Once we are in Italy, you and I will begin wrapping a special present. Or, perhaps I should say 'unwrapping.'"

Leila looked at him curiously. Then, pushing in the clutch, she turned the ignition and twisted the wheels away from the curb.

Seconds later, but for the incessant sounds of shelling in the distance, the square was empty and quiet.

EXACTLY HOW MUCH TIME had passed, she was not certain. It felt like it must have been at least an hour. Slowly, she raised herself from the prone position in which she had been lying. Every muscle in her body was quick to remind her of having recently been abused. Finally in a sitting position, she paused to stretch her arms and legs. Hunching her shoulders, and leaning forward as far as possible, she felt her back pop twice, giving some relief.

Jessica's eyes had grown accustomed to the darkness, enabling her to discern the details of her hiding place. She let her legs dangle freely, on either side of her twelve-inch-wide perch, while the circulation of blood worked its way into her extremities.

Two stories beneath the traverse beam that stretched across the width of the cathedral, her abductors had searched in vain while Jessica watched their every move.

When she had entered the church, she was desperate with fear. Dashing up the stairs to the balcony, she saw several beams spanning the width of the sanctuary. The only possibility for reaching the nearest one was a narrow ledge that ran along the wall. Desperate for a place to hide, Jessica's mind flashed back to another place and another ledge. Taking a deep breath, she started to climb.

Once over the balcony railing, she found hand and toeholds that carried her another four feet higher to the ledge. Then, pressing her body against the cold, cement wall, she eased herself along. It was a distance of about six feet, but it felt like forever until her right hand touched the wooden beam. Jessica twisted around, pulling herself onto its surface, and was just getting settled when she heard the doors open below. Lying flat, she checked the beam's edges, making certain that no part of her slender form was exposed. She thought they would have to throw a light on her directly from the balcony, or from the very front of the church, before she could be seen. It was a chance she had to accept.

Jessica closed her eyes.

Jesus, I need You once again to save me. Blind their eyes. Don't let them see me here.

Then she turned her attention to the drama far below. Once, while Dosha was shining his light up into the balcony, Jessica had almost been overcome, not with fear but with the accumulated dust that covered the beam's surface. She put her fingers over her nostrils and held her breath. The sneeze exploded inside her, with only a minuscule puff of breath and scattering of dust. She waited, afraid to move, but the feared words, "There she is!" never came.

Eventually, she was even able to smile as her kidnappers made a pretense of leaving the building, in hopes of drawing her out. They stood under the balcony, just out of sight, for a long while. Then, finally, they were gone . . . or so it seemed.

Jessica waited. As time passed, she found herself fighting off exhaustion. To fall asleep up here was inviting disaster. She had to get down. She scooted back to the wall and then twisted around until she was facing it. At this point, she did not want to look down. Getting down from the beam and onto the balcony was going to be harder than getting up. Every move had to be slow and precise.

Carefully, she worked her way onto the ledge, pausing to catch her breath while gathering up the necessary courage. Releasing the stored-up air in her lungs, she tried to relax as she inched away from the wooden beam, never taking her eye off the balcony.

Easy does it. One more step.

As she put her foot down and started to shift her weight onto it, the aging cement ledge suddenly crumbled and broke away, throwing her off balance.

There was nothing to hold onto.

Her body teetered backward, away from the wall.

In sheer desperation, Jessica lunged for the railing as she fell!

Rain clouds continued to break apart against mountains that vanished mysteriously into their murky mists. The sun never really rose; the day just grew lighter, revealing the city of Split snaked along the Dalmatian coast.

Its five- and six-story high-rises, favored by the socialists of another era, were clustered in the center of a town that once had been a favorite of Gaius Aurelius Valerius Diocletianus, emperor of the Roman Empire, A.D. 284–305. The remains of Diocletian's palace continued to attract history buffs and visiting tourists.

At either end of the "snake" were hundreds of small houses, most with red tile roofs that bleached lighter in the hot summer's sun, returning to the color of red wine under the winter rains. In front of the city, the dark blue Adriatic had, during the night, donned whitecaps that now dotted its surface as far as the eye could see. And, behind it all were the mountains.

Raindrops fell gently along the cloud-shrouded slopes this morning, on vineyards and gardens that stretched down to the sea. From those same lofty heights, mortar and artillery fire had torn into the city throughout the night.

For the moment, all was quiet, but that was about to change.

IN FRONT OF ONE OF THE RED-ROOFED HOUSES dotting the northern edge of town, a dark blue import, with a small rental sticker on the rear bumper, straddled a dirt path leading up to the door. Except for the car, the house looked abandoned. Curtains were drawn over its two small windows. The houses on either side of this one were devoid of any human activity as well.

Inside, wrapped in separate blankets on a single bare mattress, a man and woman stirred restlessly. Some pieces of clothing were draped over the top of an open door. Still others had been spread out to dry on two metal chairs and a small table in the only other room in the house.

Marwan Dosha and Leila Azari had not given up the search until after two o'clock, even though Serbian shelling of the city had made driving and walking a life-threatening experience. The fact that few people dared to venture out had made searching more simple. Anything that moved might be the girl. But there had been no further sign of her.

SPLIT'S SMALL AIRPORT TERMINAL had taken a direct hit from artillery fire three months ago. This was prior to the Serbian and Muslim leaders declaring a moratorium in order to gather around the negotiation table with UN peacekeepers, to determine a "just settlement" for the twenty-fifth time. Or was it the fiftieth? The gaping wound near the north end of the building had been patched over with pieces of wood and plastic to keep out the rain and cold. It worked as well as most things in this beleaguered nation, keeping out much of the rain and letting in most of the cold.

Actually, officials had stopped heating the building long before that. The old man said he thought it had been shut off two, no, maybe three cease-fires ago, cackling loudly over his bit of twisted humor. This morning, the scruffy-looking character, eyes haunted by a thousand days of war, whose job it had been to handle airline passenger baggage during better times, busied himself by passing hot cups of coffee to each of his visitors, compliments of an earlier UN supply run, similar to the one the Americans had come in on the day before.

Handing the phone pack to one of the soldiers, the CG walked over to where the others huddled together in a vain attempt at getting warm.

"Word has it that the shelling has begun again. Serbian troops have surrounded the city. It looks as though they are concentrating on the center of town, but air observers have identified artillery movement not too far from here. They expect that by this afternoon, the airport could go. There's one more UN flight on the way in right now. It should be here in an hour. When it turns around, we've got to be on it."

"No!" Esther fairly shouted, jumping to her feet. The inflection of her voice mirrored the distressed look she gave Banks. "Not without our daughter."

"Mrs. Cain, I understand how you feel, but we really have no choice. . . ."

"No!" she exclaimed again, starting to cry, hands clenched tightly at her sides. "You *don't* understand, Mr. Banks. You just don't. There is no way that you can understand how I . . . how we . . . feel. Our daughter has been gone three months. John and Herschel have risked their lives trying to reach her. Yesterday we stood on the wrong dock while Jessica was being stalked by a killer, half a mile away. She's out there, Mr. Banks, and she's by herself. I know that she's alive. Now, you want us to just fly away and leave her here? You've got to be out of your mind to think that we could ever do such a thing!"

John put his arm around Esther and drew her close. He could feel the rigidity in her slender body, and the pent-up emotion, and sensed that she was near the breaking point. He decided that he wasn't far from it himself.

How much more disappointment can we take without coming unraveled?

"We understand that you may have to leave, Mr. Banks," said John. "And Mr. Creston too. I won't speak for Jim or Hersch, but Esther and I stay, until we find her."

Banks looked at Grandpa Brainard and Herschel. They glanced at each other and nodded.

"We're with John and Esther," Herschel affirmed solemnly, "until this is over."

Banks sighed and turned away, but not before glancing over at the CNN news team. They had said very little, but Banks thought they would probably opt for getting out at the first chance. The others, he knew, would not come without force, and he was not prepared to go that far. He had expected as much anyway, when first he broached the subject. What a mess!

JESSICA CRAWLED OUT FROM UNDER the organ bench and stood shakily to her feet. The rose window at the far end of the nave could be seen clearly now, in the gray light that filtered through the ancient lead glass.

How long have I been sleeping?

She let herself drop back onto the bench as she reviewed the events of the night. Especially that final frightening moment!

Looking up at the transverse beam on which she had hidden, her eyes trailed back across the ledge along the wall. What she saw caused her heart to beat faster as she traced the nearly invisible path to her hideaway.

How could I have done that?

She easily made out the spot that had given way on her return, and stared for a long time, swallowing once again the feeling . . . *the incredible feeling of falling . . .*

Pushing away from the wall . . . coming off the ledge so strongly that she hit the balcony railing full force . . . knocking the wind out of her . . . fighting to catch her breath. In the same instant, she felt herself sliding backward, off the rail, frantically groping for some way to stop!

It was the inside of her upper arm that finally caught the rail, bruising the tender skin as the entire weight of her body shifted to it. Her fall slowed just enough for her to twist around and grasp hold of the top edge with her right hand, while her feet still dangled helplessly in space. It felt as though her arm were tearing away from its socket as Jessica drew on every remaining ounce of energy to pull herself up and over the rail, before crumbling in a heap on the wooden floor. When she was finally able, she crawled on hands and knees to the organ bench and wept uncontrollably. She tugged and pulled until it came far enough away from the pedals for her to get underneath. The bench offered paltry protection; but, for the moment anyway, it sufficed a young girl's need to be covered by something. . . .

Getting to her feet, Jessica pushed the frightful memory out of her mind and tugged the heavy bench back to its original place, not at all certain why she did so. Then, she walked slowly down the steps until she stood in front of the doors through which she had entered some hours before. Taking hold of the ornate handle, she pushed until it opened just enough for her to peer out through the crack. The square was empty.

It had almost stopped raining by the time Jessica emerged from the cathedral. The temperature had dropped during the night, and her clothing was cold and stiff. It had seemed at least as cold inside the church as it was outside. Her hands were a bluish white and the tips of her fingers and toes were numb. She rubbed her hands together and stomped her feet vigorously until they began to tingle.

Walking stiffly, Jessica crossed the cobblestones in front of the church, working sore muscles as she went. Nobody was around. For the first time, she became aware of the quiet. It looked like a ghost city, though Jessica was sure that behind the shuttered windows, above the empty shops and offices that surrounded much of the square, people had lived through the terror of the night with much the same fear as she had. There was no way anyone could ever get used to this.

Jessica stayed in the alleys, walking aimlessly, not sure what to do next. After a few blocks, she came onto another small public square where there were signs of human activity. Shrinking back, she watched for a while.

In front of a five-story building, with its first-floor doors open onto the square, Jessica saw people of all ages milling back and forth. Some carried old suitcases while others had simply wrapped their few remaining possessions in blankets. Two white buses were parked in front of the doorway. Near each bus, men in military uniforms, wearing white helmets, were shouting out names and giving directions as the people crowded around to board. Jessica moved further out, staying along the edge of the nearby buildings until she could see on the sides of the buses the letters UN.

UN. Mom and Dad were coming here on a UN airplane. That's what Captain Callimachus had said. Do you suppose these people are from the United Nations?

The soldier closest to her was attempting to help an old man and woman who had shuffled up to the door of the bus. Each of them were bent under the burden of blankets filled with their possessions. She heard the soldier saying something to them as he pointed to the blankets. The man's voice raised in protest and the old woman tried to climb into the bus with her full blanket. The load was too heavy, however, and the first step too high for her. A younger man stepped forward to help but she pushed him away. He stepped back protectively beside his wife and two small children and waited as the soldier tried to communicate to the old couple.

By this time, Jessica realized that the soldier was not speaking the same language as the old couple. It sounded like he was speaking French. She remembered hearing the language spoken by missionaries visiting in their home.

The soldier pointed to a small pile of suitcases along the side of the bus. The old woman shook her head violently and tried to get on once again, her best efforts resulting only in blocking the entry for others. The soldier lifted his hands in exasperation, saying something to the young man with the family. The young man shook his head. Jessica was shocked by what she heard next.

"Do you speak English?" the soldier asked.

"A little," the young father replied.

"Will you explain to these people that they must leave their things here by the bus? There is not room inside. We will put as much as we can underneath, in the baggage compartment, but tell them that people are more important than possessions. Do you understand?"

He nodded.

"They are my parents. I will try to speak to them again. They are very upset."

"Tell them that the most important thing is for us to get them out of here and to a safe place. If they don't cooperate, I'll be forced to leave them here."

The young man nodded again as a look of concern flashed across his face. Then he turned to talk to his parents. When he had finished, it was clear to Jessica that they had understood. Slowly, they turned and walked over to the pile of suitcases and boxes and dropped their load next to it. With cold and wrinkled fingers, the old woman fumbled over the knotted blanket until it opened. Reaching down, she withdrew two items and then stood back as the young man helped her retie the bundle.

Jessica watched, curious as to what the items were, when the woman turned in her direction, her back to the bus. She was crying. The old man shuffled over to her, and tenderly put his arms around her, whispering something in her ear. Then, they disappeared into the bus.

Jessica wiped at her eyes. She had seen what the old woman had in her hands and was strangely touched by it. Out of all her worldly goods, she had chosen two framed pictures.

I wonder who was in those pictures. Were they wedding pictures? Her parents? Her children?

Jessica shook her head. What things in life were ultimately too dear to lose? Right now, she could think of only one.

Life itself.

Jessica desperately wanted to stay alive. To go home. To be with her family. She continued watching as the young man, together with his wife and the two children, moved closer to one of the buses.

Shall I take the chance? It looks like they're treating these people okay. Maybe they'll help me.

She started toward the buses.

You can't trust anybody, Jessica.

The words reverberated in her mind as she stopped.

You can't trust anybody!

Jessica hesitated, uncertain of her next move.

What shall I do?

Suddenly, Captain Callimachus' face flashed across her mind. Then, Timothy Marcos and the other members of the *Evvoia* crew.

I wonder if I could get back to the ship. If the man with the scar and Leila are still looking for me, wouldn't they be thinking the same thing? They could be waiting for me to show up there. And, besides, even if they aren't, how would I ever get out to the ship?

The buses were almost finished loading. The young man was ushering his wife and children up into the bus that the older couple had boarded. If she was going to do anything, she had to make her move now.

Jessica swallowed.

Jesus, please, take care of me now.

She ran across the cobblestones and up to the soldier. He turned when he felt her pull on his arm.

"Qui va là?" he said, with a friendly grin. *Who goes there?*

"Are you with the United Nations?" Jessica asked, her heart pounding.

"Oui."

"Mister, I know you speak English," she blurted. "My name is Jessica Cain. I'm an American citizen and I need you to help me. Will you? Please?"

THE SOLDIER PEERED THROUGH a telescopic lens at the scene below. He was one of the first to have entered the city, a harbinger of what was yet to come. Though only eighteen, he had already distinguished himself in Sarajevo as a sniper extraordinaire. However, what he saw before him deserved more than a sniper's bullet. These people needed to learn, once and for all, that there was no place left for them to run. He put down the field glasses and began opening the Stinger missile container that he had carried on his back to the rooftop.

FIFTY-TWO

The mood in the Split Airport waiting area was painful, to say the least. Dan Banks tried to divert his gaze from the Cains, but every now and then he caught himself staring at them. Was it guilt stemming from their failure to have picked up the girl in time? He glanced over at Creston sitting slightly apart from the rest, hands folded in his lap, looking positively miserable. Or maybe he was simply curious as to how these parents could hold up under the pressure of such excruciating circumstances. He wasn't sure.

One thing for certain, he thanked his lucky stars that his own two kids were safe, back in America, one a senior at William and Mary College, the other a graduate student at Yale. At least he hoped they were safe—word of the spreading rash of terrorist disasters in the United States was disquieting. What if someone decided to plant a bomb at the schools his children attended? He suddenly wished that he knew just how many Jewish kids were enrolled on those campuses. Just as quickly, he chided himself over having entertained such a racist question.

Maybe I'm getting a little paranoid. And if that's the case for me, what about all the other parents in America?

Looking around the small circle, he noted that Towner was resting his leg on a pair of steel folding chairs. His back was against the wall and eyes were closed.

Sleeping? I doubt it. He looks uncomfortable. I'll bet that leg is hurting.

It did appear that Mrs. Cain was sleeping, however. About an hour ago, she had finally succumbed to the insistence of the others and curled up on a straight-back vinyl sofa. Her head rested on John's lap.

Banks had decided that he liked John Cain. He seemed to be a cool one. The account he had read in *Newsweek*, and the September Strike television special he had seen on Sky Europe had not been exaggerated, though at the time he had wondered. He was impressed with the way Cain handled himself. After giving up the search early that morning, it was John who, with Banks' encouragement, had convinced the others that they should all return to the airport and wait until it was light before doing anything further. He was certain that it had run counter to what John Cain really wanted to do, but it had been the best choice.

Banks knew that they should all get out of Split right away. Things were seriously coming apart here. Word from the UN Peacekeeping Force was not good. The Serbs appeared to be closing in for the kill. Split was going to fall, probably in a matter of two or three days. The question was no longer "if," but "when." He also knew that Cain meant it when he said they were not leaving. And, as one father to another, he admired him for it.

The old man was another likable character. He watched Jim Brainard turn a page in the small New Testament in his hand. Though Banks was not a churchgoer, it warmed him to see a man drawing strength from his faith. Somewhere deep inside, a still uncultivated part of his own spirit wished that he could do the same.

Maybe when I get home...

At first he had not made the connection with this old man and Marwan Dosha. In fact, he had wondered why John Cain had insisted on his joining them, deciding initially that he had simply not wanted his wife to travel alone for such a distance. How fortunate for them all that Brainard had been here. He was the only one who could have recognized Dosha. Who knows what might have happened if he had not?

"Mr. Banks, sir. Phone message."

The soldier with the phone pack called out from the far side of the room. Out of the corner of his eye, the CG saw Esther stir.

Why couldn't he just have brought the phone over instead of yelling?

Frowning, he got to his feet and crossed to where the young man waited, taking the receiver in his hand.

"This is Dan Banks. . . . What?" Banks turned away from the

others and lowered his voice. "Repeat that, please. . . . Are you able to verify? . . . All right. Can you bring her in? . . . I see. Well, then, we're on our way. I'm giving you back to our driver."

He handed the phone back to the soldier.

"He's going to give you directions. Before you hang up, be absolutely certain you know how to get to where he is. I don't want us winding up someplace else. Got it?"

"Yes, sir."

Banks stared out the window, gathering his thoughts as he watched several soldiers loading the last of the most recent air shipment of food and emergency medical supplies onto trucks. He motioned to the CNN team to follow him, and then walked over to where the others were seated. He saw that Mrs. Cain was sitting up now, brushing hair away from her face.

"John," he spoke quietly. "Mrs. Cain."

Towner lifted his leg off the chairs.

Jim Brainard closed the New Testament.

John and Esther sat side by side, absolutely still, her right hand clenched onto his left.

Waiting.

It was the tone in Banks' voice. Everyone knew. Something had happened. Good or bad, this was it.

"Your daughter has been found," Banks announced quietly, unable to keep the emotion from his voice.

No one moved, silently waiting to hear his next words.

"She's alive."

The next sixty seconds were sheer pandemonium! John and Esther leaped to their feet and threw their arms around each other.

"Oh, thank You, Jesus, thank You, thank You, thank You," Esther cried over and over, gratefully melding her body into John's as they held each other tightly.

Herschel limped over and pounded John on the back with one hand. With the other, he was wiping his eyes.

"I knew we'd get her," he exclaimed excitedly. "I just knew it."

Jim Brainard wrapped his arms around John and Esther. In a voice husky with feeling, he said, "Congratulations, you two. You've persevered and now God is answerin' your prayers. And, I'm lookin' forward to finally meetin' this new granddaughter of mine."

Then the questions. Where is she? How did they find her? Are you sure that she's all right?

"That's all I know for the moment. Our driver has the instructions. They don't have a way to bring her in right now. It's an area where they're moving out refugees. So what are we waiting for?" Banks smiled. "Let's get her. Go and get into the jeeps. I'll follow."

As the others rushed to leave, Banks pulled Creston aside.

"It was you who contacted the refugee points with word about the girl, right?"

"Yes, sir," answered Creston with a sheepish grin, the kind seen on a child's face when caught in the act of doing something good.

"Excellent. I should have thought of that, but I missed it."

"You've had a lot on your mind, sir."

They walked outside together toward the others.

"Sir?"

"Yes?"

"I'm sorry I messed up yesterday. I . . . there's no excuse, sir. I just blew it."

"I know you did. It surprised me, but we all make mistakes. The key is never to make the same one twice. Besides, with a few well-placed phone calls, you've made a more than adequate recovery. You're a good man, Milt. Don't ever forget it. I'm glad to have you on my staff."

Then they joined the rest, climbing into the jeeps, laughing and pounding one another jubilantly as they drove off toward the city.

THE BUSES WERE ALMOST LOADED by the time the Serbian teenager had flipped open the cover on the large plastic box. He saw black smoke pouring from the exhaust of the bus closest to him, indicating that the driver had started its engine. Carefully, he lifted the Stinger missile to his shoulder, listening to the beeping of the missile tracker that assured him that he had acquisition.

A second later, he loosed his shot.

1010 LOCAL TIME

AS THEIR JEEPS RACED into the city's central district, the streets seemed almost ghostlike, in the absence of traffic. Only a few trucks filled with armed men hurried along the city's main boulevard. A lone pedestrian ran across the street ahead of them and disappeared inside a building.

"The man I talked with said they were located near the city center, so it shouldn't be much farther," Banks said, leaning over to John. "Strange to see an entire city hunkered down like this, isn't it?"

"Exactly what I was thinking," John replied, hanging on as they rounded a corner. "Have you noticed that no traffic lights are working?"

"Yes. This is not a good day for the people of Split. I think we're getting out of here just in time."

"It should be just ahead, sir," the driver called out, as they sped past a cobblestone square.

"Look at that old cathedral, John." Esther pointed as she spoke. Isn't it beautiful?"

"It is indeed."

"When you see something like that, it is so hard to believe there's actually a war going on around us."

John smiled and drew her close. He started to answer at the exact moment their vehicle turned onto yet another square. No sooner had they driven into the open area than the driver slammed his brakes. The second jeep, but for the quick reflexes of its driver, would have rammed them from behind.

"Back up, back up!" shouted the lead driver.

Both vehicles were already retreating, and John heard Banks curse.

"Get out. Take cover!" the soldier was shouting again, waving them out of the jeep and under a narrow building overhang. John saw the young man drop down by the jeep, M-16 ready, as he scanned the windows and rooftops of the buildings opposite them. Satisfied that they were safe for the moment, he ran beyond the jeep to the edge of the square, not more than twenty feet away. Then he doubled back to where they stood, crowded together in horror and disbelief.

"Sir, it's a mess out there. They've taken out a bus load of people, probably the refugees. I see one of ours down. There are bodies everywhere."

"Can you tell what happened?"

"Could be a bomb, but my guess is a missile, sir. Probably from up there somewhere." He pointed his rifle over their heads.

"Any signs of life?"

"It's hard to say, sir. I thought I saw some people moving off to one side, but I'm not sure."

Just then, John turned loose of his grip on Esther and walked out onto the sidewalk.

"Come back, sir," the soldier ordered. "You can't go out there."

"And you can't stop me, soldier. I've got to find my daughter."

"But sir, I can't let you go. It's too dangerous."

"Leave me alone!" The look on John's face caused the soldier to hesitate. He looked over at Banks.

Banks shook his head. "Let him go. Can you get across the street and watch for snipers?"

He nodded and ran off toward a boarded-up office building.

"You, son," Banks motioned to the other soldier, "cover us. I'm going with him."

"I'm going too," said Esther, a determined look on her face.

"No, Mrs. Cain. There may still be someone up there. If there is, he's ready to shoot anything that moves."

"Mr. Banks, I expect that I've already been shot more times than any man here. Now, step aside or go with me. My daughter is out there. Dead or alive, I have a right to look for her!"

They could hear sirens wailing in the distance. Help was apparently on the way. With a sense of resignation, John held out his hand. He wanted her to stay protected, far from the horror just around the corner, but he knew Esther.

"Stay close, hon. Let's go."

"I'm coming too," declared Jim Brainard. "Might as well give them as many targets as possible."

He looked over at the soldier. "If he drops one of us, son, you nail him before he gets anybody else. Okay?"

The soldier blinked and nodded, finding it hard to believe what he was seeing and hearing. The same could have been said for the CNN crew. They had been on a lot of assignments before, but this one was more than anything they had ever experienced.

"That's an order, son," Jim called over his shoulder as he ran after the others. "Hersch, get ready to bring one of those jeeps out in a hurry."

Towner moved as quickly as he could, falling into the driver's seat of the lead vehicle and forcing the foot on his wounded leg to rest on the accelerator. All the while, he scanned every window and rooftop in his line of vision for some sign of snipers, wishing desperately he could lay his hands on a gun. A quick glance around told him that none was available.

"Stay as close to the buildings as you can," ordered Jim Brainard, as they moved toward the square, at the same time thinking how little one actually forgot between Korea and Croatia. It all came back in a flash. "Spread out and we'll make poorer targets than if we're close together."

At the corner, they stopped to take in the carnage. The bus was a burning hulk. The missile had gone straight up the tailpipe and into the gas tank where it exploded. It was hard to imagine that anyone could have survived. They saw that a second bus had pulled away into the street at the far side of the square. It was damaged, but had not sustained a direct hit. The occupants had managed to get out and were standing about, huddled in small groups, stunned and horrified by what had just happened.

John's first feeling was one of nausea at the sight of so many bodies scattered across the cobblestones. He reached for Esther to shield her from the trauma of what he saw, but it was too late.

"O dear Lord, these poor people," she cried out, stopping to stare in revulsion at the slaughter.

Just then a shot rang out. Screams followed as the refugees scattered, leaving behind one of their own lying in a pool of blood. At the instant the shot rang out, CNN's news team ran for cover. Seconds later, they stopped behind a stone wall, within fifteen feet of the sniper's victim. Without a pause, they continued filming.

In that same terrible instant, John heard two or three bursts to his left. He glanced over to see the driver of their jeep firing from a kneeling position, his arm resting on the edge of a bench that had been placed there for pedestrians to enjoy on a sunny day in Split.

"He's out of it, sir," the soldier shouted. "But we had better hurry. There may be others."

Suddenly, John saw what he was looking for.

"Over here! She's over here!" he shouted, waving to the others.

He ran to where Jessica was sitting, partially hidden behind a wheel that had blown away from the devastated bus.

"Daddy?" Her eyes were dry. "Is it really you?"

"Sweetheart," he exclaimed. Dropping to his knees, he stared at the sight of her. "O sweetheart!"

"I knew you'd come," she said simply, making no attempt to move.

Esther ran up, followed closely by Banks and Jim Brainard.

"O Jessica, my darling Jessica!" she cried as she pushed past the bus wheel and halfway reached for her before hesitating, in shocked disbelief, taking in the same sight that John had just absorbed.

"Hi, Mom," Jessica said softly. Still, there were no tears. No outward emotion at all.

Jessica's shirt was not really a shirt anymore. It hung on her, tattered and ripped, barely covering the upper part of her body, with portions of borrowed underwear peeping through, now strained and soiled and bloody. Her face was puffy and bleeding from a deep cut, high on her forehead. Her lips were bruised and bleeding as well. There were scratches on her arms and one pant leg was torn almost entirely away. Dirt and grime covered what remained of her clothing. Several open scrapes and bruises were visible as well. Esther could see where tiny rock fragments had cut well into the skin's surface.

"Are you all right, honey?" asked Esther, so stunned at the first sight of Jessica that she was now afraid to do what she had dreamed and yearned of doing for so long. Yet, even that was not the supreme astonishment. As her rescuers peered down at Jessica, their gaze was drawn to what she was holding. They watched as, with a tender stroke, she brushed the cheek of the little child cuddled silently in her arms, looking back at them.

"Sir, we've got to get out of here," the soldier pulled on Banks' coat, drawing his attention back to the immediacy of their situation.

"I know," replied Banks, and to the others he said, "Let's go. Is your daughter able to walk? We've got to move it. We're sitting targets here."

Banks' voice brought with it the urgency of their situation.

"Can you walk, honey?" asked John, reaching out to Jessica.

"Yes, I can walk."

John and Esther helped her to her feet. Her legs were wobbly and she started to sag. John put his arm around her waist.

"Here, sweetheart," Esther said, reaching for the child. "Let me take her."

"No!" Jessica's voice was sharp as she tightened her hold on the girl.

"But we need to give her to someone . . ."

"No, I can't give her to anybody. I promised."

"Come on," Banks shouted, waving the jeeps into the square. Towner and the remaining soldier wheeled both vehicles to a skidding stop in front this strange-looking group of Americans that had become a fleeting centerpiece in a war they did not understand. The scene was one of total chaos. Civilians rushed about, weeping and calling for neighbors who were no more. A single ambulance had pulled up near the burning bus, followed by a jeep with three soldiers and a mounted gun. The driver and his assistant got out and just stood there, staring. No one appeared to be in charge.

Banks shrugged. "This is hopeless. Let's go. We'll sort every thing out later."

Towner crawled into the back, along with Jim Brainard and Creston. Banks settled in alongside his driver. Esther helped Jessica and the child into the back of the second jeep. The news team crowded in as well, while John joined the driver in front.

They were halfway across the square when the first artillery shell blew out the top corner of the building directly in front of them. Seconds later, another craterlike hole erupted in the cobblestones, lifting the severed wheel of the bus high in the air before dropping it twenty feet away. Esther looked over her shoulder in horror, as mud and rock rained down on the place where, only moments before, they had all been standing. Wrapping her arms around Jessica, she hung on as the jeep skidded past the corner, leaving the square and its horrible carnage behind them.

Esther could not turn her eyes away from Jessica. She could hardly believe that, at long last, she was right here in her arms. A wave of tears ran down her cheeks. Jessica looked up at her and smiled weakly.

"Hi, Mom," she said again.

Esther wanted to speak, but was too overcome with emotion. She opened her coat and tried to wrap part of it around Jessica's shoulders. Her arm tightened around Jessica and with her other hand she hung on for both of them as they sped through the city. Every few seconds now, artillery shells, mortar, and rocket fire rained down on the city's central district. Straight ahead, dirt, brick, and pieces of roof tile sprayed in all directions from a solid hit on an apartment building. Esther ducked her head, covering Jessica and the child with her body as they passed by.

Each minute felt like an hour, until the sounds of the shelling were well behind them. At least Esther sincerely hoped that was the case. John kept looking back at them, smiling, every once in a while giving a reassuring "okay" signal with his hand. Esther noticed him looking at the child in Jessica's arms and was sure that he had as many questions as she did. There would be time enough for that later.

A sigh of relief escaped her lips as they turned off the main road toward the airport parking lot. Only they did not stop there, but kept going around to the back of the terminal, pulling to a stop near the waiting room exit they had left an eternity ago. In a matter of seconds they were inside.

Banks was instructing the surprised old codger to heat water for some tea. Creston was busy talking on the field telephone to someone. The others had crowded around Jessica while the film crew kept on doing what film crews do.

"How is your daughter?" Banks asked, pushing in alongside John and Esther.

"She looks very thin," answered Esther. Her voice filled with greater concern now that she had a chance to really look at her. "She has several cuts and bruises. There do not seem to be any broken bones or life-threatening wounds, though. I think she's in shock. And . . . wherever she got that little girl, she won't turn loose of her."

Creston tapped Banks on the shoulder. "The plane is coming in now, sir. They figure to be on the ground just long enough to release their load. Thirty minutes max, maybe less. We've got to be ready when they are. It's our last chance to get out."

Banks turned to Esther. "Mrs. Cain, ask her about the child. We've got to decide what to do with her."

Esther nodded and moved in close, kneeling in front of Jessica.

"Honey, are you feeling okay?"

Jessica nodded.

She looked at her carefully. Her green eyes were dull, lacking the luster and snap that Esther remembered.

"Who is this child, sweetheart? How did you get her?"

Jessica stared at the floor without responding.

"Honey, our plane is due in a few minutes. We've got to know more about the girl so that we can help find her parents."

"They're dead."

"What?"

"They're dead. So is her brother."

"Were they . . . in the bus?"

Jessica nodded, her countenance sad and sober now as she looked at her mother. Her eyes flickered at the mention of the bus. And all the while, the little child in her arms never once whimpered or made a sound.

"Her name is Jasmina."

Esther saw the child blink at the mention of her name and look up at Jessica.

"How do you know that? Did you know her parents?"

Jessica shook her head.

"I was talking to the . . . soldier." Jessica spoke deliberately, as though questioning her own memories as they unveiled in slow motion. "I took the chance . . . and talked with him . . . and asked if he would help me."

Esther wondered what she meant by "taking the chance," but said nothing. Her awareness was intensifying with the realization that her little girl had been through only God knew what, and that there now existed within her a deep well of experience that would need to be dipped into carefully.

"And he did help you, didn't he?" coached Esther, her hand lightly touching Jessica's bruised knee.

"Yes. He was a Frenchman, but I knew he spoke English because I heard him. I told him my name and he looked surprised. He said that someone had called earlier and asked them to watch out for me."

The others in the group looked over at Banks questioningly. This was news to them. He motioned with his head toward Creston and smiled.

"We were standing back, away from the bus, when her daddy got off. He was holding her in one arm, you know, like Daddy used to do Jenny?" She looked up at John, and then back to Esther. Her words were coming more rapidly. "He waved to us. I guess he wanted to tell the soldier something. He was only a little ways off when the bus blew up. There was no warning or anything. It just . . . blew up!" Jessica looked away, biting her lip at the memory.

The newsman peered through the eye of his camera, taking everything in, the lens even catching his coworker brushing away an unanticipated tear.

"He . . . and the soldier . . . they were between us and the explosion. I felt myself flying through the air backwards, but I landed on my side, I guess." She glanced down at her leg, with its cuts and scratches.

"There was this heavy weight on top of me. It was . . . " her voice cracked and she cleared her throat. Tears spilled down onto her cheeks now as she looked at Esther. "It was . . . the soldier, Mom. He said he would help. . . . I guess he did, didn't he?"

No one moved, mesmerized by what they were seeing and hearing.

"When I pushed him off of me, I saw the bus. Pieces of it were still falling all around. And there was her daddy . . . hurt very badly. But he moved, so I went to him to see if I could help. And that's when I saw her, still in his arms. I guess he protected her like the soldier did me. I knelt beside him and asked him what I could do, and, he spoke to me in English. He said, 'We are all dead now. No one is left. Please take my little girl. Her name is Jasmina. It is her grandmother's name. You must care for her now. Get her out of here. Will you do this for me?' I didn't know what to say, so I said, 'Yes.' Then he pushed her over to me . . . and he made me promise. 'Please,' he said, 'you must promise.' Those were his exact words. So, I picked her up, and I promised."

Her voice quivered as she looked up at her parents.

"Mom? Daddy? I promised! And then he died."

Jessica lifted the little girl until they looked into one another's eyes. Tears ran freely down Jessica's cheeks now, causing some of those listening to look away in order to gather in their own emotions. Those who saw what happened next said they would never forget it to their dying day.

There were no dry eyes left in the room.

Except for one little person who reached out her small dirty hand and wiped Jessica's tears.

FIFTY-THREE

Milton Creston was torn between the mesmerizing scene unfolding before him in the airport waiting room and the status of the C-130, sitting as vulnerably as the last bald eagle in a forest full of trophy hunters. It was against the rules of conflict for either side to target a UN plane, for they were known to be ferrying only emergency food and medical supplies. But Creston felt sure that some of the "hunters" would not be able to resist bagging such a "trophy" once it had been sighted.

His eyes moved from Jessica and the solemn little Croatian girl to the window, at the precise moment the first artillery shell hit, about two hundred yards away, throwing dirt and brush high into the air.

"Sir," Creston tugged at Banks' arm, "that round was meant for us."

Banks' brow wrinkled with a concerned frown as he walked to the window. The men who had been unloading supplies moved hurriedly to the waiting trucks. One of the UN drivers, who had been speaking over the radio pack, began motioning to Banks and pointing to the airplane. Banks nodded, tossing a knowing glance at Creston as he turned to the others.

"Excuse me for interrupting," he said with an urgency that made everyone look his way. "It is time. I must ask you all to follow our drivers to the vehicles in which you were riding. Move quickly and don't leave anything behind, because we are not coming back."

Those sitting, stood, and began shuffling with the others toward the exit.

"What about this little girl?" Esther asked, looking up at Banks.

"Bring her along. We'll see what we can do for her in Zagreb."

John turned to follow the others. As he did, the old man who had served them tea extended his hand. John took it, looking first at his wrinkled face, then, questioningly at Banks. Banks shook his head. John's gaze returned to the man again, not knowing what to say. The old baggage carrier's eyes said it all.

"Thank you," John spoke finally, gripping his hand tightly. "We are all in God's hands. I will pray for you."

The old man lowered his eyes and nodded, a pathetic smile of resignation flashing briefly across his face, as they released their handshake.

"John?" It was Banks who had called him. The rest were following Esther and Jessica through the door.

"I know," John responded, walking swiftly to catch up with the others. "I know that we can't save the whole world. It's just that, right this minute, the 'whole world' seems to be living and dying in that old man's eyes."

"Unfortunately, you are correct. The difference is that he knows."

"Knows what?"

"Wait. Let me show you something." Banks turned back to the old man. "Would you like to come with us? We will take you to Zagreb on the plane. Come on."

The old man licked his lips, as though savoring the idea, then motioned with his hand and bowed his head. Finally, eyes glistening with sadness, he looked up and shook his head, lifting his shoulders in a helpless shrug.

Banks waved understandingly and pushed John forward through the exit.

"He doesn't want to come?" John said, his voice filled with disbelief.

"I can't answer that. Under other circumstances, he might enjoy the ride to Zagreb, but Split is his home. It is the only life he knows. And, this is his war," Banks answered. "You have just won yours, so let's get you out of here."

The second artillery round fell in the parking lot on the opposite side of the terminal. John, Hersch, and Grandpa joined Creston and Banks with quick handshakes and a "thank you" to the two UN drivers who were staying behind. Moments later, they were all hurrying up into the belly of the C-130, unable to hear anything but the scream of the plane's powerful engines as the pilot prepared for takeoff. The plane began moving even before the cargo door was fully closed.

"Welcome aboard," two UN soldiers said politely. They did not smile, and were all business as they directed their human cargo to fold-down seats attached to the sides of the plane, and helped them secure their safety harnesses. There were no windows to look through. Only the movement of the huge bird as it picked up speed, and finally the moment of liftoff. No one spoke.

It seemed as though each person were waiting to be felled by an unseen hunter at the moment of final flight. But such was not to be. Safely in the sky, they stared across the empty void at each other, rewinding in silence the events of the past few hours, in order to play them back later at regular speed.

Finally, Banks broke the silence.

"Well, my friends," he said, unfastening his harness and standing up, "this has been a most interesting day at the office."

UPON ARRIVING AT THE AIRPORT in Zagreb, John and the others said good-bye to the CNN news team who were anxious to be off to file their stories. Then they were whisked away in automobiles along a main highway leading into the city.

The Consul General's wife, Dorothy, welcomed them at the Banks' residence. A large-boned, fair-complexioned woman with snowwhite hair and a warm smile, she shooed them all toward a crackling fire in a large stone fireplace. The rest of the afternoon was spent decompressing with baths or showers and, later on, a small buffet, attractively served by a Croatian maid in the small dining room. Extra beds had been prepared, including a couch which Grandpa and Hersch argued over until finally flipping a coin. Hersch called heads correctly, and elected to sleep on the couch instead of the bed.

A local physician came to examine Jessica and the child. While John and Esther watched, he carefully removed bits of dirt and stone embedded in her skin. He cleaned the small wound under her eye and the deeper cut along her hairline, advising them that stitches might be necessary and offering to do the work at the emergency room in a nearby local hospital. When he learned that they would be transferred to Germany the next morning, he encouraged them to wait and complete the additional medical work there.

It was six o'clock by the time Jessica had eaten part of a sandwich and finished drinking a glass of cold milk. Esther saw to it that she was tucked in for the night, sitting a while on the edge of her bed, answering questions about friends at home, and filling in a few details with regard to events there. She insisted on sleeping with Jasmina, who had yet to utter a word or even a sound, but clung to Jessica with the silent acceptance that this person was her protector.

Retreating from the bedroom, Esther joined John who was in front of the fireplace talking to the Banks. Herschel and Grandpa stood at the table in the next room, laughing and talking like old friends as they made a second pass at the potato salad, fresh bread, and cheese.

"How are the children?" asked John, taking Esther by the hand.

"They are resting. I'll check on them in a few minutes. Jessica insisted on sleeping with Jasmina." Esther looked questioningly at the others. "What is going to happen to her?"

"I will arrange for a local orphanage to take her tomorrow," answered Dan Banks, as Dorothy poured a cup of tea and passed it to Esther. "They are somewhat overcrowded these days, but, given the circumstances, it is the best we can do for her. If there are any relatives . . ."

"Jessica says that there are not."

"Perhaps an aunt or a cousin will surface after the war."

"If that were possible, which seems unlikely, when would it happen? How long would she have to live in an orphanage that is already overcrowded?"

Banks hesitated a moment, his eyes steady on Esther.

"What are you suggesting, Mrs. Cain?"

Esther gave John an imploring look.

"I think what Esther is 'suggesting,' " said John, placing his arm around her, "is that maybe the child could come live with us."

"You mean take her to America?"

"That's where we live, Dan," John responded with a smile. "I think it is a good idea. What do you say?"

Esther sighed with relief as she heard John verbalize the feelings of her own heart.

"Are you sure, dear?" she asked.

"I'm sure," he answered, taking Esther into his arms. They then proceeded to tell Dan and Dorothy about Jenny, who had been gone from them now for well over a year. "No one will ever take her place in our hearts, but this girl ... well ... we're in a position to help her. She needs a home and we can provide her with one. After all, Jessica did promise her father. And besides, she belongs."

"Why do you say that?" asked Banks.

"Haven't you noticed? Her name begins with the letter J, just like the rest of our children."

The four of them laughed at this wacky bit of reasoning.

Banks looked over at his wife. "Didn't I tell you that these people are truly amazing?"

She smiled and nodded, taking Esther's hand.

"I'm with you," Dorothy said. "If you really want to take her, then do it. You can work it out, can't you, Dan?"

"I'm not sure that I can, but I do have a very competent attaché. If anyone can get permission to let this child out of the country with you in the morning, he can. I'll go call Milt right now and get the process started. Excuse me." Banks turned and headed for the den that opened onto the hall.

"You've been through a great deal during the past day or two," Dorothy Banks commented, "to say nothing of the past few months. Would you like to retire early? I overheard Dan say that a NATO plane will be here to pick you up first thing in the morning."

"That sounds like a good idea," agreed Esther. "I am beginning to feel very tired. I think my nerves are finally catching up to reality and are starting to ask, 'Where have we just been?' "

The others laughed again as Herschel and Grandpa Brainard joined them in front of the fireplace. Just then, Banks returned from making his call.

"Milt is working on it, even as we speak," he said reassuringly.

"What's this that he's workin' on?" asked Grandpa, and John quickly filled the others in on what was being attempted.

"I'm going to repeat my suggestion that you all retire early this evening," said Dorothy, putting her cup down on the small table next to her. "Your beds are ready and you will need to be up ... how early is their flight, dear?"

"Six o'clock takeoff. It was the earliest we could get you out of here."

"Then that means getting up at four. I'll have the coffee made."

"Please," Esther protested. "You've done more than enough already."

Dorothy Banks' other guests murmured their agreement.

She smiled and said, "You will be awakened at four o'clock. Coffee will be ready at four-thirty. You will leave here at five and be at the airport in plenty of time. In any event, I'm sure they won't leave without you."

TRUE TO HER WORD, AT FOUR O'CLOCK her several guests were gently awakened by the maid. A half hour later, they straggled into the dining room where Dorothy Banks was scurrying about in housecoat and slippers, setting out coffee and cups alongside what looked like home-baked breakfast rolls.

Jessica looked strained, a hint of dark circles under her eyes, as she stood by holding Jasmina's hand.

"Here, honey," said Esther, handing her a breakfast roll. "You need something to eat."

Jessica shook her head.

"You have to eat something, darling,"

"Mom, what's going to happen to Jasmina?"

Esther started to answer, then stopped, glancing over at John. At the same moment, Dan Banks strode into the room.

"Good morning, everyone," he said cheerily. "Your plane has arrived and is refueling even as we speak. We'll leave for the airport in thirty minutes. Okay?"

Approving smiles and "yes" exclamations filled the room.

"And, young lady," Banks walked over and looked down at Jessica, "how are you and your little friend here?"

"Much better, thank you."

"Jessica, your mother and father talked last night about the possibility of taking Jasmina with you to America. What would you say to that?"

Jessica's eyes lit up as she stared first at Dan Banks, then at her mother and dad.

"What a cool idea," she exclaimed excitedly. "Can we do that?"

"We've been working on it and have been able to arrange for temporary custody and an exit visa. It was too late last night to do very much, but we've gone that far, with the proviso that if other family members are discovered, they will be given opportunity to ask for her. Do you know her last name?"

"I'm sorry. Her father didn't tell me her last name."

"That makes it more difficult, maybe even impossible. We'll do the appropriate things here to try to locate living relatives, but my guess is that this little lady needs a new family. And, from the looks of things, it appears that she has one."

"All right!" Jessica whooped. Kneeling down, she rested her hands gently on the child's shoulders. "Jasmina, Mr. Banks says that you can come home with us!"

The little girl stared uncomprehendingly into Jessica's dancing, green eyes.

"You probably don't understand a word I am saying, do you?"

Her eyes never wavered, totally focused on Jessica, as though there was no one else in the room. Slowly, she lifted her hand until it touched Jessica's face. She held it there for a long moment, then lifted her other hand until both were pressed against her cheeks. Everyone watched as she moved her hands away and took a step forward, laying her head against Jessica's chest.

"I think little Jasmina understands you just fine, Jessica," Banks said, clearing his throat. "I think she is looking forward to having an older sister like you. Now, let's all get something to munch on before we have to leave. You have a date at our Army hospital in Frankfurt."

Jessica looked inquiringly at her mother and dad.

"They're going to give you a physical checkup and take care of the rest of these cuts and bruises," John said, reassuringly.

"And, they're going to want to ask you some questions, Jessica," Dan Banks warned, good-naturedly. "Lots of them, I'll bet. We're all interested to know about where you've been and how you have managed these past months."

Something flashed over Jessica's countenance for an instant. A shadow. John saw it and wondered.

"Dad, can I talk to you and Mom for a minute?" There was something in her voice, a confessional tone, that John recognized. Whatever it was, she felt that it was important.

"Sure, sweetheart," he responded gently, glancing over at Dan Banks. "May we use your den?"

"Of course, right over here," he said, leading them to the door. Jasmina held onto Jessica's finger and padded along beside her. "I'll shut this and let you have your privacy."

"Thanks." John nodded appreciatively.

Jessica sat down on the sofa. Jasmina crawled up beside her and laid her head on Jessica's lap. John and Esther sat facing the girls.

"What is it, hon?" asked John.

"I . . . I'm not sure where to start. But, I guess I should tell you the most important thing. I haven't told this to anyone else, because, who would believe me? I'm only a kid."

John and Esther listened without responding.

"Do you know about the video?" Her voice quivered at recalling that helpless moment in front of the camera and those people.

"Yes, we do, honey," answered Esther. "I've seen it, but your dad hasn't. It was something they forced you to say, though, and there was nothing you could do about it."

"Thanks," Jessica said, arranging her thoughts carefully, trying to recall exactly what had been said in her presence on that last night in the house in Iran. "I didn't want to, but . . . this man . . . his name is Dosha. He was there and made me do it in front of a camera. Then, afterward I overheard their conversation when they thought I had passed out. They were speaking in English—I guess it was the only language all of them knew. I heard them talking about plans for killing a lot of people."

"Jessica, honey, if you are about to tell us something that involves the security of our nation, maybe we should invite Mr. Banks to come and listen."

"Do you think so? I wasn't sure that he'd believe me."

"I'm sure he will believe you. And it sounds as though he needs to hear what you have to say, so that he can tell the right people what you know."

"Okay," she said, shrugging her shoulders.

John opened the door and motioned to Dan Banks. A moment later, he was inside, listening carefully as Jessica reiterated what she had already told John and Esther. Then, she continued.

"The man with the scar, Dosha, talked about how they would spend the ransom money, and that he wanted more money as well. When they asked him how he was going to follow through on the things he made me read, he said that their 'freedom fighters' were already inside the country and prepared. I guess they are college students as well as some other people who have gotten into America illegally. What was it he called them? Politics asylum?"

Banks smiled. "Was it political asylum?"

"That's it. Political asylum. Oh, yes, he also said something about them being in the business world too, but he didn't say any names or anything. At least not that I remember. He said that they did not have a nuclear bomb, 'not yet,' was the way he put it, but that they do have a 'secret weapon' of some sort. This secret weapon is supposed to make thousands die when they destroy an entire city somewhere.

"They asked him questions about the city, but he never mentioned it by name. Dosha said it would be destroyed and 'tens of thousands,' those were his exact words, would die. I guess they had been talking about this place before they came to my cell."

"You were in a cell?" asked Esther, horrified.

"Not like in the movies, Mom. It was really a room with a cot where they kept me by myself. I could never leave and it was guarded all the time, so I called it a cell."

"You were right in doing so," Banks said. "It helps you keep the right view of things in your mind."

"Did they say anything more about this city?" questioned John. "Anything that would help identify its location?"

Jessica shook her head.

"I've tried to remember their exact words. I didn't pass out, but I sort of faded in and out for a while. But there is something. I don't know if I mixed it up or if this is what that Dosha guy really said. It was about the secret weapon being 'simple and silent.' Those were his words. Then, I think he said, 'That which flows from under the temple will poison the earth,' or something like that. It didn't make any sense to me."

The others were silent, absorbed in their thoughts.

"That's all you remember?" asked John, taking her hand in his.

Jessica shrugged again. "I wish there was more, but that's it."

"Okay. Time to go, everybody," Banks voice took on an authoritative tone. "We don't want to keep the pilot waiting. As soon as I get back to the office, I'll call Washington and bring them up to date. Jessica, you are an incredible young woman. You make me very proud to be an American. I hope that I'll see you again someday. Let me warn you—they are going to ask lots of questions in the hospital at Frankfurt, so be prepared. I know you'll do your best and that's all anyone can ask. So, don't worry."

"Thank you, Mr. Banks. And, thanks for coming to get me yesterday. I . . . I didn't know what to do. At first, when the bus blew up . . . well, I thought I was finally going to die. I was so scared. I kept asking myself how I could keep running, now that Jasmina was with me. I couldn't go off and just leave her, so I was praying and asking Jesus for help again, to give me courage and tell me what to do. And when I opened my eyes, there were Daddy and Mom and the rest of you. It's still hard to believe. I really thought I was dreaming."

Dan Banks laughed and put his hand on Jessica's shoulder. "I can imagine that you did, but it's no dream. You are finally back where you belong, with your mother and father. You also have a brother back home, I understand?"

"Yes, and I can't wait to punch him out. He is the worst tease in the world!"

"I'm sure he's looking forward to that. Okay, let's get on with it."

Each of her guests thanked Dorothy Banks again for her hospitality as they stepped into the two waiting automobiles. Twenty-five minutes later, they were boarding a military plane that had deadheaded in from Frankfurt. A flight attendant in military uniform greeted them as they entered and introduced them to an army physician and a registered nurse who had been awaiting their arrival. They offered Jessica a place to lie down, which she declined, wanting instead to sit next to her parents during the flight. Maybe later she would lie down to rest.

Jessica sensed that she was once again the center of attention. Only this time, she was surrounded by family and friends who loved her. Her body was sore from top to bottom and her nerves were on edge, but it didn't matter. She had never felt better in her life!

FIFTY-FOUR

Dec. 18. SEATTLE, Washington—A man, apparently of Middle-Eastern extraction, invaded the Tall Pine Shopping Mall yesterday, indiscriminately spraying bullets from two automatic weapons into a crowd of patrons waiting with their children to visit Santa Claus. He then rolled two grenades into the center of the mall. Both grenades exploded, shattering windows and wounding several people. Seven were killed and fourteen others are in area hospitals. Witnesses said that the lone perpetrator drove up to a mall entrance, got out of a car and walked inside, carrying several magazines of ammunition and the two grenades. Police were on the scene in minutes and tried to arrest the gunman as he ran from the mall. When he failed to surrender, police opened fire and killed him. He carried no identification. However, within the hour, police received calls claiming that the Palestinian Islamic Jihad was responsible and was threatening even greater violence if the US government does not cease its financial and military aid to Israel.

....

SUNDAY, 18 DECEMBER, 1015 LOCAL TIME
AMSTERDAM, HOLLAND

Lufthansa Flight 1417 broke through the dark layer of clouds at 6,400 feet. Though it was midmorning, the runway lights formed an outline similar to a lighted crucifix against the blue-green overcast that covered the airport. Ten minutes after regaining the earth, the airliner's first-class cabin opened as Lt. John Derrick and Lt. Kelly Wender exited. Lt. Derrick waited momentarily for the others, while Wender went on ahead, walking swiftly along Schiphol's B concourse. They were joined by John and Esther Cain, with Jessica and Jasmina in between. Herschel Towner and Grandpa Brainard were the last to leave the plane.

The rest of the passengers on board settled back. They were unaware of who was traveling with them in the first-class section, and thought they were stopping to take on more fuel. Though several wondered out loud as to why an adequate supply of fuel had not been taken on in Frankfurt, most settled back to enjoy the twenty-minute layover once free drinks were wheeled out into the aisles by the smiling flight attendants.

THE PREVIOUS TWO DAYS HAD BEEN spent in the US Army hospital in Frankfurt, where other released hostages had, at other times, been taken before being flown back to America. Doctors were thorough with Jessica's physical examination. They confirmed that she had not been sexually assaulted. She had lost at least fifteen pounds during her ordeal, however, and required several stitches to close the wound on her forehead. Three small sutures dealt with the minuscule cut under her eye. There were some bad bruises on her back, left arm, and leg, a cut along the left knee that required stitches, as well as numerous abrasions on her back and chest. Several more bits of stone were removed from her leg and the wounds carefully cleaned and dressed.

Esther was escorted to a local PX where she purchased clothes for Jessica and Jasmina. The girls were provided beds in the same room, but Jasmina slept most of the time with Jessica. During the first day, Jessica remained in bed, except for short walks along the hall and beyond to the counseling center. During the second afternoon, she went with her parents for a walk on the hospital grounds while Jasmina was taking a nap. Examining psychologists were pleased and somewhat surprised by the mental condition in which they found America's youngest hostage.

There were some signs of anger and depression, which the doctors deemed normal responses, considering what she had been through. She spoke thoughtfully, and seemed at ease with the mental probing, though the caution with which she spoke of certain people or events was noted, almost as though she felt obliged to protect them. During these interviews, Jessica's parents were silent witnesses, while two doctors, a member of the CIA, and a representative of the State Department posed questions and recorded answers to the harrowing story of their daughter's last three months as a hostage. They could hardly believe it was their little girl who sat across from them, recounting her agonizing experiences with calmness and candor.

Each interview was immediately transcribed and sent on to Washington. Of particular concern was the information that had already been forwarded to the State Department from the Consul General in Zagreb. Was there really a city about to be targeted by terrorists? After the incident in Boston, no one was willing to write off the possibility.

Of special interest was the sentence, "That which flows from under the temple will poison the earth." What did it mean?

Washington contacted Israeli authorities concerning its possible association with Jerusalem's volatile temple site. Maybe the terrorists were coming back to finish what had been interrupted in September. Salt Lake City's Mormon Temple was the next to come under scrutiny. Security forces were quietly beefed up at these as well as other temple sites. Pentagon staff debated as to whether the military should be involved in order to protect the populace. The CIA surveyed its Middle East and European agents in an effort to find some correlation between rumor and fact. "That which flows from under the temple will poison the earth." Was this significant? Had anyone heard it said elsewhere? Had the girl misunderstood what was being said? Nothing of substance had been forthcoming.

At first, the State Department had decided to fly the Cain entourage back to the States on a military aircraft. Then, Lufthansa, Germany's impeccable national airline, offered to clear the first-class section on one of its flights and transport them free of charge to San Francisco. When asked about his preference, John opted for Lufthansa's generous offer.

"I've never flown first class," he said, with a pleased grin, "and think of the money we'll save the taxpayers."

John and Esther agreed to give the news media a thirty-minute press conference at the hospital, thanking the world for its generous outpouring of love and compassion during their recent ordeal. Yes, Jessica is fine. No, Jessica will not be giving any interviews before we return home. Yes, she was able to rescue a small Croatian child who has been granted a temporary visa so that she may travel with us to California. No, we haven't made any future plans at this time, other than to rest and become a family again. Yes, we are very concerned about the recent wave of terrorism that has been launched against America and Israel. No, we will not comment on what we think America's response should be.

And then, after two full days, Jessica had been released.

LT. WENDER STOPPED IN FRONT of a door marked Private, directly opposite a coffee and breakfast rolls vendor who watched curiously as the others joined her. Kelly spoke briefly to the airport security guard in front of the door. He reached for a key and opened it, standing back so that she could enter. Wender disappeared briefly, and when satisfied that all was in order, stepped out, beckoning to the others. John and Esther were the first to enter, followed by Jessica and Jasmina. As soon as Herschel and Grandpa Brainard were inside, the guard closed the door.

The room in which they stood was plain, but carpeted. On the walls were two pictures of tulip fields and one of a farmhouse nestled among trees alongside a canal.

A man in a police uniform stepped forward, bowed slightly, hands behind his back, and greeted the small group in flawless English.

"Welcome to the Netherlands. We are pleased that you have chosen to stop over here on your way home. But, Reverend Cain, your visit is much too short. You and your family and friends must return again when there is more time. Let me say that our entire nation was so happy to hear that your Jessica has managed to escape from the terrorists. It is also an honor to meet you and to be able to fill your request. We understand that you have only a short time on the ground, so I will not impose on it further, except to introduce to you Ms. Annie Heergaren, with whom you have asked to speak."

The attractive young woman who had been standing near the window walked toward them, smiling.

"I am pleased to meet all of you. Especially you, Jessica." She extended a hand.

Her dark brown hair fell just below her shoulders. Blue eyes, oval-shaped nose, skin the color of milk. The comely figure, exposed three months earlier in a window in Amsterdam's red light district, was now demurely covered with a powder-blue suit, and a modest blouse.

Jessica took her hand.

"I saw you when my father and I came through Amsterdam."

"I know," Annie replied, her eyes never leaving Jessica. "I remember you. You smiled and waved at me."

"A lot of people must do that," said Jessica. "How could you ever have remembered me?"

"I'm not sure," Annie replied honestly. "It wasn't long before I began seeing your picture on our television. There was a big commotion over what your father had done in Jerusalem, as well as what was going on in America. Then, one night, a client said something that made me think of you. I wasn't sure, but I went to the police anyway. It was a lucky guess on my part that turned out to be right, and I'm just so very happy for you."

"It wasn't luck, Ms. Heergaren," said Jessica.

"The name is Annie."

"Annie," Jessica repeated. "It wasn't luck."

Annie was smiling, curious, and somewhat amused at having been singled out by the local authorities for this meeting. When an officer had first knocked on her door, she thought she was being arrested. When the reason for his visit was explained to her, she had been flattered. Of course, she would meet the young, former hostage, who had stood in front of her window one night last September waving her hand. And now, here she was, smiling at her again.

"No? If not luck, then what was it?"

"It was Jesus, making sure that I would be remembered by you at the exact time I needed it to happen."

"I . . . well . . . I . . ." Annie stuttered with surprise, totally taken back by Jessica's emphatic and direct explanation.

"You were there for me when I needed you, Annie," Jessica continued. "I told my dad that I was going to pray for you every day while we were on our trip to Israel. I guess I didn't do too well with my promise, because I forgot for a while. Things got kind of crazy, you know? But then one day I thought of you again, and I've been asking Jesus to give you the same happiness that He has given me. And, I've asked Him to give you a better job too. I don't want you to get AIDS or something, Annie. If you've got such a good mind as to be able to remember me waving to you, then you can do better."

"Well, Jessica, thank you so much. I . . . I am . . . that is nice," Annie said, obviously flustered now, by Jessica's straightforward and disquieting concern. "No one has ever before said they cared enough to pray for me. I hardly know what to say."

"God used you once, Annie, so you have to know that He's

interested in you. You were a part of what my dad calls 'God's great network.' Those are people God uses when He needs them. Anyway, I wanted to see you and say thank you for what you did."

"It was nothing really," Annie responded, quickly regaining her composure.

"It was everything," countered Jessica. "And I'm going to keep praying for you, Annie. Here, take this. Daddy found the name and address of a Christian family that lives not far from where we first saw you. They help people who want to change their lives. I hope you will go and talk to them. Maybe you can write and tell me how you are doing. Okay?"

Annie took the piece of paper in her hand. Her blue eyes were glistening as she smiled back at this remarkable youngster.

"No promises, Jessica, but I will think about it."

"I love you, Annie," Jessica took one more step and closed the remaining distance between them. She held out her arms and Annie opened hers as well. They stood in the center of the circle of people, the prostitute and the preacher's daughter, hugging each other tightly. Tears spilled out from under Annie's closed eyelids.

"Good-bye, Annie. I hope to see you again."

"Good-bye, Jessica. Perhaps we shall meet again someday."

John and Esther hugged Annie as well, thanking her for caring enough to go to the police with her concerns.

Then, as quickly as they had come, they returned to the waiting plane.

Annie Heergaren watched them until they disappeared around the corner and then walked slowly in the opposite direction toward the terminal exit, still clutching tightly the folded piece of paper the young girl from America had given her.

JOHN NEVER EXPECTED to enter San Francisco's International Airport and be overrun by media personnel for a second time. It had happened when he returned three months ago from Israel. But, what were the odds of history repeating itself like this? He had no idea.

By the time their plane touched down and began to taxi toward the terminal, they were informed that local and national television news teams were waiting in the airport. CNN had already broadcast some of the film work done in Croatia. Now, every major news reporter was hoping for more of the same kind of coverage that sells advertising and boosts TV ratings.

A twelve-year-old escaped hostage, a tiny Croatian refugee, a former member of the Navy SEALs, the man who helped save the city of Boston from a disaster planned by terrorists, and John and Esther Cain, the parents who faced overwhelming odds and bravely overcame them in order to bring their family together again. Put it all together with the Christmas season and it was just too good to pass up!

In the same VIP lounge where they had met in September, John was the first to see Jeremy standing off to the side. This time, however, he didn't stay back. John saw that he and Jessica had spotted each other at the same time. Jessica ran toward him and leaped into his arms, wrapping both feet around his legs.

"O Jeremy!" she shrieked. "I am so happy to see you!"

"Hey, sis," Jeremy said huskily, wrapping both arms around her in a bear hug. "You are a piece of work. We send you off on a little vacation and look at you. You don't come home for three months. Some people will do anything to get out of school!"

"O you . . . man, you!" she exclaimed, releasing her grip. Standing up in front of him, she pounded his chest with her fist. "I missed you so much, big brother."

"I missed you too, sis," Jeremy's eyes were wet as he blinked back the tears and hugged her again. "I wish I could have been there for you."

"Yeah, me too."

After a long moment, they released each other.

"Hi, Mom. Hi, Dad." Jeremy hugged each of them. "You guys are looking good! And Grandpa. You made sure they all came home, didn't you?"

"That's right, young fella," Jim Brainard responded with a hug of his own. "They couldn't have done it without me. 'Course this here fella helped a little. Jeremy, I want you to meet Herschel Towner."

"Hi, Mr. Towner. I'm pleased to meet you. I've heard Mom and Dad talk about you."

"Well, don't you believe anything they say. I'm really a nice guy."

"And look what we brought home," Esther said. "Well, actually, what Jessica brought home. This is Jasmina."

Esther held her up so that Jeremy could see her.

"She's beautiful, Mom."

Jeremy held out his hands, but Jasmina buried her face in Esther's neck. "She'll come to you in time. All this is just too much too soon. It wasn't until the second day in the hospital that she finally left Jessica and sat in my lap. She still hasn't said anything.

Not a word . . . since her parents died."

John saw Esther's countenance turn suddenly sober, as Jeremy put his arm around his sister. He knew what she was thinking as he watched the expression on her face.

So much pain in the world. So many who have lost so much. And yet, here we are together again, in love and with lots of hope for the future. God is faithful and good.

He shifted his gaze and nodded at an airline employee who waited patiently by the door. "Okay, gang, the sooner we face the music outside, the sooner we can all go home," John admonished genially.

At the door, he paused.

"Here, honey," he said, taking Jessica's hand. "You go first."

"No, Dad, please."

"It's okay. I'm right here with you. We're all here with you."

Jessica looked plaintively at the others, but none offered to take her place. She took a deep breath and brushed her hand nervously along the length of her hair. Exhaling, she looked up at her dad and nodded. He smiled and opened the door.

A cheer went up. Flashes. Cameras were everywhere. A sudden, unexpected panic took her breath away as she stared into the camera lenses. For a brief instant, she was back in her cell again. Voices shouted questions. People pushed and shoved.

John raised his hands above his head, signaling for quiet.

"This is all very overwhelming," he began, stepping up to a phalanx of microphones. "We're happy to see you here . . . again. But as far as I'm concerned, we've got to stop meeting like this!"

Laughter was spontaneous, followed by applause.

"On behalf of Jessica," he continued, "who has something she wants to say in a moment, and Esther, my wife, and our son, Jeremy, we want to thank you all for not letting our daughter be forgotten. You kept her face in print. You told her story and followed us all the way, via television and radio. Without you, we might never have had this happy occasion. I know that sometimes you get knocks because of the media's intrusiveness. Fact is, I've felt like saying some things about that subject a few times recently. But, for now it is enough to say, God bless you. And thanks again for everything you've done."

Again, cheers and applause, along with a few whistles from enthusiastic onlookers who were waving hastily scrawled signs that said, "Welcome Home, Jessica Cain!"

"Ladies and gentlemen, our daughter, Jessica."

More applause and voices cheering.

"All right, Jessica!"

"Welcome home!"

"Baytown loves you!"

Along with, "How do you feel? What was it like in Croatia? Tell us how you escaped." And dozens of other questions, all asked in a cacophony of voices.

John lifted his hands, once more signaling for quiet.

Jessica stepped up the microphones. She paused, gathering her nerve, though it appeared to the crowd as though she was simply waiting for them to be still. After a moment, "you could hear the silence," as the *San Francisco Chronicle* reporter wrote later in his front-page column.

"I too want to thank you," Jessica began, nervously clearing her throat. "I've been scared a lot during the last three months, but you guys are probably the worst."

There was more laughter, as those in the crowd empathized with the youngster standing in front of them. Then it grew quiet again.

"I still don't know all that has been done to help me get home. I know my parents and my brother worked hard. I guess a lot of other people did too. I know that lots of people prayed and I think that is what really did it. Jesus was with me all the time, though I have to confess that sometimes, I felt so alone that I wondered if He had forgotten where He put me."

Just then, Jessica saw Amy Foster and Shawna Pickett standing off to the left, along with their parents. She waved to them.

"Hi, Amy. Hi, Shawna. I missed you guys so much. I just can't believe you're really here," she exclaimed. Then, remembering where she was, with an excited giggle she turned her attention back to the cameras. "These are my best friends at school. Before I left, I just took them for granted, like a lot of us do with our family and friends. That's one thing I will never do again. Family and friends are too important. Anyway, I just want to say thank you again to everyone. It feels so good to almost be home . . . I'm going to sleep in my own bed tonight!"

The crowd looked at one another, smiling and nodding, each one trying to imagine how good that must seem to this twelve-year-old. They grew silent again as Jessica remained in front of the cameras and microphones.

"I guess . . . well, there were times when I wasn't sure . . . it would ever happen again, you know? I know I'm a preacher's kid and all, and I'm only twelve, so, I've got a lot to learn. But, I want you all to know how much God has meant to me while I was a hostage. I thought I was a Christian before I left on this trip, and I guess I was. But I'm a different Christian now. And I hope that someday my life will make a difference in this world, even if it's only a little one.

"There is someone new in our family I'd like to introduce to you and then I'll be quiet. I'm quite a talker, as you can tell, and there hasn't been much opportunity for that recently. It feels so good to be free to talk that it's hard to stop."

More laughter.

"This is Jasmina," said Jessica, turning and taking her from Esther's arms.

Cameras. More flashes.

"Tonight, I'm going to my old home and my old, familiar bed. Jasmina is going to her new home and a new bed. One that she's not seen before. Her family was killed in the war, in the city where my parents found us.

"I have a little sister who died in an accident. Her name is Jenny. She was so beautiful and we'll never forget her. But tonight, Jasmina is going to sleep in my little sister's bed. I really believe that Jenny will be the happiest one in our whole family when she looks down from heaven and sees her there. Maybe Jasmina is why I had to go through all of this. God knew she needed someone and He let me be there for her."

The crowd was silent, attentive to the attractive youngster and the small child that she held in her arms. Something was happening to those who looked on. It was no longer a mere news conference or media circus. People were becoming reflective. There were sniffles and damp eyes, as those standing about were suddenly confronted with what the world had become. . . . A place where children suffered the consequences of evil. . . . An arena in which gladiators cut down their offspring, while the unfeeling masses watched from the safety of the grandstand. For one brief moment, as cameras swallowed film and reporters scribbled phrases on paper, human hopes and dreams for a better future took on a most fragile form.

Lance Freeman, *Mercury-News* reporter, put it this way in his front-page story the following day:

> An almost teenager stood, holding a little child.
> Defying the coercive forces of evil.
> Faith and courage refused to give up.
> These were the latest witnesses to the faithfulness of God.
> *"I will never leave you or forsake you . . ."*

Two children whom evil brought together to harm,
but whom God intended for good
in order to accomplish what needed to be done.
They gave back the gift of hope to a cynical, old newsman.
I think maybe I'll go to church this Sunday.

TUESDAY, 20 DECEMBER, 1530 LOCAL TIME
SOUTH OF SAN FRANCISCO

AT EXACTLY THREE-THIRTY, the rental car turned off Cañada and drove through a gateway, opening onto a small parking lot. Two men got out of the car and walked toward a tall monument that looked like a displaced artifact from the Roman Empire.

As they strode through the parklike setting, they were careful to observe everything about this place. To their right was a small, colorful garden of flowers, tiered above a series of circular steps. Between the garden and the monument was a rectangular pool, lined with eight cypress trees on two sides and surrounded by lawn, giving the entrance a soft yet majestic appearance.

At the far end of the grove, flanked by live oaks and directly in front of a high wire fence, stood the monument. A perfect circle of cement and brick formed the platform surrounding an inner wall. Ten Corinthian pillars, each one reaching upward from identically carved bases, were separated from the cornice by handsomely carved capitals, depicting the leaves of the Mediterranean acanthus herb.

High on the inside of the circular cornice, there had been carved the Greek "key" design, together with a series of flowering wreaths. Since there were no corners in which to place a cornerstone, a tablet had been shaped into the inner wall and carried the message:

Erected
MCMXXXVIII

The two men leaned over the wall and gazed at the scene below. Water ran steadily from a large tunnel into a simple, blue-green enclosure, and then out again along an above-ground cement canal, finally disappearing over the weir, about a hundred yards beyond the fence. Nearby, a locked gate in the fence held a large No Trespassing sign.

"It won't be necessary," one of the men said, jerking his head toward the sign. "This will be perfect right here. Can you believe this? No security. Their most valuable natural resource, and not even one guard!"

The other man shook his head. "How do the Americans say it .. 'a piece of cake'?"

The first man chuckled and turned back to the wall for another look. He pointed to the opposite side of the monument. The other nodded as they read the words engraved in stone:

"I give waters in the wilderness
and rivers in the desert
to give drink to my people."
Isaiah XLIII-XX

"Okay, let's go," said the first man, stretching away the tension in his back muscles. "We can do it all right where we are standing. It shouldn't take more than fifteen minutes to turn San Francisco back into a wilderness and a desert!"

They returned along the gravel path to the car. As they backed up to turn around, another vehicle carrying a man, woman, and child turned into the lot. The driver smiled and waved as he coasted past them toward a parking space. Both of the men waved back, pausing at the gate to check out the sign. It read:

Pulgas Temple
Terminus
Hetch Hetchy Aqueduct
San Francisco
Water Department

FIFTY-FIVE

SCHOOL BUS FALLS VICTIM
TO TERRORIST ATTACK

Dec. 20. JERUSALEM, Israel — A busload of Israeli children,
returning from an outing to Massada, fell to an attack on the
outskirts of the city today. Tires were shot out from an am-
bush that was followed by raking the bus with heavy fire
from automatic weapons. The driver and the armed guard
were apparently killed outright, along with several children. Some were killed trying to escape. Two thirteen-year-
old boys were seriously wounded and left for dead. They
are recovering in Hadasa Hospital's critical care unit, one
listed in critical condition and the other serious, but stable.

    After expending hundreds of rounds at the helpless
bus, witnesses say that six men fled in a minivan toward
the city. Law enforcement units are searching the area, and
Israel's military has been called to a standby alert.

ISLAMIC RADICALS STRIKE AGAIN:
THIS TIME IN FLORIDA!

Dec. 22. MIAMI, Florida — A suicide bomber blew up herself and
eight other bus passengers in downtown Miami last night.

The incident is the first for this city, but the thirteenth act of terrorism inside the US, with four additional bombings reported in Israel during the past seven days, attributed by authorities to the radical Palestinian Islamic Jihad. The group appears to have stepped up its efforts to terrorize both Israeli and American citizens in an all-out effort to win support for their demands.

The President has once again made it clear that America will not bow to acts of terrorism by any individual or group. He has also restated his respect for Islam, in general, and his hope that the citizens of the United States will not associate these inhumane acts by a minority group with the peace-loving peoples of the Muslim world.

The President was questioned by one reporter, who obviously had done his homework, on the fact that a document known as the "Immunity" or "Release," preserved in Surah IX of the Koran, serves notice on all pagans who refuse to Islamize. That same Surah IX, according to the reporter, records the command to fight Jews and Christians on behalf of the Islamic religion, as a basic principle of Jihad, or martial endeavor, until they become subject peoples. With that in mind, did the President believe that these acts of terrorism were not religiously based? He refused to comment further, saying simply, "That is a question for the theologians, not the leader of a political power."

....

FRIDAY, 23 DECEMBER, 1625 LOCAL TIME
NEAR SAN FRANCISCO

JOHN MANEUVERED THE CAR through the onramp and into the right lane on Interstate 101 North and headed in the direction of the San Mateo Bridge. Esther leaned back into the seat, letting her eyes run down the handwritten list one last time. She folded it once and dropped it in her handbag, glancing over her shoulder at the boxes and bags in the back.

It had been the only one-day Christmas shopping experience that she could remember since their first Christmas together. Hectic, yes, but it was done. The Stanford Mall, filled with hundreds of last-minute shoppers like John and Esther, was in their rearview mirror. John's parents were arriving later tonight and Grandma and Papa Stevens were due in at ten o'clock in the morning. She closed her eyes, but sleep didn't come. Instead, she felt the car slow and finally come to a stop.

"What's the problem, John?" she asked, sitting up to look around.

"No problem. Just the world's longest parking lot," he replied, drumming his fingers on the steering wheel. "We've caught the commute traffic. Plan on a late dinner."

Esther sighed and settled back, reaching for the *Chronicle* they had picked up on the way out of the mall. She disliked California's wall-to-wall morning and evening commute fiasco, and once had suggested to John that employers ought to let their people go home according to the alphabet, beginning with the letter "A." That way, traffic could be more evenly absorbed by the freeway system. John had laughed at her dry wit, suggesting that she send her idea to the governor.

"REAL MEN DON'T SHOP UNTIL CHRISTMAS EVE," John had explained jokingly to Esther, earlier that morning.

"Well, I'm sure the mall will be filled with *real* men tomorrow," she responded. "In spite of the fact that we're dashing around like Santa at the North Pole, at least you don't qualify as a *real* man, John."

"Ouch. You know how to hurt a guy."

"Tough. It's what you get for making us shop so late this year. I've never done it the day before Christmas Eve. This is insane."

"Relax and enjoy. There will be great sales and we'll have a ball together—just the two of us."

And they did.

John and Esther had driven away from Baytown and across the San Mateo Bridge to shop at Stanford Mall, in the hope that no one would recognize them. Everywhere they went since arriving back home, they were stopped by people who wanted to wish them well. Parishioners from the church, friends from the community, people they did not know at all. Esther dreaded trying to get any serious shopping done until John had suggested the Stanford Mall.

When they pulled into the parking lot at ten-thirty that morning, it was already well filled, but shopping had been fun. They bought gifts for Jeremy, Jessica, and now Jasmina. Then a not-so-quiet lunch at Max's, but that was part of its charm. They waited until a table in the far corner came open and followed the hostess, as she led them to it. All through lunch, they ignored the other patrons, not like old married couples acting as though there was nothing left in the world to say, but talking and smiling as though they were newly in love. And, in fact, that was how they felt.

"I can't believe it's Christmas and we're all actually here to celebrate the season," exclaimed Esther, between bites of her sandwich. "Thinking back over this year is, as Jeremy would say, totally awesome."

"That's for sure," agreed John. "God has been good to us, hasn't He?"

"Yes. Sometimes I wake up at night and go into the kids' rooms and see them sleeping, and I think that it's almost too precious to be real. I've been waiting so long for the other shoe to drop that it seems unnatural to be getting back to a normal life again."

"I know. Several months ago, Jeremy and I were hardly able to talk. You and I were both depressed beyond words. I had my letter of resignation prepared. I honestly wasn't sure we'd make it all the way to Christmas."

"What are you going to do about that, John?"

"About what?"

"The letter."

John was silent, staring at his plate. He reached for the glass of Pepsi and took a long swallow.

"Well, it is something we need to talk about."

"Here we are, talking," Esther said sweetly, pushing back her plate.

"Well, I guess it boils down to the fact that I don't want to put the same kind of pressure on our marriage and family as we had before. Don't get me wrong. I love the ministry—it's what I've always believed God called me to do—but I love my family too. It is really hard to keep a balance between the duties and pressures of pastoring a congregation like Calvary Church and being a good husband and father. It's really hard," he said again, twisting the end of his napkin. "I'm not sure what to do."

A stillness came over the table, like an old friend, easing its way gradually into their conversation. Finally, Esther reached out and took John's hand.

"If you are worried about me, sweetheart, you don't have to. I've grown up a lot recently. I think we all have. Our family can take it, if that's what God wants you to do. At least for a few more years. I know you'll do your best to be there for us."

John smiled.

"You are the best woman in the world, my love. Every pastor should have a wife like you. Thank you. I'll think and pray about it some more. There will be time enough to talk after Christmas, but

I can't even let myself think about it right now. We need to finish shopping for all the grandparents. There are five this year, remember?" John paused and then continued, "I wish Jim had decided to join us for Christmas. Having our parents with us this year will be special, but I hate to think of him being all alone back there in Maine."

"Me too, although I think that he really wanted to be at home. And he wanted to give us some space. I believe Hersch is going to fly to Boston and spend the weekend in Booth Bay. Did I forget to tell you that?"

"Really?"

"Yes. He called yesterday to check on how we were doing. That's what he said."

"That makes me feel better. Those two became pretty good friends through all of this, didn't they?"

"We all did, my love, we all did," Esther mused thoughtfully. "So, now that we're such good buddies, let's get out of here and do the rest of our gift list. We'll join the kids in decorating the tree, and then I've still got to wrap all this stuff after they crash tonight."

"Don't forget the Christmas Eve services," John said. "The deacons are anxious for us to be at all of them. The first one starts at three."

"How could I forget? It's a marathon, by the time we're done. It is fun, though, to see everyone, especially the children. I really think it is the most wonderful night of the year at Calvary Church."

"Everyone seems anxious to see Jessica again. I didn't think she would want to go to all three services, but it seems like she does. I guess the church family is such a part of her life that getting back to it is almost as important as coming home. Anyway, not to worry. I'll help you wrap presents tonight."

"Don't."

"Don't?"

"I've seen how you wrap," said Esther, slapping at John's arm. "Come on, sport, let's get with it."

"JOHN, LOOK AT THIS." AS THEIR CAR crept forward in the traffic, John glanced over at the newspaper page that Esther held out for him.

"Right here. Look."

John's eyes darted back and forth from the picture to the on-again, off-again taillights immediately in front of them. It appeared to be a monument of some kind. He did not recognize having seen it before.

"What is it?"

"The San Francisco Water District is preparing for a celebration next year commemorating the Hetch Hetchy water project."

"So?"

"So, all the big California names are being invited to an event over here behind Redwood City. According to this article, it will happen 'at the place where San Francisco's citizens first cheered the long-awaited arrival of water as it spilled out into the waiting reservoir. It was a momentous occasion, the culmination of twenty years of politics and engineering. Today, pure mountain water still flows from under the temple to the people of the Bay Area.' "

"Flows from where?" John asked, as cars began moving again.

"That's what this gazebo-like monument is called. The Pulgas Water Temple. Ever hear of it?"

"No."

"Well, it apparently marks the end of the line for water being transferred from the Sierra runoff into the San Francisco Water District reservoir system. According to this article, there are several reservoirs in the area. It doesn't say whether they are connected to each other, but I suppose they are. Anyway, the Hetch Hetchy flows into Crystal Springs Lake. It's strange, though, isn't it."

"Strange? How do you mean?"

"Doesn't the similarity strike you as being odd? Jessica quoted Dosha as saying, 'That which flows from under the temple will poison the earth.' This article talks about water that 'flows from under the temple.' You don't suppose . . ."

John stared straight ahead as they picked up speed.

Dosha. It's Christmas and still we can't forget about Dosha and his crowd of terror merchants.

"John," said Esther, finally breaking the silence as she watched the lines around his eyes tighten, "what do you think?"

"I think it may be totally off the wall, but it's worth a call to the FBI. They've been covering everything from Jerusalem to Salt Lake City. Maybe we were wrong in thinking that Dosha was going after some holy site. Everybody has been concentrating on the 'temple' idea and passing the part about 'that which flows from under,' because we've had no idea what it meant. Even I have thought that maybe Jessica got it mixed up, in the stress of what she was going through. But, what if you're right? Maybe Dosha is planning to poison some city's water supply. How many cities do you suppose have 'water temples'?"

Esther was thoughtful for a moment. "I know of at least one," she said finally, staring at the picture on page three.

"Dosha said that his 'bribery program' was going to last until the end of December," she continued. "At that time, if we had paid up, he would release Jessica. Of course, now, we know that he had no intention of letting her go."

"So, thinking that Jessica might remember what he had said in her presence, he tried to kill her in Croatia," John interrupted, looking over at Esther. "Failing that, if you were him, what would you do?"

Esther thought for a moment.

"For starters, if I really had a time frame that I intended to work within, I might toss it out and move the clock up so that I could accomplish what I had set out to do before somebody figured it out and stopped me."

"Exactly," exclaimed John, gripping the steering wheel with growing excitement. "Now, we have no idea whether New York or Washington or Boston has a 'water temple.' But here is one, right in the backyard of the place where he struck three months ago. Maybe that was just the introduction of a coordinated and diabolical plan, and not simply an isolated terrorist incident."

"Maybe we're just crazy with speculation," said Esther, folding the paper so that the picture was on top as she laid it down in her lap. "What if we blow the whistle and we're totally wrong?"

"On the other hand, perhaps . . . just perhaps . . . the Holy Spirit is prompting and guiding us in this," answered John. "What if God led you to read that article? If that were the case, then it is no coincidence and it is certainly not our paranoia either. If this is the Lord giving us a warning, then we've got to contact the FBI."

Esther sat silently, gazing into the growing darkness outside the car. All vehicles had their lights on now and she had to hold her watch up close in order to check the time.

"How long before we get home?" she asked finally.

"In this traffic? Probably forty-five minutes. Why?"

"Because if I was Marwan Dosha, and I was hurrying to do something that would strike fear and gain the most worldwide attention, I think I know when that would be."

John looked across at Esther, waiting.

"Christmas Day might be a good time, don't you think?"

John nodded thoughtfully, letting the impact of her reasoning work its way in.

"But," she added reflectively, "Christmas Eve might even be better."

"HELLO, FBI. HOW MAY I DIRECT YOUR CALL?"

"Hello. My name is John Cain. I am the senior pastor at Calvary Church in Baytown."

"Oh, yes, Reverend Cain, and congratulations on your daughter's safe return."

"Thank you. Would it be possible for me to speak to Special Agent Duane Webber?"

"I'm sorry, sir. Agent Webber left about two hours ago and will not return until after the holiday."

"Is there someone else that I might speak with? This is in regard to the terrorist, Marwan Dosha."

"Paul Danversen is the Assistant Special Agent in Charge. I'll see if he's available. One moment, please, while I put you on hold."

John waited. An eventual look at his watch told him that a minute had passed while he listened impatiently for some human response.

"Hello," a voice boomed suddenly into his ear. "Danversen here."

"Hello, Agent Danversen. This is John Cain, from Calvary Church in Baytown."

"How do you do? We've not had the pleasure of meeting, I'm sorry. Congratulations on getting your daughter home safely."

"Thanks."

"I understand you want to discuss our friend, Mr. Dosha."

"Yes, my wife and I have come up with a theory that we think is worth troubling you about."

"Before we continue, Reverend Cain, would you please give me your social security number and your driver's license. I think I recognize your voice from television, but we have had a rash of calls in the last few days, what with all the recent problems around the country. It's only a formality, but I need to confirm that I am indeed speaking to John Cain."

"I understand," replied John, reeling off the numbers.

"Okay, thanks. Now, what is it you have for us regarding Dosha?"

John began laying out his and Esther's suspicions. Danversen listened attentively, breaking in twice to ask questions.

"You were reading a newspaper? And all this just sort of came to you?" he asked finally.

"I know it may sound far-fetched, Mr. Danversen, but we can't help but think that there may be something to this. If we are correct, and Dosha is plotting to do something to the water supply, then someone needs to act right away."

"But why San Francisco?"

"Why anywhere? Terrorism is essentially the act of thugs and madmen. We both know that they are not always the idealists they want others to think they are. I've done quite a bit of reading on this subject recently, as you might well imagine, and the experts tell me that sometimes it is just the power and the glory. In a perverse kind of way, the terrorist comes to see killing as the end in itself, rather than a means to an end.

"Why San Francisco? Maybe because his last act of terrorism here resulted in failure. Maybe because, in Europe and much of the Middle East, a lot of people view San Francisco as America's most beautiful city. To them, it is the Paris of the United States. If they could turn it into a killing field, how would the rest of the world respond? Every other city would live in mortal fear that it was next."

"Okay, I hear you. And what was that phrase again that your daughter heard him say?"

John repeated it again. "These were Dosha's exact words, according to Jessica. 'That which flows from under the temple will poison the earth.' And this statement was made with regard to a specific city."

"But no city was named?"

"Not that she remembers."

"All right, Reverend Cain. I'm going to be in touch with Special Agent-in-Charge Duane Webber and tell him about your idea. If I need you, how can I be in touch?"

John gave him the phone number and thanked him for his time. When he hung up, Esther looked at him expectantly.

"I don't know if he bought it or not, but he promised to get in touch with his boss and talk it over. I guess we've done all we can."

They sat together on the sofa and watched Jeremy and Jessica finish decorating the tree that Jeremy had purchased at a nearby tree lot that morning. It was late to be preparing the house for Christmas festivities, but the occasion was too special not to do so.

As for Jessica, her physical recovery was going very well. Cuts and bruises were healing. Doctors said that her most severe head wound would leave a very small scar that would hardly be noticeable. Emotionally, for the most part, she appeared to be progressing satisfactorily. However, Esther's "mother instinct" warned her that it would be a long time before Jessica could thoroughly process all she had been through. She promised herself again, on top of a score of earlier promises filed away in a secret place in her heart, to be there for her always.

The elder Cains had already arrived and were busy unpacking things in Jeremy's room. Jeremy had volunteered for sofa duty while the grandparents were here. Jessica was going to sleep with Jasmina tomorrow so that the Stevens could use her room. She watched Jasmina run back and forth excitedly between the tree and the piano.

What do you suppose is going on inside her little head right now?

There was still no sign of willingness to talk. The doctors believed it to be a temporary condition, resulting from the shock of the battle and the deaths of her family members. Still, Esther was beginning to worry. How long would it be before she could open up the doors that had been slammed shut inside her little mind?

FIFTY-SIX

The three black trucks rolled out of their underground storage chamber at exactly seven forty-five and headed toward Highway 84. Turning right at the corner they eased their way down the hill toward Interstate 680. At the freeway, they headed south, picking up speed. Traffic was lighter than usual, but that was to be expected. It was Christmas Eve.

**SATURDAY, 24 DECEMBER, 2035 LOCAL TIME
BAYTOWN, CALIFORNIA**

"I THINK THOSE WERE THE BEST Christmas Eve services we've ever had, sweetheart, and you did a great job."

"Thanks. The choir's songs were wonderful, weren't they?"

"However," said Papa Stevens, grinning from ear to ear, "I think Jessica's return was the present everyone looked forward to."

"I thought we would never get it settled down again after she was introduced," Esther acknowledged. "We didn't want her homecoming to divert people's attention from the service itself, but it didn't seem right to keep her away either."

"Of course not," Grandma Stevens chimed in, running her hand down the length of Jessica's hair. "And I think the way they stood and applauded for so long was not just for Jessica. It was really for Jesus, don't you agree? They were praising the One who made it all possible. I felt such a spirit of thankfulness there tonight."

"Yes, I did too," agreed John.

"I'm so glad it's finally over and everything can get back to normal," said Grandma Cain. "It seems like 'normal' has been such a long time coming to our family." John and Esther glanced at one another, sharing quiet looks of concern.

An hour of eating and visiting with the recently gathered members of the Cain family passed swiftly. At John and Esther's urging, the travel-weary grandparents retired early in order to be fresh for Christmas Day. At last, John lifted Jasmina onto his lap and settled back. It was the first time since arriving home that she had been content to let him hold her like this. On other occasions, she had wriggled away and run to Esther or Jessica. But not tonight. It warmed John's heart to feel her snuggled quietly in his arms, yielding to the sleepiness that had finally overcome her vigil in front of the tree lights. She had not touched the presents stacked underneath, but it had been a constant challenge to keep her fingers away from the lights.

A lively rendition of "Deck the Halls" was now being followed by "O Little Town of Bethlehem," Phillips Brooks' classic written for the children of his church more than a hundred years ago. It was Channel 20's annual Christmas Eve Special. Two hours of uninterrupted music, with the only picture on the screen being that of Yule logs burning in a fireplace. The first time he had seen it, he had thought, *Only in California would people sit around and watch a log burn on television.* That year it proved to be a comforting addition to the rest of their late evening, and the music selection was good. It had since become a tradition. Now, John sat staring at the image of the flickering log fire, a silent prayer rising from his heart to heaven.

Thank You, Lord, for making this the most special Christmas ever. I remember how hard it was last year. With Jenny gone, so was the spirit of the season. We were here together, but we couldn't come together. It is so different tonight. Lord, what I feel right now is priceless. Thank You for making us a family once again, stronger than we've ever been. And, Merry Christmas, Jenny. There must be a wonderful celebration going on in heaven right now. Enjoy!

Jeremy had gone to his room for a package to put under the tree and Jessica was in the kitchen helping her mother put dishes in the washer when John's attention was drawn to the crawl line beginning to make its way across the television screen.

"Esther!"

It was the tone in John's voice that caused her to drop the soup pot back on the stove and hurry into the family room. Jessica followed after her.

"Look."

John was leaning forward, Jasmina asleep in his arms, watching the crawl line message repeat itself.

> This is a special Channel 20 news bulletin: an explosion has been reported inside the 29-mile Coast Range Tunnel, part of the Hetch Hetchy Aqueduct that is the San Francisco area's primary water source. The extent of damage is unknown, but is believed to be massive. No word on casualties. Stay tuned.

The crawl line started to repeat itself for the third time. Esther stared at the screen.

"Do you think . . . " She stopped in midsentence.

John was up now, handing Jasmina to Jessica. "Put her in bed, hon," he said as he opened the drawer by the telephone and took out his book of numbers. Thumbing down to F, he opened it and punched in the ten-digit number.

"Hello, FBI." The voice was brusque on the other end, typifying someone's attitude about having pulled Agent-on-Complaint Duty on Christmas Eve.

"Hello, this is Pastor John Cain of Calvary Church in Baytown. I need to speak to Agent Webber or Danversen, please. It is very urgent."

"I'm sorry, sir. They are not available. May I take a message?"

"Look, it is absolutely essential that I . . . "

"Sir, it is Christmas Eve. I can take your message if you'll give it to me. I'll forward it to the appropriate desk."

John felt irritation building.

"Have you heard about the bomb blast along the Hetch Hetchy Aqueduct?"

The voice on the other end suddenly changed, the tone becoming increasingly cautious.

"Yes, sir, that report has just come in. Do you have information that might help us in this regard?"

"Tell Webber or Danversen that the tunnel is a diversion."

"A diversion?"

"Yes. Tell them that the real action will be at the Pulgas Water Temple near Redwood City. Get the police or somebody over there!"

"Sir? Can you confirm this?"

John was about to explode. It was the one time that he wanted to be recognized this week, and the agent apparently did not know who he was.

"This is the work of Marwan Dosha and his band of terrorists. And the longer you keep talking to me, the less time you have to stop them. San Francisco's water supply is in grave jeopardy! You need to hurry!"

"Sir, would you tell me your name again, please?"

John pulled the receiver away from his ear in exasperation, just as Jeremy entered the room.

"What's going on?" he asked, looking first at his dad and then at Esther.

"They've blown up the Hetch Hetchy Aqueduct," said Esther.

"The what?" Jeremy said, with a puzzled look.

"It's the water supply system for several Bay Area counties," John explained, handing the receiver to Esther. "Here, give the agent whatever he wants. Only make sure that he contacts Webber or Danversen."

She took the phone, a worried look on her countenance. "What are you going to do?"

"I'm going over to the Pulgas Temple."

"No, John, please . . . " her tone was pleading.

"I have to go. It may be too late already."

"I'm going with you, Dad."

John hesitated for an instant. "Okay, get your coat. I'll be with you in a second."

John ran down the hall and into their bedroom, while Jeremy went to the hall closet for their jackets. His mind racing on ahead, John fumbled with the key that unlocked the drawer. Moments later he reappeared, the handgun tucked into the leather holster that Carla Chin had presented him at his concluding lesson.

"How far is this place, Dad?"

John thought for a moment. Like most Californians, he automatically measured freeway distance in terms of time, not actual mileage.

"My guess is thirty minutes. Less if we hurry."

Esther was busy on the phone as John blew a kiss in her direction and went out the door, with Jeremy close behind.

2205 LOCAL TIME

"IT CAN'T BE FAR FROM HERE," said Jeremy, looking up from a Greater San Francisco Bay Area map that lay crumpled in his lap. They had reached speeds of ninety miles per hour while crossing the San Mateo Bridge and making their way up the long hill on Highway 92. Amazingly, John thought, there had been no patrol cars to hinder their progress. He didn't know whether to be relieved at not being pulled over or chagrined because no one had stopped them. A glance at the dashboard clock told him they had been gone from home exactly twenty minutes.

"There! Turn left!" Jeremy pointed, as the car skidded into the left turn lane and onto Cañada Drive. "My guess is that it's about a mile from here. According to the map, it should be on the right."

"Good navigation, son. You got us here. Now, when we see some sign of this place, I'll drive past slowly. If the police are there, I'll pull in. If not, then, we'll go on by, turn off the lights, and come back until we get close. If that's the way it goes, you stay with the car while I check things out."

"No way, Dad! I'm going with you."

"No!" John's voice was sharp. "You stay here."

"But . . ."

"No buts, son. Don't argue. As far as this operation is concerned, I am in charge. Just do as I say. Everything is going to be okay." John's thoughts flashed back to a dark street in Bandar-é Abbås, and Hersch's words to the same effect as they had stood outside the Fardusi compound. Then he saw it. "There. Up ahead. This is it!"

The sign was illuminated by the car's headlights.

Pulgas Temple
Terminus
Hetch Hetchy Aqueduct
San Francisco
Water Department

John slowed the car as they drove past the gate. It was shut, with a sign on the gate indicating the hours it would be open to the public. There did not seem to be any cars in the parking lot, though in the darkness, he could not be sure. They kept going until well past the gate. Then, John switched off the lights, turned the car around and coasted back, until they were about a hundred feet from the entrance. He pulled over onto the road embankment and stopped.

"All right, son, take the wheel and lock the doors. Get on the car phone and try to raise the police. If you hear or see anything out of the ordinary, get out of here. Fast. If the police show up before then, tell them that I'm inside. I don't want to get shot by mistake. If there's nothing suspicious, I'll be back in a few minutes."

"Be careful, Dad."

"Thanks. You can count on it."

John opened the door and stepped out, shutting it quietly. He felt for his gun as he walked up the road, but left it in the holster. At the gate he paused, peering into the darkness. Nothing unusual. He looked at the chain on the gate. It was wrapped around the gate frame and the padlock was in place.

Wait. . . .

He bent down to look closer.

The lock is open! It could be that the caretaker forgot to set it, but that's doubtful. Someone has picked this lock, and there's a good chance that person is in there right now.

Carefully, he unwrapped the chain and pushed the gate open. Stepping through, he glanced around the parking lot again. Nothing. The night sky was filled with twinkling stars, and a three-quarter moon edged its way from behind a passing cloud. As his eyes grew accustomed to the semidarkness, he saw something in the distance. Was it the monument? As he came closer, the shadowy outline took the same shape as the one in the newspaper.

John continued toward it, then stopped. He heard voices. At that moment, the moon moved out from behind the cloud and, in its light, he saw them. A tanker truck was backed up against the monument. Two other trucks were parked a few feet away. He made out two men standing nearby. *Wait.* A third figure emerged from the shadows and strolled over to the others.

This is it. They're getting ready to put something in the water. Marwan Dosha's words on the lips of his daughter, "That which flows from under the temple will poison the earth." Whatever it is, I have to stop them. Got to get closer . . .

The men suddenly stopped what they were doing and turned in his direction. John halted his movement, watching, waiting. He could hear them speaking in low tones, but couldn't make out what was being said. He looked for the third man, but he had disappeared. *Where has he gone?*

"Whoever you are, come forward slowly, so that we can see you." The voice was low and threatening. It came from the passenger side of the nearest truck.

Well, at least now I know where you are.

The moon was all the way out from behind the cloud now and John knew he was a sitting duck if they saw his shadow. He bent down and ran laterally off the path and onto the grass. At that precise moment, he saw the flash and heard the echo of a handgun. Instinctively, he ran toward a mound and dove for cover behind it. A second shot zinged past his ear. He hit the grass hard and kept rolling until he was behind what looked to be a tiered garden of some sort. Fumbling for his gun, he drew it from the holster.

JEREMY STOOD BY THE CAR, with the door open, listening and watching. He had made the call. *Where are they? Dad must have found something or he would be back by now. What's that?*

Jeremy's heart leaped into his throat at the sound of gunfire. Then, a second shot. Quietly, he closed the car door and ran up the roadway toward the Pulgas Temple gate.

THERE WERE SHOUTS!

It still sounded like three men, no more than that. Someone was running off to the right now. He saw the shadow and fired. *Missed him. He's still moving. Where are the others?*

John quickly surveyed his situation.

I'm too much out in the open here, but there's nowhere to go! He'll see me if I move. I still don't see the other one. Maybe he's circling around the opposite way.

The shadow he fired at had disappeared. John began inching his way along the grass on his stomach, trying to gain some additional protection from the small garden mound.

Another flash and the simultaneous sound of a gun!

Over there. It came from behind that live oak tree, off to the right.

John scrambled back the way he came, as the assailant got off another round. He grunted involuntarily as the bullet chipped the cement step, just inches above his head. Then he turned his attention back to the live oak, watching for some movement.

What I wouldn't give for a tritium night sight!

"Don't move! Drop the weapon or I'll kill you right now!"

John froze. It was a male voice with a slight accent, and it came from directly behind him. Somehow, the first man had managed to circle around and now, John knew, he had no chance. He lowered the gun to the grass.

"Stand up slowly. Keep your hands away from your body. Do not make any sudden moves or you are a dead man!"

Deliberately, John drew himself to his knees. Then he pushed up to a standing position, watching as a shadow moved toward him from the live oak. It was the second assailant.

"Keep your hands high in the air. I am right behind you,"

declared the voice. John felt the muzzle of a handgun in the small of his back, as the man ran his hands up and down John's body, confirming that there was no other weapon than the one being picked up by the gunman's partner.

"Turn around slowly," the voice ordered.

John turned until he could face the man. They were both together now, and off to the right a third man walked toward them. With the moon at their backs, it was impossible to distinguish their features. His guess was Middle Eastern, given the nature of things.

"Who are you?" the first man asked. "Police? FBI?"

John said nothing.

"Listen, my friend," the voice of the second man was oily, slick, and carried a more pronounced accent. "You have rather rudely interrupted our work here tonight, and that being the case, you are going to die shortly. I can assure you of that. We are well away from any populated area, and no one will have heard shots being fired. So, you have a choice. You may die swiftly and cleanly, or slowly and with great pain. It matters little to us which way you choose. If you wish it to be quick, however, then you must cooperate. Understand?"

"I understand," John said, concentrating on keeping his voice from showing the fear that stuck like a dirt clod in his throat.

"Once again, what is your name?"

"Cain. John Cain."

He saw the men glance at each other.

"You are *the* John Cain? The one who was in Israel last September?"

"That's me."

"Hand your wallet over. It is in your jacket. I felt it a moment ago. But, move very slowly, please."

John reached inside his jacket and withdrew his wallet.

"Throw it over here."

The man caught it in midair and opened it with a flick of his fingers. Holding it up to the moonlight, he briefly examined the driver's license behind the plastic window, before handing the wallet to his partner.

"Well, well. The great Reverend Cain has indeed paid us a visit. This is certainly much more than we could have possibly hoped for. Allah must be smiling upon us. We'll keep the wallet, thank you. It will be enough to prove to our friends that you have been eliminated once and for all. You have been a real nuisance, John Cain, you and that daughter of yours, and it will be a distinct honor to send you to an infidel's hell."

"That is the one thing I am absolutely sure you will not do to me," John responded, as an unexpected calmness settled over him, causing him to wonder if God was preparing him for the inevitable. "You cannot send me to hell. Jesus Christ, God's Son, has made certain of that."

The man holding the wallet stepped forward and, without any warning, drove his fist into John's stomach. John doubled over in pain, just in time to catch a second blow on the side of his head. He toppled like a freshly cut tree. His only sound was a low moan as he desperately tried to suck in air.

"Get up!" the man ordered, propelling the toe of his boot into John's ribs with such force that it lifted him partially off the grass. He fell backward onto his side, rolling over as he gasped for breath.

"I said get up, Cain. Come and watch what we are about to do."

Every attempt to breathe brought with it excruciating pain. He struggled to his feet, half anticipating another felling blow, but none came. His eyes focused again gradually, as the one whose boot had done the damage pushed him forward, past the reflecting pool and toward the monument.

JEREMY SLIPPED PAST THE OPEN GATE and ducked underneath a small tree, listening all the while for something. Anything. He caught his breath as more gunfire erupted. Then he saw a shadow dart from one tree to another. Finally, he made out his father lying in the grass. At first, he thought he had been hit. Then, he saw him stretch out his arms, with gun in hand, looking in the opposite direction. He opened his mouth to call out a warning, just as he heard the man behind his father shout. He saw John rise to his feet as the man moved closer. He waited, listening from his hiding place, wincing at his father's beating.

What should I do?

Jeremy turned and started back toward the gate.

JOHN STEPPED ONTO THE PLATFORM that surrounded the inner wall of the Pulgas Temple. Curious, he glanced over the side. Below it was dark, but he could hear water running. In the distance, on the other side of a wire fence, moonlight shimmered on water flowing along an above-ground aqueduct, before disappearing into the darkness.

"Have you any idea what we are doing? Is that why you have come, Reverend Cain?"

John saw that the closest truck had been backed up eight or nine feet from the cistern's cement wall.

"Having had some taste of the diabolical way your kind thinks, I must assume that you are going to try to poison the water."

"Not 'try,' oh, no. We *will* poison the water system. Of that there is no doubt. Our fellow warriors have by this time destroyed the tunnel that brings water to this region from the mountains. We in turn are about to pollute the reservoirs with plutonium chloride. It is a plan that has taken months to bring to fruition. And you, together with your daughter, have been a constant fly in the ointment.

"Actually, I would kill you now, just to get rid of you. But it gives me pleasure to know that you, of all people, will witness this greatest of victories in our Holy War. A few more minutes to watch as we kill thousands." He turned to his companion. "Ali, let us begin releasing the plutonium."

The one called Ali opened the door to the nearest truck cab and climbed in. The engine growled its protest before finally rumbling to life. Ali leaned out of the open door and shouted something in Arabic. The man holding his gun on John answered. Ali's head disappeared inside the cab and the truck began moving backward, picking up speed as it went. John watched in horror as it broke through the wall, its momentum continuing until the truck's rear wheels ran off the edge of the cistern and the belly of the tank dropped at a crazy angle against the platform floor.

The second man had slipped on rubber gloves and proceeded to lean over the edge, pressing something onto the tank's outer surface.

"Stand back," he ordered as he recovered his balance and moved toward the others. An instant later, the shaped charge of C-4 plastic exploded, creating a large rupture at the bottom rear of the tank. John suddenly felt sick as he heard its lethal contents gushing out into the water below.

"Quickly," the leader motioned to the others. "No need to use the hose on the last one now. I'm sure the Reverend Cain has been kind enough to provide us with a vehicle for our escape, have you not?"

John said nothing, calculating the distance between him and the man holding the gun, realizing at the same time that he had no real chance.

"Ali, put the next truck in position. Then go and check, just to be sure."

The second truck roared to life and slowly began moving backward toward the cistern. With a grinding crunch of metal against cement, the second tanker now hung precariously over the cistern beside the first. The man with the rubber gloves was holding a small flashlight between his teeth as he bent over a bag containing more explosives. Meanwhile, the leader prodded John ahead of him with the barrel of his gun until they stood near what remained of the cistern wall. From here, both men could see the first tanker continue to spill its radioactive material.

"I assume you know something about plutonium chloride? It comes in liquid form, is completely soluble and mixes well with water. Your fellow San Franciscans will soon be drinking sub-atomic particles known as alpha radiation. There is enough here to contaminate the entire water supply. Those who manage to escape death will leave in panic. San Francisco will become a ghost town. So will the surrounding communities. It will be months, maybe even years before an alternate water source can be created. Meanwhile, who will want to live near our little plutonium ponds? I predict the total collapse of the area's economy, Reverend Cain. What do you think?"

"Where did you manage to get this stuff?" John inquired, stalling for whatever amount of time he could get.

"We have gone to great lengths to establish connections with the scientific community in Russia. This purchase was made from reactors there that were using the PUREX refining process. To their discredit, the Russians are very bad record-keepers and never seem to quite know the exact amounts of plutonium at their disposal. Their scientists are also very poor, since the breakup of the USSR's research industry. It has been easy to make these two conditions work for us.

"A good deal of this plutonium chloride came from lines that had not been bled off until our Russian friends were able to secretly perform the task."

They watched now, as the other man lifted a small container off the second truck. So intent were they on what was taking place in front of them, that the rapidly moving dark object was not detected until it hurtled past John and slammed into the side of the man holding the gun!

The next few seconds were a blur.

The force of Jeremy's full-body blow knocked the gunman against the waist-high temple wall. A gunshot reverberated and the bullet ricocheted wildly off the brick platform. The gunman's hand went up as he tried to regain his balance, but it was too late. He pitched over the side and fell into the darkness. The man with the gloves looked up in surprise. John sprang forward and fell on top of him, pummeling him with his fists as they rolled off the platform's edge and onto the ground. He was conscious of movement nearby, but was too busy to do anything about it. A backward roll and John felt the edge of the platform. With a twisting move that sent a stabbing pain through his side, he banged the terrorist's head against the cement. The man went suddenly limp.

John looked up in time to see the one called Ali running away from the truck. Before he could say something, Jeremy darted off after him. John gasped for breath as he tried to sit up and another searing flash of pain shot across his chest. He heard a commotion out there, in the darkness, but he couldn't see anything.

"Jeremy!"

There were only sounds of grunting and gasping. Finally, all was still.

"Jeremy!" John looked around for a weapon. There was none.

He saw the shadow of a man coming toward him and, at the sight, he relaxed. He would recognize that rolling gait anywhere, even in the semidarkness. It was MacArthur High's starting point guard.

"Are you okay, son?"

"Better than you, I think," Jeremy answered, with a grin.

"Where is he?"

"Resting in the grass by the path. But, we'd better see if they have some rope or something in one of these trucks. He'll come around pretty soon. What about the other guys?"

"This one needs to be tied up. I don't know about the other one."

They rummaged under the truck seat and discovered a roll of electrical tape. Quickly, Jeremy bound the man lying at the side of the platform and then hurried off to do the same to the one he had left by the path. Inside the glove compartment, John found a flashlight. He limped back to the inner wall of the temple and turned the beam downward. How far was it? Ten feet? Probably twenty. The man lay face up, his arms outstretched in the shallow pool of contaminated water. It looked as though he had struck the cement bottom. A broken neck? Maybe he knocked himself out and drowned. Whatever, the man was clearly dead. John looked at his watch. Forty-five minutes since they had left home.

Just then, a car swung through the open gate and came to a

stop in the parking lot. Two men in police uniforms got out. One of them had a flashlight. Its beam found John just as he caught up to Jeremy.

"Police!" the man shouted, as they drew their weapons. "Down on the ground. Now! Both of you! And keep your hands where we can see them!"

John groaned, with a fresh stab of pain, as they dropped obediently to the ground.

"I've done this once already tonight," John said, grinning at Jeremy. "But somehow, it isn't the same."

EPILOGUE

"Yes, we're all fine, Grandpa," Esther said into the telephone, in reply to the concern in Jim Brainard's voice. "We're opening our presents a little later than usual this year, but, otherwise things are as normal as they ever get in the Cain household. . . . John is taking it easy on the sofa. Three cracked ribs and a small fracture in the left cheekbone. His eye looks like spoiled fruit, his lips are swollen, and he's taped up pretty good. Actually, he looks like a refugee from a barroom brawl. Other than that, he's fine. . . . What? . . . Yes, I'll tell him that Hersch offered his crutches.

"Well, the problem was that it took awhile to convince the FBI that I was for real. John ran out of the house and left me to give out his driver's license and social security number. Only he took them with him. . . . I know, what else can you expect from a preacher?

"I finally had to call Lt. Randle of the Baytown police. I met him last September, and remembered that he was a personal friend of FBI Agent Webber. When I explained the situation to him, he got things going. He contacted the FBI and local authorities in Redwood City or Belmont, I'm not sure which. Jeremy called too, from the car. But, by the time the police got there, my men had everything in control. . . . Yes, you heard right on television. Jeremy's our hero! . . . What's that? . . . Oh, I wouldn't worry, I think he still wants to work for you next summer. He's had enough excitement for a while."

Listening from across the room, Jeremy grinned and winked at his dad.

"Yes, the police handcuffed them both and hauled them in with the terrorists. One of them had John's wallet in his pocket, so it took awhile to sort the bad guys from the good... What? ... I'm not sure about that. The reservoir has been shut down and tests are being made right away. Everyone has been notified to conserve on water usage. Lots of people are afraid to use any tap water, even though it's coming from reservoirs that haven't been affected by the contamination. Bottled water is being shipped in tomorrow. It's all you see on television and it's pretty scary all right; officials are promising to let the public know everything regarding cleanup procedures. Some are saying that the best option is to pump the contaminated water into the Bay and let the tides take care of it.

"They have engineers heading out to the tunnel too. They will check out the extent of the damage and submit a proposal for a temporary alternate water source that will give them time to re-open the tunnel.

"Dosha? ... Unfortunately, nobody seems to know where he or the woman disappeared to. Our guess is that they are somewhere in Europe or the Middle East. We don't think either of them is here in the States, but who knows? Yes, it is a bit unsettling to think about it. I hope they are caught soon. We'll all feel safer. ... Okay, I'll tell them. Merry Christmas to you and Hersch. We love you."

Esther put down the telephone and smiled at the others. Everyone was crowded into the family room. Grandparents Cain and Stevens sat on chairs that had been placed in a semicircle. Jeremy was on the floor with an arm around Jessica. John, careful not to move any more than he had to, lay stretched out on the sofa, a little groggy from pain medication, but otherwise alert and enjoying the scene. Esther walked over and knelt down by him, pecking his forehead with a kiss.

Jasmina seemed at home today, more relaxed and contented than usual.

Esther shifted to get comfortable and, as she did, her eyes caught movement in the pool outside the family-room door. It was the pool sweep. John called it "the beloved ghost" that had haunted them ever since Jenny's death. She looked again. Its ethereal qualities seemed to have vanished. She smiled.

It's just a pool sweep now.

Esther ran her hand across John's chest.

"I love you, you big lug," she whispered.

"I love you too," he replied with a puffy smile.

Her gaze turned back to Jasmina, who was touching a Christmas tree light with her delicate fingers. Today, no one tried to stop her. Suddenly she whirled around, ballerina-like in grace and motion, one hand held high and the other pointing away from her.

Has someone taught you that? mused Esther. *What other secrets are hidden inside your little mind and heart? We may never know.*

Jasmina stopped and began walking toward Jessica and Jeremy, carefully planting one foot directly in front of the other, arms stretched out as though she were on an invisible high wire. Finally, she looked up and smiled.

What happened next caught everyone by surprise, a moment of astonishment that was followed by gales of excited laughter.

The little Croatian said her first word.

"Jes-see-kah."

Coming in Summer 1996
• *Pursuit* •

THREE PEOPLE'S LIVES are about to be forever changed by their pursuit of truth and love.

KRISTIAN LAURING grew up in the church, the only son of Reverend Peter and Sarah Lauring. Bright, outgoing, and extremely verbal, everyone was certain he would follow in his father's footsteps. Everyone, that is, except Kris, whose rebellion against the faith of his childhood ultimately breaks his parents' hearts. As the popular host of America's newest and most controversial television talk show, Kris slashes at society's traditional mores and creeds while pursing media acclaim.

KATRINA LAURING, his beautiful sister, responds differently to their growing-up years. Quiet, introspective, and dutiful, she sees the beauty of belief and the safety of her family's conservative convictions. But she too will defy her parents and venture into an exotic, mysterious world where her faith finds more questions than answers and courage is tested by extraordinary events. In the midst of it all, Katrina encounters a love that breaks an inviolable rule.

IBRAHIM SEVALI grew up in a single-story building of white-washed concrete, three rooms in all, or four if you include the unattached verandah in front. His parents worked in the fields. So did most of his ten brothers and sisters. But Ibrahim's keen mind and unusual thirst for knowledge sparked his spectacular rise from a poor, rural Turkish family to a respected post at the University of Istanbul.

When Ibrahim discovers an ancient manuscript, hidden for centuries in a Cappadocian cave city, he understands it will be the gateway to fame and fortune. Its contents confirm what Muslims have been saying for centuries. Yet, if made public, its message will tear apart the delicate fabric of the Christian and Jewish world. In his dilemma he makes another discovery, that of a lovely American woman who touches both his heart and his soul as she searches for honest answers to her own questions of faith.

Three vastly different people suddenly find their lives woven into a tapestry of success and failure, faith and danger. From simple small-town life to the mesmerizing beauty of San Francisco, from the high-tech of modern television to the highlands of ancient Cappadocia, from quiet seminary halls to the exotic intrigue of the mosque, three people pit the power, piety, and passion of their lives against the mysteries of religious faith and the elusive reality of truth.